WORLD
QUAKE 3

BOOKS BY MARK HOBSON

Fiction
World Quake
World Quake 2
Wolf Angel
A State of Sin
Dweller Under The Roots
Grey Stones
A Murmuration of Starlings
Now May Men Weep

WORLD
QUAKE 3

By
Mark Hobson

COPYRIGHT © 2024 MARK HOBSON
ALL RIGHTS RESERVED.
THE MORAL RIGHT OF THE AUTHOR HAS BEEN ASSERTED.

ISBN: 9798344545073

PUBLISHED BY HARCOURT PUBLISHERS

EXCEPT WHERE ACTUAL HISTORICAL EVENTS AND CHARACTERS ARE BEING USED FOR THE STORYLINE OF THIS BOOK, ALL SITUATIONS IN THIS PUBLICATION ARE FICTITIOUS AND ANY RESEMBLANCE TO LIVING PERSONS IS PURELY COINCIDENTAL.

BOOK COVER DESIGN BY KEN DAWSON

FOR LOTTE

THE EARTH WILL BE CHANGED INTO AN IMMENSE CEMETERY; THE CORPSES OF THE WICKED AND THE JUST WILL COVER THE FACE OF THE EARTH.

THE FAMINE THAT WILL FOLLOW WILL BE GREAT.

MARIE JULIE JAHENNY OF LA FRAUDAIS, FRANCE.
THE BRETON STIGMATIST.
EXERT FROM PROPHECY OF THE THREE DAYS OF DARKNESS.

PART 1

THE DESCENT OF MAN

Chapter 1

INTERNATIONAL SPACE STATION
LOW EARTH ORBIT
260 MILES ABOVE THE EARTH'S SURFACE

FLIGHT ENGINEER MADISON LEITNER HAD lost track of time. She wasn't sure of the exact date. She thought it might be Friday, which meant they'd passed over into August. However, yesterday she had spent hours cleaning the Harmony habitation node with a handheld vacuum cleaner sucking up floating crumbs and dirt, a job that was always reserved for Tuesdays. That made her question if it was really Wednesday today.

Madison could have checked her Station Support Computer to confirm the date, but she had turned off all non-essential equipment, including the SSC units, a few weeks ago to conserve energy. She felt that counting the days and marking them on an imaginary calendar in her head was necessary in the beginning to keep her self-discipline. But as the days turned into weeks and the weeks into months, it became clear that all she was doing was marking the passage of time since the planet and her entire world were irreparably damaged. The longer the gap, the more she felt disconnected and isolated from her past. All she had left were memories, like an invisible thread that connected her to the people and things she used to know.

Moreover, since the station orbited Earth once every 128 minutes, keeping track of the days was meaningless.

On DAY 1, Madison and her fellow crew members were awed and terrified as they watched the planet being torn apart. Madison, however, soon became cold and detached in the face of the catastrophic event. The other crew members were pointing their fingers and chatting excitedly as if they were spectators at a sporting event, noting key moments such as the colossal landmass of China rippling with seismic waves like a tumultuous ocean, Northern Europe disappearing beneath a series of mega-tsunamis, and New York and Manhattan's skyscrapers reduced to molten slag. But while Mission Commander Montgomery and Science Officer Beaufort could barely contain their excitement at what they were seeing, Madison's thoughts were already focused not on the broader implications but instead had zeroed in on her personal tragedy.

It was difficult for Madison to comprehend the enormity of billions of people dying. Although she knew this was a landmark turning point in human history, the scale of the catastrophe made it hard to process. Instead, she watched the earthquakes, floods, and volcanic eruptions like some merciless, unflinching deity. Meanwhile, in her mind's eye, she saw her family running for safety, trapped under debris, or swept away by the rushing waters.

World Quake 3

As the world was ending, Madison thought only of her husband and two sons. After the dust settled and the shock had set in for the three astronauts, Madison was overwhelmed with feelings of selfishness.

Commander Montgomery, who was always quick with a few smart-alecky comments about the ISS being the safest place to be, became a shadow of his former cocksure self and sank into a deep depression from which he never emerged. Now, he was dead at his own hand. Science Officer Beaufort was dead, as well, killed by Madison in self-defence, leaving Madison all alone.

Later, confirmation of the news she dreaded the most had come. Her dear husband, Harry, and their sons, Danny and Sean, all perished on DAY 1. There would be no last words or messages telling of her love and devotion. No fairytale reunion was possible. All Madison could do was hold on until she ran out of water, air, and food.

But what was the point? She'd asked herself this question a hundred times and still had no satisfactory answer. It would be easy for her just to turn off the life support system and surrender to the inevitable. However, that would only lead to a slow and painful ending through suffocation. Another option was to float out of an airlock without an EVA suit, but she didn't fancy being blasted with radiation, causing her saliva to boil. Beaufort had died this way, and it hadn't been a pretty sight.

In the end, it came down to one thing, Madison concluded: she was no quitter.

It had been drilled into her from an early age by her parents to never give up on her ambitions and hopes. They encouraged her throughout her teens and twenties when she was in college, and later when she joined the Air Force and was selected for astronaut training. Her instructors at Houston and the AsCan Centre in Arizona further instilled a spirit of endurance, perseverance and adaptability. NASA had a saying that perfectly fit this mood of defiance:

We as humans evolved as creatures who could learn to adapt to any situation, no matter how harsh. We as a species of explorers will meet many setbacks... but humans will not give up.

Simply put, Madison had a pugnacious side to her.
Or, to put it another way, Madison would continue to flip the bird to the cosmos.

She had grown so used to the isolation and peacefulness that when events took a dramatic change two days later, Madison wondered at first if she was hallucinating.

She was currently at the station's water recycling unit, trying to figure out why it was malfunctioning. The International Space Station collects water from the crew's urine, sweat, and breathing vapour. In return, the system extracts oxygen from water in a well-balanced process that should provide drinkable water and breathable air. However, the recycling unit wasn't perfect, and the balance was never 100% efficient. Thus, some water still had to be brought from Earth. Even if the supply from Earth is cut off, there should still be enough water for several months. But something was wrong with the equipment. Madison had already replaced the unit's distillation assembly, yet the instrument panel still showed it was on the blink.

Currently, the water recycler was only functioning at 50% capacity. If it stopped working altogether, she would be in trouble.

Madison floated away from the complex machinery and kicked it in frustration. Another red warning light appeared. Great.

She flicked through the maintenance manual, her body gently falling towards the planet's large gravity mass 260 miles below. When her stockinged feet touched the hatchway, Madison flexed her knees and pushed away, boosting herself upwards. Grabbing a handgrip, she swung back towards the water recycler and frowned in consternation.

A beeping sound caught Madison's attention. She noticed a flashing green square on the panel interface. She tapped it and looked at the monitor, where she saw a readout that caused a slight flutter of alarm. It was the proximity alert, warning her that something was approaching the station. Despite this, Madison told herself there was nothing to be alarmed about. It was probably a stray tool, such as a socket wrench, or a satellite drifting too near because of orbital decay.

She attached the manual to the bulkhead, pushed herself towards the nearest observation cupola, and peered through the transparent dome.

From this position, Earth wasn't visible. All she could see was one portion of the solar array angled towards the sun and, further away, lots of stars. The proximity alert picked up any space debris within one hundred miles, so the chances of spotting anything small were remote, but she searched around for any errant objects. After a minute, she was about to give up when something caught her eye: a dark shadow moving across the sea of stars.

Whatever it was, it was big. And it was closing in fast.

Something flashed rapidly on the front of the moving thing, temporarily blinding and confusing her. She closed her eyes and rubbed away the dark afterimages that swirled in her vision. Madison had barely opened them for a second look when the station suddenly shuddered. She gave an involuntary gasp before the station vibrated again, this time accompanied by a rapid tattoo of metallic clangs like someone was bashing the outside with an enormous hammer. Klaxons sounded throughout the station, and the emergency lights flickered and dimmed before brightening again.

Something had hit them. Some piece of space junk had slammed into the station. It was the only explanation.

More flashes beyond the cupola broke through Madison's terror, and she watched dumbfounded as the dark object was joined by a second and then a third. They moved in a phalanx formation, which instantly told her she wasn't looking at space junk because they were manoeuvering with a purpose, now changing direction.

Madison dragged herself down the capsule and through the hatchway into the next compartment, from where she'd have a better view. Pressing her face to the viewport, she could barely comprehend what she saw.

Three Soyuz spacecraft glided towards the station with their stubby solar panels resembling insect wings. Each craft mounted a railgun on its front, spitting shimmering flames towards the ISS. Madison watched the rounds travel arrow straight through the vacuum, their tracer-like glow producing a wonderful pyrotechnic display. The rounds hit the station about two-thirds of the way down, setting off dozens of mini-explosions that shattered the four-inch-thick hull of aluminium and Kevlar. The pieces of sheathing burst outwards and sparkled as they caught the sunlight. Another burst of fire destroyed the D700 radio package, and its pair of dishes spun away with a rending, twisting sound only audible inside the station. With the communication array destroyed, any hope of reconnecting with survivors on Earth vanished. Madison felt her fear, which was ever present like a shadow at the back of her mind, suddenly increase tenfold.

The breach in the hull posed a threat to the entire station's integrity. Fortunately, to avoid a catastrophic depressurization, the hatches connecting each section of the station closed automatically, isolating the damaged compartment. This did not silence the high-pitched sound of oxygen escaping nor prevent the station from listing to one side, causing Madison to roll over.

Thankfully the wall was padded with foam and she bounced off without harm. She clawed her way back to the viewport. The Soyuz spacecraft had ceased firing, and the lead vehicle used its altitude thrusters to steer a course to the closest CBM. Once the Soyuz was mated to the Common

Berthing Mechanism her crew would be able to board the station.

The sudden turn of events left Madison shell-shocked. In moments her situation had gone from risky to critical, with far-reaching consequences that were difficult to comprehend.

The brief battle in space had come to an end. Despite all parties agreeing never to use weapons in space the Russians had seized the moment and launched an audacious attack against the International Space Station. This meant the Baikonur Cosmodrome, or a similar location, had survived the earthquakes and was still operational. On the other hand NASA appeared to be in total disarray with no communication with their astronauts in space and no ability to prevent the Russian attack.

Madison recognized the sounds of the Soyuz spacecraft's docking mechanism as it sealed onto the airlock. She had only a few moments to plan: should she resist or surrender? But even as she floated there in indecision, Madison knew fighting was senseless. Even if she could find an improvised weapon, grappling with well-organized and likely well-armed cosmonauts was a crazy idea. There would only be one outcome.

Madison backed away. She could slow the Russians down by sealing off different sections of the ISS and then retreating to the furthest part of the station. This wouldn't buy her much time but would send a clear message that the Russians couldn't have everything their way.

Madison turned around so she could pull herself through a nearby hatchway. She stopped abruptly because a man was blocking the opening. He had a short and stocky physique, which suggested he had spent considerable time in space. His round face had small features and he was holding a handgun, which he pointed directly at her.

"Please come with me, Mrs Leitner," he said with a thick Russian accent.

Chapter 2

SOMEWHERE OVER THE ENGLISH COUNTRYSIDE

PEERING OVER THE SIDE OF the wicker basket, Scott Cook watched the countryside passing below. Even after a week of travelling by hot air balloon he still couldn't get used to the dizzying views.

Their first attempt at flight had nearly ended in disaster. With the balloon securely fastened to a mooring rope, he and Fabian had taken the balloon up several hundred feet using small bursts of the propane burners. Initially everything seemed to be going fine until Scott shouted down to the others, instructing them to unfasten the line. As soon as the rope was released a strong gust of wind caught the large envelope and swept them away.

"Jeez!" Scott had shouted. "Open the vent!"

They'd been blown sideways at a 45-degree angle, forcing the two men to hold on for dear life. Luckily the wind took them away from the coast and over the fields and country lanes. Scott's wife and the others had chased after them, shouting and calling out, but they were soon left behind as the balloon gained speed and altitude.

Fabian pulled at the control line to open the small vent hole at the crown of the balloon, which would release the hot air and allow for a safe landing. But either he pulled too hard or the line was frayed because it snapped and came away in his hand.

"That's not good," Fabian shouted, making the biggest understatement of the year.

The basket was being thrown around violently and they were in danger of falling out. Scott let out a loud curse. If only his friend Alan Pritchard were still here. Alan would know what to do. Alan had saved them from many tight situations since the earthquakes. For one, he wouldn't have untied the guy ropes; that was a rookie mistake on Scott's part. But Alan was no longer with them. He'd died on their journey back home. So the responsibility of finding a safe place to live fell on Scott, and discovering the hot air balloon at that moment felt like a big stroke of luck. It was much easier to fly over the destroyed land than to travel on foot.

That was the idea, anyhow.

What Scott hadn't considered was his own foolishness.

Scott's brain worked overtime as he gazed up at the balloon from the bottom of the basket.

"Get me up there, Fabian," he shouted. "I'll have to do it by hand."

"Are you crazy?" the young Dutchman responded.

"I don't need to go high. Just above the burners."

He gestured towards the frayed end of the control line. When Fabian saw what he meant, he buried his head in his hands, groaned incoherently, and said, "I'll go. You remember I'm a better climber than you, right?"

That was true. Fabian's climbing abilities and physical prowess had been extremely valuable numerous times.

As the hot air balloon continued to race out of control over the countryside, Fabian struggled to his feet and held one of the uprights supporting the basket. The balloon's sharp tilt made it slightly easier for him to climb onto the wicker rim, but it also meant he was dicing with death: one misstep, and he'd be over the side.

Scott anxiously watched Fabian climb past the burner, avoiding the hot blast valve. Then Fabian stretched his arm as high as possible, just reaching the loose end of the control line. He wrapped it around his wrist and then tugged.

The hot air balloon immediately started descending, catching them both by surprise. Scott, who was holding onto the bottom of the basket, was fine, but Fabian's feet slipped and he was left hanging by a thread.

"Hold on!" Scott shouted needlessly. "We're going down fast!"

They dropped like a stone and the ground rushed up to meet them. Scott watched through a gap in the basket as they flew over a stand of trees and a road cut by several deep fissures. They barely avoided a wrecked farmhouse before crashing into a large greenhouse in the back garden. The basket snagged on a high wall surrounding the plot of land, bringing them to an abrupt stop. In the chaos, Scott saw his friend thrown through the air before the basket overturned and trapped him underneath.

Scott was too stunned to move at first. After a few moments he regained his composure and tried to get out from under the basket. He was afraid that Fabian might be lying on the ground, injured and bleeding.

Crawling on all fours, Scott emerged to find his friend sitting among the crushed fruit and vegetable plants. He was dishevelled and had tousled hair, but otherwise he was fine.

"I'm never falling for your crazy ideas again," Fabian said, munching on a juicy tomato.

Both men escaped serious harm, and by the time their companions arrived, Scott and Fabian had already cleaned themselves up. It took them the rest of the day to retrieve and inspect the balloon for damage. Fortunately, the balloon was still operational.

Following the terrifying experience, they chose to spend their first night back in England at the farmhouse and try again in the morning. They found signs that the property had been deserted in haste because the larder was well-stocked with canned produce and the garden overflowing with fruit and vegetables. They took advantage of the abundance of food around them and started a campfire to ward off the slight evening chill despite the mild summer weather.

Scott and his wife Sara were still dealing with a tense situation after learning that Louise Swann was pregnant with Scott's child. Even though Sara had forgiven him for cheating, finding out about the baby brought up a lot of problems for their future. For the time being they called a truce and enjoyed a restful night's sleep.

The day after their first go with the balloon, Scott, Fabian, and Tammy Dahl, the leader of the scout group they had met outside Amsterdam, made another attempt. This time they learned the basics of ballooning through trial and error. It was much more difficult than they had anticipated. They could figure out how to climb and land, and the basket was equipped with an altimeter to measure their height and a windspeed dial. But once they were airborne, they had no control over the direction they travelled.

By the middle of the afternoon, they felt confident enough to try once more. They decided to take a short flight, and they took off once everybody was on board. They only flew a few miles (it was hair-raising for them all, particularly the children) before landing in the middle of a large field. Reasonably pleased with their progress, they decided to camp there for a second night.

On the third day, they set out to find a place they might call home. To conserve the propane gas and avoid risks, they would only travel during the daytime.

It soon became clear that finding a safe place to take refuge wouldn't be straightforward. The country all around took on a different aspect from above, and the few available maps were of little help because the landscape had been drastically altered by the recent earthquakes: most of the roads and railway lines were blocked by landslides, bridges had collapsed, and rivers changed course. Many towns and villages had been destroyed by fire or reduced to rubble. In the distance to their right, the Norfolk Broads sparkled in the morning sun like ribbons of quicksilver. Further away, on the horizon, The Wash seemed to have increased in size threefold, and the town of King's Lynn had been washed out to sea. Through their binoculars they could see the twin towers of the town's Minster poking above the waves several miles offshore.

They floated silently above the English countryside, with only the occasional roar of the balloon's burners breaking the peace.

It wasn't all grimness. In the aftermath of the disaster, there were some signs of nature's resurgence. They saw flocks of waterfowl skimming the marshy ground, herds of deer roaming the deserted streets, and wild ponies chasing each other across fields. On the fourth or fifth day, a swarm of brightly coloured butterflies appeared, flitting and dancing around their balloon, drawing laughter and sighs of wonder.

But they saw no signs of human life. Not living, at least.

On the outskirts of one large town, Scott noticed long earth banks arranged in orderly rows along with abandoned earthmovers and bulldozers. He realized that these could only be mass graves marking the location where many people had been buried in a hurry. There was no activity in the area, which could mean that the gravediggers had completed their grim task and there were no more dead to bury, or they themselves had perished.

Later in the afternoon, Louise drew their attention to a long line of abandoned vehicles on an undamaged stretch of motorway. The queue lasted over a mile and they soon saw what had caused the logjam.

"Would you look at that," breathed Tammy.

The motorway passed right alongside a large reservoir. The concrete dam had ruptured and the water had gushed through the breach, carving a muddy defile and crushing everything in its path. Hamlets and villages stood no chance against the onrushing flood. The motorway beyond this point had crumbled under the crush of water, and they could see countless cars and trucks buried in the dried-up mud. Sadly, hundreds if not thousands of people had lost their lives in this disaster. It was clear that the survivors had no chance of receiving help or being rescued from the wreckage.

Scott lowered his binoculars and could think of nothing to say.

Beyond the ruptured dam stretched open moorland ascending to lines of hills. It meant they'd come further than any of them realized. The southerly winds had carried them to northern England, likely somewhere around the Peak District or the Yorkshire Dales. Scott took out the maps and spent a few minutes studying them.

Just then, the propane burners over his head gave a series of laboured coughs before cutting out. Scott looked at them in alarm.

Fabian fiddled with the controls.

"What's happened?" Scott asked, quickly folding up his maps and joining him.

"There's no pressure coming from the tanks," replied Fabian, operating the blast valve trigger.

"What does that mean?"

"It means," said the young man with a shrug, "that we are out of juice."

They'd been lucky to get this far, Scott told himself as he leaned over the basket and looked at the ground a thousand feet below them.

"We need somewhere to put down," he told the others.

They continued to drift for a few minutes with the wicker basket creaking quietly in the breeze. As they passed over a hill topped with limestone, a small village appeared on the other side with an expansive green next to a crumpled church spire.

"That will do," someone said.

Scott gently pulled the repaired control line to open the vent, and the balloon started a slow descent towards the ground. A minute later, it touched down on the village green with scarcely a bump.

The grown-ups hopped out, secured the balloon, and then helped the children down. The balloon envelope slowly deflated.

Scott gazed around. At the edge of the village green was a drystone wall. He strolled over for a closer look and found a small graveyard on the other side. During the earthquakes, the village church had partially collapsed. The spire had fallen and spilled over the churchyard into the car park next door like a giant's game of Jenga. In contrast, the nave remained intact, although it was now exposed to the elements where the collapsing spire had torn away the porch. From his position he couldn't see the aisles and wooden pews, but near the altar was an impressive organ caught in a shaft of sunlight. From under the church roofline, a pair of stone gargoyles scowled down at him.

Scott walked down the wall and went under the lychgate while reading notices for a village fête and a charity line-dancing event. He stopped on the pavement and looked at a white-painted pub called The Shepherd's Rest. At one time it would have been a picturesque country inn but unfortunately the upstairs had been gutted by fire, which had spread to the neighbouring properties. A swarm of flies was feasting on the body of a dog lying in the gutter.

The sound of his friends' voices drew Scott back to the centre of the village green.

Tammy approached him.

"Louise was just saying that as we were coming down to land, she noticed a large caravan park on the outskirts of the village. They might have propane tanks. What do you think, Scott?"

Everyone was looking at him and waiting.

The village was strangely silent, and he felt uneasy, though he couldn't quite figure out why. After the disaster, his intuition had become so heightened that it remained vigilant for any potential danger. It wasn't exactly blaring out an alarm, but something wasn't right.

Then Scott berated himself: it was the end of the world. Was he expecting a welcoming committee or gaily dressed children dancing around a maypole, perhaps?

"It's worth a look," he said.

He glanced up at the sky. A bank of clouds had closed in, threatening rain showers.

"Me and Tammy will go. On the way, we'll check out the village. The rest of you search around for somewhere we can spend the night. But don't wander too far; stay within sight of the balloon. We can pitch the tents here if you can't find anywhere suitable."

The circle of expectant people all nodded.

After Louise gave them directions, he and Tammy left the rest of the group and crossed over the grass. They passed through a playground and a metal gate before arriving at a road that bordered the village green. They set off walking and soon found themselves passing through the centre of the deserted village.

The unsettling silence continued to make Scott nervous. He wondered where everyone had gone. Looking around, Scott noticed the quake damage was haphazard and unpredictable, and they had seen this pattern in other places too. While a row of houses lay in splinters on one side of the street, small shops looked untouched on the other. The contrast was stark. There should be some survivors, he reasoned.

Scott walked towards a small convenience store. Looking through the window he noticed that the shelves were empty. Next to the store was The Jubilee Tearoom, which had also been ransacked by looters, leaving overturned chairs and tables but nothing left at the food counter. Somebody had been here searching for supplies but they'd apparently moved on. Scott wondered if all the survivors had been evacuated. Perhaps the authorities weren't taking any chances considering the breached dam was only a few miles away. He wasn't sure if this made him feel better or worse.

Tammy led him away from the row of shops and pointed out the village market hall. The quakes had destroyed the old structure, snapping the stout timber pillars like they were made from balsa wood. There was an overturned pushchair on the ground, and a child's pink coat fluttered in the breeze.

They moved steadily through the village. Scott had long since grown immune to the horrors left by the worldwide earthquakes and floods, but he still felt drawn to the ghastly sights. They held a spellbinding fascination for him, and he asked himself how much more of this the human mind could soak up before reaching a breaking point.

As they moved forwards, they came across several vast heaps of debris that obstructed their path. Wooden telegraph poles leaned at odd angles, creating criss-cross patterns against the sky. The smell of leaking gas and damaged sewer pipes was all around.

It took them three times longer than expected to walk through the village but they eventually made it to the caravan park.

It was a small affair, mainly comprising several large static caravans with a sprinkling of glamping pods. Near the entrance was an intact bungalow presumably where the site manager lived. Damage here was minimal, and it would have made a good place to spend the night, but they both decided it was too far from the balloon.

It didn't take them long to find what they were looking for; the site was well-stocked with propane tanks. Behind the bungalow was a fully fuelled quad bike and trailer. They set to work loading the propane tanks onto the trailer and securing them with bungee straps.

While working, he and Tammy were interrupted by a strange noise. It was a high-pitched ululation coming from a distance, and the hills around them made it difficult to determine where it originated.

They stopped what they were doing and looked around. When they heard the noise again, Scott thought it sounded closer and coming from a different direction. This sent shivers down his spine. Tammy, who never went anywhere without her crossbow, shifted it onto her shoulder.

"What is it?" Scott asked as the wailing faded away.

"Sounds like dogs."

The shrill yowling came again.

"Or wolves."

"We don't have wolves in England," Scott reminded her.

"Didn't Scotland reintroduce them several years ago? They could have made their way south."

Scott wasn't sure on that score: he'd read about the idea, but such stories come and go.

They decided to crack on. After securely strapping down the last tank, Tammy took the quad bike controls while Scott sat behind her. Then she turned on the ignition, pressed down on the right-hand foot pedal, and thumbed the throttle. The bike's four large wheels gripped the grassy field and they set off.

During the return journey, Scott carefully watched their surroundings. He looked forward to rejoining the others.

• • •

Their companions had managed to find a good spot to spend the night. Across the village green was a small daycare centre with an open view of their balloon. They placed candles around the classroom, unrolled their sleeping bags, and rustled up a supper of cold baked beans and sausages.

After finishing their meal, Louise gathered the children around her and began reading a storybook. Even the older children came over to listen as if they, too, longed for a return to more innocent times.

Scott sat against the back wall, watching the scene unfold before him. It was like a flashback to their old lives, and he couldn't help but think of all the kids he had taught in class. He remembered Fawad, who was the only one from his class to survive the quake only to be killed by the school caretaker, Mr. Finch. But for one night, it was as if none of that had happened.

Later, after the storytelling, Louise and Saskia, the teenage girl, let the children rummage through the selection of toys, which mainly targeted young toddlers but kept them entertained.

Sara came over and sat next to Scott. She leaned her head against his shoulder and they exchanged smiles.

After settling into their sleeping bags, the children drifted off to sleep, and the occasional murmur broke the classroom silence.

One by one, the adults fell asleep until Scott was the only one still awake.

Scott heard the howling again coming from somewhere. This time, he noticed a new sound accompanying it — a whistling and fluting noise that rose and fell. It took him some minutes to figure it out. It was the wind blowing into the church and through the organ pipes.

The blend of sounds made a haunting melody.

Chapter 3

CHICKAHOMINY INDIAN RESERVATION
LITTLE GREENBRIER RIVER
WEST VIRGINIA

OF THE THREE MEN ESCORTING them to the reservation, Young Little Wolf was the most aggressive, Kenny Leland decided. He would prod Kenny with his foot whenever his pace slowed down or if he tried to look around. And whenever Kenny or his friends, Bethany and Alex, exchanged words, Young Little Wolf would ride up to them on his prairie pony and bark at them, as if he were looking for a fight. Kenny had a feeling that the confrontation could have turned violent if it hadn't been for the young man's father, Two Moon.

Finally, Two Moon had enough of his errant son. They had a brief and heated talk, which ended with Young Little Wolf trotting to the head of the group with a sullen expression. After this, they proceeded without incident.

The tense confrontation back at the riverside, when Kenny and his friends woke to find the newcomers going through their personal effects, was still fresh in Kenny's mind. In hindsight, the three men's sudden arrival was unsurprising, as only a few miles separated Kenny's campground and the Indian reservation they'd seen the day before. It was now clear that they had been under observation right from the start. Kenny felt like an idiot because they had been foolish enough to trespass on someone's land. He only hoped their naivety would not cost them dearly.

Kenny had tried to appeal to them by explaining their mistake and promised they would leave immediately. Two Moon, whom Kenny guessed to be around fifty years old, had responded with little more than a command to follow him. Kenny suspected that Two Moon didn't have the authority to decide what to do about their trespass.

They had no other option but to follow the command. Kenny was concerned about what would happen to their things, particularly their guns, while they were away, but the three American Indians showed little interest in their belongings. It didn't really matter, anyway, if Kenny, Bethany and Alex never came back.

From their campground, they retraced their journey of the day before. They bypassed the town of Lansing and were led under the dense tree cover on Mount Sewell's flanks and past the gnarled tree they had passed yesterday. It took until mid-afternoon before they came within sight of the Indian reservation, and by the time they entered the small village, all three of them were footsore and thirsty.

As they'd observed yesterday, the village was a mixture of lodges, tepees, and a few run-down motorhomes. A group of men were repairing a cluster of cars parked at the back of the village. The school bus was nowhere to be seen. People were busy with their assigned tasks, but many stopped to look at the newcomers. Soon, a small crowd including several children followed them.

In the centre of the village, a few people were sitting on deckchairs around a burning oil drum. One of them was an elderly man who appeared to be at least one hundred years old. He wore a large sheepskin coat with the hood up, even though the sun was shining warmly. Next to him, a young person in a red and black flannel shirt and headscarf was playing with a litter of kittens in a cardboard box.

Kenny and his friends were brought before the elderly man. Two Moon spoke to him in his native language while the man in the sheepskin coat watched them closely with his tired eyes. Kenny felt uneasy under his watery gaze, so he glanced around and realized that the news of their arrival had spread as the crowd around them had doubled in size. All eyes were on them.

He caught Young Little Wolf's baleful stare. Kenny refused to back down and stared back.

The elderly man's voice drew Kenny's attention. He spoke with strength and eloquence, pointing a bony finger at Kenny from his coat's long sleeve. Two Moon translated his words.

"He asks, what brings you big bellies here? He who takes the fat, why have you built a home on our sovereign land?"

Kenny was caught off-guard by the derogatory remark. He was unsure how to react until he saw a playful twinkle in the elderly man's eyes, which made him think it was merely a tongue-in-cheek insult.

"We are just trying to find a secure place to live. Please excuse our ignorance; we have been through many hardships during our journey," Kenny said, opening his arms and shrugging. He continued, "We are tired of wandering and struggling to survive." Bethany and Alex nodded in agreement beside him.

Two Moon passed this on to the venerable chap, who was warming his hands on the fire.

"He asks that you tell him of your experiences," Two Moon prompted.

Kenny took a moment to collect his thoughts before speaking. He recounted everything that had happened, starting from his time at the observatory in the Canary Islands. He then mentioned his flight to London and the earthquakes that occurred there. He went on to describe their journey to Iceland and the eruption of the volcano. Kenny also spoke of their travels with the President, which caused a stir among the listeners. Finally, he talked about their arrival at Little Greenbrier River. By the time Kenny finished speaking, he felt emotionally exhausted.

Two Moon and the village leader had a lengthy discussion, which Kenny wasn't part of. As they conversed, the boy with the cardboard box sidled over.

"Do you want to buy some kittens, mister?"

Kenny said in a friendly voice, "Sorry, Kid."

Two Moon shooed the boy away.

"He asks me to tell you that your arrival coincides with our departure along The Second Trail of Tears."

Kenny didn't know what the trail of tears was, but it sounded like the villagers would soon be embarking on a journey of their own. He asked Two Moon why they would leave here when it seemed a good place to remain.

Two Moon seemed to acknowledge this with a phlegmatic smile, and he looked at his sneakers.

"There is a large community of our folks, thousands of us gathered together in a strong and safe location. There are too many dangers for us here since The Great Cataclysm, and too much blood will be spilled if we stay. If we are to survive, we must join our families."

"Do you mean there's a risk of more earthquakes?" Bethany asked.

"He who takes the fat wishes us harm," Two Moon answered, using the odd phrase for a second time.

"People are drumming you out, you mean?" said Kenny.

"It has always been this way."

"But this is your sovereign land. You've lived here since before our folks arrived in Europe," Alex added.

The elderly man spoke again, and Kenny thought he understood English more than he pretended.

"There's another reason why we have to go," Two Moon said. "Come with me, and I'll explain."

Two Moon walked through the village, followed by Kenny and his friends. The villagers dispersed, and Kenny felt some of the tension inside him ease. After a minute, they approached a gable-roofed lodge made of elm bark. Two Moon opened the door and stepped inside, beckoning them to follow.

It was gloomy inside, with only a pair of lanterns and a small fire lending any light. They filled the interior with acrid smoke that caught the back of Kenny's throat. A group of women and girls were present but they quickly moved aside to let the new arrivals through. At the back of the room, a woman with facial piercings was sitting on a wooden pallet holding a child of five or six in her arms.

As Kenny's eyes adjusted to the dim light, he saw that the child appeared unwell. She had no hair other than a few wisps, and her face was pale. Her lips were dry and covered in mouth ulcers. There was a faint medicinal smell in the air, mixed with a sweet hint of corruption.

Two Moon told them that the child had a malignant brain tumour. The diagnosis was pretty bad. She was getting treatment before The Great Cataclysm, but now without further care, she was unlikely to make it.

The girl's mother looked up at them and smiled sadly, before gently rocking the child to and fro.

"We have medicines to slow the tumour and control seizures, but she needs surgery. We are told that the large community has doctors who can help."

Alex asked, "Is the outpost or settlement far from here?" as a frown darkened his features.

"It is across the border of Kanata."

"Canada? That's a heck of a journey for this young lassie," Alex exclaimed.

"The poor thing," Bethany breathed.

"When are you leaving?"

"As soon as we can. In a few days, with luck."

"How do you plan on getting there?" asked Kenny.

"We have many vehicles and horses."

"But the quake damage?" Kenny pressed.

"There are many alternative routes to freeways and highways," Two Moon replied, and for the first time, he had a hint of a smile on his face.

"Yesterday, we noticed a yellow bus."

"Yes, two of our young men have found a workshop in Lansing and are fitting it out with bunks for our children."

Kenny chanced a smile back, saying, "You have everything in order."

Two Moon took them outside, and they blinked their eyes in the afternoon sun.

"We're really sorry for your difficult situation," Kenny said, speaking for all three of them. "If there's anything we can do to compensate for our transgression."

"The child's fate is out of our hands," Two Moon stated pragmatically.

"So," Kenny said hesitantly, "what happens now?"

"Let me speak to my grandfather," Two Moon replied.

They reached the group seated by the burning oil drum, and Two Moon started talking with the elderly man. Young Little Wolf didn't seem happy with the direction their conversation was taking because he shot Kenny a dark look. Maybe, Kenny reasoned, he'd suffered a lifetime of grievances.

Two Moon broke away and rejoined Kenny's party.

"He asks me to tell you that he understands your plight and that he shares your troubles. But entering the area without permission is a grave matter."

Kenny became wary again.

"Although it seems that your actions were caused by carelessness rather than malice. For that reason, my grandfather grants you permission to stay, but you must remain beyond the mountain. If you betray our trust, then measures will be taken."

"Are you saying we can return to our campground?" Bethany asked.

Two Moon turned to her and nodded.

"You may visit the town for supplies and hunt for game in the woods, but do not cross over the mountain further than the old tree."

Kenny said, "We understand," and breathed a sigh of relief. He extended his hand and wished them luck finding their folks and getting help for the sick girl.

Two Moon offered them bottles of spring water from a cooler, and then the three of them began their journey back. From the village, they hiked up the northern side of Mount Sewell and arrived at the visitor information boards on the broad summit. On the opposite side of the trail stood the tall and gnarled tree that had been struck by lightning. This would now be the boundary between the two groups of survivors.

Kenny thought about the girl suffering from a brain tumour. He was no expert, but he felt that her chances of survival were quite low. Even if they managed to cross the border and locate the large community of survivors, and assuming there were indeed doctors there with the necessary skills to treat her, recovering from such a serious illness would require months, if not years, of ongoing treatment.

Kenny had a feeling that Two Moon shared his feelings but guessed there was more to their journey than trying to save one girl's life or escaping roaming bands of genocidal maniacs. The dangerous trip provided them with a sense of purpose, a goal to achieve, and a degree of control over their own destinies. Heaven knows that everyone who had managed to survive this far needed something to hold onto, something to motivate them beyond mere existence. Otherwise, what would be the point?

They made it back to their campground by the downed plane without any trouble and were relieved to see that nothing had been stolen, including the Humvee and guns. Although Two Moon's sons had made a mess, it was nothing major. Kenny realized that they needed to improve their security since they might not be so fortunate the next time uninvited people showed up unannounced. They were eager to finish building their new home as soon as possible.

It was dusk and too late to work that day, but when morning came, they set to work enthusiastically. They completed the frames for the cabin's walls and then hoisted them into position using ropes and the Humvee's towbar. They then used mallets to split cedar shingles to cover the walls. If treated with linseed oil, cedarwood would last for decades before rotting.

After two days of hard work and two nights of sleeping in shifts inside the crashed plane, the cabin walls were almost complete. They spent the morning filling the gaps between the cedar shingles with moss. Now, they were ready to begin working on the roof.

"We need to go into town for supplies," Alex announced. "Using the railway sleepers for the corner posts is fine, but they'll be too heavy for the roof."

"What do we need?"

Alex, in his role as a construction worker, took notes while talking out loud, tugging at his small beard and sucking in air through his teeth.

"We need timber for rafters, hardwood sheets, bitumen for waterproofing, nail guns, and other power tools."

Kenny suggested they get their hands on a generator to charge them.

"Lansing is a small town," said Alex, "but there should be a Home Depot or a couple of lumber yards."

Kenny looked around at the peaceful countryside. He wasn't stoked about going to an urban area, but they had to take the chance to finish building their new home.

Chapter 4

GORNERGRAT MOUNTAIN
BERNESE ALPS
SWITZERLAND

THE VAST FIELDS OF BASALT rock extended for miles. For two days, the earth had spewed out continuous lava flows from deep within its core, melting the snow and glacial ice and transforming the high alpine passes into a barren moonscape. It took a further three days for the ground to cease shaking and cool sufficiently to allow Timo Lehmann to venture outside.

The proton beam emanating from the crater at Lake Geneva, which was once the location of the Large Hadron Collider, disappeared as the tremors subsided. Timo assumed that the two events were related unless the ATLAS detector, the world's largest particle accelerator, had finally run out of power.

While he was waiting in the hotel, Timo constructed a few homemade bottle thermometers using glass bottles, water, alcohol, straws, and red food dye. He also took the time to convert his rough notes into a more detailed and scholarly document. In addition, he kept himself and Genny in good physical shape by exercising her on the bar terrace and jogging with her through the hotel corridors.

Finally, on the Friday following the latest round of geological upheaval, Timo estimated it was safe to go out and explore.

Timo discovered a Bernese Trek backpack among the abandoned hiking gear in the hotel lobby. He decided to use it to carry the thermometers and put his notepad inside a small tote bag. He then pulled on a pair of good boots and some outdoor clothing. Finally, he bid farewell to Genny, leaving her alone in the Tower Suite as he set off.

It was a beautiful day with cloudless skies and good visibility. He followed one of the pathways to the edge of the terrace railings, clambered over, and dropped three feet onto the rocky ground.

The uneven basalt surface felt unstable at first, but after a few steps, he soon grew accustomed to walking over it. Under the thick soles of his boots, the ground was warm but not hot, and pieces of quartz glimmered in the sunlight. Small pillars of steam vented into the air here and there while an unpleasant sulphur odour lingered in the atmosphere.

Walking across the rocky terrain, Timo was amazed by the diverse shapes formed by the hardened lava streams. Some basalt rocks had an unusual hexagonal form, while others were globular masses resembling petrified oil slicks. Others resembled crazy paving, emitting curls of smoke between the cracks.

He carefully descended the slope, passing through shadow where the valley once held glacial ice a thousand feet deep but was now filled with house-sized boulders. Timo remembered the intense seismic activity and volcanic eruptions that shattered the Monte Rosa massif. He realized that if something similar were to happen right now, he would either be buried under a mountain of debris or instantly incinerated in a flash of superheated steam.

He selected a location for the first thermometer, inserting it between two chunks of basalt near a deep borehole. Timo patiently waited as the red dye crept up the straw, marking its position with a pencil. He then took out his notepad and quickly wrote down the reading and details about the surrounding terrain before moving on. After walking another 500 metres, Timo stopped and placed the second thermometer, noted the temperature, and repeated the process every half a kilometre.

He was searching for a spot to place the last thermometer when he suddenly came upon a rocky ledge. He stopped just in time, lurching over the drop. Once he recovered his balance, he leaned forward to peek at what was on the other side. Shaking his head because he couldn't tell from this angle, he stepped back from the edge. He then made his way around the shelf of rock and approached it from the side.

Timo peered into the opening of a large cavern sheltered beneath the ledge. He felt the heat coming from beneath the earth and could smell the distinct odour of hot metal that he had come to associate with lava. This suggested that he was looking at a big magma chamber bubbling with geothermal energy.

Timo's face started tingling from the heat in a few seconds. He realized it was unsafe to stay in that place for too long. He hurriedly set the last thermometer and made his way back to the hotel, retracing his steps. He was back inside within half an hour.

The evening found Timo inside the mountaintop observatory, where the walls of the large dome were covered with star charts and lunar maps. On the desks there were several instruments: a spectrometer to measure components of light, a small MCP to measure particles and photons, and a bolometer to gather electromagnetic radiation readings. To keep himself warm, he had also brought a thermos of oxtail soup with him.

As Timo stood in the observatory, the main telescope towered over him. It was a 36-inch parabolic Crayford focuser telescope made of strong but lightweight carbon fibre, fitted to a roller-bearing assembly. The telescope was user-friendly. All Timo had to do was input a set of coordinates, and the dome would rotate on its drives. The ceiling shutter would slide open, and the telescope's computer would locate whatever celestial object or constellation he wished to observe, revealing the night sky in all its glory.

Tonight, the panorama of stars appeared particularly stunning, glittering over the snow-capped Matterhorn.

But something wasn't right. Timo was a nuclear physicist and expert in quantum mechanics, but like most scientists, his knowledge extended to other fields such as plasma and radiological engineering, magnetic resonance, and astronomy. After the events of DAY 1, Timo and his colleagues at CERN worked tirelessly to fix the disaster. They quickly discovered that the close transit of the Moon with Earth had triggered a chain of events that destabilized the planet's iron and nickel inner core, heated up the molten outer core, and caused fluctuating magnetic field readings. To counter these issues, they ran the Large Hadron Collider's proton beams at seven trillion volts and successfully slowed down Earth's core. Sadly, new dangers had emerged as soon as one set of problems had been resolved.

Timo went through his papers until he found the logs he had kept during his previous evenings of observing the night sky. He licked his fingertip and turned the pages back and forth, periodically peering through the telescope's eyepiece. In the viewfinder, he could see the constellation of Scorpius with its bright orange star, Antares.

Timo frowned deeply. The constellation of Scorpius was in the wrong place. Normally, at this time of year and this latitude in the northern hemisphere, it should be low in the sky and hidden behind the mountain range. But the star Antares was high overhead, winking down the length of the telescope.

Timo entered new coordinates into the computer and waited as the dome moved around. Then he peered through the eyepiece once again. He noticed that Sagittarius was not in its usual position, too. This constellation was typically visible south of the equator, but now it was just appearing behind the Matterhorn's pyramidal peak.

Timo leaned back in his chair, closing his eyes and squeezing the bridge of his nose in frustration. Something had gone horribly wrong with Earth's axial tilt. After studying the data, there was no other conclusion. The moon's altered prograde orbit had wreaked havoc on Earth, dragging the planet over onto its side. Normally, Earth spins on a 23.5–degree tilt, which causes the seasons. If the planet tilted more, it would throw the world into further chaos. Earth would experience a decades-long winter that would cause untold suffering.

During Earth's long history, the planet has undergone a complete reversal of tilt every 13,000 years, returning to the same 23.5-degree tilt after roughly 26,000 years. The last time this happened was during the Last Glacial Period (LGP), or the Last Ice Age as it is known in popular culture. LGPs have occurred throughout Earth's history, and a handful of times, these glacial epochs have led to what scientists call a *Grande Coupoure*, or an extinction event.

Timo tried to recall everything he knew about extinction events:

Around 2.4 billion years ago, Earth witnessed its first mass extinction event which is now known as the Oxygen Catastrophe. This event occurred due to the emergence of a bacterium that had the ability to produce oxygen as a byproduct of photosynthesis. As the bacterium thrived and multiplied, it released unprecedented amounts of oxygen, causing a significant shift in the composition of the Earth's atmosphere. This sudden influx of oxygen was toxic to many of the existing species on Earth, and as a result, they perished, leading to the extinction of almost 85% of all species. This event marked a significant turning point in the history of life on Earth, leading to new species better adapted to the changing environment.

Around 360 million years ago, the planet experienced a significant and devastating event that resulted in the extinction of a vast number of species. This event, known as the Late Devonian Epoch Extinction, is believed to have been caused by a global cooling period that decreased sea levels. As the sea levels decreased, the oceans experienced widespread anoxia, which is the reduction of O_2 levels. This anoxic environment made it difficult for many marine species to survive, and as a result, an estimated 70% of all life in the sea was wiped out, such as trilobites, marine arthropods, and coral reef species. It took millions of years for the Earth to recover from this event.

250 million years ago, before the reign of the dinosaurs, a series of massive volcanic eruptions occurred in the Siberian Traps region. These eruptions spewed out copious amounts of toxic greenhouse gases, including sulphur dioxide and carbon dioxide, that raised global temperatures and transformed the oceans into a highly acidic environment. The event proved fatal, and around 70% of life on land and a staggering 90% of life in the sea perished, marking it as one of the most severe mass extinctions in history. Scientists have called this event The Great Dying.

Approximately 70,000 years ago, a catastrophic event occurred at the Toba Caldera Complex in present-day Indonesia. This event is referred to as the Toba eruption and is widely recognized as one of the most significant volcanic eruptions in Earth's history. The Toba eruption resulted in a colossal amount of ash being released, causing a global volcanic winter that lasted for six to ten years. This volcanic winter, in turn, contributed to a cooling episode that persisted for the next one thousand years. In addition to the environmental impact, the Toba eruption had a profound effect on the genetic makeup of humans. The sudden drop in temperature and the resulting famine likely caused a significant genetic bottleneck in the human race. Some estimates suggest that the human population may have dropped to as low as one or two thousand individuals, which had long-lasting consequences for the species.

It was reasonable to wonder if Earth was heading for another *Grande Coupoure,* a mass extinction event. If it was, then humanity might not survive such a culling. However, Timo tried to reassure himself that such events take tens of thousands, if not millions of years, to unfold slowly. Although it might seem like a blink of an eye in terms of a planet's lifecycle, it was an impossibly long stretch of time for the human brain to comprehend. Timo's immediate concern was to survive each new day.

After shutting down the telescope, Timo gathered his things and walked back to his hotel room in the Tower Suite. Genny must have heard his footsteps because he could hear her claws scratting at the door. As soon as he stepped inside she greeted him by smothering him with drool and wagging her tail so much that she nearly fell over. After five minutes of hugging and frolicking on the couch, Timo finally managed to disentangle himself from her clutches.

After settling her, Timo took a seat at the writing desk to update his extensive notes.

Chapter 5

**WHITE OAKS
BELLE HAVEN
VIRGINIA**

DEPUTY ORVILLE GEDDES OF THE Belle Haven Sheriff's Department holstered his sidearm and looked down at the dead man. He was a big fella whose bare stomach spilled over the top of the blue workmen's trousers he'd been wearing. The front of the trousers were undone because the man hadn't time to do them up properly when Deputy Geddes arrived unexpectedly. Now he was dead, with his body peppered with five still-smoking bullet holes and his bushy beard turned crimson.

Deputy Geddes felt a fuzzy sensation inside his head. It was like his skull was stuffed with cotton wool and was in sharp contrast to the red-hot rage he'd experienced after gunning down the teenage looters over at Groveton Mall. When the call came over the patrol car radio, he'd reasoned that, as a law enforcement officer, it was his duty to serve the people of this parish to the best of his abilities. Since the declaration of Martial Law, he had been granted a lot of leeway in executing his powers. Thus, Geddes calmly drove along the abandoned country roads with one purpose in mind: to bring order to his jurisdiction.

He'd arrived too late to prevent the lady from being attacked but had stopped her from being killed. Deputy Geddes turned away from the dead man to find her squatting against the wooden shack and fastening her torn blouse.

"Pardon me, ma'am," Geddes said and removed his hat and used it to shield his view as the woman dressed.

Geddes waited until she was finished and then escorted her to the car.

"There's a field hospital over near Artillery Ridge," he told her quietly. "There will be specialist folks there, professional types, who can offer you support. I'll get you there in no time."

Deputy Geddes glanced in his rearview mirror, but the victim said nothing back and she shrank away into the shadows. After her ordeal, she had to be terrified. Why should she trust him, or any other man for that reason?

They didn't speak further during the car ride. To reach the refugee camp, Geddes had to cross a US Army pontoon bridge over the Rappahannock. He drove up onto the row of barges which spanned the river, and the car's tyres vibrated over the metal decking. On the far riverbank, he turned onto Monroe Road and through a set of gates.

The camp was spread across a large field and consisted of lines of tents and galvanized huts, water bowsers, soup kitchens, numerous portable toilets, and a makeshift hospital tent like something from an episode of M.A.S.H. Thousands of people, dressed in the same clothes they were wearing during the earthquakes, milled around. The air was foul with the smell of unwashed bodies and desperation. The entire place was surrounded by high fences strung with razor wire.

Deputy Geddes shook his head and wondered how things had got so bad. His was the most powerful nation in the world, but now it was like a Third World country.

He drove slowly through the throngs of people, ignoring their pleas for help and the sound of bare hands smacking against the car windows. He pulled up outside the hospital tent and looked over into the back seat.

"Sorry, we'll have to go through the crowds. Are you ready, ma'am?"

She gave no response. Geddes donned his hat, pushed open his door, and jumped out. He was immediately besieged by a swarm of people. Emaciated and jaundiced faces, young and old, squeezed in on all sides. With little ceremony, Geddes pushed them away, reached around for the passenger door, and hauled out the woman. He carved a path through the crowd, even as one lady tried to press her newborn into his arms. Then he lifted the tent flap and ducked inside.

The interior reminded Geddes of the sports hall at Donovan's Corner, but on a smaller scale. Wounded and ill citizens filled the whole space. Most had been hastily patched up, and there was a strong smell of gangrene where wounds had been left to fester. Near the back was an army medic up to his knees in gore and sawing off a man's leg. An orderly tried to keep the flies away.

The woman alongside Geddes flinched, so he gently shepherded her away from the unsettling scene and led her towards a screened-off part of the tent. A female doctor was bending over a prostrate form, while on the next bed, an army chaplain was administering last rites.

"Excuse me, miss. I have someone who needs your help."

The doctor turned to Geddes and gave him a distant, vacant stare.

"Can't you see I have enough on my plate?" she muttered.

Then she looked at the woman with Geddes, and her eyes softened minutely as an intuitiveness seeped through her exhaustion. She pointed at an opening in the tent wall. "Through there. They will see to her."

Geddes took the lady across and peered into the adjacent tent. He saw that there were about a dozen people inside, of varying ages and genders. Some of them appeared to be sedated while others were weeping quietly. Two female staff members were moving about the tent, attending to them. But before they could step through, the female doctor called Geddes back.

After pulling the bedsheet over her patient's face, she took the woman by the elbow and said, "Leave her with me."

"Thank you kindly," Geddes replied, fanning his face with his hat to dispel the smell. He lingered a moment, looking at the scene.

"If there's nothing else, we are rather busy," the doctor prompted, not too subtly.

Geddes nodded and stepped outside. The crowd had dissipated, and he took a deep breath, trying to clear his head. The air outside wasn't much better than in the hospital tent. Geddes leaned over his patrol car, drumming his fingers on the metal roof as he scanned the area. The camp was in disarray and with no clear leadership in sight. Just a few days ago, there'd been a visible military presence here, with soldiers in uniform conveying a sense of order and control. But now, other than a few medics in green fatigues attending to the sick and injured, they seemed to have pulled out, leaving the camp occupants to fend for themselves. In their wake, they'd left the camp teetering on the edge of anarchy.

He heard a commotion coming from one of the nearby huts. Outside, two groups of men were involved in a scuffle, and he was about to go over and break it up when a rumbling sound above stopped him. Thinking it was a helicopter passing overhead, he was surprised to see three C-130 aircraft flying in formation just above the treetops.

Geddes watched as, in their wake, a group of around ten or twelve parachutes gracefully descended from above. Each chute was carrying a large, heavy crate slung beneath it, and they swayed gently in the breeze as they drifted slowly downwards. The aircraft banked and peeled away over the trees, their turboprop engines beating the air.

The moment the parachutes appeared, people in the camp stampeded towards them. There was a rush of running feet and a loud clamour of voices. Tents were knocked over and those who were unable to keep up were pushed aside. Anyone who fell to the ground was trampled into the dirt.

The parachutes came down in the field next door, and when the lead figures reached the fence, they clambered over it. Geddes watched in horror as people became entangled in the razor wire at the top. Those behind simply stepped on them to pass over. Others were caught against the bottom half of the fence, and Geddes could do nothing but stand and watch as a crush developed. Children screamed as they lost their parents in the mêlée. He saw people fainting, and worse still, some were asphyxiating.

Geddes snapped out of his shock and rushed over, calling for order. He reached the human stream and was immediately swept off his feet and carried along. The people were pushing and punching each other. In the chaos, his hat was knocked off, and someone's elbow hit him hard on his nose, causing blood to pour from his nostrils.

Once again, Deputy Geddes tried to calm the crowd down, but his voice was drowned out by the noise and the confusion. He drew his sidearm and fired three shots into the air. For a moment, there was a brief silence, but it was short-lived. As soon as the crowd saw some people dropping down into the field and rushing towards the crates, pandemonium broke out once again.

The soil under his boots became soft and squishy as if he were treading through mud. But to his horror, he soon realized that he was actually stepping on people. Geddes barely had time to process this before another human wave swept his feet off the carpet of bodies, and the human river surged forwards.

Geddes twisted his head to see people being crushed to death against the fence. Then, under the weight of bodies, the barrier buckled and gave way. Those at the front stood no chance; they went down and hundreds more steam-rolled over them.

The collapsing fence at least released the pressure and the crowd burst into the spacious field. Geddes managed to wade his way to the fringes, gasping for his breath, and then watched the horror continue to unfold.

The mob spilled over the field in a mad dash for the airdropped crates. They left dozens of broken and bleeding bodies in their wake. When they reached the first one, they clambered over the pallets, tearing at the fastenings and digging inside. One man emerged holding a box of food like a sports trophy, whooping and hollering. Then a fight broke out as they battled over the contents of the crate.

The remainder of the baying mob veered away and made for the other crates, which had come to rest near the trees. Suddenly, several vehicles came tearing out of the woodland and accelerated towards the containers. Geddes saw they were pickup trucks mounted with guns, and he looked on as they slid and snaked over the field, racing against the hungry people to reach the crates first. The trucks easily beat them. Two of the pickups slewed to a halt and their occupants trained their guns on the approaching mob. As the crowd wavered and drew to a stop, the people in the remaining pickups hurriedly loaded up the crates, turned around, and raced for cover.

Driven mad with hunger and despair, the outraged crowd watched helplessly as the trucks made off with the supplies. There wasn't a thing Geddes could do. He considered hurrying over to his car to give chase, but knew it was pointless: the thieves would be long gone.

Deputy Geddes turned to look at the field and campsite. He saw a trail of destruction marked by the dead and dying. A few of the injured were heading back through the hole in the fence, helped by colleagues or medics. Meanwhile, most of the crowd hung about silently or looked up at the sky more in hope than expectation.

As Geddes made his way back to the campsite, he noticed that a field triage spot was being set up just outside the hospital tent. The scene was chaotic, with people rushing around and shouting instructions to each other. Dozens of victims were lying on the ground, each wearing a brightly-coloured armband - red, yellow, green, or black – to indicate the severity of their injuries. People were screaming and writhing in pain. Amid the pandemonium, Geddes caught sight of the female doctor whom he had seen earlier.

"It's not the first time this has happened," she told him as he drew near.

Geddes glanced down at the patient she was treating; it was the lady he'd seen holding a newborn. The lady's lips were tinged with a bluish hue.

"Yesterday, we had a delivery of blood," the doctor was saying. "Those same delinquents rode off with the entire batch."

"Why?" Geddes could barely think about anything except the baby.

"They're racketeers looking to make a mint. The lowest of the low. Absolute scum."

The doctor looked him up and down and then turned away.

"You lot aren't doing your job," she added under her breath.

Chapter 6

INTERNATIONAL SPACE STATION
LOW EARTH ORBIT

FOLLOWING THE RUSSIAN TAKEOVER OF the International Space Station, Madison was mostly confined to the Harmony habitation node. She was only allowed to use the washrooms twice a day, but always under the watchful eye of at least one cosmonaut. Notwithstanding her captivity, Madison tried to sneak glimpses of what her captors were up to whenever she was escorted through the station. Despite the Russians' best efforts to conceal their plans, Madison was able to learn quite a bit.

For instance, the day after the Russians boarded, another Soyuz spacecraft and a Soyuz MS-20, a sixth-generation vehicle with a bigger cargo compartment, arrived in orbit. This brought the total number of cosmonauts onboard from 9 to 15. The new crew members spent most of their time repairing the damage caused to the ISS. They also used the Soyuz as sleeping quarters.

In addition to carrying out repairs, the Russians were also busy extending the station. Madison watched through her viewport as they skilfully manoeuvered a large capsule from the MS-20 to the far end of the station and began bolting it into place.

This additional capsule was unlike any other that Madison had seen before. First, it was a different shape from the other segments of the ISS. The capsule was more like a vertical drum mounted within a tubular framework, with its own solar arrays and only one square hatchway. It also didn't seem large enough to be habitable, certainly not for long periods. The Russians ran various tests revealing several remotely operated clamps spaced evenly around the framework. Additionally, the capsule could rotate independently from the rest of the station.

Madison was prevented from seeing more when she was ushered away from the viewport. It wasn't until the next day, as she was being escorted to the washrooms by her female custodian, that she crossed paths with the Commander of the VKS, the Russian Aerospace Forces, Leonid Khrenov. He was the same cosmonaut she had encountered after the brief space battle.

Madison, as an ISS crew member, demanded to be informed about the purpose of the new capsule.

Khrenov, in his green flight suit adorned with the VKS chest emblem, stared back with an unwavering gaze.

"Roscosmos are violating their agreements with NASA and ESA; you can't do this," Madison pointed out.

Khrenov's face twitched slightly, as though the first hint of a smile threatened to spoil his bland features. But he seemed to lack the muscles necessary for normal smiling, so his smile was more of a sneer, like the mark of a branding iron.

"NASA is finished," he said in accented English.

Madison was taken aback by Khrenov's remark and before she could respond, he had already moved away. She should have asked him what he meant because his words seemed to confirm her worst fears. She also wanted to inquire about the whereabouts of the 'special cargo' – the hermetically-sealed locker containing the Declaration of Independence, the United States Constitution, and the Gettysburg Address. Surely they must have it in their possession? Madison watched Khrenov as he floated through the station, her brow knitting together.

On her way back from the washrooms, Madison tried to talk with her custodian, Liliya Trimenko, a freckled redhead.

"What is it like down there?" she implored. "Are there many survivors?"

All she got in return was a disdainful glance.

"What harm can it do by telling me?" Madison pushed, desperate for any news, however vague.

Liliya Tremenko took a deep breath and pushed out her chest.

"The Russian Federation is unbowed. We have suffered no earthquakes, and our people are content. Only the capitalist West is on its knees," she replied, spitting out the last part.

Madison let out a resigned sigh.

"We have achieved great victory with our annexation of the Russian Orbital Station," Liliya added, "and this is just the beginning."

Madison didn't press the matter further and followed silently as she was led back.

• • •

During the next 24 hours, work outside the space station continued non-stop. The Russian team continued to assemble the new capsule. As the hours passed, more components were unpacked and transported through the vacuum by men and women wearing Russian-made semi-rigid spacesuits. Madison observed their movements whenever she had the chance, anxiously watching as they installed a dozen objects that resembled telegraph poles onto the clamps. And slowly, a horrible, sickening sensation developed in the pit of her stomach. She couldn't shake off the thought that perhaps the Russians were building some sort of weapons system.

It didn't appear to be a rocket launcher. The elongated rods did not seem to have rocket nozzles for propulsion, and their pointed nose cones were too tapered to hold a guidance system. But it was clear that the Russians had developed a lethal piece of hardware.

As she dozed in her sleeping pod that evening, it came to her. Madison jolted awake, bumping her head against the wall. She quietly unzipped her sleeping bag and drifted through the doorway. The station was quiet, and the lights were dimmed. There was no sign of her custodian, which made her wonder if the Russians had stopped caring about her discovering their intentions.

Through the window, she could see a few small figures moving around outside. Their white suits stood out against the dark expanse of space. As the space station floated above

Earth, she could see the strange apparatus with its sleek rods pointed towards the planet.

Rods from God. That's the fanciful name the concept was given during the Cold War. A kinetic orbital strike. A hypothetical plan to attack the planet's surface with tungsten projectiles dropped from orbit. Although it sounded like something out of a pulp science-fiction novel, both the US and the Soviet Union had developed conceptual designs for satellites capable of turning it into reality. A kinetic bombardment had the advantage of being able to deliver the payload from low earth orbit at very high speeds, making them almost impossible to defend against. There would be no need for warheads because, travelling at Mach 24, the tungsten rods would hit the earth with such force that they could penetrate hundreds of feet underground, delivering as much kinetic energy as tactical nuclear weapons but without the radiation. Moreover, there would be no launch warning, and the time from launch to impact would be just a few minutes; much quicker than the time taken by an ICBM.

It had been thought that the idea was purely speculative, as neither side had the technological expertise required to push the boundaries of what was possible. But scientists working secretly in Russia's hidden laboratories had managed to turn the unthinkable into a usable tool of war, at a cost of billions of rubles. Now, at a time when the United States and the West were most vulnerable, Russia was about to strike with its latest superweapon.

• • •

Madison had trouble sleeping and she rose well before her eight-hour rest period expired. The Russians had brought fresh supplies of food with them, but Madison found it unpalatable, so she settled for a small portion of rehydrated cereal and green tea for breakfast. Madison's captors ate their meals separately and rarely interacted with her. They no longer kept her under constant guard. When Madison caught sight of Khrenov and Trimenko, they were deep in conversation. Did their austere expressions seem more smug, or was she just imagining things?

In the middle of the morning there was a new development. Madison was watching the cosmonauts returning to the airlock, but instead of the usual shift change, once they were on board, the station started to vibrate slightly. The vibration began to get stronger and turned into a groaning sound of metal being stretched. Then the station shifted laterally, which caused Madison to drift a little bit to the side.

They'd fired up the station's rockets. This wasn't uncommon as they often did this to prevent orbital decay. But usually, the rockets were triggered for short bursts only to make minor adjustments. This time, the engines stayed on, and their dull roar could be felt and heard throughout the station. It became clear that this was not a minor adjustment but rather a significant change in the station's position.

Madison scooted over to her sleeping pod, booted up her Station Support Computer, and quickly accessed the station's private network. She used the built-in iris camera in section 2 to scan her eyes and log in. Madison opened the navigation readout to check the International Space Station's current position and trajectory. The station was currently gliding on a transfer orbit that would take it over the North Pole. The computer anticipated they would soon enter an elliptical orbit, with a low perigee. This meant that their new orbital path would take them closer to Earth's surface than usual, and when she saw which region they would be traversing, her heart skipped a beat.

In approximately twenty minutes, they would pass over Hudson Bay in Canada and enter the United States. Madison tried to identify any significant targets under their flight path. One possibility was Grand Forks Air Force Base in North Dakota. The base used to house Minuteman ICBM silos during the Cold War, but more recently became a surveillance radar station and part of the Air Force Space Command intel ops network. South of Grand Forks was Ellsworth AFB, located just outside Rapid City, which currently houses B-1B strategic bomber aircraft and is a centre for next-generation cutting-edge unmanned weapons systems. Both bases would be attractive targets, but they would most likely have already been destroyed by the earthquakes. So why would the Russians want to hit them with a kinetic bombardment from space?

Chewing her lip, Madison pinched the onscreen map and zoomed in, her eyes flicking rapidly over the monitor.

Bingo.

NORAD, the joint US/Canadian Air Defence Centre. It was situated in a highly secure subterranean complex that was deeply buried beneath Cheyenne Mountain near Colorado Springs and was designed to serve as the nerve centre for all air and space defence operations in the event of thermonuclear war with Russia or China. In addition to its primary role as a military command centre, Madison also knew that NORAD had been earmarked as an alternative seat of Government. This meant that should the US Government be incapacitated or destroyed in a nuclear attack, NORAD would serve as a temporary base of operations for the continuation of government.

The Russians were going after the biggest target of all. They must have intelligence that the President was there. But Madison struggled to understand what they hoped to achieve. Did they envisage Russian jackboots marching on American soil when all that remained was rubble? Or was it the last, desperate act of a dying regime?

Madison turned off her computer and left the sleeping pod. She wasn't surprised to find Liliya Tremenko waiting for her. Liliya was holding a small handgun, and she gestured with it towards the hatchway.

Madison floated in place, her hair forming a halo.

Liliya edged closer and said, "Please move."

"Or else? If you shoot me, you'll put a hole in the hull."

"You want to see, don't you?" Liliya said.

The worst part was that Madison wanted to witness what was about to happen, even though it horrified her. They made their way through the station until they arrived at the Zvezda Service Module, the Russian section.

Five or six cosmonauts were crammed into the capsule, leaving little space for Madison. Khrenov was present, but he barely acknowledged her. She hadn't visited this area often, so it took Madison a moment to refamiliarize herself with the interior. In typical Russian fashion, everything appeared antiquated and retrograde but functional. A Russian flag was pinned to one wall, and a picture of Yuri Gagarin hung above the galley table. She found a spot by one of the windows and waited.

Her Russian counterparts went about their task with quiet efficiency. There was a total lack of small talk, just the sound of fingers tapping keyboards accompanied by the dull background noise of the station's engines.

As Earth turned beneath them, the remnants of the city of Denver came into view, which was little more than a faint smear at this altitude. She heard a command barked in Russian, and the rotary launcher mounted on the station began to revolve in a series of jerky movements as it searched for its target.

"Today is great day for my people, Mrs Leitner," Khrenov said in broken English.

There was no countdown, but soon after he spoke, four of the tungsten rods fell silently from their clamps, five seconds apart. Madison watched as they dropped away and disappeared within moments. The next few minutes slipped by agonizingly slowly. She became aware that she was holding her breath and had to consciously remind herself to breathe. Finally, an expanding shockwave like a ripple on a pond appeared in the arid land far below, followed by three more. In moments, they were hidden from view under a veil of dust.

It was over just like that. It was almost anticlimactic, and she chided herself for expecting something more spectacular.

On the ground, it would be a different matter. Madison could picture the death and destruction as the four tungsten rods impacted the mountain and pushed far underground into the heart of the command centre. The blast wave from the kinetic orbital strike would throw the subterranean complex right off its spring supports, sending personnel to the floor in a heap and shattering ankles. She could imagine their screams as thousands of tonnes of granite crashed down from the mountain, flattening the bunkers and everyone inside. This would be accompanied by a wall of superheated gases hot enough to incinerate all remaining life. The noise of the man-made earthquake would be heard hundreds of miles away.

Madison felt a sharp, throbbing pain in her head as if echoes were bouncing up from the impact site. Hot bile squirted into her throat, and her eyes leaked tears. With great effort, she brought her emotions under control. She sensed somebody moving closer and thought it was Khrenov. But it wasn't the Commander of the VKS come to gloat. It was the woman, Liliya Tremenko. Madison felt her hot breath against her ear.

"Keep watching," Liliya whispered, her voice trembling with excitement. The gun jabbed into Madison's lower back. "We have so many targets."

Chapter 7

**PEAK DISTRICT NATIONAL PARK
NORTHERN ENGLAND**

FOR THE FIRST TIME IN years, Scott's insomnia was in remission (it took the end of the world to cure it), but it felt as though every time he closed his eyes, someone or something would interrupt his sleep. It started with aftershocks or distant rockfalls, then the alarm bell at the survivors' camp near Amsterdam, and once to inform him of the death of a child as they'd crossed Doggerland. Now, someone was shaking his shoulder and whispering his name, and he was fed up with it.

He'd been dreaming of the time Sara's parents visited them during the Easter holidays a few years back. Every morning, they would take a brisk walk along the lakeshore, and during these walks, Scott would point out different types of wildlife and plants they passed, naming the trees and birds (he'd become an expert at recognizing them, due to his regular dawn musings).

On the way back, Sara's father, Lucas, started to become agitated. Even though they walked this same route every day,

Lucas was convinced they were going the wrong way. He insisted on following a path that led deeper into the woodland, which led to an argument with Celine, which soured the mood for the rest of their holidays.

Scott later recognized this as the first sign of something wrong with his father-in-law. It came before the swearing, before the bruises appeared on Celine's arms and wrists, before Lucas' wanderings from their house in Amsterdam.

In his dream, that evening Scott and Lucas sat on the veranda enjoying a beer as Lucas picked out various star constellations, some of which appeared different than they should. While reciting their names, Lucas turned and gave Scott a sly wink, as if they shared some big secret that only men understood. Scott began to laugh because he got it, and this set Lucas off. The big man playfully jabbed Scott in the ribs. Just then, the veranda door slid open and the women came out to join them, and the dream faded into the sound of someone whispering, "Scott, wake up."

It was still dark inside the classroom, but an orange tinge on the ceiling hinted at the sunrise. Tammy Dahl leaned over Scott, her finger pressed against her lips. She beckoned him to follow. Trying not to groan from moving his stiff limbs, Scott shimmied out of his sleeping bag and joined her by the cloakroom in the hallway.

Scott rubbed his eyes and said, "I'm guessing this early wake-up call isn't for good news."

Tammy shushed him and closed the classroom door.

"What's the problem?"

"One of the kids has gone walkabout," Tammy told him.

"What?" Scott came instantly alert.

"I woke up early and had to use the bathroom. That's when I noticed the main door was open."

It was still ajar, emitting chilly air.

"Did you search outside? Have you checked all around the daycare?"

"I've looked everywhere."

"What about the swings in the playground?" Scott asked, stepping over to the exit.

"I've looked everywhere," she said again, grabbing his arm. "He's gone AWOL, for sure."

Scott cursed lightly.

"We have to tell the others and start a search."

"Wait," Tammy said, not letting go of him. "We don't want to start a hullabaloo and frighten the boy's friends, do we?"

Tammy was right, as usual. The last thing they needed was a bunch of hysterical children.

"The two of us will go and search the village," Tammy suggested. "We know our way around, and with some luck, we'll find the boy in no time."

"I'd best leave a note for Sara."

"Be quick. I'll meet you out back."

Scott quietly returned to the classroom. He searched for a crayon and some paper and quickly wrote a message. He left the note in a spot where his wife would see it. Then he grabbed his coat and headed outside. Tammy was waiting for him by the quad bike.

"Will it wake up the others if we use this?"

"Not if we wheel it around the green before we start the engine. If they're still about, it might frighten away those wolves, and we can cover more ground on the quad."

Scott had momentarily forgotten about the howling they had heard the day before. He scanned the area, but the wooded hillsides were shrouded in mist.

"Do you know how long he's been gone?"

Tammy shook her head as she uncoupled the trailer.

"He could be anywhere," Scott said under his breath and gestured towards the half-demolished church. "We should check there first."

"I doubt we'll find him there. We need to think like a child thinks, Scott. Where is a boy that age most likely to go?"

Tammy was probably on the right track, and Scott tried putting himself in a child's shoes. If the boy woke up and wandered off, what was the first place he'd make for? Where would he wind up? Maybe he was hankering after his old life, some remnant of how the world used to be. Despite the distractions of modern technology, today's children still enjoyed simple pastimes such as playing in the park, riding a bike, going to McDonald's, or visiting the arcade. As they trundled around the village green with the quad bike, Scott shared his thoughts with Tammy.

"Let's start with the high street, check out the toy shops, fast-food places and anywhere else promising. After that, we'll look around the parks and playgrounds. Maybe he just fancied a walk."

"At this time of the day, in an unfamiliar place? He's aware of the risks."

"It sounds absurd, but we can't rule it out. Kids deal with things differently to adults."

Scott, as a teacher, ought to know that better than most. He had lost count of the number of times his pupils behaved contrary to expectations. Whether it was dealing with their parents' separation, the death of a family pet, or an outbreak of acne, they often surprised you. When it comes to children, expect the unexpected.

When they arrived at the road, Tammy started the quad bike and Scott rode on the back. They weaved around stationary vehicles and strewn rubble, searching for any signs of the missing boy. As they approached the first row of shops, they slowed down to a crawl, scouring the broken storefronts and calling out his name. After a few minutes, they reached the ruined market hall having seen no sign of him. Tammy came to a stop at a junction. To the left was the entrance to the caravan park, and to the right was a narrow lane lined with more stores.

Scott pointed at the road leading to the right.

"Let's try that way," he said, raising his voice over the noisy engine. Tammy nodded in agreement and steered around the wreckage. However, they soon found themselves caught in a maze of obstructions and had to backtrack in search of an alternative route. More than once, they passed unstable buildings that leaned dangerously over the roadway, and broken shards of glass littered the ground, crunching under the quad's wheels. Scott couldn't help but worry about the boy's safety. With so many hazards around, there were countless ways he could have an accident or become trapped.

After searching for ten minutes without success, Tammy drew to a halt again and turned off the engine. The quad bike's throaty roar faded and a heavy silence settled over the village like a heavy blanket.

"So where did everybody go?" Scott said.

"What do you mean?" Tammy said over her shoulder.

"The inhabitants. Where are they?"

"Evacuated by the army. Moved to transit camps. Upped and left of their own accord. Remember the broken dam just up the valley?"

"I don't mean the survivors. I mean the dead. There should be bodies lying around, half buried beneath the rubble. I don't see any signs of digging equipment or rescue gear. It's bizarre."

"Don't knock it, Scott. I've had my fill of stiffs."

"Me too. But I just have a bad feeling, that's all."

"That, my friend," Tammy said, patting his knee, "is the new norm. Let's just concentrate on finding the boy and going back."

Scott ground his teeth and peered around at their surroundings.

"Look, there's a sign pointing to the railway station," he said.

"I see it."

The small station lay at the bottom of a deep cutting lush with overgrown gorse. It boasted a quaint ticket office and two platforms connected by an old footbridge. A train had derailed and lay in a zig-zag pattern, its carriages crumpled and ripped open like sardine cans. Tammy parked alongside the edge of the platform, and they both hopped off. Scott stepped over to the nearest carriage, scrambled up onto its tilted side, and poked his head into one of the broken windows.

He was met with a messy and disordered scene of torn metal, ripped upholstery and left-behind luggage. A potent smell of spilled diesel filled the air, and he noticed several large bloodstains. But there was no sign of the passengers. Scott called out the boy's name, just on the off chance he was playing hide-and-seek, but there was no answer. He slid back down onto the platform.

Meanwhile, Tammy had wandered off. Scott could hear her footsteps inside the ticket office. Suddenly, she called his name. Scott scooted over and went through the doorway. She was leaning against a wall, her arms folded and smiling broadly. Scott soon saw what amused her.

The boy was standing in front of a vending machine, eagerly looking at the goodies inside. There were soda bottles, packets of crisps, and chocolate bars galore. He'd already got his hands on a small tub of ice cream; the evidence was smeared all around his mouth. Tammy and Scott watched as he vigorously shook the vending machine until a packet of salt and vinegar crisps fell loose and appeared in the chute at the bottom. In a flash, the boy grabbed the packet, tore it open, and started stuffing handfuls of crisps into his mouth.

"Enjoying yourself?" Scott asked.

The boy made various appreciative noises, gave them a thumbs-up, and went back to his feast.

Reluctant to spoil his delight, Scott joined the boy and gave the vending machine a hefty whack on the side. More goodies tumbled free.

"Cool, man," the boy said, bits of crisps flying from his mouth.

They waited until he'd stuffed his pockets and then steered him outside.

"We need to have a chat about you wandering off like that, young chap," Scott started to say.

"A quad bike! Freaking awesome." The boy raced over the platform and sprang into the leather seat, gripping the handlebars. He made loud engine sounds. "Is this ours? Can I have a go – please!"

Tammy and Scott walked over to the small child, exchanging looks as they flanked him.

"Maybe when you're a little older," said Scott.

The boy looked up at him with sincerity.

"I'll be eleven years old soon. My birthday is coming up."

"When?"

He turned his head to face Tammy.

"The last day in August," the boy replied.

Scott racked his brain as he tried to figure out today's date but he'd lost track of the days.

"We'll see," he said.

"That means no. When a grown-up says 'we'll see' it always means no."

Scott gave him a forced smile, then patted his small shoulder and said, "No promises, but we'll see. But how do you suggest we take the quad bike with us in the balloon, Mr Smart Alec?"

"Oh, yeah."

Scott saw the boy's face crumple with disappointment. "In the meantime, you can ride upfront on the way back if you like."

"Cat's Pyjamas!"

Scott didn't have the foggiest what that meant, but he took it the boy was cool with the idea.

This time, Scott took the controls with the boy on his lap. Tammy sat behind him with her trusty crossbow slung across her back. They rode up the pedestrian slope and passed a burned-out shell that was once a thatched cottage adorned with colourful hanging baskets.

To avoid the blocked roads, Scott took a different route back. He went over a packhorse bridge and followed a fast-flowing brook.

"Go faster, mister!" the boy shouted.

"This thing's a beast," Scott replied.

The boy bounced up and down and imitated the quad bike's engine with loud enthusiasm.

"You want to go faster?" yelled Scott. "Hold on to your hats!"

He spun the handles and raced through a set of gates. Just ahead was a square bowling green. Bouncing over the wooden trough onto the flat surface, Scott spun them around in circles at breakneck speed, turning a set of doughnuts for the boy. The boy let out a loud whoop of excitement, and Scott found himself joining in the fun.

Scott raced off the bowling green and peeled across a sports field, the quad bike's wheels ripping through the overgrown grass and leaving furrows in their wake.

"Scott, will you slow down for Pete's sake," Tammy urged, her grip on his back tightening.

Scott laughed loudly, but he cut his speed as they hit the tarmac again. Up ahead was the market hall.

"That was fun. Just wait until I tell the others," the boy said.

Scott fist-bumped him, saying, "Wasn't it?"

All that remained of the village square was a solitary telegraph pole entangled with loose wires; it reminded Scott of a maypole. The rest of the square was in ruins, resembling the aftermath of the Blitz in East London. The destroyed market hall was surrounded by piles of rubble, some as high as dozens of feet. Atop the highest mound was a beaten-up piano, looking out of place against the sky.

"We should get back," Scott told them as he navigated around the labyrinth of debris. "The others might need a hand getting the balloon ready."

They were halfway around the square when movement up ahead caught Scott's attention. He slammed on the brakes, coming to a halt. A hundred meters away, a man emerged from the shadows and stepped into the roadway, blocking their path. A vicious-looking mastiff was at his side, straining at a thick rope tether. The dog's jowls hung low, drooling saliva that dripped onto the ground.

As they watched, a second man appeared. He wore loose-fitting cord trousers and a black donkey jacket with a sheepskin hunting cap perched on his head. He also had a ferocious dog, a mongrel that appeared ravaged by some disease. He clutched a homemade weapon in his other hand – a baseball bat bristling with sharp-looking nails.

"Shit," Scott said to himself, too quiet for the others to hear over the engine sound.

"Looks like we have more company, Scott," Tammy said, tapping him on the shoulder. Behind them, three additional figures – a woman and two men – had appeared from the ruins. They were all armed to the teeth and with them loped a pack of dangerous hounds.

"What do they want, mister?" the boy asked. "Are they angry because I stole the ice cream?"

"I don't think so, little man."

Just then, one of the dogs emitted a horrendous-sounding howl, a mournful noise that chilled Scott's blood. The other dogs took up the sound, their strident ululation swelling in volume.

Then the man with the mastiff shouted something, and he let go of the rope tether. The dog bounded towards them, snarling with deadly venom.

Chapter 8

LANSING
WEST VIRGINIA

IN THE AFTERNOON, AFTER SNACKING on army rations and energy bars washed down with strong coffee, Kenny, Alex and Bethany got into the Humvee and left their campground. They drove through the shallow waters of the Little Greenbrier and followed the blacktop road until they reached the crossroads. This time, instead of turning towards **KEEGAN'S TIRE MART** and Sewell Mountain, they went straight ahead, past the Dollar Store, and over the rail tracks. After five minutes, they arrived at the edge of town.

Based on their maps, Lansing had only one main street extending for eight blocks or so, containing a handful of stores, several bars and diners, and little else. There was no downtown or centre; instead, the municipality was spread out lazily along the valley as far as the next conurbation. They shouldn't have any trouble finding a Home Depot or a similar store where they could get a generator and building materials.

They turned the corner onto Main Street.

Kenny came to a stop. "Crap," he muttered.

They'd thought Lansing would be mostly deserted, much like all the other places they had passed through during their travels. After leaving the army base at Fort Knox, they had barely encountered any other living person until Two Moon and his sons arrived. If the town lacked people, they could quickly load up the Humvee with whatever they needed and head back home.

What confronted them was a snake pit of disorder.

Firstly, Lansing was anything but deserted or sparsely populated. It was a bustling hub of activity, with people everywhere they looked. Men, women and children hurried along the pavements or crowded the street corners, while traffic crawled along Main Street. There were even people on horseback, which added to the chaos.

Secondly, it appeared to be a place where rowdy behaviour and drunkenness were the norms. The few bars Lansing boasted were so packed that their patrons overflowed into the street. Brawling in the gutters or puking your guts up seemed the most popular activity of the day. The sound of breaking glass or screams barely garnered any attention. Lansing was a free-for-all.

The only thing Kenny could compare it to was a frontier town in the Old West. All it needed was some tumbleweed blowing down the street to complete the picture.

"What do we do now?" Bethany asked as they surveyed the disorderly scenes.

"We need that kit. Without it, we won't finish the cabin," Alex pointed out.

Kenny hesitated momentarily, his attention drawn to a man fastening his horse's reins to a lamppost. The man disappeared into one of the dimly lit bars. Suddenly, a loud commotion erupted from inside, and a second later, the man came flying out the window, crashing to the ground with a thump. Nobody batted an eyelid.

"Kenny?"

"I heard you. Look, this doesn't change a thing. So let's go in, get the stuff, and get out again. We won't mess around, and we'll mind our own business. Agreed?"

His friends agreed.

Kenny eased the Humvee forward, trying to find a safe path through the crush of people and vehicles. The town was so congested that moving at more than a walking pace was impossible. He and his companions fixed their eyes on the road ahead, hoping to blend in and avoid drawing much attention.

Halfway down Main Street, they noticed the town hall still stood tall and strong despite the earthquakes that had rocked the region. As they got closer, they saw that instead of the usual Stars and Stripes flag flying high on the flagpole, a new flag bearing a shovel and musket was flapping in the wind. On the lawn out front, someone had constructed a wooden stockade. It was a rough and hastily constructed enclosure made of logs and boards. Kenny peered out of the corner of his eye and saw several people huddled inside the stockade, looking scared and confused. A sign on the side said:

THIEVES AND RAPERS

"You have to be kidding me?" said Alex from the backseat.

"Don't stare," Kenny instructed, although he found it impossible not to look for himself. The sight was a stark reminder of how much the world had changed. One of the prisoners caught his eye, the man's face a mixture of dread and pleading. Kenny looked away sharply.

With a sense of relief, they made it to the top of Main Street and turned off onto the quieter back lots. Soon after, they spotted the orange Home Depot signage they sought.

The warehouse perimeter was surrounded by parallel lines of concertina wire, making it appear like a high-security facility. A queue had formed at the entrance, and armed guards kept a sense of order. Kenny and his companions left the Humvee and made their way across.

As they approached, Kenny spotted a man sitting at a desk taking people's details before they were allowed to enter. People leaving the warehouse were being frisked on their way out. Compared to the rest of Lansing, it all looked well-organized.

They waited in line until it was their turn.

"What do you want?" the man said without looking up. He was middle-aged, balding, and wearing small round glasses—in another life, he might have been an accountant or a pharmacist.

Kenny recited a list of what they needed. The man wrote it down.

"What do you have to exchange?" he asked.

"Sorry, I don't understand."

"What currency?" Again, he didn't look up.

"We don't have any money," Kenny told him.

"Money is no good here. Money is worthless now." He sighed heavily, like he'd repeated the same thing too many times today, and pointed at a sign tacked to the fence. "This is all we accept."

The three of them read the notice.

DURING THE ONGOING NATIONAL EMERGENCY
ONLY THE FOLLOWING CAN BE EXCHANGED FOR GOODS
BY ORDER OF THE NEW VIRGINIAN CIVIL DEFENCE FORCE

GOLD OR SILVER
ALCOHOL
TOBACCO
MEDICATION/ANTIBIOTICS/ALLERGY MEDICINE
RUBBING ALCOHOL
READING GLASSES
RECHARGEABLE BATTERIES
CONDOMS/MORNING-AFTER PILL
FEMININE PRODUCTS
FISHING GEAR
PEPPER SPRAY

**WATER PURIFICATION TABLETS
PANTYHOSE
GARDEN SEEDS
BABY FOOD
POWDERED MILK**

"Pantyhose!" Bethany exclaimed.

"I've seen Marines use them to prevent tick bites and leeches," Alex told her. "You can also use them to filter water."

Kenny read the full list and then told the man behind the desk, "Sorry, but we don't have any items to exchange."

"Then I can't help you," said the man, briefly making eye contact with Kenny before moving on to the next person in line. "Next."

"Wait. We really need this stuff, d'you understand?" Kenny protested.

"If you don't have anything to trade, then that's the end of it."

The man signalled with his finger, prompting one of the armed guards to move a little closer.

"Now get out of here."

Kenny was about to say more when he felt Bethany tugging at his shirt sleeve, pulling him away.

"He can't do this. People are trying to survive."

"He can, and he did," Alex pointed out.

As they moved away, a skinny youth stepped into their path from where he'd been loitering near the fence. He seemed hyped up and all jittery, like he was tripping.

"I can get you in there," he said to Kenny. He showed him a piece of paper. "You can have my docket if you like."

"Won't you need it yourself?"

The youth shook his head. He had little spots all around his nose and mouth.

"Nah, I can get some more, no problem. Here, take it." And he held out his hand.

"Thank you, thank you very much."

Kenny was about to take the docket when the youth added, "Your lady is pretty. It won't take me long."

Kenny bunched his fists, and if it hadn't been for Alex, he would have lamped him one.

"Easy there, pal," his friend said. "We mind our own business, remember?"

Back at the Humvee, it took Kenny five minutes to calm down.

"Those mercenary bastards. Their little racket is costing lives," he growled as he marched back and forth.

"Now we know why people took all the gold from Fort Knox," Bethany said.

Alex broke away and started to rummage around in the Humvee's rear. He returned with a heavy metal crate they had found at the army base.

"Come on, I have an idea."

They followed him back to the security fence. By then, the spotty youth had slipped away. When they reached the front, Alex dumped the crate onto the desk, drawing a furious look from the man in the glasses.

"Will this do?" And Alex snapped open the lock and lifted the lid.

Inside was one of several M5 automatic rifles they'd discovered in the armoury blockhouse, alongside the claymore mines and boxes of army rations. There were several clips of ammo tucked in next to the firearm.

"This is a next-generation rifle, fresh off the production line," Alex said, sounding like a salesman at an arms fair. "They are so new that the army was still testing them. You're looking at some serious firepower here, my friend. I doubt if you'll see another gun like this anywhere else."

The man in the glasses called the armed guard over again, and they spent a few moments inspecting the weapon and talking in low voices. Afterwards, he turned to Alex.

"Where did you get this?"

"Perhaps it's best not to ask. You know how things can be."

"Do you have any more?"

"Just the one," Alex lied effortlessly. "Well?"

The man at the desk chewed on the matter for a moment and then wrote out a fresh docket, tore it off, and handed it over.

"Get what you came for and then leave. Don't come back."

They passed through the security fence without further issue and made their way into the cavernous warehouse. Finding a flatbed trolley, they started searching the aisles. The store was dimly lit because the only sources of light were daylight coming through the front windows and a few battery-powered lamps scattered around. No music or announcements were made over the speaker system; all they could hear were occasional whispers and faint footsteps. They passed a few people—mostly men picking up building materials like themselves—but didn't speak with any of them.

They loaded the trolley with sheets of hardwood, some lengths of 4 x 4 timber, and half a dozen 1-litre tins of bitumen. After that, they went to the electrical department and found the necessary power tools. Finally, they searched for generators and found a surprising number to choose from. They decided to settle for a 220V gasoline generator.

They headed back outside, where someone checked the items on the trolley against the list on the docket. Meanwhile, another person approached and frisked them to ensure they were not trying to sneak out with extra items. After everything was in order, they made towards their Humvee.

Kenny pondered who was running the show. He assumed those who held real authority had either fled or been run out of town. In his opinion, the New Virginian Civil Defence Force appeared to be a local militia. It was a pity that they were not doing a better job maintaining law and order in the town, but then he remembered the people penned up in the stockade. He wondered how they had ended up in that situation. Establishing their guilt or innocence was not a priority; their future seemed bleak.

They loaded the Humvee and headed out of the parking lot. They planned to stop at the tire mart for gasoline on the way back to their campground, but first, they needed to leave Lansing. Retracing their route, they slid back onto Main Street.

The crowds had increased, if anything. Almost the whole street was thronged with people, slowing traffic even further. Kenny noticed that everyone was moving in the same direction and wondered why. Suddenly, he heard a bell tolling.

The brassy noise rang out at regular intervals as if summoning people.

A small gap in the crowds allowed Kenny to see they were converging on the lawns in front of the town hall. A cheer went up, and he heard peals of laughter and merriment. The droves of people pressed in even tighter, and Kenny had to steer onto a side street so that he wouldn't run over anyone.

Abandoning the Humvee, Kenny, Bethany, and Alex followed the crowds onto the grass and elbowed their way to the front. A big lady wearing a lopsided judge's wig read out a proclamation, her voice carrying over the tumult. She sounded drunk.

"The local assizes found the accused guilty of petty larceny, banditry, and extortion to satisfy his perverse desires. The sentence will be carried out immediately. Bring the rogue forward."

Two strong men appeared and dragged out a prisoner from the stockade. The terrified man was then paraded before the jeering spectators.

With a jolt, Kenny recognized the youth from the warehouse. He'd been roughed up, and his nose was all bloody, but there was no mistaking that spotty face. Just an hour ago, he'd been bothering them; now, here he was, having been seized, found guilty of various crimes, and about to face his punishment – the whole crazy circus put on for the enjoyment of a throng of delirious citizens.

The condemned – and Kenny had few doubts that his punishment would be grim – was stripped and made to stand atop a wooden scaffold. The baying mob screamed insults and spat at him or found the whole display side-splittingly funny, especially when the youth wet himself.

Then the woman produced a fist-sized stone from somewhere and placed it at her feet. On her command, the pair of men forced the youth to lie on his back with his spine across the stone. Then they tied his wrists and ankles to the scaffold, leaving him spreadeagled.

Someone fetched a timber board and lay it flat over the youth's body, leaving only his head uncovered. The crowd suddenly grew hushed, the atmosphere electric with tension. Kenny looked around and saw a sea of expectant faces.

The woman, who may or may not have been a real judge, leaned over the young person lying on the ground.

She slurred her words as she asked him, "Do you have anything to say?"

"Please let me go," the youth begged so quietly that only those near the front could hear him.

The woman turned to the crowd, announcing with a roar, "He pleads guilty!"

The crowd erupted and clapped with all their might. Kenny wanted to close his eyes, but he forced himself to watch.

The first heavy cast-iron weight was placed onto the board, drawing a long and loud groan from the youth as it pushed down on his chest. Then they added a second, even heavier one, and his groan evolved into a spluttering wheeze.

Kenny considered intervening. Nobody deserved this, no matter what they had done. It was barbaric. But he knew if he meddled, there was a good chance he'd suffer the same punishment.

By the time a third weight was added, the crowd was going wild. To them, this was prime-time entertainment, no different than when the multitudes gathered to watch people put to death at Tyburn in medieval London or the Bastille in Paris. The weight pressing down on the youth was too much for his bones to bear, and his spine splintered with a loud crunch. Then his ribs snapped, piercing his lungs and causing him to gasp helplessly. Bethany could no longer watch, and she turned away and buried her face into Kenny's chest.

"More, more, more," chanted the crowd, and the woman duly obliged them by adding a final cast-iron weight. A pool of blood spread out over the scaffold, but the youth still lived. His head lolled feebly from side to side and from deep in his throat, he made pitiful mewling noises.

The woman stepped onto the board, the extra load dislocating the youth's shoulders and knees and crushing his internal organs. Shit squirted from his arse, raising an uproarious cheer. She reached down with a knife, sliced off his tongue to silence him once and for all, and tossed it into the mob. A scuffle broke out as people fought over it.

At last, the youth gave a rattling gurgle, and his suffering was over, bringing the gruesome spectacle to an end. The audience fell silent.

"The next sentence will be carried out at daybreak," the woman announced as she stepped off the board and tottered off-stage.

The people started to drift away.

Behind them, a new prisoner was shoved into the stockade, replacing the dead youth.

Kenny's mouth dropped open.

World Quake 3

It was Young Little Wolf, the youngest son of Two Moon.

Chapter 9

PEAK DISTRICT NATIONAL PARK
NORTHERN ENGLAND

IN THOSE FRAUGHT MOMENTS AS the dog bolted towards them with unrelenting ferocity, Scott was certain they were done for. The animal closed the gap with a singular mission to inflict harm; to tear them to pieces with its powerful jaws. It stormed along the rubble-strewn street, a charging mass of muscle and bone, and leaped. But then, when it was seconds from setting upon Tammy, Scott heard a sudden *twang*, followed by a brief *thrum*. To his amazement, the dog suddenly changed direction in mid-air, its body snapping back as though on an invisible tether. It landed in a cloud of dust, thrashing its limbs in fury, and Scott saw a crossbow bolt sticking out of its forehead.

Scott was so caught up in watching its death throes that Tammy had to shout to break the spell.

As she reloaded her crossbow, she snapped, "We need to leave now, or we'll become their main course."

Several more dogs came running towards them followed by their human handlers. Scott didn't hesitate and stepped on the accelerator. The quad bike blasted forwards, nearly tipping them all off the back. He aimed directly for the man in the donkey jacket, praying they would close the gap before he had time to swing the baseball bat.

His prayer was answered. At the last second, the man leaped out of the way, but as he rolled sideways, his weapon struck Tammy on her back. She yelped as the nails bit deep into her skin. The mongrel ran alongside the quad bike, snarling and snapping at them. Tammy quickly recovered her wits and kicked out, and the dog joined its handler in the dirt.

Scott spun the handlebars to avoid colliding with the man's buddy, whose features seemed ossified into a permanent scowl. The quad bike took a serpentine passage between heaps of rubble, kicking up a rooster-tail of debris in its wake. Over the roar of its engine, Scott could hear the angry shouts and barking of their pursuers.

Directly in front of them, the gutted ruins of a Georgian townhouse reared up, its interior exposed like a doll's house. Scott didn't have enough time to change course, and they catapulted through the building, passing underneath a chandelier and exiting through the back door into the rear garden. The tyres made a crunching sound as they drove over the broken glass from a shattered orangery.

Scott stole a quick look at the boy seated in his lap, whose face was a blend of sheer terror and exhilaration. *Hold on kiddo,* Scott thought to himself.

They hurtled out of the garden through a gap in the fence. Passing by the back of a row of shops, they had to duck under washing lines to avoid getting tangled in the laundry. It was odd how out of place some things could be in the aftermath of the Apocalypse.

Scott had no idea whereabouts they were because keeping a sense of direction was impossible. Even if he knew their location, Scott wondered if it was wise to head back to the village green or if it would be better to draw their pursuers away. But things were happening too fast to decide. He saw two of the dogs streaking towards them from the right, followed by their handlers.

Tammy raised her crossbow, but just as she fired, the quad bike passed over some debris and her shot went high.

Scott ignored her swearing and veered between two shops, pinning his hopes that the ginnel was wide enough. The dogs followed, their barking bouncing off the walls. There was just enough room, and they burst out of the far end of the passage and slewed across a badly tilted footpath. Seconds later, they found themselves hurtling over parkland. Scott increased his speed.

"Make for the trees," Tammy hollered in his ear, pointing towards a wooded area. "See if we can lose them!"

"Won't we get stuck?"

"There should be a trail, a shortcut to the caravan park; I think I saw it yesterday when we went to get the propane."

"You think?"

"Trust me. Then it's a short run to the church."

Scott hoped Tammy's internal compass was working better than his because he was totally lost.

Again, Scott was unhappy about leading their pursuers to the classroom. He could only hope Fabian had the hot air balloon primed and ready for a quick getaway. A quick glance over his shoulder revealed they had little choice because the hunters were already in the park.

They bumped and bounced over a playing field and entered the shade beneath the trees. The earthquakes had torn up the shallow soil, uprooting some trees and leaving others leaning precariously. The trackway was little more than a narrow animal spoor winding between the trunks, but Scott preceded along it as fast as he dared.

They'd need to find somewhere to hide from their pursuers if they hoped to shake them off. Scott thought that might fool the people but not the dogs. He cast about for a hiding place and after a few hundred yards he spotted the remains of an ancient-looking packhorse bridge tucked away in the foliage. The arch had collapsed many years ago, but the bridge was covered with vines and it blended in, so might serve. Scott steered off the track, drove the quad bike through the undergrowth, and approached the structure. Beneath the nearside buttress was a damp and shadowy cave. He carefully guided them inside and killed the engine.

The hair-raising chase left all three of them breathless, sweating, and covered in dust. The boy started coughing, and Scott cupped a hand over his small mouth while trying to steady his own panting.

Gradually, as their breaths grew fainter, new noises emerged around them, coalescing into birdsong, buzzing insects, animals moving through bushes, and moisture dripping from the cave walls. Scott felt a sudden peacefulness, and although he knew it was an illusion, the feeling had an appeal.

All too soon, barking dogs and muffled voices wormed their way into the tranquil setting. The voices grew more substantial as they drew nearer, revealing their pursuers' frustration.

"Keep looking," said one man. "They have to be in here somewhere."

They could hear twigs snapping underfoot and crunching leaves; they were almost on top of them. Scott gripped the handlebars, ready to bolt from cover.

"Go on, girl. Go and find them."

There was a snuffling from an animal's snout as one of the dogs sought out their scent. Scott's entire concentration zoned in on the noises as they came closer.

Then the ugly mongrel came into view, its scrawny head and bloodshot eyes almost within touching distance as it sniffed the ground near the packhorse bridge. Scott felt the boy's body tense.

The dog moved nearer. It was shivering with sickliness; there were spots of blood around its jaws, and its flanks were blotchy with mange. It paused, and for a heartbeat, Scott thought it had found them because it seemed to be looking straight at them. But then it cocked its leg against the bridge, had a pee, and turned to wander away. They watched it disappear through the bushes.

"You not picked them up, girl?" came the voice.

More footsteps overhead; the man was standing on the bridge.

"Any sign over your way, Mary?" the man called.

"Nothing," answered a faint female voice. "I think they went deeper into the trees."

"Fuck," the man muttered and then he jumped down off the bridge. His tread grew fainter.

Just then, the boy spluttered and coughed again, the sound magnified by the cave.

"There they are! Under the bridge! Go get them, girl!"

Scott didn't hesitate. He started the ignition, thumbed the throttle, and gave the machine everything as he launched them out of the cave. The mongrel and one of the men disappeared under the front wheels. There was lots of shouting and screaming, and in the next instant, Scott and his passengers were blasting through the woodland at full pelt, the engine buzzing like a chainsaw.

Twigs and leaves slapped against their clothes and skin, and their reckless passage sent a flurry of birds flapping into the sky, their wings beating furiously as they tried to escape the commotion. Scott's senses were alert to any signs of danger. Tammy was clinging to his back, but she got off another shot. Scott couldn't tell if she hit anything; he only cared about putting some distance between them and their pursuers.

Exposed roots coiled over the trail like serpents, threatening to tip the quad bike over. They went under a fallen tree, the trunk just grazing their heads. The trail made several tortuous turns and then dipped towards a shallow watercourse. They splashed through mud, getting soaked. Then the quad bike climbed the opposite bank and they flew over the rim, landing with such force that it rattled Scott's teeth. He barely kept control.

The trail gradually widened until they passed a nature information board, and then they cannonballed into the morning sunlight. To Scott's huge relief, he saw they'd arrived at the caravan park. He wasted no time and swiftly drove around the caravans and glamping pods, heading straight towards the entrance.

His eyes were gritty with dirt and his heart was pounding against his chest. Scott exited onto the road and risked a quick look over his shoulder; the people and dogs were just leaving the woods, still in hot pursuit but far enough behind to give them breathing room. He realized they had a chance to make it out of this alive.

Tammy collapsed against his back; whether from relief or pain, he didn't know.

"Are you okay?" he shouted.

"Yes," she answered through gritted teeth.

"Once we're in the air, we'll take a look at you."

As soon as the words left his mouth, the quad bike suddenly veered sideways. Scott looked down and saw that one of the tyres had burst; the thick rubber tread was disintegrating and falling apart. He hit the brakes, narrowly avoiding a collision with a wall.

They had to continue on foot. Without a word, the trio hopped off the quad bike and started pegging it through the village. Scott took the boy by the hand and led them into the maze of destruction, where they'd have a better chance of losing their pursuers.

They climbed a mound of rubble, possibly once a library or bookshop judging by the scattered pages, and then slid down the opposite slope. Scott looked left and right, his mind working out their options. He went left, away from the high street. Scaling an even higher pile of bricks, he stole a quick glance at their surroundings, ignoring the noises of shouting and barking behind them. In the near distance he saw the toppled church spire and beyond it was the curved top of the inflated hot air balloon. Scott silently thanked Fabian before setting off again.

Back at ground level, they hurried along a road and then edged around a large hole in the ground, trying to ignore the smell of fractured sewer pipes. A red Royal Mail van, with its roof crushed under the weight of fallen debris, was obstructing their path. On the right was a building with a small triangular opening where the door once was, and Scott stooped down and squeezed through it. The boy went in next, followed by Tammy.

They were inside a small furniture shop, where the floor had tilted at an angle, causing most of the contents to fall against an inside wall. Scott grabbed a mattress and with Tammy's help, used it to plug the opening. Crab-walking through the dimly lit interior, they reached the cash office at the back and went out through a fire exit.

Crossing the backyard, Scott guided them by an overturned milk float, their feet nearly adhering to a big puddle of curdled milk. At the end of the street, he recognized a place—it was the convenience store they'd checked out the evening before. Meaning they didn't have much further to go – just around the next bend, down a short road to the playground, followed by a mad dash over the green to the balloon.

They found the man in the donkey jacket and his female companion waiting for them around the corner. He was holding the baseball bat while the woman had a bicycle chain which she spun around in circular motions, forming a knuckle-duster around her hand. Two dogs, their teeth bared, were at their feet.

The man and woman started walking towards them, closing the gap, and Scott heard the boy whimper. A quick look confirmed how petrified he was: tears were rolling down his cheeks and his legs were trembling with exhaustion, making Scott doubt he could run for much longer. Scott bunched his fists at the same time Tammy levelled her crossbow.

But then the dogs gave a whimper and slunk off, and a moment later the ground trembled. Under Scott's boots, the roadway slid in two directions at once, nearly unbalancing him and reminding him of funhouses at the seaside. The shaking increased and a deep rumbling sound came from deep underground, as if tectonic plates were grinding together. It was an aftershock, the first they'd felt for days, and its unpredictable nature made the man and woman hesitate.

A dark shadow fell over both groups of people, and everyone turned to see the wall of an already weakened tenement block suddenly start to tilt and lean outwards. Scott picked up the boy and leaped to safety, praying Tammy was doing the same. Out of the corner of his eye he saw the man in the donkey jacket push his companion out of his way as he ran. The woman was not so fortunate; she gave a blood-curdling scream as the wall fell and buried her. The noise and dust became mixed with the aftershock, and when everything settled again, they saw her lifeless arms and legs poking from the fresh pile of rubble. The man in the donkey jacket had fled.

Beside him, Tammy was bent over and spitting from her mouth. The boy's hair was white with dust, making him look old. Scott's knees were bleeding. They had escaped by the skin of their teeth.

The road ahead was choked with wreckage. The masonry hadn't settled, so it was too risky to climb over. They would have to find another way. The boy looked done in so Scott hoisted him in a piggyback, retraced their steps, and cut through the delivery bay behind the convenience store.

From somewhere ahead came the loud roar of the hot air balloon's burners. They must be near.

Tammy drew ahead and took a cautious peek around the next corner.

"It's clear."

They'd arrived at the church car park. All the vehicles had been crushed under the fallen spire, but there was a passage via the churchyard.

"We'll have to go through the church," Tammy pointed out.

Scott was too fatigued to answer; instead, he just nodded and staggered along in her wake.

A minute later he spotted the balloon through the ruined nave. Everyone had boarded the basket except Fabian, who waved encouragingly. The sight boosted Scott's flagging spirits.

"Almost there, kiddo," he told the boy, whose snot-encrusted face was buried in Scott's shoulder. The boy mumbled something back, and his arms tightened their grip around Scott's neck.

They preceded across the churchyard, their feet clattering over the gravestones. They entered the church's ruins, which now resembled some felled creature with roof beams for the ribcage and the pipe organ as its stilled heart. What they experienced next reinforced the sensation of being inside the belly of the beast.

Scott felt, and then heard, something crunching under his boot. He looked down and saw a small skull. As he removed his foot, the bone turning to dust, he told himself it was an animal skull, but the size and shape disabused him of that notion because it was unmistakeably human, *and small.* Tiny finger bones attached to arm bones bore this out. Everywhere, there was an overpowering mephitic smell, a corruption that clung to the back of his throat like bottled gas that had escaped from an ancient tomb.

Scott raised his head and his field of view widened. Bones. There were bones everywhere. Not just a carpet of them, but so many thousands that they covered the aisle and pews like snow drifts. Complete and in-complete skeletons of people, all mixed up together. He saw femurs and clavicles and vertebrae and jawbones, young thorax and scapula, geriatric spines and pelvis and ball-sockets. Their whiteness was startling, and an awful thought that they'd been picked clean took hold of Scott's hamstrung mind.

Now they knew where all the people were. Their bodies gathered together and dumped inside this once-holy sanctuary which now approximated hell on earth. A boneyard.

Scott's horror was interrupted by the aggressive barking of a dog.

Tammy heard it too because she whispered to him, "We have to keep going," and began to free-climb over the human detritus.

"Keep your eyes closed, kiddo," he said softly to the boy. "Whatever happens, keep 'em shut."

Breasting the piles of bones was a graphic example of what a person would endure to stay alive, and it was an episode burned into their memories until their dying breath. Scrabbling and clawing through brittle skeletons, with bone dust clogging their airways and coating their skin and becoming a part of them, ascending and descending and ascending the waist-high drifts, avalanching beneath cascades of gnawed rib, tibia, kneecap and pubis bones.

Scott closed his mind to the images, refusing to acknowledge them as individual people because thinking of them as men, women, children, or *babies* would have broken him.

Wading through the last heaps, they reached the other side and stumbled into the open. Ignoring the gargoyles' fixed gaze, they gambolled over the drystone wall and began jogging onto the village green.

Fabian shouted words of encouragement while pointing urgently, prompting Scott and Tammy to turn their heads and look. The man in the donkey jacket hurried through the playground with his mongrel, intending to intercept them. Scott struggled to run faster, but his legs felt like jelly and he fought to stay on his feet. He could hear the mongrel panting right on his heels. Tammy, who was just in front, suddenly dropped to one knee, aimed her crossbow, and fired. The red fletching flashed brightly as it skimmed past Scott's head. He heard a high-pitched animal yelp.

When he drew level with Tammy, she slung the crossbow over her back and shouted, "Let me help!" They each slipped an arm under the child's knees, locked wrists behind his back and lifted him up.

Fabian fired the burner, and the balloon slowly lifted from the grass. Scott and Tammy helped the boy into the basket and climbed in after him. Scott fell in a heap on the wicker floor.

The man racing after them roared as he realized his prey was about to escape. From where he was seated, Scott saw a pair of dirty hands grip the edge of the basket. As the man's feet left the ground, his knuckles turned white, and he was left dangling in mid-air.

They continued to ascend. First, they reached six feet off the ground, then ten, and finally fifteen. But the man, who was psychotic with rage, refused to let go. Instead, he pulled himself up, and centimetre by centimetre, his terrifying face appeared over the basket's rim. His eyes and face were jaundiced, and when he grinned, Scott saw his teeth had been filed to points and were discoloured with dried blood. He was simultaneously laughing and panting. He flung one arm over the basket and then one leg and the basket tilted, making the children scream.

Then the man emitted a peculiar gurgle as a crossbow bolt hit him square in the face, and just like that, he disappeared over the side. There was no scream of terror, just a dull thump like a heavy sack falling to the ground. The basket righted itself and they sailed away from the village.

Chapter 10

GORNERGRAT MOUNTAIN
BERNESE ALPS
SWITZERLAND

THREE EVENTS HAPPENED IN QUICK succession that caused Timo's position to rapidly worsen. Individually, they may not have had much of an impact, but when combined, they delivered a triple blow with devastating consequences.

He had planned to stay in the mountaintop retreat for the duration. He knew that his chances of survival were slim, with a life expectancy ranging from a few days to a few months if he was lucky. But he decided to enjoy the hotel's luxuries while he could, indulging in the delicious food and wine from the restaurant, soaking in the hot tub with its breathtaking views, and taking daily walks with his dog.

One morning, he was abruptly awoken by loud clanking and rattling noises.

Timo sat bolt upright in bed, thinking to himself *This is it. This is how it all ends.* But before he'd even rolled out of bed and put on his white towelling robe (he'd be damned if he'd be caught starkers!), Timo grasped that the sounds didn't herald a new round of geological upheaval. The hotel wasn't shaking on its foundations and the panoramic window wasn't thumping with pressure waves.

The racket was coming from the heating system and hot water pipes.

Timo had never really considered what he would do if the system malfunctioned. Like most people, so long as he had hot water and warmth at his fingertips, he hadn't given it much thought. But as he walked through the hotel corridors with Genny at his heel he realized he had a problem on his hands. The vibrating air ducts and the clanging pipes made it clear that something was not right.

In the hotel basement, Timo found a floor-standing boiler that was very different from the wood-burning biomass boiler at home. The hotel boiler was a hybrid heating system that included a hot water cylinder and a fancy touchscreen control panel. After spending a few minutes pressing various symbols and icons, Timo was able to display a digital graphic of a pressure gauge. The gauge was glowing red and in the centre of it there was a flashing digit displaying a reading of 3-bar. Timo touched it, and the number changed to 20 PSI.

The boiler pressure was too high. It shouldn't exceed 1.5-bar. Timo searched for an access panel. Inside were the boiler's innards of pipes and tubes. He tinkered around, checking valves and nuts, and noticed water was dripping from the filling loop, which was the backup hose that supplied water to the system. There were two valves that maintained the pressure, one acted as a stop valve and the other as a double-check valve to ensure the water didn't flow back. The double-check valve was out of position, so Timo reached inside to give it half a turn. Unfortunately, as soon as he touched it, the hot water scalded his hand. He quickly searched for a rag, twisted the valve, and heard a faint hissing sound as water flowed through the hose. He watched as the pressure gauge dropped slowly down to a safer level and turned green in the process. After a minute or so the air ducts and pipes settled down, he replaced the access panel, and left the basement.

Later that morning, he got to thinking about his parents.

Timo had an unconventional upbringing. As a child, he lived in a house located in Bern's Old Town that had originally belonged to a wealthy family. But during the financial crisis that hit Switzerland in the 1990s, the family lost all their wealth overnight. The house was left vacant and abandoned until a group of squatters took over the property. They transformed the mansion into a drug den, which became a popular destination for the hippie culture that was experiencing a resurgence at the time. Timo's parents were students who had spent time in Amsterdam's coffee shops, and they joined the squatters in the house. Timo was born a year or so later.

Like many free-spirited dropouts, Timo's mum and dad embraced a nonconformist approach to religion. Theirs blended different beliefs and faiths, not quite a cult, but a hotchpotch of creeds and denominations. They rejected conventional values.

Two or three days a week, the group of freethinkers would spout their crackpot nonsense shrouded in hemp smoke, sitting on bean bags and playing the sitar or thumping away on mridangam drums. When they weren't discussing peace and love or trying to relive their 70's drug-induced fantasies, they transformed the once-beautifully maintained lawns and gardens into sprawling vegetable plots or reared chickens and goats. They gathered organic waste materials, including animal dung and human waste, left it to decompose to produce methane, and then converted it into electricity. They cultivated their own strains of skunk in the greenhouse. It was all very bohemian, like a modern-day Eden. A New Jerusalem.

Timo, by this time a young boy, hated it. He hated the constant change of people coming and going and staying for only a few days. He hated the psychedelic murals, the all-night parties, the days spent busking for a few francs. But more than anything, he hated feeling lonely, without any friends his age.

When he was seven or eight years old, his parents took him on a pilgrimage along the old hippy trail that went through Nepal and Southeast Asia. By then, the popularity of this druggy subculture was waning. The era of Jimi Hendrix was now a distant memory, replaced with Nepali gangsters pushing their death poppies. One evening, while they were staying at a hostel on Old Freak Street in Kathmandu, they were robbed. His parents – the last hippies standing – returned home with Timo.

In their absence, the commune in Bern had changed. The libertine, carefree and pleasure-seeking lifestyle Timo's mum and dad sought had been replaced by strict religious teachings poorly disguised as education. The new way of life required everyone, including young Timo, to work tirelessly from sunrise to sunset. Mum and Dad, normally too spaced out to care, did little to fight the changes.

On his sixteenth birthday, Timo packed his bags and left, never to return.

The transformation in his life was dramatic. Out went the hippy-drippy subculture. Suddenly unshackled by its claustrophobic start in life, Timo's mind expanded in a way far better than any psychedelic drug could achieve. He sought knowledge the polar opposite of his parents' beliefs. Their frame of reference was nature's balance with the mind and seeking enlightenment through sexual liberation and free love. Timo was more interested in science and technology. He enrolled in evening classes and won a scholarship to EPFL in Lausanne, Switzerland's foremost university for quantum mechanics and particle physics.

Mum and Dad's insistence on raising their son in a cloistered commune in the belief that he would imbibe their unconventional beliefs and way of life backfired. Instead of becoming a reflection of their offbeat lifestyle, their son went in the opposite direction.

Timo was a hardworking student fully invested in his studies. His passion for learning impressed both his peers and tutors alike. His exceptional academic performance led him to be shortlisted for a placement at CERN, sight of the world's largest particle accelerator beneath the Franco/Swiss border.

Despite his successes, Timo's parents were less than thrilled with his career choice. They expressed their disapproval in their letters to him, hoping to gently persuade him to return home. As time passed, the gap between Timo and his parents grew wider, and their attempts to sway him became more insistent. Eventually, Timo decided to cut all ties with his family.

That was several years ago now. Timo barely thought of his parents as his work at CERN consumed most of his time, leaving him little room to think about anything else. Only on special occasions like birthdays and Christmas did he ponder about them.

When Doomsday struck and humanity collapsed, Timo's chief consideration was to save the planet. He didn't have time to worry about a couple of old hippies who may have already passed away years earlier.

It was strange why he would think of them at this moment. Unusual and unsettling.

• • •

It was time to check the thermometers. Timo donned his outdoor gear and set off over the hardened lava streams.

He had only taken a few steps when an excruciating pain in his tummy doubled him over. It hit him so suddenly that Timo spluttered unintelligibly. It felt like someone had grasped his intestines in their fist and twisted them. He'd never felt an agony so intense and his eyes watered.

As quickly as it hit, the pain subsided. Timo straightened and gently probed at his midriff. He wondered if it was something he had eaten earlier that day. He wiped his damp cheeks with the back of his hand and turned to glance back at the hotel towering over him. Timo contemplated whether to return to the hotel and take some indigestion tablets. But the small effort of twisting set off another bout of pain, this time starting in his lower back and side before flaring through to his lower intestine and groin.

Timo cried out. A tsunami of torture gripped him, and without warning, he vomited over the rocks. He started to shiver, partly because of the bellyache and also from fear; Timo knew any illness took on a whole new level of significance.

After about a minute, the pain stabilized. Timo couldn't think how that could be: one moment, he was crying in excruciating agony, and the next it had shrunk to a dull, but manageable ache. It seemed to come in waves, and when it hit, it was never in one place: sometimes it was in his side or his back, or it might shoot down his ureter like someone was poking their finger inside him. Was it a urinary tract infection? Gall stones?

During one lull, Timo staggered back along the pathway, hoping the respite lasted long enough for him to make it inside. In his room, he had an emergency backpack filled with warm clothes, food and medical supplies. He'd reached the corridor leading to the Tower Suites when a fresh lance of pain knifed into him, pitching him against the wall. He scrabbled for purchase but couldn't stop from sliding onto the carpet, spewing all down his clothes. He continued on all fours. After a further minute, he was squirming on his belly and wailing. He could feel his energy levels plummeting.

He finally reached his room. With superhuman effort, he strained for the door handle, his fingers trembling as he tried to grasp it. His dog suddenly appeared, wagging her tail and thinking it must be playtime when she saw her master bellying across the floor. Timo pushed her away, crawled towards the backpack, and scrambled around inside. Bringing out his first-aid kit, he peeled off the lid and rummaged through the spilled contents until he found a foil of painkillers. Timo dry-swallowed three capsules.

At length, Timo made it onto the bed and lay face down on the pillow, feeling wretched.

Timo woke up several times in a delirious state. At one point, he opened his eyes to see his dog happily gobbling up the vomit that had spilled out of his mouth while he slept. Later on, Timo mustered up the strength to drink some water and take more pain meds. The pain came and went, but it was always there, lurking in the background. Exhausted, Timo pulled the duvet over his head and slept some more.

• • •

His dog was lapping his face, its rough tongue scraping the skin. Timo peeled open his gungy eyes to find Genny hovering over him, looking down.

Timo tried to move his body and was surprised to find that he could do so without experiencing severe pain. Although his throat was dry and his limbs were stiff, the pain in his stomach had temporarily subsided. Whatever the illness was, it had left Timo feeling drained. All he wanted to do was rest for a while longer. But as soon as he rolled over and closed his eyes Genny nuzzled him insistently and whined in the back of her throat.

"I'll be all right. I just need to sleep."

Then Timo spluttered as something scratched the back of his throat. After a brief episode of coughing, he pushed himself up onto his elbows and looked around the room. Everything appeared familiar but he felt there was something not right. Then he saw the wispy smoke silently sliding under the door.

It took a few moments for his woozy brain to work out what it meant. Genny, who was already two steps in front, jumped off the bed and started to trot anxiously around the room. A cold slice of realization broke into Timo's torpor. There was a fire somewhere in the hotel.

Merely thinking that sent a flutter through his chest like a moth was trapped in his ribcage. It summarily stayed all other thoughts, even this morning's illness.

Timo pushed the covers aside and stood by the bedside on wobbly legs. He moved towards the door and placed a palm against the wood. It felt cold. Trickles of smoke coiled through the slender gap, and he could detect a very faint smell of burning. He suspected the fire was elsewhere in the building. If he was wrong, and the blaze had already reached the corridor outside, then opening the door would be a mistake. But what choice did he have? There was no other way out.

"Stay here," Timo ordered the dog. Then he opened the door a fraction, slipped outside and closed the door behind him.

The corridor was filled with hazy, grey smoke. It brushed the walls and rippled over the carpet. The smell of burning was sharper and more pungent, but there were no visible flames. Timo progressed down the corridor and peered around the first corner. The gauzy smoke grew thicker, generating more coughing, which in turn induced a sharp twinge in his midriff. Holding his waist, Timo reached the head of a short flight of stairs that led down to the bistro. On the wall he saw a fire extinguisher and quickly grabbed it before descending the stairs to investigate.

He used his shoulder to push open the door to the bistro. The lights were turned off to conserve power but the interior flickered with orange light. As quickly as he could move his wearied body, Timo crossed the room, carefully navigated around the bar and chairs, and stepped through the staff door. In the back, a bubble of hot hair wafting up from the basement made him recoil. As he raised his arm to shield his face, Timo was horrified to see flames licking up the walls and rolling beneath the basement ceiling. He could hear the roar as the fire fed on the wood doors and fittings.

Timo realized that the small fire extinguisher was hopelessly inadequate. Even as he watched, flames started to sprout from the basement entrance and spread up the stairs towards the bistro. The heat was unbearable, and he couldn't stay there for more than a few seconds. He quickly turned around and retraced his steps to his room.

Timo swiftly gathered a few things, stuffing extra clothing and food into his emergency backpack. He remembered to add his journal, notes and maps. Genny was scampering around his feet and barking fearfully as Timo had one last look around the room. If he'd forgotten anything, then it was too bad. Then he scooped up the puppy, tucked her inside his coat and put on the backpack.

In the corridor once more, Timo retreated in the opposite direction to put some distance between themselves and the raging fire. He'd only been in the room for a couple of minutes, but in the meantime, black smoke had begun pouring out of the air ducts and filling the hotel corridors.

Timo wafted his hand to create a path through the thickening miasma as he moved forwards in a crouch. The pain in his midriff mercifully held off, which was one good thing.

Timo had thoroughly explored every corner of the hotel during his stay and had memorized the layout of each floor. If he turned left, he would reach the area of the building overlooking the café terrace. He pushed open a door and found himself in one of the laundry rooms, which led to a short passage and some service lifts. Taking a lift would be too risky, but there was an emergency exit around the corner. Timo slammed the push bar down and stepped outside into the cold afternoon air. He took a few deep breaths and then started jogging along an iron walkway that ran down the length of the hotel.

He clattered down the rusted fire escape. From nearby he heard breaking glass, and when he craned his neck to look he was met with a daunting sight. Flames the colour of the setting sun were prancing from windows higher up in the building. The fire was spreading rapidly, leaping from floor to floor with unsettling ease. He had come close to being trapped and had barely made it outside in time.

He continued his descent and reached the path at the bottom. From there, it was a short jog to the café terrace. Timo made his way through the tables and chairs until he reached the retaining wall. On the other side of the wall was the old snowfield. Due to the recent earthquakes, the snowfield had turned into a vast plain of rocks and boulders.

Timo stopped to take a breath and turned to look back. The grand mountaintop hotel was well ablaze by now. Tongues of flame darted from almost every window, looking like inmates flapping their arms from a prison. A mighty crash came from the corner tower that housed the observatory, sounding like an avalanche of roofbeams and tortured steel. Timo watched as the steel dome tilted and sank in slow motion as the supporting floor gave way. Then the dome slipped off the tower and rolled and bounced down the mountainside, clanging like some huge bell. A gout of hot flames erupted from the top of the tower, causing him to move away from the intense fire. Genny, who was under his coat, cried miserably.

The second tower, containing their plush suite of rooms, was likewise burning like a Roman candle. He could see countless windows along the hotel's façade shattering, showering glittering shards down to the ground. Timo pulled up his coat's hood and retreated out of harm's way.

Timo was transfixed by the burning building before him. He couldn't help but feel a sense of awe and horror in equal measure because the building had been his sanctuary and now he was losing his last refuge.

He stayed for ten minutes as the hotel went up in smoke. The walls started to cave in, sending sparks spiralling into the sky.

Finally, he turned and walked away. Staying there would not serve any purpose. They had to find a new place to take shelter. Being out in the open as evening approached would be a death sentence as the temperatures would plummet at this altitude once night fell.

Timo went in the direction of the funicular station, hoping to follow the tracks down the mountain to Zermatt. But when he rounded the corner, he was disheartened to find that all that remained of the station and engine room was a heap of debris. The rail tracks, which zigzagged down the mountainside, were twisted and buckled as far as the eye could see.

Timo crossed to the nearest viewpoint binoculars, only to realize that they were coin-operated. He unslung his backpack and rummaged around until he found his own pair and then trained them on the distant slopes and mountains. He could plainly see the Jungfrau and the Matterhorn, as well as the Italian lakes in the distance. But the Monte Rosa massif was no longer there, shattered by the quakes and magma eruptions. The remains now blocked the pass to Zermatt. As for the town itself, it had been washed away by the meltwater from the glaciers.

Timo lowered the binoculars and felt his body sag. He could see no way off the mountain. At his back, the hotel continued to blaze. To make matters worse, the pain meds were wearing off.

He peered through the binoculars once more, turning in a full circle, and stopped.

A short distance away was the entrance to the underground magma chamber. Timo put the binoculars away, put on the backpack, and made his way onto the lava field. After a strenuous walk over the basalt rocks, he arrived at the cave's entrance twenty minutes later.

As he approached the entrance, the warmth emanating from it was palpable but not as hot as before. A quick check of the thermometer confirmed this. There was no steam venting out of the ground, either.

Timo gazed at the darkening sky and the lengthening shadows. Genny wriggled inside his coat as she sought warmth.

Steeling himself, Timo ventured inside the cave.

Chapter 11

EAGLE ROCK NATIONAL FOREST
FRANKLIN COUNTY
BLUE RIDGE MOUNTAINS, VIRGINIA

FROM THE REFUGEE CAMP, DEPUTY Geddes tracked the thieves as they headed northwest through Murray Gap to Boone Mill. Once a prosperous timber town on the James River, after the Civil War Boone Mill became famous for its distilleries and breweries. Following World War II, many of its menfolk moved out to build the hydroelectric dams two counties over and never returned. Later, Boone Mill was known for its ink parlours, a mean Creekside Grill and an antique emporium.

Before the earthquakes, Boone Mill had a population of 239 in the 2020 census. Now it was a deserted backwater of tumbledown shacks and neglected backyards. The thieves decided it was an ideal place to spend the night.

The female doctor's words had stung Deputy Geddes, especially since he was trying his best to hold things together. But there was only so much one cop could do. After she had calmed down and things had settled following the botched airdrop, she'd explained how the bunch of racketeers had plagued the whole state, moving from town to town and hoarding up all the supplies of food and medicine. Geddes was angry that the military hadn't stopped them, but they had already left days ago, abandoning the people they had pledged to protect. During the ride to Boone Mill, he hadn't encountered any army patrols or checkpoints.

Tracking the ragtag convoy of pickups laden with their plunder wasn't difficult. On the way, they'd ransacked a drug store, a nursing home that had survived the earthquakes, and an equine veterinary clinic, killing a handful of people in the process. Finally, after two days of violence, the snakes made camp in the woods just outside Boone Mill.

Geddes observed them through his binoculars from the cover of a stand of pines a short distance away. He'd picked a spot where the sun wouldn't reflect off the lenses and where he was screened by ground cover. His patrol car lay beyond the ridgeline out of sight.

Looking down the slope, he studied their small campsite. They had set up a large army tent with a canvas awning to protect them from the hot sun. Overall, there were four men present – two of them were busy gathering firewood, one was digging a fire pit, and the last person was standing at a fold-out table beneath the awning preparing food. Their pickups were parked in a semicircle around the campsite, resembling a wagon laager.

The two men who had gone to collect wood for the fire returned and dumped their branches on the ground. The third man promptly complained, waving his arms. A heated argument ensued, but at this distance, Geddes couldn't hear what they were saying. Then the two men wandered off, sat on camping chairs, brought out a couple of beers from a cooler and started playing cards. The fourth man came over while gesturing with his arms for the man digging the fire pit to make it wider. This caused the man with the shovel to throw it away and stomp off.

Geddes gave a wry shake of his head. Their complete lack of discipline was a gift for him.

He watched and waited through the long afternoon. The man who had gone off in a huff returned and a fire was started. The aroma of cooked fish soon reached Geddes. More beer was consumed, and they seemed to settle their differences as they got drunker and louder.

By this time, it was evening. Stars appeared overhead. Deputy Geddes rubbed his tired eyes and flexed his stiff limbs, but he stuck at it, not once breaking off from monitoring the thieves. From somewhere nearby, an owl hooted.

Just then, three of the men slipped their guns over their shoulders and climbed into one of the pickups. The engine sputtered and coughed a few times before finally roaring to life. Geddes watched as the pickup bounced along the uneven dirt road, kicking up dust. Its taillights grew smaller and smaller until they eventually disappeared into the darkness.

Now where in the juices had they gone? Had they set off to continue their pillaging spree, or did they have a secret rendezvous with someone? Geddes wasn't too concerned about their whereabouts, because it now meant only one person remained to guard the campsite.

It was a stroke of luck quickly compounded by another; the man left behind decided to relieve himself. Geddes could not believe how lax their security arrangements were. He had a perfect chance to snoop around. Geddes waited until the guard slipped into the trees and then prepared to leave his hiding spot.

As Geddes was about to get up, he noticed a shadowy figure lurking in the darkness just beyond the reach of the campfire's light. The figure moved cautiously, darting from tree to tree and stopping every so often to look around. Geddes was intrigued as he watched the person gradually approach the tent.

Whoever it was, they saw an opportunity. They slipped past the fire and ducked under the awning. A kerosene lamp hanging from one of the tent poles illuminated the face. Watching through his binoculars, Geddes saw the person was a young man in his early twenties. He was stocky and had dark hair and lean features. Geddes lost sight of him as he went into the tent.

Geddes felt suddenly tense. If the guard taking a leak returned to find an intruder combing through their spoils, it would end badly. The young man was wagering his life.

Just as Geddes was thinking about the potential trouble, the guard emerged from the forest, zipping up his pants. Geddes braced himself for an almighty ruckus. But the guard simply returned to his spot by the fire, kicked off his boots to warm his feet, and continued drinking.

Geddes contemplated the idea of creating a diversion to allow the young man to escape. But he was hesitant to reveal himself at this point. Maybe he ought to let them sort it out between themselves; after all, looters were looters.

He watched the campsite. After ten more minutes, the sound of the pickup reached him. It came rumbling down the dirt road and the three men piled out. The man by the fire fetched a tarp and between them, they covered something in the back of the truck.

They all returned to the fire to warm their hands and their backs. They added more wood, and the person in charge of food pulled out something wrapped in foil and placed it in the embers. Geddes, who was feeling the chill, wished for a warm bed and some hot food.

There was no sign of the intruder, he could be hiding inside the tent or have slipped out the back. If he was lucky, Geddes thought, he might get away with his recklessness. But he wasn't.

As midnight approached, it was inevitable that the thieves would soon retire. Three of them stood up, stretched and yawned. They threw their beer cans away and said goodnight to the fourth man who was likely on watch duty. He gave them the finger and everyone laughed.

No sooner had the lookout dragged a blanket around his shoulders than the peace was shattered by an uproar from inside the tent. The man leaped to his feet, knocking over his chair in the process. As he brought his gun to bear, his colleagues reappeared, dragging the unfortunate intruder out into the open. There followed more raised voices, and in a flash, things turned ugly. Geddes flinched as one of the thieves drew back his fist and punched the young man in the jaw. Even from his hiding place, Geddes heard the loud smack. The blow was followed by two more punches, these to the solar plexus. The young man grunted and doubled over. He was forced upright, giving Geddes a view of his bloodied lip and frightened eyes.

There was further hollering as they questioned him. The young man's answers mustn't have satisfied his interrogators, because they set on him en masse, punching and kicking him to the ground. The beating didn't let up for over a minute. When one of the thieves – the one who'd been on watch duty – used the butt of his hunting rifle to hit the side of the young man's head, Geddes reflexively drew out his sidearm and took aim.

But before he could pull the trigger, the others turned on their colleague. As their victim lay on the forest floor, unconscious or dead, they berated him. Geddes had a feeling they were not too pleased he'd allowed an intruder to enter their tent while he was supposed to be keeping lookout, or maybe he'd overstepped (unlikely, considering they'd already committed murder that day). Regardless of the reasons behind it, Deputy Geddes watched as they took their anger out on the lookout.

In the meantime, and much to Geddes' relief, the prostrate figure on the ground stirred.

The arguing stopped. They watched their victim crawl on his belly towards the trees for a few seconds like they were toying with him. Then a pair of the thieves hauled the young man to his feet and tied him to a tent pole. A rag was pushed into his mouth to act as a gag. They slapped him about some more, and the three not on watch duty stomped back inside.

The lookout adjusted his chair and leaned back, holding his rifle in his lap. He scowled at the semi-conscious young man.

Geddes returned his sidearm to its holster and resumed his vigil.

•   •   •

Geddes was surprised they hadn't killed the man outright. At any moment, he expected them to put a gun to his head and pull the trigger. But as the long hours of darkness gradually gave way to dawn, and the thieves made no move to end the man's life, it became clear they intended to keep him alive.

Geddes realized just how lucky he had been. One more minute, and he'd probably be the one tied to the post. He thought of the saying, "One man's loss is another man's gain" but didn't feel bad about it because he didn't know anything about the man currently tied up. Maybe he deserved to be in this hole. But the night's events had only added to Geddes's own problems.

He wasn't aware of falling asleep because the next thing Geddes knew, he was woken by the sound of car doors closing. He quickly grabbed his binoculars and saw the thieves had packed up their campsite and were getting ready to leave. Their prisoner lay in the back of a pickup, hogtied but conscious. Geddes hurried back to his own vehicle.

The small convoy of pickup trucks drove through the dense woods of maple and beech trees, following the dirt road. Geddes trailed behind about a quarter of a mile back.

As he drove, Geddes' mind raced as he tried to think what to do next. He could just pull them over. But then what?

Arrest them and confiscate their plunder? What was he supposed to do with four prisoners and a badly beaten man? Assuming the trigger-happy roughnecks came peacefully, that is. He couldn't exactly call for backup. Apprehending them would not be simple.

On the other hand, he could just deal with them the same way he'd dealt with the looters at the shopping mall. But they'd been a bunch of teenage delinquents, whereas these guys were dangerous bandits armed to the teeth. The situation was tricky.

He was still weighing up his options and trying to devise a plan when the convoy turned off the dirt road, crossed a stream, and rode up onto a blacktop—the first real road Geddes had seen since leaving the refugee camp. From cover, he watched them accelerate. A mile or so away, he could see a small town.

A few minutes later, Geddes drove past a roadsign. They were in Lansing, West Virginia.

LANSING
WEST VIRGINIA

Kenny, Bethany and Alex drove straight over to the Indian Reservation, ignoring the warnings to keep away. They hoped that the village elders would make an exception this time, and they were right.

They quickly explained what they'd witnessed outside Lansing town hall.

"Young Little Wolf looked to be in a bad way," Kenny concluded.

"Did he see you?" asked Two Moon, an undercurrent of anger making his voice quiver.

"I don't think so. They'd beaten him so badly he could hardly stand up, let alone pick us out from the crowd."

Two Moon and his grandfather talked for a moment in low voices.

"He only went looking for medicines," Two Moon told them. "For the girl."

Kenny glanced at the gable-roofed lodge, remembering the child within.

"Without her drugs, her seizures become worse. She only has enough for two more days, so my son said he would find what she needed. When he did not return last night, we grew worried. Now you bring us distressing news."

"The whole town has become a hellhole, with armed goons running the show," Alex said.

"Who is in charge?"

They told Two Moon of the drunken lady in the wig, to which he nodded wisely.

"It sounds like the town mayor. She's been a thorn in our side for years, constantly threatening to expand the township onto our ancestral land."

He looked at them with a hard and penetrating stare.

"How long did you say we have, before they...?" He left the sentence unfinished.

"Until daybreak."

"Then we have no time to waste."
"What do you plan on doing?" Bethany asked.
"What we have always done. We horse trade."

•   •   •

They drove to Lansing in the Humvee, Two Moon bringing his eldest son with them. Before leaving the reservation, Little Bird fetched a hunting rifle with a scope. The plan was to negotiate some kind of bargain to secure the release of Young Little Wolf, but if the mediation failed it was clear that they would have to resort to a different course of action.

At the town hall, they were stopped on the lawn by one of the gun-toting militiamen.

"Where do you think you're going, Tonto?"

"I want to speak to my son."

"That joker? So, you're the one responsible for siring him, are you?"

He exchanged a laugh with one of his chums.

"Just let me see him. So I can check that he's alright."

The thug glanced over to where Young Little Wolf was standing, holding onto the stockade with his hands. Even from a distance, it was clear that his face was swollen and bruised, with dried blood on the side of his head. His clothes were torn and dishevelled.

"He looks alright to me, Pop. Why would he not be alright? Are you impugning my good character by suggesting I'm not treating him kindly? What do you say, Cody?"

Cody, the other militiaman, shrugged and said, "I don't know what impugning means, but he seems fine to me."

"There you go. Nothing to worry about."

"Just move out of our way and let us pass," Little Bird said, his hand resting on the stock of his rifle.

"And what do you intend to do with that peashooter, Geronimo?"

Mercifully, before things spiralled out of control, Two Moon laid a calming hand on his eldest son's shoulder and gave a subtle shake of his head. The thug smirked.

"This is ridiculous," Kenny said in frustration. "You don't have any right to hold him."

"Fuck me, if it ain't Kemo Sabe himself. Well, FYI, we have every right to hold him. He was caught red-handed stealing essential medicines, hombre."

Kenny sighed, looked to one side while he counted to five, and then stared the man square in the face.

"It's clear that you're just a hired gun to do the mayor's bidding. Letting the prisoner go is way above your pay grade; I understand that. So, do us a favour, and take us to see your boss, there's a good fellow."

"Yeah, we want a chat with the big cheese, dummy," added Alex.

After a few more verbals ping-ponging back and forth, the militiaman grew bored and escorted them inside, where the spacious civic building was lit with beams of light shining down from the cupola onto the marble floor. After their weapons were temporarily confiscated, they were led up a spiral staircase, their footsteps echoing throughout the grand interior. On the top tier, the militiaman stopped before a set of mahogany doors, knocked, and then pushed them open.

"It's your funeral," he said with a snigger and left them.

They found themselves in an airy room that had previously been the town mayor's office but was now decorated like a garish boudoir. The floor space was occupied with dozens of shop mannequins wearing expensive dresses and jewellery, their sightless eyes indifferent to the trashy décor. A birdcage was hanging in one corner of the room, and inside it was a canary. A massive plastic palm tree filled an entire window. The room was furnished with 19th-century candelabra, walnut cabinets, and pine tables. The octagonal walls were adorned with gilt-framed oil paintings of public dignitaries who now sported felt-tip moustaches and monocles. A familiar-looking judge's wig was placed on a bust of Abe Lincoln that sat on the edge of the mayor's desk. The same flag that was hanging outside was draped over the wall behind the desk. In the room next door, they glimpsed a king-sized bed covered in leopard-print cushions.

In the center of the spacious room, the town mayor rested comfortably on a pink chaise lounge. Her appearance was reminiscent of a Hollywood movie star from the 1930s. She wore a semi-transparent dressing gown with fluffy fringes and held a cigarette holder. On a side table next to the chaise lounge, there was a glass of sherry and a bowl of grapes. A teenage girl was kneeling on the floor, diligently varnishing the mayor's toenails. Another militiaman was leaning against the nearby wall.

Upon seeing her guests, the mayor attempted to focus her watery eyes with little success. She squinted, her lower lip protruding. It was clear she was still intoxicated.

"Sho, sho, my little mouse," she told the girl. "I have visitors."

The teenager dutifully withdrew from the room.

"Come forward, then. I grant you an audience, dears. Let me hear your entreaty," she said while beckoning with her cigarette holder and giggling.

They moved closer and stopped in front of the chaise lounge. Kenny suddenly craved a cigarette upon smelling tobacco smoke.

"It's about my son," said Two Moon.

The mayor looked him up and down with feigned nonchalance.

"What of him, dearie?"

"You have him tied up outside like an animal. I want him released."

"Oh, what on earth has he done to deserve that?"

The mayor turned to the guard.

"What has this man's son done to deserve that, Mungo?"

The guard stepped forward and whispered in the mayor's ear.

"I see," she replied, and then to her visitors, "Well, the man is a malefactor from what I hear. Therefore, we have to make an example of him."

"He was just looking for drugs for a sick little girl! She'll die without them!"

"Do keep your voice down."

"But can't you give him a break?" interjected Kenny. "Show your people that you can be merciful when required?"

"My people? I believe that justice is what my people demand. They appreciate a firm hand, can't you see? If I had a quarter for every person asking what you've just asked, then I would be a wealthy woman. Thanks to my leadership, our community has developed a strong sense of togetherness. Everyone here knows the rules and the consequences of breaking them."

"From what we saw, this town is lawless," Alex murmured under his breath.

"What was that? If you have something to say, then say it out loud. And what kind of accent is that, pray tell?"

"I'm a scouser."

"Duh?" the mayor said with a shrug.

"I'm from Liverpool."

"How very quaint and English. Well, my dear friend, we have different ways here in West Virginia. Ways that have been successful for hundreds of years."

"Oh yeah, we saw how you do things earlier," Alex came back at her.

The mayor appeared unfazed. "Did you like the show? It was my idea and more engaging for the spectators than executing him by firing squad. I took inspiration from your country's extensive history of torture and punishment. Your people certainly knew how to extract a confession during their puritanical reigns of terror."

She reached over and popped a grape into her mouth.

"The next time, I might try the Judas Cradle. Are you familiar with the Judas Cradle?"

"We're going nowhere with this," Kenny said before the mayor could go into gruesome detail.

The mayor spread her hands and smiled widely.

"You have no authority to do what you are doing," Bethany said, and Kenny saw twin red spots appear on her cheeks.

"On the contrary. Since martial law was declared, I have unlimited authority to make and enforce any laws I deem necessary to maintain order and prevent damage to property and loss of life throughout the county." She hiccuped loudly. "Or something like that."

"Martial law only applies to a military authority. You represent a civilian body."

"Oh, poo poo. As you may have noticed, the army has abandoned the people, so I had to create my own militia: it's called the New Virginian Civil Defence Force. That was my idea, as well. Do you like our new flag?"

"They are not a militia," blurted Alex. "And you are not a military commander. You're nothing but a tinpot dictator in some piss-poor town. It's a fucking free-for-all out there."

Next to him, Kenny cringed. Losing their composure wouldn't be helpful or wise. Although he couldn't blame his friend, as the entire situation was insane. He also noticed that Little Bird looked about ready to implode. The guard and he were engaged in a macho staring contest.

The mayor sighed loudly before pronouncing in an airy voice, "I will think on your petition and determine what is to be done by the morning. Now, see these people out will you, Mungo."

"Bloody provincials," Alex muttered as they turned to go.

They'd reached the set of doors and were just stepping through when Two Moon said in a calm voice, "You can have our land."

"What?"

"You can have all of our land marked by the boundary markings. The whole reservation. You've been after it for a long time. So it's yours. If you free my boy and give us the drugs we need."

"Close the door, Mungo," the mayor ordered. She wriggled her toes to dry the varnish and drew steadily on the cigarette holder. Then she looked at Two Moon and said, "Explain."

"We will be departing soon. So, we will relinquish control and ownership of all the land on both sides of the river and across the mountain, which falls under our sovereign territory. It will be transferred to the township with immediate effect. This includes all the resources and properties. The land is rich and fertile, which you are going to need if you plan on surviving long-term."

"And you'd do that? Your claim goes back thousands of years. But you'd be willing to just hand it over?"

"Like I say, lady mayor: we are leaving. You'd be a fool to turn the offer down."

"Well I have to say, this is unexpected," the mayor replied after a moment of reflection.

She wasn't the only one surprised. Everybody in their party, including Little Bird, was dumbfounded by the proposal. Another thing: the reservation also included their own plot of land by the crashed plane.

"Unexpected and tempting. Why are you in such a hurry to go?"

Two Moon was wise enough to refrain from saying anything provocative, such as the danger his tribe was confronting from the militia - an issue he had previously hinted at. He also chose not to bring up any topic related to Canada. Instead, he dismissed her question with a wave of his hand, stating, "It's not important."

The mayor wasn't so drunk not to know when she was being lied to. She finished her cigarette and exhaled smoke towards the high ceiling.

"Is there something that I should be aware of? A portent of impending doom, perhaps? Have your ancestors passed down some innate connection to Mother Nature from generation to generation? Should we expect a plague of locusts or a fiery comet to burn across the heavens? I'm sorry if I sound like some vile racist from a banana republic, but as mayor of this town, it is my duty to put the residents' safety above all other considerations, including the acquisition of your land."

She waited for a few seconds, enjoying lording over them. Kenny could see right through her, however, and knew it was nothing more than a monumental display of hubris.

Like some sagacious ruler seeing the bigger picture, she nodded sagely.

"On consideration, your son's crime was relatively minor, and the punishment already administered to him, together with his brief imprisonment, will hopefully act as a deterrent against future lawbreaking. I will grant him a reprieve."

She looked at Kenny, adding, "There, you see I can be compassionate. It's given me a nice, warm feeling inside, I must say."

She waved them away imperiously.

"The matter is closed. Mungo, release the prisoner and give them whatever drugs they require. Also, arrange immediate transfer of land rights with our friend here."

As they descended the stairs, Bethany leaned in close to Kenny. "That was close," she intoned in his ear.

Fifteen minutes later and Young Little Wolf was reunited with his father and older brother. He needed help walking, and from the way he struggled for breath, they suspected that he might have a broken rib. Moreover, he was badly concussed. They helped him get settled in the back of the Humvee, and then one of the guards approached them carrying a cardboard box that contained essential medicines. The guard silently handed over the box and then marched away.

"I'm sorry," Two Moon said, and Kenny wasn't sure if he was apologizing for giving up the land or making them homeless.

"The way I see it, you had no choice," Kenny assured him.

"The little girl is all that counts," added Bethany.

"That woman," Alex said, pointing his thumb over his shoulder at the town hall, "Who does she think she is: the Queen of Sheba?"

"She was drunk with power as well as liquor." Kenny started the engine, saying, "Let's go and pack."

• • •

Deputy Geddes didn't know what to make of things.

Upon reaching the outskirts of town, he pulled over into the parking lot of a Dollar Store. He didn't want to attract attention by driving around in his patrol car and wearing his uniform, so he entered the store and found a set of clothes his size from the looted shelves. After shoving his sidearm down his waistbelt under his shirt, he strolled into town, hoping to blend in like an ordinary guy.

Within five minutes, Geddes was certain that he had made the correct decision. Lansing, a small and unremarkable town just weeks ago, was every cop's idea of hell. Order had given way to unruliness and chaos. What passed as law enforcement — men driving around in pickups brandishing guns — did little to curb the town's descent into anarchy. If anything, their presence seemed to embolden the disorderly behaviour that had taken hold.

He made his way down Main Street, doing his best to remain inconspicuous. He reached the town hall to find the prisoner penned inside a makeshift calaboose on the lawn. Geddes saw the lifeless corpse of another jailbird up on a wooden scaffold.

His attention was drawn to a group of people arguing with two guards before they were marched inside the building. Parked at the side of the road was a Humvee. Geddes knocked about for a while, hoping to speak with the prisoner, but a second guard glowered at him and told him where to go.

Geddes crossed the lush grass and settled onto a stone wall. From his vantage point, he observed his surroundings and waited. Patience was the name of the game. He was clearly outgunned in this town, so a confrontation was out of the question. Recovering the stolen supplies from the airdrop was still his main objective, not breaking the prisoner out of jail. For the time being, he needed to size things up and find out what dynamics were at play around here.

After some time, the people exited from the town hall. Geddes watched as the guards crossed over to the pen and pulled out the prisoner. The young man was so weak from the beating that he almost collapsed. To Geddes' surprise, the guards handed the prisoner over to the group, and they helped him to the Humvee. A minute later, someone gave them a box, which Geddes could see had a red cross on the side, and then they drove away.

Geddes was trying to figure out what was really happening. It was clear that some sharks were hoarding the supplies of food and medicines meant for the refugees, but he couldn't understand why they would free a prisoner who was destined to face the same fate as the dead man on the scaffold. It seemed like either the group from the Humvee had paid a very large amount for his release or they had significant influence.

Geddes regretted not stopping the Humvee because the group might have some valuable information. Feeling as though he'd achieved little, he walked away. But as he crossed over the railroad tracks at the edge of town, he noticed the same Humvee parked near the Dollar Store. He increased his pace.

The group had gathered in the parking lot and were examining the freed prisoner's injuries. Geddes walked towards them without trying to hide his approach, and they turned around when they heard his feet crunching over the gravel. They all immediately grew tense.

"Take it easy. I don't want any trouble," he said, trying to dispel their fears.

"Who are you?" one of them asked, placing an arm around the shoulder of the sole female.

"I'm Deputy Geddes." He fished out his badge and held it up. "That's my vehicle," he added, pointing to his patrol car which was just visible around the side of the building.

The man studied his badge and then looked at the clothes Geddes wore but did not comment.

"You're a cop?" the woman asked.

"Well, from the Sheriff's Department, but yeah, I guess so."

"You going to book us for illegal parking or something?" asked one of the other men, a short chap with a crabby attitude.

"Nothing like that," Geddes said.

He noticed the freed prisoner's injuries looked even worse up close.

"I think your friend there is gonna need more than just TCP and cotton wool to patch him up."

"We have this," replied the first man. So far, the other three – all Native Americans – hadn't spoken; they just watched him with deep suspicion.

"Listen: I saw what happened to him late last night."

They all exchanged looks.

"You did?"

"Yessir. They did a real number on him."

"Did him up like a kipper, more like," growled the angry one, who sounded like John Lennon.

"I also watched what just happened at the town hall. Whatever you said to free him must have had some effect because I know how these things work; believe me, I've seen enough of it over the last few weeks. A small town run by power-hungry people with small-minded views who are taking advantage of the current clusterfuck – pardon my French. He's a lucky young man. How'd you manage to exert influence like that?"

"How we did it isn't important," said the woman. "What matters is getting away from this place. Now if you don't mind, we have to be going."

"Sure, I don't blame you," Geddes said and stepped to one side. "But I'm just thinking: the next bunch of people they round up mightn't be so lucky as your friend."

"It's got nothing to do with us," said the angry one. "Like our lass says, we gotta go."

Geddes remained silent for a moment before gesturing towards the box on the backseat of the Humvee. He drew attention to the label on the side. "Steroids and PCVs. I may not be a doctor, but I do know those are used to treat brain tumours."

As soon as he spoke, the three Native Americans went still, their expressions suddenly turned pensive.

"What of it? Look, just who are you precisely?" asked the one with a chip on his shoulder.

"I told you, I'm a Sheriff's Deputy."

"That badge doesn't prove anything. For all we know, you could have killed the Rozzer and taken his car. Do you think I'm as thick as a docker's butty, mate?"

Geddes struggled to understand the man's strong dialect.

"I also know drugs won't be enough," Geddes went on, instead. "The patient will need chemotherapy and surgery."

"So?"

"So let me help," Geddes answered. "I'm your friend, not your enemy. Tell me your story and I'll share mine."

"Bloody Mary, what is this, Jackanory?"

But the other man, the one who appeared to be in charge, tried diffusing the situation by stepping between the two men. "What did you say your name was?" he asked.

"Geddes. Orville Geddes. And yours?"

"Kenny."

He introduced each of his friends and then started telling their story.

After finishing a potted history of how they'd each survived the apocalypse, Geddes and Kenny felt more comfortable in each other's company. However, Alex Bartle, a sailor from Liverpool, was still wary and didn't trust him completely.

"I don't see what you can do about it," Kenny said after learning about the stolen supplies. "They have their whole operation buttoned up pretty tight. It's the same at the warehouse."

"Fighting a one-man crusade will only get you killed," warned the woman. "Anyway, cop or no cop, nobody can be judge, jury and executioner. Going down that path is no different from the town mayor."

"I hate to say it, but I think you're correct, ma'am."

"Call me Bethany."

She looked around at her fellow survivors as though she was weighing matters up in her head. Then she came to a decision.

"Perhaps you should put your energies into something more useful. Something which might make a difference," she said further.

"Such as?"

"You said that you wanted to help us. So help us. Help us help the sick little girl we told you about."

It seemed that her words took everyone by surprise, going off their expressions. Even the Native Americans. The oldest of the three men finally spoke.

"What are you saying?"

Bethany Waghorn smiled at Two Moon.

"I'm saying that we should go to Canada and do everything we can to get her the help she needs. *All* of us."

Chapter 12

INTERNATIONAL SPACE STATION
LOW EARTH ORBIT

THE RAUCOUS PARTY WAS IN full swing. Russian heavy metal music blared through the speakers, the volume turned up to nearly unbearable levels. The cosmonauts were celebrating what they called their "great victory" aboard the newly-named "Russian Orbital Station", and were eager to let loose and have some fun. Commander Khrenov opened a case of vodka, and the alcohol flowed freely as they toasted their success. They laughed, joked and shared stories, and it didn't take long for them to get intoxicated.

Madison was invited to the party but when she declined, Liliya Trimenko sneered at her for it. How could she join in after the holocaust the Russians just carried out, Madison fumed? Following the destruction of the US/Canadian Air Defence Centre at NORAD, the Russians fired their Rods from God Superweapon at Peterson Space Force Base a few miles north of Cheyenne Mountain, flattening the classified facility. Next on their hit list was the Buckley Strategic Command HQ, also in Colorado, home of the US defence satellite communication link led by Space Delta 4. Other targets followed one by one: STRATCOM Command Centre - Raven Rock Mountain Complex underground citadel – The National Military Command Centre 500 feet below the Pentagon. Piece by piece, the Russians pulverized what remained of the United States military and governmental command structure, cracking open the subterranean bunkers like eggshells and killing everyone inside.

After a while, it became like watching a computer game. Detached and business-like, the Russians went about their cold-blooded master plan like emotionless bots. The few times Madison caught Khrenov's attention, he looked right through her with wintery, gelid eyes that chilled her down to the bone. The Russian capsule felt like a cryogenic chamber.

The only positive thing to come out of Madison's presence was when she noticed a familiar object tucked into an alcove at the back of the capsule. It was the hermetically-sealed locker containing the 'special cargo'. The locker was strapped to the wall to prevent it from floating away, but it appeared to be untouched. Interestingly, someone had placed a discarded jumpsuit over it as if they had forgotten about it.

Madison gave nothing away, maintaining a stoic demeanor as she watched her nation being bombarded. Later, she pretended to be so spaced out from shock and raw emotion that when she asked to be excused, nobody thought anything of it. Madison left and went back to the Harmony habitation node.

About an hour later, the station's engines cut out and they glided back into their regular orbit. Five minutes after that, the music had started and the drinking quickly got underway.

Russians being Russians, they drank the vodka as if it were water. Madison went to her sleeping pod and waited. She waited for four hours. Just when she thought the party would never end, the music stopped abruptly. When she checked the cameras, she was pleased to see the cosmonauts sleeping soundly and snoring.

Madison logged into the station network. For weeks now, the station's water recycling unit had been malfunctioning. First of all, she'd stripped down the whole thing and put in new filters. Then, when that hadn't worked, she had replaced the distillation assembly, only to be interrupted when the Russians arrived. Drinking water wasn't the issue because they'd brought lots more with them. It was the oxygen they drew from the water that was the worry. In an emergency, they could draw oxygen from the liquid rocket propellant. Which is what gave Madison an idea.

NASA uses liquid hydrogen and liquid oxygen for rocket fuel, whereas the Russians use a cocktail of RP-1 and Syntin, a variant of liquid oxygen. One of the ingredients of RP-1 is nitrous oxide, better known as laughing gas.

Madison accessed the life support interface on the computer display. She selected the icon for the larger of the two Soyuz spacecraft, the MS-20, which was currently empty of crew. The fuel tanks showed 85% RP-1, which would be enough to hide what she had planned. She needed to determine the amount of nitrous oxide required per crew member to make them all unconscious. On average, an astronaut consumed 2 pounds of oxygen daily, but Madison only needed a fraction of that amount in nitrous oxide. After calculating the numbers, she entered them into the software controlling the feed pumps.

Nitrous oxide is odourless and colourless to human senses, but she deactivated the environmental systems that would sound an alarm when dangerous gases were detected. Then she put on her emergency breathing mask and pressed the button to activate her plan. After that it was just a case of sitting back and marking time as the anaesthesia spread slowly throughout the station, borne on the low-level centrifugal air currents.

Side effects of nitrous oxide include dizziness, disorientation, loss of balance, impaired memory, euphoria and a fit of giggles. Larger quantities could lead to hypoxia and death, but even though she hated Khrenov and his crew for what they had done, Madison had no intention of committing murder. She just needed them out of the way for a while, with no chance of them interfering in her scheme.

When she judged enough time had elapsed, Madison turned off the flow of nitrous oxide. She emerged from her pod and floated through the station, comforted by the hiss and click of her breathing mask. Upon arriving at the Russian capsule, she found the crew heavily sedated and bobbing up and down, blissfully unaware of their situation.

Madison conducted a path through the clutch of passed-out people and halted in front of the control panel. Compared to the American consoles, the Russian equivalent was very retro, consisting of dials, knobs and levers. It took her a few moments to figure out which control did what, but she soon discovered how to operate the rotary launcher. There were still several tungsten rods attached to the clamps, and when the space station was passing over the Pacific Ocean, Madison released them to fall harmlessly into the sea. Then she turned off the launcher motors and powered down its batteries.

While in the middle of sabotaging the launcher, Madison noticed Khrenov drifting nearby in a semi-conscious state.

"What are you doing?" he slurred, his face contorted with an uneven grin.

"I am destroying your small toy, Comrade."

Khrenov giggled loudly, exclaiming, "What a wonderful idea!"

Madison patted him on the head and said, "There, there. Go back to sleep, you little troublemaker."

Khrenov closed his eyes and floated away.

A few minutes later and Madison had successfully disabled the Russian weapon permanently. To ensure that they wouldn't have the opportunity to repair or rearm it, she used the console to disengage the MS-20 Soyuz spacecraft and sent it sailing away through space along with its cargo of spare parts.

Next, Madison moved across to the alcove and retrieved the 'special cargo'. The locker was weightless In the Micro-g environment, making it easy for her to pull it through the station to the airlock. Once there, she unlocked the docking mechanism and entered the smaller Soyuz craft. The Soyuz craft was always kept fully fueled and ready with enough supplies to last a few days in case of an emergency evacuation from the ISS. As she closed the hatch behind her she whispered a farewell.

"So long, chumps."

Madison felt no remorse about abandoning the Russian cosmonauts up here. Stranded, they'd no longer pose a threat to anyone. Whether they were rescued or not, she didn't care.

After securing the locker she ran through the pre-flight checks, strapped herself in, and then launched the craft away from the International Space Station.

It was time to embark on the next phase of her mission.

It was time to go home.

Chapter 13

HADRIAN'S WALL WORLD HERITAGE SITE
NORTHERN ENGLAND

IT WAS WELL PAST MIDNIGHT, and the storm was getting worse with each passing moment. The wind was growing stronger and the driving rain was lashing their bodies with increasing ferocity. Scott huddled down beneath the makeshift shelter, holding onto the canvas roof to prevent it from being blown away.

After their narrow escape from the village, the air stream carried the balloon in a north-easterly direction, passing over the moorlands, pastures and deserted farmhouses. The passengers were all stunned and frightened, trying to process the bombshell revelation they had just witnessed, unable to accept the discovery that some survivors in remote areas of England had resorted to cannibalism.

Was the practice widespread, or was it confined to just a few locations? It could explain why there were large regions without any human survivors. Sure, the earthquakes, floods and other natural disasters had claimed millions of lives, but it was still surprising that there weren't more people like themselves trying to survive. But if you and your family were starving, desperate and with no hope of help, who knows what level you would resort to?

Another possible explanation for the countryside's empty state was the accident at the Whitehaven Nuclear Power Plant. In the immediate aftermath of the massive earthquake that destroyed Windermere, a mandatory evacuation was ordered for the area, driving the survivors out.

Which was worse: being killed by bloodthirsty cannibals or a slow and painful demise due to radioactive fallout?

Looking around at his fellow survivors, Scott knew they were all asking themselves the same questions. Louise, in particular, had more to lose.

As fortune would have it, they didn't have much time to think about the matter. Out of nowhere, the weather took a turn for the worse. Strong winds began to hit the balloon and when Scott glanced around he was disheartened to notice huge thunderhead clouds forming on the horizon. The balloon spun and bounced about in the strengthening thermals.

"Hold on, everyone. We might ride it out."

It quickly became clear their course would take them right through the heart of the storm. Being at the mercy of the wind, there was nothing they could do but pray. At least the prevailing winds were taking them further away from the contaminated zone.

A sudden upwelling of air sent the balloon rocketing up like an express elevator, causing Scott's stomach to drop. In the next instant, they were plunging like a stone and everyone on board screamed in unison. The basket bucked like a bronco as a million zephyrs of air, all moving in different directions at once, sent them on a helter-skelter track through the wind-tossed sky. Fabian made a valiant effort to keep control of the situation, but it soon became apparent that it was a hopeless task. After a minute, Scott shouted for him to join the rest of the group in hunkering down. Meanwhile, Sara and Louise huddled together, which was a further sign of their truce and growing bond. Together, they did their best to keep baby Phoebe safe.

A cloudburst hit them, pouring down an intense amount of rain and drenching them in seconds. Over the sound of the wind, Scott could hear the rain drumming against the balloon envelope like a rat-a-tat tattoo. Darkness descended as the clouds bunched together, turning day into night.

As the storm raged on, memories of a similar tempest that they had encountered while crossing the North Sea flooded Scott's mind. It felt like a lifetime ago, and so much had transpired since then. The feeling of ceaseless motion was identical, and the merciless battering of the wind resembled the surge of colossal waves. They were jolted around the wicker basket in the same manner as they had been tossed about in the wheelhouse of the fishing vessel. The only thing absent was his dear friend, Alan Pritchard.

The clouds suddenly illuminated with a bright, white light, revealing their mountainous sizes. Thunder roared overhead. Scott observed fork lightning dancing around them, crackling the air with millions of volts of electricity.

Scott felt the balloon dropping again, and in the brief stuttering of fulgent lightning, he saw the rocky ground swiftly filling his vision at warp speed. They were about to crash land into a drystone wall. He shouted a breathless warning but had no idea if anyone heard him.

Then the basket hit the ground, ploughing a groove in the soil before slamming into the big wall. Their world turned sideways as the basket was upended.

Scott wriggled out of a tangle of limbs and crawled from the basket into the midst of the raging storm. Using the wall for support, he pulled himself up and looked at their surroundings. They'd come down in the middle of nowhere; all he could see were rolling fields and heath dotted with a few stubby trees that clung to the barren landscape. The wall was several feet tall and wound its way over the undulating ground in both directions. The place seemed familiar to Scott; he remembered being there before on a field trip with Alan and their school pupils last winter. It was the last place he ever imagined landing.

What to do next was more pressing than their location. They needed to find shelter from the wind and rain or risk hypothermia. Scott retreated into the overturned basket.

"Is anyone hurt?" he asked loudly.

There were a few groans, but everyone shook their heads.

"Righto! Let's grab our things and find some shelter."

"Can't we stay in the basket?" asked Louise. She was holding her stomach, and Scott hoped it was just the reflexive gesture of an expectant mother. She looked tired.

"I don't think it'll last long in this weather," Tammy Dahl said.

"She's right. It's time to abandon the balloon. Get your skates on, folks!"

They all huddled together in the pelting rain, their raincoats providing little protection. Scott struggled to remember the details of their field trip, wishing he had paid more attention to Alan's lesson. Scott had been tasked with keeping the children in line that day, while geography and history were his friend's areas of expertise. If he was right, they had crash-landed right against Hadrian's Wall, which meant that every third of a mile there should be the remains of watchtowers that once provided shelter and living quarters for the Roman soldiers. If they could reach one then it might offer some respite until the storm passed.

Scott took the lead. It was difficult to make progress because of the gale-force winds blowing from the south, so when they came to a stile, Scott guided them over to the wall's sheltered side. They stuck together like a herd of livestock, with Scott acting as the shepherd driving along his flock of lost lambs.

After a few minutes, one of the watchtowers emerged from the curtain of rain. It was a small square structure divided into several rooms, but the walls were only a few feet high, making it look more like an unfinished DIY project than a Roman fort. A flash of lightning floodlit a crumbling mosaic floor. There was no roof to speak of. Scott scolded himself; what had he been expecting after two thousand years? They'd just have to make the most of it.

Scott scrambled down to the subfloor level and chose a room that butted up against Hadrian's Wall. He removed his backpack and fished out a tent.

"You'll never pitch it with this wind blowing!" Tammy yelled.

"I don't plan on trying, but if we stretch it over our heads it might keep the rain off," Scott hollered back. "See if you can find some stones to weigh down the corners!"

While Tammy and Fabian went searching, Scott unrolled the canvas sheet. The wind immediately caught it and almost blew it away. With the others' help, he spread it wide. Using heavy rocks, they secured the canvas onto the stone foundations, creating a waterproof roof.

Despite being cold, wet, and thoroughly miserable, everyone was grateful to be out of the worst of the storm. Scott switched on one of the flashlights to take a look around at the children's faces. Nobody spoke much; they just sat huddled together for warmth, blowing on their hands or wiping their snotty noses. Glancing at his watch, he noticed it was early evening. They were facing the prospect of a long night beneath the makeshift shelter.

Maybe a sing-song would lift the children's spirits. He began singing "Ten Green Bottles," and a few of the children joined in at first, but their voices dwindled as they reached the third or fourth verse. Scott then looked into his backpack for some food, but all he could find was a tin of peach slices and a packet of stale crackers. He glanced over at the boy they had been searching for in the village.

"How about you share some of those goodies, eh? What do you say?"

The boy, seeing that his friends needed a boost, generously shared his booty and within five minutes they were all scoffing bars of Twix and cheese and onion crisps.

Finally they all settled down and one by one they fell asleep. Tammy tried to resist, but even she succumbed despite her sore back, leaving Scott alone with the canvas roof. He didn't mind though; it gave him time to think.

As he sat lost in thought, memories of the recent balloon ride and the chase through the village returned. He thought about the Roman Legions manning Hadrian's Wall, trying to stay alive just like they were today. Scott wondered what lay ahead.

Scott quietly pulled out his Ordnance Survey maps and studied them under the flashlight's glow. He remembered the terrain from the balloon and was able to work out their approximate location – just east of Sycamore Gap. There was a lake and a farmhouse nearby, and it seemed like a good idea to explore the area in the morning. But they needed a more permanent plan. They had to find a place to settle down. Going back home to Windermere was out of the question due to the contamination. Scott thought that the coast could be an option. If they could find a fishing harbour similar to the one they had stayed in before crossing the North Sea to Amsterdam, preferably one with no religious sects like The Children of Morningstar, it would be perfect. The village should be evacuated, remote and with an endless supply of seafood.

Scott spent the night poring over the maps, tracing various routes with his finger and considering multiple possibilities. As the storm began to die down towards daybreak, an idea finally came to him. He carefully folded up his maps and drifted off to sleep.

• • •

In stark contrast to the stormy night, the following day dawned sunny with clear blue skies. Surfacing from under the canvas shelter, the grown-ups stood blinking like prehistoric people leaving their cave while the kids went tearing across the heath, bursting with energy.

Scott gathered the adults together and spent a few minutes running his plan past them. Then they held a vote, and it was unanimously accepted.

They had a long hike ahead of them so they decided to camp here for a day to rest and dry their gear. They pitched their tents on a south-facing slope with good views of the surrounding area, giving them ample warning of anybody approaching. The spot was way off the beaten track, but after yesterday's scare, Scott wasn't prepared to take any chances; he warned the kids to stay close to the campsite.

While they settled in, he suggested to Fabian that they should check out the nearby lake and farmhouse. Tammy, who was their top marksman with the crossbow, would stay behind and guard the rest of their group. They each took an empty backpack and followed the trackway down to the lake.

With the sun on their backs and insects buzzing around them, it was easy to imagine that everything was good with the world. Somewhere in the gorse bushes, a songbird was singing. Fabian, who was wearing his signature sunglasses, talked about shooting his wildlife blogs using drones, the outward-bound group where he met Tammy, and other fond memories. Scott was happy to listen.

As they approached the lakeshore, the glistening body of water came into view. At the near end, the shoreline was lined with reeds while a sandy beach lay further along. At the beach, the track divided into two paths: the left one continued around the lake, while the other went up a hill covered with low-growing woody vegetation. They stopped to rest and examine the map. The farmhouse should be located on the other side of the hill, assuming the quakes hadn't changed the landscape or that the farmhouse hadn't collapsed.

"Come on," Scott urged his friend.

They scrambled up the hillside in single file, forcing their way through the spikey shrubs. Near the summit, they moved laterally around the flank of the hill because experience had taught them that standing on skylines wasn't a good idea. The shoulder of the hill was dotted with boulders, screening their approach and providing good cover.

The farmhouse lay at the end of a small valley. They studied it through their binoculars. The house was made of stone, had red shutters and doors, and a slate roof. One of the chimneys had collapsed, causing the gable end to cave in and leaving a pile of debris.

Across from the farmhouse there was a long outbuilding with an open side. The building was divided into three different bays. Inside, Scott could see a few overturned milk churns and a stack of hay bales. Near the farmhouse door there was a kennel, but they did not notice any other indications of a dog. The yard was overgrown with weeds. Beyond a drystone wall was a long expanse of pasture, but there were no cows or sheep in sight. Overall, the place had a desolate air to it.

Leaving cover, Scott and Fabian picked their way down the slope. Approaching downwind to mask their unwashed smell, walking with light steps, without speaking, and pausing every few yards to listen, they neared the farmhouse.

Unlatching the gate, the two of them walked across the yard. The outbuilding was to their right, and as they passed by, they noticed an old tractor in the shadows at the back. Its engine cowling was open and several spark plugs had been ripped away, leaving exposed black and red wires. A pair of grimy overalls hung on a hook nearby. In the next bay were several large plastic barrels of liquid fertilizer. The air was thick with a strong smell of sour milk and mildewy animal feed.

Fabian took a quick look through one of the farmhouse's ground-floor windows, trying to see between the closed shutters. When Scott raised his eyebrows, Fabian made an OK gesture with his hand, indicating that it was safe to enter. Scott unfastened the latch and pushed open the door.

They found themselves in a small entrance hall. Through a door on the right was a typical farmhouse kitchen: it contained a large table and chairs, an oak dresser filled with china, copper pans, and a wood-burning range. A bead curtain hung in one corner of the kitchen. Scott's attention was piqued by a folded note on the tabletop. The note had a handwritten message on it.

Johnny – it began – it breaks my heart to have to tell you that your mum didn't survive the earthquake. She was badly injured and passed away two days after the disaster.

We have buried her in the small garden at the back of the farm. It's too painful for me to stay here anymore, so your uncle Mick and I have left and will make our way to Spen House at the Salterhebble Crossroads. We will wait for you there. Please do your best to reach us as soon as possible.

Our love and thoughts are with you and Lauren.

Dad xxx

Scott returned the note to the table and wondered if the family had ever been reunited. He and Fabian searched the kitchen for a few minutes. On the counter, they found a bread tin with a mouldy loaf inside. Scott walked across the kitchen and pulled back the bead curtain, revealing a small pantry. Inside, a pair of dead hares hung from a string, surrounded by a swarm of flies. In one corner of a shelf he spotted a sealed jar of jam, a few tins of soup and a plastic container filled with dried lentils. They put them in their packs.

Returning to the entrance hall, they ventured into the parlour. The first thing that caught their eye was the sight of clothes that were still hanging from a dryer over an open fireplace. They appeared to have been there for some time because they had badly disintegrated. On the hearth they spotted a pair of worn-out men's work boots and some tattered women's slippers. In a rocking chair there was a ball of blue wool and knitting needles. The farmhouse had an eerie and abandoned feel to it as if the residents had left in a hurry.

Beneath a sagging timber lintel, a narrow set of stone stairs led to the upper floor. In the main bedroom, they were confronted with the damaged portion of the farmhouse. There was a vast, jagged rent in one wall where the gable end had caved in, leaving the room exposed to the elements. The wallpaper hung in tattered strips, and the rug squelched with the remnants of last night's deluge. On the bedframe rested a heavy timber roof beam, while the bedsheets were stained with patches of dried blood the colour of autumn russet.

The house contained nothing else worth saving so they went downstairs and back outside to the yard. They poked around for a bit, mostly out of curiosity. In a cramped corrugated toolshed they found an antique reaping machine with horse tracers still attached and a two-wheeled cart filled with bits of cast iron pipes.

They retraced their route to the lake.

While they were strolling along the shoreline, Fabian noticed something and pointed at it.

"What is that? In the water?"

They approached the water's edge for a better look and spotted something floating on the surface.

"Fish!" exclaimed Fabian. "Dead fish! There's a bunch more of them over there too."

The silver scaly bodies were everywhere, some floating on the surface and more caught among the reeds at the edge.

"They must have been poisoned. D'you think it was the fallout from the power plant?"

"I doubt it," Scott replied. "We're too far away."

"Well, something killed them. Every fish in the lake is dead from the looks of it."

He removed his sunglasses for a better look.

"What do you think it was, Scott?"

"My guess is the quakes released poisonous toxins from subterranean aquifers. Let's avoid getting our feet wet."

"So, we're not having fish for dinner then?" Fabian asked.

"And no swimming for the kids, either."

They hurried back to the campsite to warn the rest of the group.

PART 2
TRAIL OF TEARS

Mark Hobson

Chapter 14

**BERNESE ALPS
SWITZERLAND**

THE CAVE TURNED OUT NOT to be a cave after all. It was a lava tube, an underground tunnel formed by slow-moving magma beneath the earth, known scientifically as a pyroduct. The walls of the lava tube were etched with horizontal grooves, tide marks indicating the various levels the lava had reached after spewing from the subterranean magma chamber. The ceiling of the lava tube was adorned with a forest of knobbly stalactites, more generally called lavacicles, which reminded Timo of shark teeth. As the flashlight beam passed over the floor, mineral deposits sparkled like crystals in a magical grotto from a fairytale.

Despite the freezing air outside, the atmosphere below the surface was oppressively humid. Timo and Genny were standing above a gigantic magma chamber, which held vast amounts of lava. It was frightening to think of what would happen if it suddenly flooded into the lava tube.

It was also very smelly.

But Timo was willing to endure the bad stench of sulphur and the risk of a bone-melting death if the alternative was dying from the cold. He also needed to rest again as the pain in his stomach had returned. Though it wasn't as sharp as before, it was still severe enough to leave him feeling nauseous. Timo gathered the strength to lay out a sleeping bag and he held Genny close as they spent a long night together.

Timo woke up feeling relieved that the pain had again decreased to a bearable level. He prepared some food for Genny and gathered up their gear as she ate. The entrance to the tunnel was now filled with daylight, so Timo stepped outside to take a look. In the distance, he could see that the once grand hotel had been reduced to a smouldering pyre. The air was thick with smoke.

Returning to Genny, Timo peered into the lava tube. The tunnel, which was about fifteen feet wide and twenty feet high, appeared to stretch endlessly into the distance, descending into the earth at a shallow decline. Timo wondered how far it went. Did it lead to the magma chamber? He'd read about similar lava tubes in Iceland and Hawaii and remembered that they could extend for miles. Some eventually headed back to the surface.

Could it possibly be a way off the mountain? All the other egress routes were impassable. The only way to know was to investigate further. It would be risky because there were multiple ways it might end badly: death by lava, death by noxious gas poisoning, and death by a cave-in, to name just a few.

"What do you say, girl?"

His dog didn't express any opinion; she simply looked up at him with her big brown eyes.

"I suppose I'll just have to make the decision for both of us, then."

Timo attached her lead and they set off.

As they penetrated deeper into the tunnel, the light from the entrance slowly faded. Very soon, the white glow from the flashlight became their only source of illumination. The circle of light bounced around the tunnel, disorientating Timo.

The walls were decorated in an array of red and green hues, creating a mesmerizing sight. Running his hand across the surface, Timo was struck by their smooth texture, as if the rocks had melted under the intense heat. Remarkably, there was an absence of moisture, with no water dripping from the ceiling or trickling down the sides. It occurred to him that with enough supplies, it would be possible to remain down here for an indefinite period of time - if you were willing to put up with the obvious dangers. In fact, stone-age humans might well have sought shelter and lived in such places.

From time to time, they would hear various sounds. Pinpointing their source was hard because they seemed to come from different directions — sometimes from ahead, other times from the tunnel walls, and occasionally from deep beneath their feet. The noises changed, too, ranging from deep, grinding rumbles to high-pitched tones that were almost beyond the range of the human ear. Genny appeared to pick up on things that Timo didn't because she would cock her head and emit fearful little whines in the back of her throat. More than once, Timo had to coax her to continue, and he briefly considered going back. But doing so would only take them back to square one.

The dark void looming over Timo's head created the illusion that the tunnel's ceiling was descending as if it intended to crush them both. He knew this was just a trick of the mind, but he found it difficult to shake off the notion.

Ahead of them, the tunnel telescoped into the darkness. They had been walking for approximately twenty minutes, covering about half a mile, when Timo noticed they were now going uphill. Taking a breather, he checked his compass: they were heading north and should be directly beneath the alpine massif blocking the pass. Timo couldn't help but feel a glimmer of hope.

They continued onwards and a few minutes later the impenetrable darkness ahead slowly lightened. Timo picked up the pace. At length, the subterranean passage was lit by a bright beam of daylight lancing down through a skylight in the tunnel ceiling.

As they stepped into the light, basking in its radiance, Timo realized that the jagged hole was too high to reach. But Timo refused to despair. Leaving the beam of light, he hurried forward through the passage and sure enough a second and then a third skylight lit the way. Eventually they found a rockfall that provided a sloping path to the surface.

Genny appeared to have overcome her fear as she tugged on the lead, eager to leave the dark passage. Timo patted her on the head and then found a safe route through the opening. Blinking against the bright sunlight that greeted them, Timo and his dog stood at the lip of the skylight and looked around.

It was a beautiful sight.

But not what he'd hoped for.

Instead of seeing green meadows covered in alpine flowers, sunlit streams and pretty waterfalls, they were confronted with an endless vista of snow-capped peaks. Mountaintop after mountaintop extended as far as the eye could see, marching over the horizon. Instead of leading them safely down the high pass, the lava tube had brought them out at the very apex of the Bernese Alps mountain range. Timo couldn't figure out how this could be; he was certain they would emerge further down the valley near the ski resort.

For the first time, Timo felt they were truly finished.

• • •

Nature's total ascendancy was overwhelming. Timo felt insignificantly small in comparison. He wanted to drop to his knees and curse at the injustice.

From where he stood, Timo had an unrestricted view of the mountain peaks standing in ranks to the horizon. Away to the north, he recognized Switzerland's majestic Three Peaks—the Eiger, Mönch, and Jungfrau—the Ogre, the Monk, and the Young Maiden. According to legend, the Monk protects the Young Maiden from the Ogre.

On the right, Timo could easily identify the Simplon Pass, which Emperor Napoleon used to lead his army over the Alps, mimicking his hero Hannibal of Carthage in 218 B.C.

In the canton of Valais loomed the prominent peak, the Weisshorn, with wisps of cloud trailing off its challenging East Ridge.

Timo felt tears welling up in his eyes. He sat on a nearby rock and took a moment to compose himself. Genny came over and sat in front of him, staring up. It was as if she could read his mind, sensing his despondency.

Don't give up, her brown eyes seemed to say.

Together, we can do this. Me and you.

The dog turned to look across the spectacular panorama like she was telling him: *That is the way.*

Timo gave a humourless laugh and scratched her forehead.

"You make it sound easy, girl."

She wagged her tail and licked his fingers.

"Do you know what we would be up against? The distance from here to Bern is about sixty miles as the crow flies and at least double that on foot. We'll need to cross mountains and glaciers, navigate rivers, and hike through forests. Most roads and bridges will be destroyed. It will be freezing cold at night, and neither of us is dressed or equipped for mountaineering, in case you hadn't noticed."

Genny gave a bark and started to prance excitedly.

"You're crazy, do you hear?"

What was crazy was him sitting on a mountainside and having a surreal conversation with his dog, discussing the idea of crossing the Alps in simple hiking gear. It was as absurd as George Mallory attempting to climb Everest in hobnail boots or Ernest Shackleton crossing the stormy South Atlantic in a rowing boat for sixteen days before climbing over South Georgia's mountain range.

Even stranger was how easily he had chosen Bern as a possible destination. Once again thoughts of his parents seemed to have slipped unnoticed into his subconscious, calling to him from the past.

For a long time, Timo stared at the snowy peaks, hands gripping his knees and his body rocking gently in the wind. Finally, he came to his feet.

"I don't believe we're doing this," he told Genny.

He began searching in his pack for his woolly hat and gloves.

"It's a stupid idea."

He scooped up his dog, placed her into the backpack with her head poking out of the top, and wrapped a scarf around her neck.

"I've no idea how you managed to talk me into this."

As he prepared for the enormous task ahead of them, Timo carefully deliberated on the best approach for the journey. Keeping it simple was the key. Going directly north wasn't an option because of the rugged terrain of the mountains. His plan was to proceed through the lower slopes and tributary valleys, steering clear of the treacherous boulder fields. When it became necessary to climb, it was best to use the spurs and passes. This wasn't about conquering mountains, nor was it about finding the shortest route. He was willing to double or even triple the distance if it meant avoiding a fatal accident – even a sprained ankle would be as bad in their circumstances.

The lava tube skylight was located halfway up a steep snow-covered bank on the side of a long ridge. Their first task was to descend to the bottom. Then they faced a demanding climb up a second slope. Following that they would encounter a series of four ridges and spurs that resembled the knuckles of a clenched fist. Timo estimated that if they could get past these obstacles by dusk, they would have made good progress on the first day. He looked around for the best way down, but one way looked as good as another, so he chose a path at random and began his journey.

From the cave opening, the gradient didn't look too bad. But after a few dozen yards, it was clearly much steeper than he had anticipated. The deep snow made the going even more perilous; he had to scrape holes for his feet and move in sideways steps. It wasn't long before his calf muscles began to ache.

The way grew sheer. Timo began a continuous dialogue with a God he didn't believe in. Then he slipped and fell on his backside and suddenly started to toboggan down the slope on his back. He dug his heels into the snow to try and arrest their descent, but it didn't help, and soon they were sliding faster and faster.

The snowy landscape rushed past in a blur and they narrowly missed a series of jagged rocks. Everything unfolded so quickly that Timo didn't have time to react. All he could do was experience pure fear – fear of plunging over a precipice, smashing his head open on a boulder, or the terror of Genny tumbling away and being lost forever. He screamed; he couldn't help it because the sound was squeezed out of him by the pressure against his chest. Then, all at once, the ground levelled out and their speed began to slacken.

He lay in the snow, looking up at the mountain peaks and blue sky, his heart thudding away in his chest. Then he picked himself up.

"Are you all right, girl?"

He felt a pair of paws on his head and hot breath on his cheek.

"Thank God," and he started to laugh uncontrollably.

They granted themselves a short rest and then started up the next slope. It was tricky going and soon became a tortuous climb up a deceptively large spur. He laboured uphill, one foot at a time, and sucked in great gulps of the rarefied air. The height and exertion became a terrible strain and when he stopped for a breather, Timo was disheartened to see they hadn't even reached the level of the lava tube on the slope behind them – in fact, they were only a third of the way to the ridgeline.

After another twenty minutes, Timo halted for a short meal. He dug a hole in the snow and placed his small Primus stove in it. Lunch consisted of crushed biscuits boiled up into a thick sludge, which was hot and unwholesome but which lined their stomachs.

While they were eating, Timo noticed a menacing bank of clouds forming on the horizon. The afternoon was getting on, and it had taken them two hours to reach this point with another two hours needed to reach the ridge. They were way behind schedule and Timo realized that his estimates of today's progress had been way too ambitious. He seriously needed to reconsider his calculations.

It was impossible to reach the series of four spurs today. Now the goal was to reach the top of the ridge and then descend the other side before dusk. Somewhere in the valley there would be a crevasse or a small cave where they could shelter for the night.

They started up again. The ascent became steeper but Timo set a fast pace in his determination to beat the approaching storm clouds. His legs became wobbly from the exertion. Upwards and upwards they climbed.

Finally, at about four in the afternoon, they struggled to the top. The ridge was so sharp that Timo could sit astride it, one leg on either side. He peered over the edge. Beneath him was a precipitous drop ending in a deep chasm one thousand feet below. To the left was a chaotic mess of shattered ice cliffs descending to a line of glaciers. It was too sheer a drop to make it down from this position. The only way was to shuffle along the saw-toothed spine of the ridge until it descended in a series of stone shelves to the valley below. He could see some distant trees down there, which meant they could build themselves a big fire. With this thought in mind, Timo started the hazardous journey along the ridge's backbone.

It was slow going. The risk of a misstep wasn't helped by a strong wind gusting over the ridgeline. Timo had to grip the rocky crest with both hands while keeping both legs on one side of the ridge. This meant his body was twisted at an odd angle, making him dangerously off balance.

He could hear Genny making nervous mewling noises from the backpack and after a few minutes she burrowed down out of sight.

The crooked ridgeline descended like a set of stone terraces, some no wider than a step. Timo placed each foot carefully, hoping the rocks didn't collapse beneath his weight. As he went lower, the wind dropped away, and it was with a feeling of relief that the descent grew more straightforward. He traversed across the face of the ridge at a linear angle.

After descending in this manner for several hundred feet, he reached a point where the headwall ran parallel to the narrow valley. Soon after, Timo lowered himself down a wide crevice and reached the snowy spur in the shaded side of the ridge. They'd made it down just in time because heavy snow flurries blew on a brisk wind.

Timo could barely see the end of the valley through the falling snow. He bent into the wind and pushed himself forwards. The narrow valley turned northwards, and he followed it as it passed a line of mountain ash. He began looking for a suitable shelter and soon noticed an overhanging ledge that sheltered a shallow cave.

Half an hour later and they had a roaring fire going. Timo cooked some tinned stew as they settled into the sleeping bag.

Later, the bad weather cleared, revealing the stars above. Timo tried to remember their names but he was too tired.

He slept soundly while curled up with his dog.

Chapter 15

CHICKAHOMINY INDIAN RESERVATION
LITTLE GREENBRIER RIVER
WEST VIRGINIA

THEY SPENT THE REST OF that day and all of the following day making their final preparations to leave the Indian Reservation.

After dropping Two Moon and his sons off at the village, Kenny and his friends drove the Humvee to the site of the crashed plane, with Deputy Geddes following behind in his patrol car. They loaded up the trailer with essentials, including weapons, ammo, food, and camping gear. Deputy Geddes was genuinely impressed with how well-kitted out they were. After securing everything, they drove over Mount Sewell and reached the Indian village to find arrangements well in hand. Eager to assist, they joined in and offered to help wherever it was needed.

The school bus had been converted into living quarters for the younger kids. All of the seats had been removed and replaced with bunk beds. The rear section was partitioned off, and behind the partition, a small medical area was created for the girl with the brain tumor. It contained a larger bed covered with soft blankets, an IV stand, and medicine racks.

Bethany found herself volunteering as a nurse/childminder to help the girl's mother and to keep the little ones entertained during what promised to be a long journey to the border. Meanwhile, Alex set to work improving the security arrangements. He removed one of the bus skylights and replaced it with a homemade machine gun emplacement. On the bus roof, he welded one of the new M250 machine guns to a circular turret that revolved in a full 360-degree circle by pulling on a hand crank. Underneath, he slung one of the pilot bucket seats from the crashed plane. When he was finished, he proudly tried it out, making *rattattat* noises like he was playing wargames.

While all of this was happening, Kenny and Deputy Geddes (he insisted they call him Orville, but to Kenny, a cop was a cop) held a meeting with Two Moon to discuss the convoy's configuration. It was decided that Kenny would drive the Humvee at the front of the convoy, with the other vehicles and school bus in the middle and Geddes bringing up the rear in his patrol car. The convoy would be shielded by a screen of men on horseback – videttes – thrown out to the sides and front. They would patrol several miles ahead to watch for potential dangers.

It became apparent at some point that they were being observed from afar. On the hilltop, several tiny figures were spotted. On the far side of Little Greenbrier they noticed pickup trucks parked in the scrub. Everyone agreed that it had to be the town militia who was watching them and they were making little effort to stay hidden. As long as both sides kept their distance there shouldn't be a problem but the standoff was tense nonetheless.

When everyone was ready, they all got into their vehicles and started their engines. Two Moon was the last to get in. From the Humvee, Kenny watched him taking one final look around. Then he took his seat on the bus, and with little fanfare, the convoy departed.

They'd only travelled about a mile when the militia swooped down on the reservation. The convoy pulled over and everyone watched in heavy, sombre silence as the militiamen proceeded to ransack the village, setting fire to the lodges and the grand elm bark hut. More than a dozen columns of dark smoke curled into the windless sky. They fired their guns in celebration as their pickup trucks rumbled through the village. Then, two figures could be seen hoisting their new flag above the village's totem pole, drawing a loud cheer. The flag, with its image of a crossed shovel and musket, was visible for miles around.

Kenny could only imagine the pain this act of ugly sacrilege caused Two Moon and his kinsfolk. It was a testament to their character that they chose to suppress their emotions rather than react.

Kenny followed the planned route they had decided on. After leaving the reservation, the first part of their journey was along an unscathed portion of Route 19 until they reached the Hemlock Cabins near Ames Heights. At this point the road led them to the New River Gorge Bridge. Constructed of steel alloy, with a central arch of 1,700 feet spanning nearly 800 feet over the densely forested river gorge, the bridge served as a vital link between Fayette County and the central section of the Appalachians, a range of mountains stretching all the way to Canada. Or at least it used to; now the scene was one of utter devastation.

The earthquakes had swiftly obliterated the engineering marvel. This breathtaking structure, constructed over the course of three years, succumbed to the tremors in a mere twenty seconds. The entire structure had plunged into the yawning gorge below, dragging numerous vehicles and their occupants down with it. At the bottom of the deep chasm, colossal steel spars had come to rest in big piles of rusting scrap metal.

Unlike the bridge in St Louis, which was just about passable, there was no chance of crossing the gorge. Kenny, who vividly remembered the terrifying episode when he'd almost fallen to his death into the Mississippi, was quietly relieved. But Two Moon's people had already selected an alternative route. Rainbow Valley Road, an old dirt track following the riverbank, led to the small town of Hawk's Nest. According to Two Moon, they could cross a shallow ford downriver from a small waterfall.

It was ten miles from the collapsed bridge to the town. Kenny set an unhurried pace due to the men on horseback. The convoy crawled along the rutted track with the broad river flowing in slow, languid currents to their right. Occasionally, pieces of flotsam floated past. Kenny observed half-sunken rowing boats, a carpool roof, and water towers, as well as a logging truck with a yellow cabin sunk midstream.

The riverbanks had been remoulded by mudslides in some areas, leaving trees uprooted as the ground avalanced into the river. The mud had hardened in the sun, setting like concrete.

Amidst the scenes of quake damage, they encountered some peculiar sights. Around a corner, they spotted a man wearing shorts and a vest, casually sitting on a sofa placed on top of his trailer. He reminded Kenny of Jeb and his cat and cheerfully waved at the passing convoy. The bus driver honked in response. Further down the dirt track, they had to pause as a herd of deer drank from the river, unfazed by the nearby humans. Shortly after, they came across an overturned firetruck. The vehicle had come to grief on a sharp bend, toppling over and coming to rest among tall stalks and reeds. Through the shattered windscreen, Kenny could see human-shaped silhouettes.

The river became shallower as it ran over smooth rocks. Kenny could see the ford up ahead. He steered the Humvee onto the riverbed, drove over the rounded stones, and up the far bank. Two Moon's older son was waiting on horseback, and he leaned out of his saddle to talk with Kenny.

"We've found something that I think you need to see," Little Bird said. "About half a mile from here."

Kenny didn't like the ominous tone in the man's voice.

"What is it?" he asked.

"Just follow me."

Kenny waited until Two Moon stepped down from the bus and joined him in the Humvee before setting off through the trees, leaving the convoy to make its way over the river. Little Bird guided his horse along an increasingly narrow trail.

Kenny followed some twenty yards behind, driving in low gear to avoid scaring the horse. Tree branches scraped at the Humvee's bodywork.

Kenny looked at Two Moon and asked if he knew what this was about. His companion just shrugged, his eyes piercing the leafy canopy.

After a few minutes they arrived at a clearing. The place looked familiar. He, Bethany and Alex had been here before. It was the old grist mill by the mountain stream that they had stumbled across several days ago. It was a pretty spot in the shade of leafy trees. The water wheel had long since stopped grinding corn, and the flashing on the roof was full of holes.

Kenny turned off the engine, wondering why they were there. He joined Little Bird and together they walked over a wooden footbridge covered in vines. Near the door Little Bird paused and gave Kenny a red neckerchief. Then he tied his own around his neck and over his nose and mouth.

"You're going to need it," he warned Kenny in a muffled voice.

Kenny quickly tied the neckerchief over the lower half of his face, and when Little Bird pushed open the creaking wooden door, Kenny felt the weight of some terrible torment drag him down. He really didn't want to go inside but found himself stepping over the threshold into the grist mill.

As soon as he was inside, he was surrounded by a swarm of blue bottle flies. They bombarded his face and crawled across his eyes. Kenny swatted them away with his arms. Along with the flies came a smell like something from the grave, a cloying miasma that infiltrated the neckerchief and seeped into his nose and mouth. The strong mephitic stench clung to the back of his throat like phlegm.

Kenny looked around, and as his vision adjusted to the dim interior, various details slowly emerged. He could see the gears and drive shafts of the old machinery, several abandoned cornmeal bins in the corner, and what looked like some lumpy old sacks spread over the floor. But then he noticed spindly, bony things splayed at unnatural angles, remnants of pale breasts like hessian sacks with nipples that oozed gelatinous milk, and children's fingers clutching the air like frozen claws. Craniums shattered with exit wounds.

The floor was carpeted with human detritus, and the whole was alive with a seething mass of maggots. It took a Herculean effort not to flee from that place. Kenny felt a wave of dizziness pass through him and he closed his eyes and counted to ten. When he opened them again he saw that Two Moon had joined them. Father and son moved among the corpses, outwardly unaffected by the grisly scene—or so it seemed.

Kenny tried to speak, but his words came out garbled, so he had to try again.

"Who are they?"

Three words were all that he managed. Then he fled out into the daylight, tore off his mask, and spewed into the bushes. After he finished retching, Kenny walked away and leaned against a tree, staring off into the woods. He had snot dangling from his nose and he wiped it with his sleeve.

He sensed someone approaching and looked over his shoulder to find the two men standing beside him.

"Who were they?" Kenny asked for a third time.

"Descendants of the Chactow, we think, from the Eastern Woodland Nations. They were moved west to Oklahoma many lifetimes ago."

"They were all shot. Executed," Kenny said back to Two Moon. "Even the children."

"There are more of them in the woods. Buried in shallow graves," said Little Bird.

He directed them to a group of fresh mounds of soil a short walk away. Kenny stood looking down at them.

"We can't let the others know about this," he thought out loud.

"They deserve to be told," replied Two Moon.

Kenny looked at the woods around them.

"Do you think the people responsible are still here?"

"Maybe, maybe not. These folk have been dead for several days, so their killers might be hundreds of miles away."

Or they could be seated in the mayor's office at the top of Lansing's civic building, lording it over everyone, Kenny thought.

"The other day, you said something strange. *He who takes the fat wishes us harm.* That if you stayed, blood would be spilled. And if you wanted to survive, then you had to leave. You talked about a Trail of Tears."

Kenny looked at him squarely.

"You knew this was coming, didn't you?" he went on. "That it was happening elsewhere, and it was only a matter of time before it happened here."

"We had heard rumours. That people west of the Mississippi were being forced off their land. But this is the first proof we have seen that it is widespread. Something made the Chactow flee here. Like us, they tried to escape, but in their case, they failed."

"Is that why you cut a deal with the mayor – to prevent more bloodshed?"

"This is history repeating itself," Two Moon said in way of answer. "All of this has happened before."

There was an eerie stillness as the group of men surveyed the burial site. Kenny was unconvinced. It seemed too easy to simply leave their reservation without putting up a fight. Just the same, the prospect of a violent clash with the town militia was even more daunting, so who was he to judge them? Plus they also had to consider the sick girl. Yet none of it sat well with him.

Kenny didn't dwell on the matter any further because all of a sudden a powerful aftershock rocked the woods. Small tremors had become so frequent that they barely paid them any attention, but this one was stronger than most, and it felt a little different as well. The earth thumped beneath their feet in a series of blows as if something below was whacking the ground and trying to get out. Kenny watched the soil over the graves become agitated, with loose pebbles bouncing around like magic beans. A face appeared as the ground gave up its dead and Kenny turned away from the ghoulish sight. Around them, thousands of birds took to the air.

Then the shaking abruptly stopped and a hush enfolded the woods.

"I don't know what that was," whispered Kenny, "but it didn't feel like an earthquake to me."

"I think you're right. More like a shockwave from an explosion."

They left the burial site and returned to the grist mill. Once aboard the Humvee, Kenny followed Little Bird back to the river.

Nobody had been harmed. While they'd been gone the rest of the convoy had completed the crossing without incident. But everyone was talking about the strange affair, with all manner of theories doing the rounds. Some said they heard distant thunder accompanying the shaking. The consensus was that whatever it was, it happened far away from them.

Chapter 16

SOYUZ SPACECRAFT
LOW EARTH ORBIT

TO FLIGHT ENGINEER MADISON LEITNER, going home didn't necessarily mean returning to the United States. Anywhere on Earth would do, as long as she survived the violence of re-entry.

As the Soyuz craft drifted away from the International Space Station, she said into her mic, "Houston, this is Nuada. We have achieved good separation here."

Of course, there was nobody in Mission Control at the Johnson Space Center to hear her. But if there had been— if there had been no earthquakes, tsunamis, and volcanoes, no Rods from God superweapon—Madison could picture the scene in her mind. She could visualize the white-haired, bespectacled Flight Director loosening his blue tie for the thousandth time, dabbing the perspiration on his forehead with a handkerchief, and then saying in his Texas drawl, "Nuada, Flight. Looks peachy down here."

The Flight Director would glance up from his small monitor to the large screen covering the entire wall at one end of the room. This status board, commonly referred to as the 'Big Board', displayed precise data regarding the Soyuz craft's return to Earth, which is the riskiest part of any space mission.

He would fidget nervously, his eyes darting here and there, checking and rechecking the readouts, and living off copious amounts of black coffee to keep himself focused.

The stress he experienced would be somewhat alleviated by knowing that every member of Red Team - the twenty-six other people in the room - was going through the same tensions and fears, with everyone sharing the burden. Not to mention the thousands of scientists, technicians, and engineers whose collective skills made human space flight possible.

But none of that support was available for Madison.

Instead, she would have to do this the hard way, on her own.

"Nuada, Flight," Madison said in a deep voice as she imitated the Flight Director's voice. "We're getting good data here. Your velocity is 35,415 feet per second. Range to splash, 1,750 nautical miles. Entry Angle 7.2°"

"Roger," Madison replied in her own voice. "My CMC guidance dials look good."

"Switch on your 8-ball and DSKY. We are three and a half minutes from entry interface. Start your first aerobrake manoeuvre."

Madison examined the outdated flight controls on the Soyuz spacecraft's flight deck, amazed that the fifty-year-old systems were still functioning. The Entry Monitor System panel showed trajectory information, the scrolling display indicated velocity versus deceleration, and the Roll Indicator provided data on the craft's pitch and re-entry angle. The Russians liked to brag that things worked just fine and were as reliable as a Kalashnikov, and they may have had a point. But what she was doing had never been attempted before: a single crew member trying to bring home a spacecraft without help from Mission Control.

"Houston, horizon check is about 5° above the 31.5° line in the window."

"We concur," Madison replied in the Flight Director's voice.

"We'll be in blackout in seventy-five seconds," Madison announced to nobody. "Switching from Programme 63 to Programme 64."

"Roger that, Nuada."

Madison reached up and flipped a series of switches above her head. Her arm strained against the steadily increasing G-forces, marking the first tenuous layers of atmosphere exerting their decelerating forces on the spacecraft.

"Entry Initialization complete," she said. "P64 has us. Forward heatshield beginning to glow."

"Great stuff, Nuada. Our readings are 6-Gs but easing back to 3-Gs. You should notice the difference anytime now."

"Glad to hear it, Houston," remarked Madison as her facial muscles stretched taut.

"Your velocity is at 36,565 feet per second. Range to splash is 1,315 nautical miles."

Through the small window beside her, Madison watched as the horizon gradually darkened while the Soyuz descended into the planet's stratosphere. The roll indicator showed normal.

"I'm vectoring along the corridor nicely, and Gs are dropping. My altitude is 55,000 feet. Entering comms blackout now."

With the apex cover, or heatshield, wrapped around the forward compartment of the Soyuz, the craft started to shake violently as it descended into the upper atmosphere. From outside, she heard a faint whistling of thin air passing over the hull. The comms blackout lasted for three minutes and forty-five seconds and it felt like an age as Madison counted down the seconds. Far below, she spotted the deep blue ocean catching the bright sunlight.

"1,2,1,2,1,2,1,2,1,2,1,2. This is Nuada. Do you copy, Houston?"

"This is Flight. It's good to hear from you again," Madison answered herself in the fake Texas drawl. "Recovery ship has radar contact. SWIM 1 taking off from the Saipan now. Bring her in, Flight Engineer Leitner."

At 24,000 feet, Madison jettisoned the heatshield and armed the chute pyrotechnics. Immediately after this, she turned on the controls for the Landing Systems, which would trigger the timers and barometers to gauge the outside air pressure; if these readings were out, the chutes wouldn't deploy correctly.

When the Soyuz re-entry vehicle passed below 10,000 feet, Madison flicked a switch to release the drogue chute, followed seconds later by the three large main chutes. This would suspend the craft at such an angle to cause it to hit the water "toe first". Immediately after, Madison felt a sudden deceleration of the capsule. She dumped the excess propellant, seeing it float by the window in a cloud of red vapour, obscuring her view. When it cleared, she saw that one of the chutes hadn't deployed properly.

"I have one streaming chute," she said into the mic.

"Stand by for a hard impact."

The Soyuz smacked into the ocean, the impact shaking every bone in Madison's body. She was thrown against the seat restraints, feeling something tear in one shoulder. She didn't have time to dwell on the pain. The spacecraft temporarily submerged beneath the waves and then bobbed back up like a cork.

"Splashdown. Mark splashdown," she announced, before quickly unbuckling herself. As she scrabbled for the inflatable life raft, Madison could feel the Soyuz rock on the sea swell. From outside came the dull sound of the floatation collar inflating to prevent the spacecraft from sinking.

Madison carefully turned the handle of the post-landing vent, expecting a rush of fresh air. Instead, she was met with a forceful blast of seawater that drenched her face. It streamed into the crew compartment before trickling to a stop. Madison cursed herself for neglecting to operate the Cabin Pressure Release valve before splashdown.

After wiping her eyes clear, she fumbled with the exterior hatch and finally managed to unlock it. As she pushed it open, a cool breeze blew in. She took a moment to fill her lungs with the glorious air, inhaling the lovely briny smell. She had forgotten how wonderful Earth smelled.

She took the life raft and pushed it through the opening, then flung it clear of the craft while simultaneously pulling the inflation lanyard. There was a tiny popping sound as the air canisters detonated, and in seconds, the large orange life raft began to mushroom out and take shape before stabilizing itself in the water.

Madison tied it to one of the handgrips and returned to the Soyuz's crew compartment to retrieve the locker containing its precious cargo. Then she squeezed her body through the hatch, biting her lip against the agony in her shoulder. She thought that she had also taken a blow to the head but now wasn't the time to worry about her injuries. For now, she was more concerned about a short circuit causing a fire, so she had to quickly get away from the craft.

Sitting on the outside of the blackened and scorched hull, which was still hot to the touch, she threw the locker into the raft. Then, after double-checking to make sure she hadn't forgotten anything important, she stepped off the Soyuz and into the life raft.

The interior was quite spacious, with enough room for three cosmonauts. It contained an emergency rations pack, a pair of paddles, a transmitter beacon, some flares, a first aid kit, a fishing line, a knife, a compass, and an anchor. On the roof, there was a light and a rainwater catchment hose. Additionally, there was another light below the waterline to help guide someone back to the raft in case they fell in.

She untied the mooring line and used one of the paddles to push away from the Soyuz. She rowed about twenty feet away and realized she had made the right decision to leave the spacecraft as wisps of smoke began to escape from the hatch and vents. As she moved further away, small yellow flames started to appear.

In just thirty seconds, the craft was belching black smoke and crackling with electric sparks. The floatation collar caught fire and started to deflate, causing the Soyuz to tip over. Water was now gushing through the hatch into the crew compartment. Madison watched with a sense of sorrow as the craft sank beneath the waves. The only sign that it had ever existed was the parachute canopies floating on the sea's surface and the bright orange life raft bobbing in the vast ocean.

Madison struggled to keep a sudden feeling of terror at bay. She had known there would be no rescue helicopter to lift her out of the water and take her to a navy carrier, no ticker tape parade through Manhattan, and no interview with Time Magazine. She should have been greatly relieved to have made it down alive, even with a busted shoulder and a sore head. However, the magnitude of her new circumstances - adrift hundreds of miles from land with no help on the way - felt like a heavier burden than the planet's gravity.

She needed to remain level-headed and think logically. Madison had always prided herself on her ability to keep calm in a crisis. However bad her current predicament was, being marooned at sea was preferable to being stranded in space.

She decided to check her injuries. As she cautiously flexed her shoulder, a sharp twinge shot through her arm when she attempted to lift it above her head. It didn't feel like a dislocation, more like a torn muscle. The impact during the splashdown had also left her with a throbbing sensation on her forehead. When she felt with her fingers she discovered a small gash wet with blood. Again, she didn't think it was severe, but she'd have a nasty-looking purple bruise there by the next day. Coupled with the broken nose from her fight with Science Officer Beaufort, she must have looked an alarming sight.

Madison shimmied across the life raft and leaned over the side to splash water on the injury. Then she opened the first aid kit and rummaged through the contents until she located a pack of Steri Strips. She applied them to the cut and then rubbed in some Vaseline.

Madison put away the first aid kit and then checked the emergency rations. According to the writing on the packet, there were nine high-energy bars in sealed foil packs, containing a balanced diet for survival at sea. The ingredients included saturated fats, carbohydrates and vitamins C, B_1 and B_6. Madison thought they would taste terrible, but if they kept her alive, so be it. There were also several plastic packs of fresh drinking water.

She then turned to the compass, which was probably the most important piece of gear in the life raft. It was one of those fancy models that you typically found on yachts and pleasure craft. Madison had a vague idea of where she had come down; somewhere in the North Atlantic and three or four hundred miles off the US Eastern Seaboard. The compass would play a crucial role in determining whether she made it to the mainland or not. Basically, she needed to head west. If the currents took her east she was screwed because no amount of paddling would see her reaching shore.

Madison reminded herself that it was about overcoming one obstacle at a time. Humans are wired to survive, no matter what it takes. That's how we evolved from hunter-gatherers to landing on the moon. The earthquakes might have zeroed out most of that supremacy, but staying alive was still ingrained in our DNA.

Chapter 17

**GREAT SHUNNER FELL
NORTHERN ENGLAND**

OVER THE NEXT FEW DAYS they saw further evidence of the deadly toxins now polluting the rivers, streams and lakes. As well as dead fish, they came across the distressing sight of deceased horses and cows scattered across fields and meadows, and then as they reached the uplands and moors of Shunner Fell, dozens of sheep carcasses. They all shared two things in common: they were found near drinking holes, and they all had white foam around their mouths.

The contamination was more widespread than Scott had hoped. Instead of being confined to the lake, the freshwater supply was affected over a large area. Initially, this wasn't a concern as they had their own drinking water. But as the days passed and their provisions ran low, Scott became increasingly worried.

So far, they had avoided villages and towns, instead traveling across open fields and staying near hedgerows and low walls. Occasionally, they encountered country lanes and, since Scott didn't expect any cars to be around, they followed them for several miles. The objective Scott had set them was a crossing of Great Shunner Fell Moor in a few days, before striking northeast around the city of Newcastle. Although fit and healthy adults could probably do it quicker, they had set shorter, easier stages because of the children. But as they journeyed on and encountered numerous dead animals, Scott reluctantly brought up the subject of replenishing their provisions.

"If we can find an isolated hamlet, we could raid it for food and water," he said one evening around the campfire.

A few of the grownups vetoed the idea on the grounds that it was too dangerous, but their objections were not very strong as everybody knew they had limited options.

Pointing at the map, Scott went on.

"Newbiggen is a small village, just a few houses at a crossroads. There's sure to be a petrol station or a convenience store."

"But what if it's like the last place?"

Scott didn't need reminding; he remembered the church filled with gnawed bones all too well.

"Look, we'll scout it out first and if anything seems suspicious then we'll find somewhere else."

They set out early the next morning, following a sheep trail over the moors towards Kirkby Gill, a valley with steep hillsides leading down to the village. About a mile from the first houses was the Worton Viaduct, the only remaining bridge over a wide and sluggish river. The viaduct had been unused for years and was overgrown with weeds, and the brickwork was crumbling. But even after the recent earthquakes, it appeared sturdy enough. Taking their chances, Scott and Tammy walked across to the middle span and, from its vantage point, turned their binoculars onto the village.

Newbiggen was anchored on a minor crossroads. As far as places went, it was an unspectacular hamlet of about a dozen shabby-looking dwellings and a single pub that had seen better days. Scott thought he could see a tiny post office/general store, but it was hard to tell through the fine drizzle that had started to fall. There was something strange about the buildings that he couldn't quite put his finger on. He couldn't spot any earthquake damage, but there was something odd.

"I don't see any people," Tammy said, interrupting his thoughts.

"Or signs of any defences."

They looked at one another and nodded in unison, and then called the others to join them.

Having crossed the river they approached the hamlet across a muddy field.

What they found next took their breath away.

It was a sunken village.

Scott had seen documentaries about it on TV. It was called soil liquefaction, a rare phenomenon that sometimes happens during earthquakes. If the ground was shaken vigorously enough, solids such as roads and pathways lost all cohesion and behaved like liquid or quicksand, sucking vehicles and buildings into the earth, only for the ground to set hard again.

They walked through the village, filled with astonishment.

The things they saw:

Houses partially sunk into the ground so the height of the bedroom windows was at shoulder level.

Cars and vans tipped up and sucked down, with only half of the vehicle showing.

Manhole covers pushed up, resembling huge mushrooms.

Lateral cracks sprouting tall weeds.

Sand blows – or miniature sand volcanoes – scattered around like molehills.

A woman and a pushchair fused into the ground outside a bus shelter.

A dog on a leash with only its head above the surface.

People trapped in cars, or, if they fled outside when the quake struck, in the street or their gardens, their corpses forever half-entombed in solid ground.

It was a surreal experience, a peculiar blend of captivating fascination and morbidity that held a hypnotic power over them. Of all the strange sights and oddities they had encountered during their travels, from the ancient land bridge of Doggerland to a WW2 German submarine, the village of Newbiggen stood out as the strangest of them all.

They gathered near the post office.

"I'll go in while you lot wait outside," Scott said. "If you hear me shout out, then make a run for it."

"What about you?" asked Sara.

"I'll be right on your heels."

He turned to the boy who had gone AWOL the other day.

"And you - no wandering off, okay?"

"Who, me?" the boy replied with a cheeky grin.

Scott needed to enter the post office and general store by going through the flat above, which was now at ground level, and then heading down. With Fabian's help, he jimmied open an upstairs window and climbed inside. He found himself on a landing. There was a bookshelf against a wall filled with volumes about British birds. On the top shelf next to a cordless phone was a plate filled with loose change and sets of keys, while on a small stand was a Sunday newspaper that looked like dried papyrus. Scott picked up the phone but of course it was dead.

He moved along the upstairs hallway, trying doors randomly. The first one opened to a broom cupboard, the second was locked, and the third revealed a bedroom. Scott recoiled in shock at the sight on the bed.

It was an elderly lady. He could only tell this from the grey hair and pink slippers because everything in between was a mass of squirming, feasting rats. They had burrowed into her face and hollowed out her stomach and chest to reach the soft organs underneath. The bed sheets were covered in a large rust-coloured stain, and small rib bones showed through the tiny bodies and scaly tails. The rats paid him no attention because they were too busy with their repast. On a nightstand, Scott noticed an inhaler, a row of pill bottles, and a set of false teeth in a small glass tumbler. In the corner next to the window was a zimmer frame.

He left the room and closed the door. He felt oddly embarrassed as if he had intruded on a private affair, which in a way, he had. Whether the lady had died a natural death or taken her own life, Scott didn't know. She may have lain there for days, bedridden and wondering why her carer never showed up. Scott backed away and walked to the end of the hallway and around the corner.

There he found a staircase leading down to a door. Pushing it open, Scott entered the dim and now subterranean post office. The aisles were strewn with envelopes and rolls of bubble wrap. A photo booth had toppled over, crashing through the lottery machine and staff counter. In the cash office near the back, there sat a large safe with its thick steel door half open, the inside packed with money.

Scott moved between shelves until he found a drinks fridge. Taking a cardboard box, he filled it with plastic bottles of tepid water and then carried it back up the stairs and passed it to those waiting outside.

"We had a vote while you were gone," Fabian said once Scott had climbed out of the window.

"Oh, yeah."

He gazed uncertainly at the circle of faces.

"Am I going to like this?"

"Louise is tired. It's not easy for her slogging over the moors in her condition," Sara said.

Scott looked at the young teacher's assistant. She cut a sorry sight with her hood up against the rain, and her face was drained. She was carrying his child, and Scott was acutely aware of the constant danger of her taking a fall.

"We're all exhausted, Scott. This weather looks settled for the day."

Scott looked at the leaden clouds and the mist gathering on the surrounding hills. With the weather closing in, there was a danger of them getting lost and wandering around in circles. Or becoming separated.

"We need a proper break. With hot food inside us and somewhere warm to sleep," Sara went on and hugged baby Phoebe. "It will do us the world of good. Then, when we are fully rested, we can press on."

Scott wasn't thrilled with the idea of staying in the village, not after their last experience. But he knew Sara was right. They had been on the go for weeks, ever since leaving the survivors' camp near Amsterdam. They had travelled hundreds of miles by boat, balloon, and on foot, in hot sunshine and driving rain, all the while being hounded by people intent on killing them. And they still had a long way to go before finding somewhere they could call home. Scott worried that if they continued, it was only a matter of time before they lost more people. They needed to ease up.

He insisted that they find somewhere secure and, if not impregnable, then at least defendable.

"I don't trust these houses," he said as he gestured at the sunken village. "There's no telling what damage has been done to their foundations."

He decided it was best not to bring up the topic of the rats. Instead, he tasked them with finding a place to stay. They searched for a while and eventually discovered a suitable location just across the crossroads.

Behind the village pub was a large stable block and cow shed at the edge of a potato field. It was unaffected by liquefaction, and the lower half was made of solid breeze blocks, while the upper part was a spacious and dry timber hayloft. The only way to enter the hayloft was through a trap door and ladder, which could be drawn up after them if they came under attack. There was a skylight in the hayloft that would make a good escape route. The young lad with the wanderlust attitude appeared with an aluminium ladder he happened to find (Scott thought of giving him another ticking off for straying away, but held his tongue for now) and Scott adapted it as a drawbridge by lowering it horizontally from the shed roof to the pub roof next door using a rope.

Guards were appointed for the nights on a three-shift basis of two hours each. The roster included Saskia and two of the more responsible teenage boys. They developed a set of alarm signals using different whistles and owl hoots. If they needed to abandon the shed, they agreed to use the viaduct bridge as a muster point.

They brewed up their midday meal—lentils, potatoes, and Scotch broth blended into a stew—then Tammy and Scott decided to survey the surrounding area. First, they ascended the shed roof for a clear overview.

"There are lots of blind spots," he said, pointing towards several locations where individuals or groups of assailants might approach without being noticed. "Our field of observation stinks."

"Yes, but if we channel any raiders directly towards us, we can deal with them more effectively."

"How do we do that?"

Tammy showed him how to make various booby traps. She used fishing lines and rape alarms to set tripwires. Then she made homemade traffic spikes by hammering nails into lengths of garden hose she found in the shed and laying them over the roads and farm tracks.

"These will shred their tyres or cut their feet to pieces," she said with a wolfish grin.

She had other ideas that would turn the area into a fortress. Taking some wooden clothes pegs, two electrical wires and AA batteries, she demonstrated how to make basic alarm devices that would produce loud and fiery sparks when sprung by snares.

Red smoke bombs triggered by blank shotgun cartridges.

Pungee pits.

"Have you ever considered joining the military engineers?" he quipped.

"Being a camp supervisor is enough for me."

"You learned all of this prepper stuff from the Scouts?"

"Some of it, but not all. Necessity is the mother of invention."

After setting their traps to ward off attackers they sketched several maps clearly marking out which areas to avoid. These maps would be handed out and pinned up. It seemed a little excessive for a temporary stopover, but Scott wasn't willing to take any chances. Nobody wanted another encounter with ruthless predators.

Chapter 18

BERNESE ALPS
SWITZERLAND

EACH DAY, THEY WOULD WAKE up when the sky was still pitch black, have a hearty breakfast, and set out in the dark. After the nerve-wracking experience of navigating the treacherous terrain of the Alps on the first day, Timo's biggest fear was being stranded high up on a mountainside after nightfall. Any mountaineer will tell you that the most hazardous part of a climb is the descent, especially if climbers feel a rush of exhilaration upon reaching the summit and may not exercise the same level of caution on the way down as on the way up. Fatigue sets in as the day wears on, and with the end in sight, the risk of accidents increases. To make matters worse, navigating these dangers in the dim light of twilight raises the likelihood of mishaps.

Put simply, it was better to go up in the dark when feeling rested and fresh than to descend in the dark feeling exhausted.

Both of them quickly adapted to the new routine, even though their days of hiking and climbing were tiring and their progress was slow. One day, the weather was so bad that they spent their time sheltering from the elements, using their free time to rest and plan their route.

The following day, conditions were much better. The weather was fine and there was a light southerly wind. They made good progress during the morning as most of the hiking to that point was along gentle inclines to low-altitude valleys. But by late morning, Timo faced a long climb across a yellow band of limestone slabs. He had to traverse a long slope with a consistent 30-degree angle and the steeply pitched ground made his footing uncomfortable. Due to little snow on the ground, Timo had to walk on the points of his hiking boots. Under his feet were loose scree and icy rocks, making the mountainside unstable and slippery. Below him was a broken terrace just two hundred feet away, followed by a long fall to the glacier below.

Timo did his best not to glance down, focusing instead on the task at hand. After some time, he discovered a long ledge that stretched across the slope. He carefully made his way to the far end, manoeuvering around a buttress. As he turned the corner, he suddenly found himself exposed to a dangerous crosswind. It hammered into Timo, gusting somewhere around 60 miles per hour, he estimated. It made a hell of a noise as it screamed over the ridgeline. Timo held on for dear life, gritting his teeth.

The outcrop, a broad wall of hard rock, loomed over him like the sharp bow of a battle cruiser. It was a daunting obstacle, made more lethal by the vicious crosswind that howled and whipped over its cruel face. Seeking refuge from the relentless gusts, Timo retreated from his exposed position to the shelter of the buttress, his gaze scanning the rugged landscape for an alternative route.

He couldn't go around the outcrop. Neither could he go up, because that led to the summit, which would add hours to the day's journey. So the only choice was to go down and underneath the fortress-like buttress.

Inch by inch, Timo made his way down the steep gradient, each meticulously placed step taking him closer to the cliff edge. He passed from the band of limestone slabs into a shaded section of the mountainside, finding himself treading on ground that resembled loose roof tiles. There was more snow here, but it was the soft, powdery kind that wouldn't stop him if he slipped.

As he made his way closer to the broken terrace, the going became increasingly treacherous. With about twenty feet left until he reached the sheer drop, he changed his direction and began to move sideways, adopting a cautious, crab-like crawl on all fours. The only thing preventing a potentially fatal fall was the firm grip of his rubber soles on the slippery tiles.

The intense mental and physical strain of climbing with so much care and always one miss-step from death almost became too much. All the time, he was thinking this had to be one of the most remote and inhospitable spots on earth. The wind drove powdery snow into Timo's face, blanketing his skin and snow goggles and sticking to his eyebrows. The foothold ledges narrowed to just inches, and he was breathing hard from the effort and the terror.

For over one hour, Timo made painfully slow progress over the greasy tiles. Eventually, he neared the shoulder of the mountainside. He could hear the wind beyond making peculiar vibrating sounds where it blew over the serrated ridgeline. Clambering around the corner, he expected a sudden squall to throw him off, but he was elated to find the wind was much weaker at this level. He crawled forward towards a pair of boulders that offered a sheltered spot and sat back with a groan of relief. Timo could hardly believe he'd made it.

He looked at his surroundings. He was at the edge of a broad snowfield that funneled up to a cone of snow near the top, below a big stone platform with cracks and fissures. Across the snowfield there were some scattered boulders and then a sheer vertical wall that rose several hundred feet high. Lower down, the ground descended in a series of folds like a flight of giant steps, each one overhung with a cornice of packed snow.

Timo gave himself five minutes and as he was about to start his descent, he noticed something out of place. Just below the cone of snow, he spotted a piece of red material flapping in the breeze. Getting up, Timo crunched through the snow to take a closer look.

When he was still ten yards away, he realized that it was a body. The red material he had seen was a parka coat partially gathered underneath the corpse. Timo drew nearer, seeing more details.

The body lay face down, fully extended and pointing uphill, with both arms outstretched and its fingertips dug deep into the frozen gravel like it had been attempting to stop itself from sliding down the mountainside.

Timo knew straight away that the corpse was old and had been there for quite a while. Other than the parka, most of the clothing had been stripped away by the relentless wind. The skin appeared to be unnaturally pale, like alabaster, bleached of colour by the dry air and constant freezing temperatures. He saw where birds and other wildlife had pecked at the flesh. The head and face were buried in scree and stones, so he couldn't see its features, but Timo thought that it had once been a man because of the well-preserved muscles and powerful physique. One leg was broken in two places; the thigh and the ankle bone were both snapped and jutting out at unnatural angles. Coiled around the waist were several strands of rope, tightly constricting the ribcage. Lastly, the feet were dressed in worn brown leather boots with frayed red laces, although the crampons appeared to be in good condition.

Timo sat on his haunches, gazing out at the rugged mountainside as he imagined the harrowing scene. A seasoned mountaineer had suffered a horrific fall down the mountainside, breaking his leg as he bounced from boulder to boulder. Desperately trying to arrest his rapid descent, the climber had flung out his arms to grip the ground before finally coming to rest at this spot. His climbing partners had been helpless to prevent the accident and faced the heart-wrenching decision to leave him behind. The fallen climber, maybe drifting in and out of consciousness, succumbed to the cold and his injuries and lay here undiscovered until now.

Timo felt an air of melancholy settle around his shoulders. Discovering this single body, alone in the mountains for all of this time, had a deeper impact on him than the countless earthquake victims. It seemed like a lonely spot to pass away, yet it was also a beautiful and peaceful setting. It felt somehow appropriate for someone doing what they loved the most, scaling the snow-capped peaks.

He didn't wish to disturb the dead man, but Timo felt obligated to learn a bit about him. He slid off his backpack, mindful of his sleeping puppy nestled inside. His gaze settled on a walking stick wedged into a cranny just a few feet away. Going over, he bent down and picked it up.

Timo saw that it was one of those vintage German wooden walking sticks that were popular during the 1970s, adorned with little tin badges from places like Dinkelsbühl, Boppard, Lake Titisee, and the Austrian Tyrol. So, the climber was well-travelled and enjoyed outdoor activities. He was likely middle-aged, fit and had passed away around forty to fifty years ago.

Returning to the body, Timo carefully pulled the red parka free and searched through its pockets. He found a box of soggy matches, a small tin of meat lozenges, a wood-handled pocket knife, a red bandana for the hot days and a pair of mittens for the cold days. Zipped into an inside pocket was a crinkled driving licence. Timo carefully peeled it open. Inside was a small faded photo of a chap with thinning wavy hair. The licence was issued in 1973 to one **Günter Braun of Dusseldorf, West Germany**.

Timo replaced all of the items. At the last minute he decided he ought to take the crampons, thinking the dead man wouldn't mind. Then Timo wedged the walking stick into the snowy ground beside the body as a marker. He stood for a moment of quiet, pulled on his backpack, and continued his journey down the mountainside.

Timo's familiar caution returned. The topography from this point appeared easier, but he knew that looks could be deceiving. He focused on finding a safe path offering firm footing, trying to push thoughts of the dead mountaineer out of his mind. The ground was a severe, ice-covered grade, and it was difficult to know where the packed snow was stable and where it could give way under his weight. He was especially worried about the snow cornices overhanging the steps, so he skirted around them, following the ground where it resembled a large half-moon-shaped basin.

Getting used to wearing the crampons over his boots took some time. Walking on their spiky prongs felt odd like he was skittering over the icy surface. The secret was to dig his boots in hard with each step, which slowed things down even further. After a little experimenting, Timo picked up a steady, if measured, rhythm.

He worked his way along the crest of the ridge until he came across a small gulley, and then started his descent. After twenty minutes, the walls of the gully became steeper and a small stream of meltwater flowed down the centre. As Timo made his way, hopping from rock to rock and using the sides of the gully for support, the stream increased in depth and he found himself wading through water that climbed to his knees. The water was frigid, fed by the snowy uplands, and soon his fingers and toes grew numb.

After another twenty minutes of steady going, the gully had levelled out but had transformed into a deep gorge with perpendicular sides. Without climbing gear, there was no way to get out, so Timo had no option but to follow its course. Before long, the stream turned into a fast-flowing river. A few stubby trees appeared along the top of the gorge, and some even sprouted from its sides. The sounds of birdsong filled the air. Encouraged that he had passed below the snowline into the grassland regions, Timo pressed determinedly forwards.

Shortly after, the ground became more even on the other bank. He decided to cross over, which was no easy task. He had to leap from one boulder to another, risking an icy ducking at best and, at worst, a horrible death by drowning. Thinking the climber's walking stick would have been useful, he spent a few moments searching for a tree branch. Suitably equipped, he set off.

He jumped onto the first rock, wobbled for a second before finding his balance, and then moved to the next. After four or five rocks, Timo had reached the midpoint and now faced a five-foot jump to the next one. Since there was no space for a run-up, he planted the end of the branch into the riverbed, gripped it with both hands and pole-vaulted across the gap. Timo's feet landed on the slick boulder and his crampon-covered boots skidded, sending him sideways. He dropped the branch and whirled his arms in circles, but he was never going to regain his balance and he went under the surface.

The cold made him involuntarily gasp and his mouth filled with water. Weighed down by his backpack, Timo panicked. He gripped the pebbly riverbed to stop himself from being washed away. The river was only a few feet deep and he was only submerged for a few seconds but it felt like much longer. He rose to the surface, regained his footing, and stumbled through the shallows to the far bank, abandoning all attempts at staying dry.

When Timo made it to the muddy riverbank, he fell to his knees and coughed up a lungful of icy water. He quickly removed his backpack and tore off his snow goggles before unfastening his bag. Everything inside was soaked, including his spare clothes and food. But right now, he didn't care about that; all that mattered was checking on his puppy.

He scooped Genny out. She was sopping wet and shivering from the cold, and when her head flopped to one side, Timo feared the worst and nearly cried out. But then she opened her eyes and gave a powerful shake of her body, showering Timo with water droplets. She gave a few high-pitched yaps and then licked his face.

• • •

A short walk from the boggy riverbank, Timo found a pleasant meadow filled with alpine flowers and decided to camp there. Overlooking the river, he discovered a fallen tree trunk with a spacious hollow underneath. The hollow was dry and sheltered, and because it faced west into the afternoon sun, he was able to lay out his wet possessions to dry. After that, he relaxed, stretched out his aching limbs, and savoured a moment of pure relaxation in the sun's soothing rays. Genny, unfazed after her watery ducking, played in the lush grass.

In the morning, he planned to strike out for the Simplon Pass. This would involve a strenuous hike through the rocky notches near the village of Gondo, followed by a cautious journey across the marshy Canton of Valaise to the Rhone

River. The Simplon Pass was located just on the other side. It consisted of a series of winding switchbacks that straddled the mountain pass between Italy and Switzerland, reaching a peak of over 6,500 feet above sea level.

Afterwards, they faced a two-day journey north to the picturesque town of Grindelwald. Timo doubted it still looked like it did on the postcards and holiday websites. Then they had a further two-day journey west to Interlaken. From there, the route to Bern should, in theory, become easier.

He hoped to reach the city outskirts in about a week to ten days, accounting for potential delays such as bad weather or rest days. Timo didn't know what they would find there, but given the devastation in Geneva, he was certain that it wouldn't be good. He would wrestle with that problem at the proper time.

Just then, Genny came bounding across the meadow, cutting off his thoughts. She hurried over to their makeshift shelter and burrowed into their sleeping bag. Moments later, Timo heard the faint rustling sound of someone approaching.

He quickly put on some clothes and hurried out from under the tree barefoot. Just then he saw a goat emerge through the grass. The goat was sniffing around the riverbank, looking for wild turnips. When it spotted Timo, it stopped and gazed at him with its docile eyes.

It was a female Alpine ibex. Normally they are found high in the mountains, defying gravity by clinging to sheer rock faces. Occasionally they would wander down to lower altitudes. Timo knew that even with small horns and a blank stare, the female of the species could be dangerous.

Looking at the goat, Timo was about to shoo it away. However, when he heard his stomach grumble, he found himself salivating at the mere prospect of eating cooked goat meat.

But catching a wild mountain goat was no simple task. At first he tried talking gently to it and holding out a handful of nettles. The goat continued to look at him with a blank expression, so Timo very cautiously closed the gap.

"There, there, girl," Timo said, feeling stupid because what do you say to a goat anyway?

After a minute, the animal summoned enough courage to gingerly stretch its neck forward and tentatively began nibbling on the nettles. Timo allowed it to graze for a moment as he made more cooing noises. Then, when he thought the goat was at ease, he made a lunge for one of its stubby horns.

In the blink of an eye, the goat twisted and turned away, nearly ripping Timo's arm from its socket. With a powerful kick from its hind legs, the goat sent him falling face-first into the lush grass. As he lay there, Timo watched the goat gallop off.

But the animal didn't go far; instead, it headed down to the river and started drinking water.

Returning to their makeshift shelter, Timo searched through their gear. Soon after, he emerged with a lasso made from the neck strap of his map case.

In his second attempt at catching the goat, he fared just as badly as his first. Getting the lasso to snare its horns or feet proved hopeless. He had seen animal wranglers on TV make it look easy – there were even videos on YouTube of kids doing it before they could even walk – but it was impossible.

Timo ended up straddling the goat's back, crying for help as it gamboled in circles around the meadow.

As the slapstick circus act unfolded, Genny couldn't resist peeking out of her hiding spot and happily wagging her tail.

Timo, bruised and battered, had one final idea.

They roasted the goat carcass over the crackling, popping embers of their fire as the sun dipped below the horizon. Once ready, man and dog eagerly dug in, savouring every tender bite. Set against the backdrop of the untamed wilderness, it was a meal they would not soon forget.

Earlier, Timo had driven the goat upstream to the boggy riverbank, close to the spot where they had fallen in. The dumb animal quickly found itself mired in the mud, and ignoring its bleating cries, Timo had closed in to deliver the *coup de grace* with a big stone.

He felt guilty afterwards. Both of his parents were strict vegetarians and had raised their son the same way. But that all changed when Timo went to McDonald's with his friends and tasted a Big Mac for the first time. Even so, there was a big difference between ordering, say, lamb chops from a menu and killing and butchering an animal with his own hands.

Timo was determined not to waste a single part of the carcass. They would use what they couldn't eat in other ways.

For example, strips of rawhide could be used to make bolas, a type of hunting tool. Bolas were similar to slingshots and were weighted with small stones. When hunting, they would be aimed at prey to entangle their hindquarters, bringing them down long enough for the hunters to finish them off.

After being dried and cured over the fire, the animal's hides would make durable clothing. Goat fur, on the other hand, is soft and insulating, making it perfect as bedding.

Caught up in these thoughts, Timo sensed that they might actually prevail.

Chapter 19

SNAKE RIVER
APPALACHIAN MOUNTAINS

A FEW MILES FROM THE TOWN of Bainbridge Ferry on the Snake River, they stumbled upon a sunken riverboat. It had been converted into a floating casino and appeared to have broken loose from its moorings before fetching up here.

Kenny stopped the Humvee and got out. The convoy behind him came to a standstill, engines running.

The boat had got into difficulties in the faster-flowing waters a mile upstream before foundering on rocks. She had then capsized as water flooded through the hole in her hull. The riverboat's bow was pulled under, lifting the keel clear of the river. Now, the only parts showing above the waterline were a single smoke stack and the paddlewheel at the stern.

Amidst the flotsam and jetsam floating in the river were dozens of corpses, rich wheeler dealers gambling away their fortunes, or tourists having a whale of a time until disaster struck. Now, swarms of water insects hovered in clouds or crawled over the dead. Several bodies had washed up on the riverbank. Their faces had puckered up and gone all wrinkly, and their bellies had bloated.

Kenny returned to the Humvee and the convoy set off again.

A few miles further north, they stopped once more, this time for something much worse.

Later, Kenny tried to compare it to all the other horrors they had seen in an attempt to understand the human depravity involved. But in order to bracket it as the inevitable aftermath of a widespread tragedy meant delving into the darkest recesses of man's mind. Even then, he doubted he would fully grasp the true evil at hand. The only thing relatable was the horrors of the Nazi death camps.

In a large sward of pastureland edging the river, a wholesale slaughter of men, women, and children had occurred. As he walked through fields of dead, their stiff and cold limbs ready to snag the unwary, the horrors bore down on Kenny's already tormented nerves. A heavy stillness hung in the air. With it came an unusual smell. For some reason, it reminded Kenny of sweet potatoes cooked just as they turned bad.

He walked over the undulating ground, trying to avoid the spilled insides of the disembowelled or the brain matter of the executed, but soon the bottom of his trousers was caked in bloody mud. Several other members of the convoy had joined him, and each of them walked with their heads down, lost in thought.

The perpetrators had made no attempt to bury the dead or hide their crime. The bodies lay thick upon the ground where they had been murdered, their bodies heaped together and their limbs interlaced. Some had gunshot wounds, others stab wounds, while many had been bludgeoned around the head. It was akin to a battlefield where no quarter was given and no prisoners were taken. But Kenny figured this had been no fair fight between two well-armed opponents. Instead, these people – and they were all Native Americans, each and every one of them – had been rounded up, brought to this spot, and butchered.

There were also suggestions that some of the victims were tortured. Near some bullrushes next to the river, Kenny came across a girl of about five or six. She'd had her ears cut off and her eyes gouged out, both legs amputated at the knee, and by all appearances, was made to walk on her stumps. Kenny stood looking at her still form, too shocked to cry but unable to understand the level of degenerate corruption needed to inflict such evil. It was a canker of the soul.

He heard someone approaching. Their feet made swishing noises through the tall reeds. Kenny turned to find Deputy Geddes, wearing his civilian clothes, standing a short distance away. His hands were balled into fists, and despite the crumpled hat he wore, sweat trickled down his ashen face in grimy rivulets.

Geddes looked around at the piles of dead.

"I was trying to count them," he mumbled. "It felt important, you know? Someone's gotta keep track of this. But once I hit five hundred, I just gave up."

Kenny couldn't think of a response.

"This isn't just forced displacement," Geddes carried on. "It's ethnic cleansing."

"They think we are a bastard class of humans," a new voice cut in, causing Kenny and the Deputy to turn around, seeking a welcome distraction.

Two Moon approached, his features seemingly set like concrete in a blank expression, and his eyes glazed with a thousand-yard stare.

"They aren't happy with driving us off our land. Instead, they want to eradicate my people and destroy our culture forever."

"And the disaster gave them the perfect opportunity," Kenny said. "The perfect excuse."

"Oh, they don't need much of an excuse. It goes back hundreds of years. Greed is the root cause. They covet our farms and reservations. Greed and envy."

Two Moon walked to the river's edge and saw the dead girl. Kenny searched for a flicker of emotion, some sign of compassion. But the Native American revealed nothing; it was like he had detached a part of his brain from the horrors around them.

"The Indian Removal Act was official government policy in the eighteen-hundreds and the President's top priority. It became a religious quest to him."

"But that was two hundred years ago. I thought it had been resolved in the courts?"

"Does it look like it has been resolved, Kenny? Look around you."

"This is fucking shit, man," Deputy Geddes said. "It's shit, shit, shit."

He cupped his hands to his mouth and hollered aloud.

"There must be some survivors," he told his colleagues and hollered again. There was no reply, the only audible sound being the rhythmic chirping of crickets over the water. The scorching sun beat down relentlessly on their shoulders.

Deputy Geddes removed his old Sheriff's hat and used it to fan his face. Then he shielded his eyes and pointed along the riverbank. The others noticed a pair of scavenger birds squabbling and fighting over something lying in the mud. It was just another body. But then they heard a low moan and saw it moving.

They wend their way through the greasy grass, jumped down to the river, and then waded through the shallows, letting the water wash off the blood and guts. The scavengers flapped away.

Lying amidst the reeds they found a tribal elder, a man in a sleeveless denim jacket. He had been shot in the stomach and the birds had commenced pecking at the gaping wound. The man's face was sickly and sallow, and his chin crusted red where blood had gushed from his mouth. The river lapped around him, making him move in the gentle swell, and Kenny wondered if they had been mistaken: the man appeared to have passed away. But then the eyes fluttered open and his fingers squeezed at the muddy bank, and he drew in a long, rattling breath.

Two Moon knelt beside the old man and carefully unbuttoned his shirt collar. Kenny watched his brown eyes search out each of their faces like he was hoping to anchor onto something remotely compassionate. He finally settled on looking up at the blue sky.

The man didn't have long to live. That was obvious to them all, and he suspected he knew it too. Speaking gently, Two Moon coaxed a few details out of him.

In a croaky voice, the wounded man said:

"Long time we travel. People feel bad when they leave Old Nation."

Kenny had to lean closer to catch the words.

"Women cry and make sad wails. Children cry and many men cry. The big bellies come, and the lady chief gives the order to kill. Firing and death all around, and grass trampled flat. People die very much."

The old man's voice started to taper away, and just before he slipped into unconsciousness, he uttered, "Left me for dead. Many days pass. Now, I am ready."

Later, they painted the old man's face red, the colour of life, wrapped his body in a shawl, and buried him by the river. The women immersed themselves in the water, turning east and west, and commenced a keening lament, and those on shore picked up the eerie wail.

Kenny and his friends watched from the side as the death rituals went on into the early evening. With dusk fast approaching, they all returned to their vehicles or horses.

After continuing along the Winchester Turnpike, they reached Bunker Hill and stopped for the night. Due to security concerns they chose to form a laager, a circular defensive formation with their vehicles, and posted lookouts. They parked the bus in the middle.

Alex continued to improve their security by installing machine guns on the pickup trucks and adding a metal grill to cover the bus windshield. Kenny watched him for a while and then boarded the bus, slipping behind the partition into the medical area.

Bethany was looking after the little girl so the child's mother could rest. When she saw Kenny, she walked up to him. There was an anxious expression on her face and she looked jaded, which worried Kenny. When Bethany went in for a long hug, he knew something was wrong.

"Her symptoms are getting worse," she told him. "The seizures are growing more violent and she's losing her vision in one eye where the tumour is pressing against the optic nerve."

Kenny looked over her shoulder. The girl was currently sedated. She looked tiny and vulnerable. She held a Teddy Bear in one hand.

"The steroids help reduce the swelling in her brain, but that's only a temporary treatment. To shrink the tumour, she needs targeted cancer drugs like inhibitors and antibodies."

"Is she in pain?"

"Some of the time. Morphine helps to keep it under control, for now."

"All we can do is make her comfortable," Kenny offered.

"But Kenny, we don't know what we're doing. Without informed knowledge, we might be doing everything wrong. We could be giving her the wrong drugs and the wrong care. Should we switch to other kinds of treatment? We just don't know."

"Hey there," Kenny said in a soothing voice and wrapped his arm around her shoulder. "Don't start on a guilt trip. Self-reproach won't help anyone, and you've got to stay strong for the girl's mother."

He could feel Bethany trembling against his chest. She took a deep breath to hold back her tears, determined not to break down. When she looked up she said softly, "We're running out of time. We need to get to Canada soon to give her a chance."

"We're going as fast as we can, but the terrain is rough. Add to that the earthquake damage and the human threat. Two Moon's folk know of all the backroads and secret paths, but it will be a gruelling ride."

"Then I'm scared, Kenny," she said, glancing at the sleeping child. "I'm scared of what's going to happen next."

That evening, as they lay under tarps, neither of them could sleep. Bethany was too preoccupied with worrying about the girl, and Kenny couldn't stop thinking about the people slaughtered beside the river. So around two in the morning, he snuggled up to her and they spent the next few hours talking in hushed tones. They were both relieved when morning came and the convoy started moving again.

The morning passed without incident as they followed a serpentine mountain road through the forested landscape. To the west of Baltimore, they crossed the Maryland state line into Pennsylvania, and the road began to steepen.

As they ventured further, they came across the aftermath of a recent forest fire. At first, they noticed only a few blackened trees, but soon there were hundreds and then thousands of them. The entire landscape was filled with charcoal trunks stripped of branches or reduced to stumps. The air was smoky, with a crisp, bonfire smell that irritated their throats. The ground was covered in so much ash that the roadway was barely visible. The higher they ascended, the more extensive the damage appeared. Before long, the trees lay in uniform rows on the ground, all pointing in the same direction, reminiscent of images of the aftermath of the Tunguska Event in Russia in 1908. It seemed that a similar incident had occurred here, with a massive blast causing a powerful shockwave that flattened entire forests. As they silently contemplated the devastation, they all remembered the distant thunder and the ground shaking at the grist mill.

Mystified and more than a little frightened, they pressed on. Turning back and finding another circuitous route around the wasteland was out of the question. They all knew time was of the essence.

The ash-covered mountain road wound around the hill's shoulder and they encountered a chain-link fence across their path. A sign read:

WARNING: RESTRICTED AREA. BY ORDER OF THE UNITED TELEPHONE COMPANY

There was a hole in the fence where someone had driven through from the other side in a hurry as if they were fleeing from something. Kenny, driving the Humvee at the front, passed between the fence posts and continued along the road. Half a mile ahead there was a second fence. Two nearby guard towers had toppled over. Another sign warned:

RAVEN ROCK MOUNTAIN COMPLEX - SITE R.
THIS INSTALLATION HAS BEEN DECLARED A RESTRICTED AREA.
UNAUTHORIZED ENTRY IS PROHIBITED.
ALL PERSONS AND VEHICLES ARE LIABLE TO SEARCH BY ORDER OF THE COMMANDER.

It seemed to be an army camp or command post, and Kenny briefly felt hopeful. Perhaps there were personnel and medical facilities here. However, his hopes vanished when he saw the destruction on the other side of the fence.

Whatever had happened here had left the ground scarred and altered in fantastic ways. Nothing was where it should be, and the land was oddly slanted and buckled. The only way Kenny could describe it was like some giant had picked up the mountain, broken it up, and tossed the pieces back down to earth. It defied all other explanations.

Kenny looked beyond the second fence and saw several burned-out helicopters on a helipad. Nearby was a cinder block structure that might once have been a security building or a fire station but was now mostly destroyed. The upper stories were gone, shorn off at head height. In the parking lot, the vehicles had melted into a modern sculpture due to the intense heat of the explosion.

Elemental forces had scorched or napalmed the soil. Kenny wondered if a nuclear explosion had done this, but they had seen no mushroom cloud in the distance and no blinding flash of light. Was it a volcano, then? He doubted it; this was different from the eruptions in Iceland.

He joined Geddes by the fence.

"I think I know what this place is," the Deputy said to Kenny.

"It looks like some kind of top-secret base," Kenny said, gesturing towards the sign.

"That's not the half of it. They call it the *Underground Pentagon.* It's a cutting-edge subterranean command centre that would kick into action if there was a third world war. This place has everything you could think of - its own power plants, water reserves, a hospital, living quarters, stores, gyms, you name it. It's like a whole city down there. They built it so thousands of government officials could survive underground for months and run things."

"If it's so secretive, how do you know all of this?"

"How do you think?"

"The internet," both men said in unison.

"Well, something went very wrong with their planning," Kenny smart-mouthed.

He thought of the bunker beneath Downing Street and how everything fell apart because of a military coup. This was way worse.

"Let's take a quick look around."

Kenny went over to the bus and called up to Alex.

"If we're not back in ten minutes, hit the road. Don't waste time looking for us."

"Ten-four."

Geddes came across a gap in the fence and managed to widen it enough to slip through. On the other side, they encountered several cracks that had burst the ground open, exposing deep holes. They cautiously navigated around these and then scrambled over the rubble-strewn approach road. On their left was a twenty-foot-high portal leading into the hillside. A set of blast doors had been blown clean off their hinges, ending up fifty meters down the hillside. The opening was scorched black.

From the entrance, a passage supported by steel roof spars telescoped into darkness. Together, they moved deeper into the tunnel. Kenny sensed they were going downhill because his feet slid forwards with each step. The floor felt strange, and when he glanced down, he saw in the diminishing light that the concrete resembled melted slag or sandflats covered with lugworm casts. Only incredibly hot jets of flame could make concrete run like that.

A lingering smell of hot metal backed up his suspicions. As they kept going, it grew stronger, and they heard weird clanging and rapping sounds of metal slowly cooling down. It was unbearably hot, and they were soon drenched in perspiration. The air was also thick and muggy, making it hard to breathe. Kenny started to worry that there might be noxious or combustible gases present; the idea of death by asphyxiation didn't fill him with joy.

They passed several doors, but they had partially dissolved and fused with the tunnel walls, appearing like melted plastic. One of them had a viewing window, but it was so distorted that it offered no clue as to what lay on the other side.

As they walked, Kenny couldn't shake the feeling that the walls were closing in on them, squeezing the air out of the subterranean complex. The weight of millions of tonnes of rock above gave him a sense of dread, as if at any moment it could come crashing down to trap and crush them.

Then, a pale and suffused light appeared further down the passage. It guided them, calling them forwards despite the dangers from infiltrating any deeper into the hillside. A moment later, they emerged on the edge of a vast, cathedral-like space.

"Oh, boy," Geddes said, the cavernous chamber lending his voice a Doppler effect.

Before them was the eviscerated hub of the once bustling underground city. A colossal hole stretching a hundred feet in diameter had carved out the heart of the bunker, reaching down at least a thousand feet. Each floor of the underground complex, from office spaces to the dorms, corridors, storage areas, canteens, sick bays and utility rooms had been cored out and left exposed, their walls and floors sliced clean through like sardine cans. Wisps of smoke curled upwards from the bottom of this vast pit while the remnants of steel girders glowed a fiery orange. Broken pipes gushed water cascading down the walls of the immense borehole. High above, a jagged hole in the mountainside allowed sunlight to stab into the subterranean refuge.

They stood in rapt silence like they had been put under by the incredible sight. Kenny felt fascinated and frightened simultaneously. He also felt incredibly small as he wondered what herculean forces had been unleashed to crack open the mountain. A persistent murmur of anxiety bubbled in the pit of his stomach.

"It must have been an explosion, right?" Geddes was saying. "Maybe the power plants blew up."

"I don't think so, mate. Look at those beams and struts. They're bent downwards."

He pointed out a mass of crossbeams overhead.

"Whatever did this came from above," Kenny added.

It took a couple of seconds for the implications to sink in. "This was intentional? Is that what you're saying?"

Kenny nodded.

"Like a missile, d'you mean? Jeez."

Then another thought occurred to the deputy.

"Where are all the people? There should be bodies or parts of bodies, at least."

It was a valid point. Kenny wasn't in a hurry to see more dead people, but it might give them a clue about what caused this. Had the detonation immolated them to ash? Or perhaps a firestorm had sucked them into the fiery pit below, similar to what happened to the residents of Dresden during the World War Two RAF air raids.

Kenny and his friend didn't have time to think any further because at that moment they heard the sudden, rapid sound of gunfire from outside.

They exchanged a brief, startled look.

"The convoy," they said in unison once more.

Then they turned and started running.

Chapter 20

THE NORTH ATLANTIC
SOMEWHERE OFF THE US EASTERN SEABOARD

MADISON WAS RESTING IN THE bottom of the life raft. The gentle pitch of the ocean swell and the soft sound of waves lapping against the raft's rubber sides managed to soothe her nerves. The meds she had taken for her shoulder injury slowly melted away the sharp edges of pain, and a welcomed calmness settled over her. For the first time in weeks, she felt totally at peace.

The swaying and rocking motion felt quite similar to the sensation of being weightless in space, she figured. There wasn't that big a difference between being stranded aboard the ISS and marooned at sea. Floating two hundred and sixty miles above the planet or at the mercy of the ocean currents off the American coast pretty much amounted to the same thing. In a way, it was almost liberating. She wasn't bailing out and giving up the fight, but when your options were as limited as Madison's, there was no point in agonizing over it.

All through that first day, the wind built steadily, blowing from the southeast and kicking up a steep, irregular chop.

Madison kept a close eye on the compass, hoping that the prevailing wind would keep pushing the raft closer to the coast. In the afternoon, a school of porpoises followed her for a while, remaining at a safe distance but appearing curious.

After resting, Madison attempted to determine the speed of the raft as well as keep track of its direction. Lacking proper instruments, the only way to gauge their speed was by dead reckoning. She marked the mooring line with a series of knots at regular intervals and attached one of the paddles to the end. Then, she threw the rope overboard. The paddle provided enough weight to pull the line behind the raft as the wind pushed the craft along. After letting the mooring line out for thirty seconds, Madison counted the number of knots that passed through her fingers. The life raft was traveling at nine knots, equalling nine nautical miles per hour, or just over ten miles per hour. That speed was relatively safe for a small craft like the life raft, but if the wind and currents picked up, she would be in for an adventurous – and wet – ride.

Night came on. Although the moon and starlight lent the wave crests a ghostly paleness, Madison strained to see what threats would emerge from the darkness next. At one point, a shooting star trailed across the heavens, and she briefly thought of Commander Khrenov, Liliya Trimenko, and the other cosmonauts, wondering what they were currently doing.

Madison drifted in and out of sleep, the wind vibrating against the PVC roof. During her moments of wakefulness, she considered what she would do if she made it ashore. Until now, she hadn't given it much thought; all her energies were simply put into reaching American soil. That in itself would feel like a victory. It was hard to explain this even to herself other than feeling an overwhelming need to reclaim at least some control of her own destiny.

She wondered what she would find: death and destruction, most likely. Flattened towns and cities, disease and lawlessness, refugee camps everywhere. Or maybe she was the last person on Earth, like in the movies. Out here at sea, with nothing but the fish for company, that felt like a real possibility.

Nope, there would definitely be a bunch of people still alive, for sure. But whether the living envied the dead was a whole other story.

But what if she did wash up on a beach or a rocky cove somewhere? If she arrived at a FEMA shelter or first-aid station, would anyone be interested in hearing her story? Wouldn't they have more urgent concerns than dealing with some crazy lady claiming to be an astronaut and carrying items she said were of historical value?

Aside from the practical challenges of safely reaching land, Madison had no idea what would come next. She again reminded herself to tackle one problem at a time, turning those words into a mantra in her head.

Madison drifted off into another fitful sleep with these thoughts meandering through her brain.

She woke up the next morning to something bumping against the bottom of the raft. She thought it might be the porpoises returning for another playful frolic. As she reached for the zipper, the life raft was suddenly wrenched sideways and then sent spinning, causing her to freeze.

Had she struck a sandbank or a shoal? Could she have reached the shallower coastal waters so soon? Or perhaps she'd hit a piece of flotsam. She tentatively pulled up the zipper and rolled back the canvas flap.

Low, troubled clouds nearly touched the lumpy sea. The wind was still out of the same quadrant. Madison tried to see past the swell, hoping to spot land; all she saw were rollers surging forwards, their white crests hissing, the waves looking like they meant to girdle the planet. There was no sign of the porpoises, nor seaweed to suggest they were approaching the shoreline.

Another bump under the raft sent it corkscrewing around, causing Madison to grasp hold of one of the grab handles on the buoyancy tube. She watched wide-eyed as the rubber bottom of the raft bulged upwards as something pushed up from beneath. The protuberance moved around for a few seconds before retracting. Just as Madison poked her head outside, she caught a glimpse of a shark's dorsal fin slipping through the sea.

The moment she saw it, a chill ran down her spine and her mouth dropped open. She watched the shark swim around the life raft. Madison didn't know much about sharks; she could barely tell the difference between a tiger shark, a basking shark, and a great white. But she knew they all had one thing in common - big jaws filled with sharp teeth. She also remembered that they were attracted by vibrations and could smell blood from miles away. Frustrated, Madison hit the rubber buoyancy tube, thinking about how she had splashed seawater on her head injury the day before, and now there was a son of a bitch shark circling her little boat.

What was she supposed to do? They attacked boats, right? She'd seen the movie. If the shark clamped its mouth on the rubber tube, the raft would deflate in seconds. Then she would be in the water doing the doggy paddle and imitating fish food. What did they say if you found yourself under a shark attack? Smack it on the nose to screw with its senses. Even better, whack it on the gills. Madison grabbed one of the paddles, fervently hoping the shark would get bored and swim away, but she was prepared nonetheless.

The shark swam around for a minute, maintaining a cautious distance. Then it abruptly altered its course and started heading directly towards the life raft. Madison's heart raced as she watched the dorsal fin cut through the waves. At the last second it slipped beneath the surface and glided right under the flimsy raft, causing it to lift up on a pressure wave. Bracing herself for a potential attack, Madison couldn't shake the horrifying image of the shark's razor-sharp teeth chewing through the rubber bottom; the last thing she would ever see would be those same teeth tearing and shredding her legs down to the bone.

Nothing happened. There was no violent attack against the life raft, just the irregular movement of the boat rising and falling in the chop. Madison raised herself onto the buoyancy tube and tried to see over the top of the roof, but her view was blocked by the triangular canopy. Slipping inside, she flumped across the rubber bottom on her hands and knees, ignoring the twinge in her shoulder, and reached the small viewing port. Pressing her face to the transparent plastic, she desperately tried to see where the shark was.

There it was. Forty yards behind the life raft and turning this way. The head briefly popped up like it was taking a peek. Then the tail thrashed back and forth, the head went back under, and the fish came right at her. It closed the gap in seconds and, with a mighty smack, it clocked the side of the life raft. Madison screamed and fell onto her back. The boat turned clockwise in one full circle, but instead of biting through the bottom, the shark was shoving the raft before it. She could hear the fish thrashing beneath her, the thin rubber bottom providing the flimsiest of barriers separating her from its teeth.

The raft surged through the water. Madison feared that one of the guy lines had become tangled up with the shark's fins. She worried that if the shark dived down, it would drag her and the raft with it. But this scenario – terrifying though it was – hardly had time to germinate in her mind when the small boat was flipped clear, jolting Madison into action. As she quickly got to her knees and looked over the side, her eyes locked with the chilling sight of the shark just mere feet away. She could see its long, sleek form just below the surface as it swam in a figure-eight pattern, its small black eyes fixed on her.

There was no doubt that it was a great white. You didn't need to be a marine biologist to understand that.

Again, it attacked. Madison had a close-up view right into its mouth as the jaw prepared to clamp onto the buoyancy tube. Instinctively she lashed out with the paddle, striking it directly on its snout. The creature reared away with a big splash and seemed to shrug its body as it dived out of sight.

Gritting her teeth against the throbbing pain from her tortured shoulder and panting for her breath, Madison stared at the foaming water where the shark had been seconds before. If it reared up again, she would aim for the eye with the stubby end of the paddle. Just don't drop the paddle, she told herself. If she lost it over the side, then she really would be up against it.

The raft shuddered again. It felt like something large and powerful was grinding against the rubber bottom. Madison felt the material stretch taut beneath her kneecaps. In her head, she pictured the shark probing for weak spots. Perhaps the predatory creature wasn't interested in the taste of PVC, instead preferring to snack on human flesh.

The scraping from below stopped and the raft steadied itself, now only moving with the ocean swell. Madison took this moment to think about turning the raft's supplies into a makeshift weapon. She debated whether to fire the signal flare at the shark, knowing that if she missed or if the flare had little effect, she would have wasted one of the rounds. Alternatively, she could use the knife from the emergency kit and stab the shark, but there was a risk that she might slip and puncture the buoyancy tube instead. She also didn't fancy getting up close and personal with it. If she had a pole that she could tie the knife to, like an improvised boat hook, that might work. But there was nothing suitable onboard.

She turned swiftly at the sound of a big splash. The shark surfaced once more, its powerful movement churning the water into a frothy white turmoil. Its head shook vigorously from side to side, and its body trembled. She estimated its length to be about nine or ten feet, its body an aqua blue. As it rolled onto its back, revealing its white belly, the shark made one final thrust with its tail before plunging into the cold depths.

Madison waited. After ten minutes with no more sightings, she let out a sigh of relief.

• • •

After some time, she noticed signs that she was getting closer to the shoreline. Pieces of debris were floating on the surface, gathered together like a log boom. The largest piece was a typical small-town church roof and spire. A pair of gulls sat on the top, looking at her as the life raft floated past. She also recognized a carport, white picket fences, a children's trampoline, telegraph poles, and a lot of other flotsam.

Even if the coast of America was still a hundred miles away, she felt confident she was heading in the right direction. As she paddled around the obstacles in the water, her main concern was attracting the shark's attention, but she also had to be careful not to get tangled in the debris. A little later, she passed a capsized catamaran, remnants of a timber jetty or boardwalk, a rusty minibus, and finally a whole house with its roof on fire.

The floating wreckage gradually dispersed until she was in open water again. On the western horizon was a long cloudbank, which she told herself must hide the coast.

In the later part of the afternoon, the school of porpoises made a return. They splashed around the life raft and snorkeled alongside the buoyancy tube, drenching her in water. Madison watched them quietly, reflecting on how little had changed for sea creatures. In fact things may have improved for them, with fewer manmade threats such as fishing nets, disruptive sonar and pollution.

The porpoises moved away from the raft, now swimming in circles and growing agitated. Then they stopped dead, and a quiet tension filled the air.

With sudden violence, the shark drove straight up out of the sea, its jaws smashing together, engulfing one of the porpoises. Madison had no time to cry out. In half a second, the unfortunate mammal was nearly ripped in two, the front and tail only held together by its innards. The shark had come half clear of the water and then it belly-flopped down with a huge splash, taking the porpoise with it. The rest of the pod scattered, zig-zagging through the waves. The sea turned red, and the shark went into a frenzy at the taste and scent of its kill.

Part of the dead porpoise was thrown clear, and it had hardly touched the water when, from out of nowhere, more sharks appeared. The water began to roil as they fought over the morsel. More of them whipped around the water, squirming and snapping at more tasty pieces. Fins crisscrossed the surface. The water exploded into a maelstrom of chaos. Madison watched from the life raft in terror, unable to look away from the gruesome spectacle.

Slowly, as the porpoise was devoured, the ruckus settled down. With their blood lust satiated, the sharks started to leave until only a handful remained, cruising back and forth through the pink-tainted sea. Eventually, only one was left, and although Madison couldn't be certain, she was sure it was the same one that had attacked the raft.

She waited, expecting at any moment that it would resume the skirmish. But perhaps the shark remembered being whacked on the snout and didn't want to repeat the unpleasant sensation.

At long last it turned away sharply and sliced through the water. Within seconds, Madison had lost sight of it. She only realized she had been gripping the life raft so tightly that her knuckles had turned white when her hands started hurting. She let go and ran them over her face.

They came away smeared red. Her face was splattered with hundreds of blood droplets.

Chapter 21

NEWBIGGEN VILLAGE
GREAT SHUNNER FELL MOOR
NORTHERN ENGLAND

SCOTT WATCHED THE HARE AS it ambled across the high moorland tundra. The animal had acquired a brownish summer coat because, even at this time of the year, the weather often became unpleasant at these elevated altitudes. One moment, the landscape of dwarf birches, grasses and lichen-encrusted rocks could be bathed in blue skies and warm sunshine; the next, a bank of clouds carrying driving rain could blow in, catching the unwary off guard.

Scott lay on his stomach with just his face showing over the top of a small knoll. Beside him was the young boy. Scott had brought him along to keep him out of trouble because, despite Scott's best efforts, he had a habit of disregarding the rules and giving everyone a headache.

In Scott's coat pocket was a bunch of round pebbles that he had scooped out of the river. As they continued to watch the hare minding its own business, unconcerned or oblivious to the presence of two humans, Scott reached down and chose one. He gripped it in his hand, feeling its weight and estimating the distance. Then he slowly rose into a half-crouch, pulled his arm back like a baseball pitcher, held his breath, and hurled the pebble as hard as he could.

The pebble struck the hare just behind the head, stunning it and sending it staggering sideways.

"Come on," yelled Scott, shattering the peaceful silence.

He and the boy jumped to their feet and ran across the moor. They reached the stricken animal together, but the boy hesitated when he saw the hare writhing on the ground and shaking its head. His expression of joy turned to agitation bordering on distress.

Scott noticed the change in the boy's demeanour. He squeezed his narrow shoulder.

"I know it's not nice, but we've got to eat. Catching fish is too risky because of the bad water."

Scott fell to his knees and reached for the hare, which started to squirm and kick with its hind legs.

"Look away if you like, son."

"I'm okay," said the boy, his face strained but determined to be a man.

Scott quickly wrung the animal's neck, then stood up with the hare in his hand.

"This stuff is packed with protein, and as long as we cook it properly, it should be totally safe to eat. The ones to avoid are those that are already dead because the poison is already inside them. It kills them instantly, we think. A living creature means a healthy creature."

He stuffed the dead animal into his backpack, saying with a grin, "That was a damn good shot if I do say so myself." He winked at the kid. "Pardon my language."

"That's not swearing," the boy said. "Bloody and shit are swearing."

"Where did you learn words like that?"

"They teach us English in junior school. Everyone at home speaks it."

"I'm sure they do," Scott said, noticing that the Dutch boy barely had an accent. "But not those words. Did Fabian teach you to swear?"

The boy shrugged, twin red spots colouring his cheeks.

"He might have done," he replied, attempting, but not entirely succeeding, to suppress the mischievous grin on his face.

"That figures."

They walked across the moorland side by side. As bleak and hostile as the landscape seemed it was also startlingly beautiful, with multicoloured bushes and mosses stretching to the horizon. It also offered a ready supply of meat in the form of cattle, hares and other game. The summer air buzzed with the sound of insects.

As they traversed the low hills in long, tireless strides, the two hunters searched for signs of more game, such as animal footprints, spoor or torn bark on the dwarf birch. Scott had discovered a red grouse nest filled with eggs the previous day. Closer to the village, there were blackcurrant, redcurrant and blackberry plants, and they planned to thoroughly pick them on their way back.

Gradually, their path started to descend from the more exposed part of the moorland. They went around a marshy area and followed a trackway between two hills as it debouched into a wide valley with isolated stands of conifer trees. In the distance, they could see the rooftops. They would arrive at their temporary home in about half an hour.

As they walked by the trees Scott heard the boy sniffle. When he glanced over, he noticed tears running down the boy's face.

"What's up, son?"

"Nothing."

"Come on, spill the beans. Better to get whatever's bothering you off your chest now before the others notice."

He put his arm around the boy.

"Is it the dead hare?"

The boy shook his head.

"What then?"

"Just stuff, you know? It doesn't matter."

As a teacher, Scott had gained firsthand insight into children's thinking. When a tearful twelve-year-old boy claimed everything was all right, it clearly wasn't. Scott brought them to a stop and found a nearby boulder to sit on. He patted the stone and the boy hesitantly lowered himself beside him.

"You know, a problem shared is a problem halved."

The boy frowned like he didn't understand.

"I mean, talking about things might make you feel better. And anything that you tell me will stay just between me and you. Scouts honour."

The boy squirmed around and Scott thought he was about to stand up and walk away. But then he unexpectedly began to shake as tears flowed more freely, and he cried, "I miss my mum and dad."

That one short sentence cut deep into Scott's heart as profoundly as all the harrowing things they had seen and done since DAY 1. It overwhelmed him with a sense of guilt, of how he'd been so busy with simply trying to stay alive that he hadn't spared a thought for the children. Like everyone else, they had been to hell and back, but they'd also carried the heavy burden of knowing that their parents were, in all likelihood, dead. They were orphans, all of them.

Here was this young boy, yearning for the comfort and security that only his family could provide. It went a long way to explaining the boy's behaviour, the restlessness and tendency to wander off alone, like he was searching for something lost forever. While Scott couldn't provide what he wanted, he could offer a warm embrace and a handkerchief to wipe away his tears.

He allowed the boy to cry, patiently waiting as he exorcised a portion of his sorrow. Then with a few more sniffles and hiccups of his breath, the boy started to tell Scott of the day the floods came.

It had been a beautiful day in late spring.

A group of teenagers and their adult supervisors had spent a week at summer camp near the town of Edam, famous the world over for its cheese. The teenagers were part of an outward-bound group for troubled kids foisted out by middle-class parents too busy to handle them. The camp offered activities such as sailing, kayaking, raft building and exploring the nearby nature reserves.

"At first, everyone wanted to do the exciting stuff," the boy told Scott as they sat on the boulder. "Nobody wanted to do birdwatching, pond dipping or go on nature walks."

That all changed when they met Fabian, the cool kid shooting nature blogs with drones, and Tammy Guide, their troop leader, who used to live on the streets but had turned her life around. Suddenly, everyone wanted to hang out with them because Fabian and Tammy had similar tough starts in life and could relate to the children better than the other supervisors.

"They were awesome. They had life figured out, and they didn't treat us like we were a waste of space. Fabian was already part of the group before Tammy, so he was kind of in charge of us. But then Tammy showed up and she was a natural leader. They were amazing together. Fabian taught us how to use the drones and edit his videos. He had tonnes of followers online, so he really knew what he was doing. And Tammy was super laid-back; nothing seemed to bother her or make her angry – as long as we followed her rules."

The bunch of kids spent most days either in the nature reserve or at the top of one of the birdwatching towers, from where they flew the drones and captured great footage. One morning, they had spotted some nesting waterfowl through their binoculars and Fabian wanted to get some overhead shots. He suggested they take a short walk over the sand flats by the sea, and at the last minute, Tammy decided to join them. So the little party pulled on their wellies and raincoats and set out from the campsite, following the line of the sea dyke for about a mile before venturing over the wetlands.

"It was a warm, sunny day, the sort of day when city kids finally learn to love the countryside," said the boy. "Fabian flew the drones over the nests, and he even let me take a turn. But we couldn't get a strong signal to download the footage, so we decided to return to the camp and try from there. By then, most of us were muddy and wet from the mudflats, and we were tired. So back we hiked."

They had just reached the camp, he told Scott, when they noticed a commotion. Several groups of people were gathered together, talking animatedly. Initially they assumed someone had fallen ill because a few of the adults were rushing around and looking flustered. Then they heard a radio playing, and Tammy led the group over to investigate.

"We were just in time to hear something on the news about an earthquake in London, which we all thought was strange, you know. Not LA or Turkey, places where they have quakes, but London. Then the guy on the radio started sounding all weepy and blurted something about a really bad flood coming our way. We get floods all of the time in the Netherlands, but the way he said it made us all a bit frightened. Then he changed it from floods to a big wave. He said one of those whatsits?"

"A tsunami?" suggested Scott.

"Yes, a tsunami was heading our way. It was going to be huge and cause a lot of damage. That's when a few of the campers ran off and jumped in their cars and drove away real quick, like. They didn't even bother taking their caravans or tents; they just took off. After that, people's phones started ringing. All the boys and girls in our group had calls from their parents and they started bawling their eyes out, and for the first time ever, Tammy looked really scared. My phone didn't ring, and I checked to make sure it was on, which it was, but my mum or dad didn't call or send a text or anything."

Scott wrapped his arm around the boy and squeezed hard. He went on with his tale.

"After that, a group of campers decided to climb onto the sea dyke, thinking that it would be safe and that the sea defences would hold the wave back. They even started filming the scene with their phones."

Scott could easily envision the scene: spectators lining the sea defences, clamouring for a ringside seat and determined to capture the historic event. A few might even have taken out selfie sticks and live-streamed it on social media.

Nothing happened for a long time, the boy recounted. Just when it appeared to be a false alarm, the people on the dyke started shouting and pointing. Some of his friends were eager to see, so they hurried up the steep bank. Tammy very wisely told the rest of her group to climb the tower.

"We were all up on this platform, kind of like a lookout post, and we were staring out at the sea. That's when we spotted it."

Scott, whose wife had recounted her own eyewitness experience of the mega-tsunami hitting Amsterdam, was captivated by the boy's story.

"What did it look like?"

"At first, it looked like a strip of white cloud or mist on the horizon. We watched it come closer, and all the birds started flying away, and we could hear farm dogs barking in the distance. Those on the dyke still thought it wouldn't reach as high as the banking. One lady even brought a deckchair to sit on. But then when the tsunami was about a mile away, all the water in the wetlands suddenly drained away, like the tide was going out. I think that's about when they suddenly realized how much danger they were in, and they started running for their lives. Some ran down the banking, while others ran along the top of the dyke. But it was too late."

The people fled through the camp, screaming and trying to escape in their cars. The mega-tsunami towered over them, higher than a two-storey building. From their perch atop the tower, Tammy's group watched helplessly as the seismic sea wave crested over the dyke without slowing and crashed down. Cows in the field next door were swept up by the inrushing water, their lowing barely audible beneath the deafening roar of the waves.

Some campers attempted to climb the tower, but at that point, the water surrounded them, and they had no chance. Only two stragglers managed to climb to safety, both friends of the boy. They held onto the ladder as the water engulfed them.

The entire area was devastated. Tents, caravans and camper vans were completely wiped out, disappearing as if they had never existed. Those on the tower could only watch on in horror as people below desperately struggled to stay afloat, but the force of the wave was overwhelming. Some drowned, while others were crushed by floating debris, their flesh and bones pulverized to nothing. Many of the others suffocated in the thick mud. Even those who had ventured out on kayaks or sailing vessels faced the same fate as they were mercilessly swept along by the relentless deluge.

The tsunami carried away farm buildings, fishing boats, and bridge trusses from the Ije River, carting them miles inland. A second wave followed the first. Travelling faster than a person could sprint, the torrent poured down the N247 motorway leading to Edam, engulfing and sweeping away dozens of vehicles in its path.

Clinging to one another, shivering from the biting cold and overwhelming fear, the young boy and his companions bore witness to the once-charming town being pummelled. Water poured into the narrow streets, washing away broad sections of the town. The entire waterfront, from the yacht harbour in the north to the idyllic cottages at Landal in the south, cracked free and slid into the sea. The boatyards, a cement plant, bustling docks and warehouses disappeared beneath the waters.

In addition to the raging waters, a new danger emerged—fire. Near the fishing wharves, a group of large petroleum tanks had burst open, their contents catching fire. Burning gasoline spewed out in all directions, sending sheets of flame across the harbour.

"It was like this huge burst of flame and smoke, and it was glowing bright cherry red," the boy told Scott.

The burning oil slick moved away from the tower like a big tide of fire, spreading the inferno even further. As the survivors looked around, all they could see was a chaotic sea of floating wreckage and columns of black, greasy smoke rising skyward.

The waves rolled south towards the suburbs around Amsterdam. Everything was obliterated. The R-Net train line was destroyed in seconds. Peering through their binoculars, the onlookers watched the astonishing sight of 125-tonne diesel locomotives being overturned like mere children's toys, the rails being broken apart, and the rolling stock being knocked into a tangled mess.

All through that first day they clung to their refuge, hearing the cries of the wounded grow fainter. As night fell, the horizon glowed orange from the enormous fires burning in Amsterdam's docklands. Over Schiphol Airport, they watched passenger jets flying in circles, unable to land; one by one, their lights fell to earth.

At the first light of dawn, they discovered two children had grown so weak they had passed away, while a third died from hyperthermia before midday. Stranded on the tower, the bunch of terrified children repeatedly tried calling their families, but the network was down. They anxiously waited to be rescued, praying for the sound of helicopters. But as the hours passed, their hope began to dim. The scale of the disaster was unprecedented.

Realizing that their survival depended solely on their own actions, Tammy and Fabian started to make plans.

Sitting on the boulder, the young boy fell silent. It struck Scott that the youngster was a tough little scamp, probably more resilient than he realized himself. All the children had to be to have made it this far. But at the end of the day, he was just a child all alone in the world.

Scott knew the rest; Tammy and Fabian had given him the basics of how they had built their little community and searched far and wide for fellow survivors. That's when Scott and his friends entered the story.

"I'll find them someday, my mum and dad, just like you found your wife and baby girl."

"You hold onto that thought, lad," Scott said, ruffling the boy's hair.

He stood up and patted his backpack.

"How about we go and make some supper? I'll teach you how to clean and cook this thing?"

The boy nodded and they started down the slope towards the distant rooftops. After a few strides, the boy slipped his hand into Scott's.

Chapter 22

**THE SIMPLON PASS
SWITZERLAND**

THE HIKE TO THE HIGHEST part of the mountain pass was long and rigorous, but fortunately, most of it was on paved roads. After reaching the ruins of the alpine village of Gondo, Timo and Genny successfully crossed the Rhône River and began ascending the formidable mountain ridges that run along the Swiss and Italian border.

The climb exacted a punishing toll on Timo's calf muscles as the winding roads seemed endless, zig-zagging higher and higher. But at least the weather was favorable, with mild temperatures and clear skies. Genny enjoyed being off her dog lead, trotting ahead or exploring the grassy verges and munching on the flowers.

Timo was hopeful that the worst was behind them. Even though they still had some distance to cover, the way ahead was mainly characterized by gentle foothills and alpine meadows cut with shimmering mountain streams, at least according to Timo's maps. But he was still worried about how the earthquakes might have altered the terrain. Moreover, he knew that the weather could unpredictably shift at any moment.

To ensure they stayed warm during the cold nights, they now had a blanket made from goat fur. Timo also wore leather gaiters to protect his legs, and he had fashioned a warm dog coat for Genny. His backpack contained portions of goat meat that had been carefully cooked, smothered in rock salt, and wrapped in greaseproof paper to keep it fresh.

He felt more optimistic than he had in weeks. They had an ample supply of food, lots of accessible fresh drinking water, and a clear destination in mind. On top of that, the tremors had subsided at long last.

After they finally reached the top of the pass, Timo was worn out. He sat down to have lunch while taking in the mountain air. They were way up at 6,500 feet above sea level, and the view of the green hills overlooked by forested slopes and peaks was jaw-dropping.

Later, as they started to descend, Timo's attention was caught by a movement across one of the meadows. At first he thought his eyes were playing tricks on him and he had to shield them from the sun's glare.

In the distance, several figures were moving aimlessly about. They were the first people he had seen since reaching Zermatt, and he had grown so used to the isolation that the sight took him aback. Instinctively, he wanted to shout and wave, if only to hail some fellow survivors. But then he remembered the husband and wife with the small child and how they had tried to kill him. So, rather than call out, Timo watched from a safe distance.

There were four or five people, a mix of men and women, all dressed in white. He couldn't see their faces clearly from this vantage point, but their directionless meanderings struck him as peculiar. They appeared to be walking in erratic patterns, moving in one direction before turning around and walking back or just going in circles.

They didn't spot Timo, so he quietly called his puppy over and continued down the road.

A few minutes later, he spotted two more individuals, this time under some trees. They wore the same white clothes and seemed engrossed in something in the tree branches. Timo was certain that he could hear them singing.

As he peered through the dense foliage, Timo's eyes fell upon a large building nestled within its own grounds. It slowly dawned on him what he was seeing. It was one of two things: either a secluded private clinic or a wellness centre. The figures dressed in white were unmistakably guests who had ventured outside. Timo wondered why there weren't any staff around. He didn't want to walk over and find out what was going on because then he'd feel like he had to help, and he didn't want that extra responsibility.

He watched them for several minutes, and after they passed from sight, Timo carried on. The road bypassed the woods and then dropped down a steep hillside, slaloming first one way and then the next. To the west, he saw a small lake nestled between two peaks. Consulting his map, they should reach a tunnel up ahead where the road burrowed through the mountains for about a mile. If the tunnel were still usable, it would lead to the small town of Brig, near the impressive Jungfrau mountain. Timo hoped to find a place to shelter in the town. Alternatively, an emergency mountain hut would suffice.

They trudged on. The tunnel came into view around the next bend, and Timo breathed a sigh of relief. They drew near to the rectangular tunnel mouth and peered inside. It curved away through the mountainside. Sunlight streamed through a series of openings along the right-hand wall, illuminating the interior. It appeared to be in remarkably good condition.

Timo entered, walking with crisp strides, his footsteps resounding off the concrete walls. Genny stayed close to his heel. It reminded him of their journey along the lava tunnel and was just as nerve-wracking. Timo's pace quickened, not wanting to stay inside the enclosed space for one second longer than necessary, and when the tunnel exit appeared to their front, he jogged the final two hundred metres.

Glad to be out in the open again, Timo stood by the roadside and looked down at the charming town of Brig.

Renowned for its cozy inns, its thermal baths, and the baroque palace that acted as the centrepiece of the picturesque alpine spa town, it was a popular tourist destination. A devastating fire had swept through it from one end to the other. It was still smoking. All that was left was a jumble of roof tiles and charred roof beams.

Immune to such sights, Timo felt nothing. Later, he would write about it in his journal, adding it to his other observations. In the future, if he was still alive, he might look back and recall with sadness the fate that had befallen this and other places he had come upon. But for now, he needed to stay focused and couldn't afford the luxury of grief.

They had only gone a few more steps when, with no warning, Timo's lower gut was wracked with excruciating pain. It had been days since the last bout of illness and with the journey through the mountains on his mind he had almost forgotten about it. But now it returned with a vengeance.

Timo hissed through his clenched teeth and bent over as the wave of agony gripped him. Genny, who was a few feet in front, turned to look. Timo's vision went blurry, all the strength went out of his legs, and he fell forwards headfirst onto the hard surface of the road, knocking himself out.

• • •

The ringing of a bell woke him up. Timo's head felt like it was stuffed with cotton wool, and it took a while for the distant peals to filter through his dulled senses. He slowly opened his eyes. For several seconds, the residual image of his mother's face lingered like an imprint on his retinas. He must have been dreaming of her. When he blinked, the illusion disappeared, and Timo became fully alert.

He lay on a hard mattress atop a wooden bed frame inside a small, stark room with bare stone walls. Other than the bed, the only items of furniture were a stool and a side table. On the floor was a chamber pot. A tall window let in weak daylight, as well as the sound of ringing.

Timo rolled onto his side, his bare feet meeting the cold floor, causing him to gasp. As he sat up, a dizzy spell passed through him and his head felt sore. Someone had wrapped a bandage around it.

Presumably, the same person had removed his clothes because now he was wearing a pale blue hospital gown. But he still had his underwear on underneath, which provided him with a modicum of dignity. Despite the simple clothes and surroundings, the small room felt cozy.

Timo didn't know how he had ended up in this place. The last thing he remembered was falling over and hitting his head on the road. After that, everything was a blank. For that matter, he didn't have a clue where he was or what had happened to his dog.

Timo stood up, but a sudden sharp pain in his stomach made him wince. He leaned against the wall for support and lifted his gown. Timo noticed a clean dressing on his lower abdomen, just above his groin. As he peeled back the edge, he saw several stitches underneath. It dawned on him that someone had performed a minor surgery on him while he was asleep. Panic briefly washed over him at the thought.

Once the twinge of pain subsided, Timo went to the window, mindful not to lose his balance on his weak legs. Instead of glass, the window contained a set of iron grilles. He held onto the grilles and peered outside. All he could see was a tall, crenellated wall, and further beyond, a muddy field where longhorn cattle were roaming. Standing on his tiptoes, he could just barely glimpse a section of a courtyard two or three levels below.

He wondered if he was inside a castle. There were certainly a number scattered throughout this region of Europe. It dawned on him that he might be in the clinic he had seen earlier, and the recollection of seeing the patients aimlessly wandering about didn't inspire much confidence.

Wherever he was, finding himself indoors after spending several nights seeking shelter in caves and under trees felt incredibly strange. Despite the room being basic, the simple act of sleeping in a real bed felt like an unexpected luxury.

The bell stopped ringing, its chimes fading into silence, and Timo moved across to the door, eager to get some answers. He turned the latch and pushed. The door didn't budge. He tried again but to no avail. The door was locked, and the discovery left him so disconcerted that he momentarily stepped back in bewilderment. That confusion quickly turned into irritation and he pounded on the wood with his fist while clutching his waist with the other hand.

"Hey, open up!" he shouted, his voice sounding hoarse.

Swallowing, he called out again.

"I said, open this door!"

He heard footsteps approaching. A key turned in the lock, and Timo stepped back as the door scraped open. He was about to continue with his tirade, but the person standing before him was so unexpected that he was temporarily lost for words.

A young man with rosebud lips peered out from under a hooded brown robe, his bespectacled eyes twinkling with merriment. He tilted his head and smiled warmly.

Timo quickly regained his composure and fired off a series of questions: "Who are you? Where am I? And what the Devil is going on?"

"Please, do not overexert yourself," the man responded, speaking in heavily accented English. "It's important for your recovery that you rest."

Timo felt another twinge in his stomach, confirming the hooded figure's words. He had to make a conscious effort to calm himself. Peering over the man's shoulder, he could see a stone passageway leading to a flight of steps.

"My name is Brother Edwig," the robed figure introduced himself, pulling Timo's focus back to him. "Welcome to the Monastery of the Holy Trinity."

"A monastery?" Timo blurted before he could think of anything better to say. "I'm in a monastery?"

"Indeed, and not just any old monastery, my friend. For hundreds of years, pilgrims travelling along St. Peter's Pilgrimage of Grace from the Basilica di San Pietro to Krakow have visited to see our collection of holy relics. We have the finger bones of the Apostle Saint Peter, the head of Saint Oliver, and most importantly, the holy prepuce preserved in an alabaster box of muskroot. Would you like to see them?"

"Not right now, but thank you anyway. Can you tell me precisely where we are?"

"I've just explained."

"I mean our location in relation to the nearest town or village?"

"Ah, I see," the robed man said as he placed his palms together. "Well, as you may be aware, most of the hamlets no longer exist. But in regards to where we found you –"

"Where you found me?" asked Timo.

"Yes, one of our brothers found you unconscious in the roadway, and he brought you here. He couldn't leave you like that. To answer your question: our monastery is only five miles from that spot."

"What about my dog? I had a small puppy with me. Please don't tell me he ran away."

"He is safe and sound and currently in the refectory."

Feeling a little happier upon hearing that Genny was okay, Timo lifted the hem of his hospital gown again and pointed at the dressing, asking, "What about this?"

"Oh yes," the man calling himself Brother Edwig said. "As soon as you arrived, it was clear that you were very ill. Luckily, some of my fellow brothers here know a little about medicine. We had to perform a quick but important procedure while you were out cold."

"What kind of procedure, exactly?" Timo asked while poking at the dressing. "What was wrong with me?"

"You were suffering from renal calculi, also known as kidney stones. They are very painful indeed."

"You're telling me," Timo said under his breath.

"Normally, kidney stones pass naturally, but sometimes they become lodged in the ureter. When that happens, there is a risk of infection and even sepsis. It was crucial that we surgically remove them."

Timo scratched at his temple and said, "I suppose I should thank you?"

"There's no need. We're just happy we found you when we did and thankful for your progress."

Timo was pleased to know the debilitating pain shouldn't return, but he still felt frail.

"How long have I been here?"

"Just overnight. Did you sleep well? I know it's not the Ritz."

Timo just smiled and nodded. Then he asked, "Why was my door locked?"

"For your own well-being. We didn't want you waking up and getting yourself lost. Until you know your way around, the labyrinthine passageways inside the monastery can be confusing, particularly at night. Since the earthquakes, we have been forced to use lanterns and candles. And we don't want you taking a fall over the walls, do we?"

Timo forced a grin. "I guess not."

Brother Edwig lightly clapped his hands together. "Now, you must be hungry. The bell you heard was our summons to dinner. So, chop chop, my friend. Let us eat, and on the way I will give you a quick guided tour."

Timo stood in the doorway and gestured towards his outfit.

"Oh, silly me," giggled Brother Edwig. "I will fetch your clothes. Please wait inside your cell for a moment."

Timo watched him scuttle away, uneasy about Edwig's choice of words to describe his room. A minute later, he returned with Timo's neatly folded and laundered clothes.

Brother Edwig waited in the passageway while Timo got dressed. He informed Timo through the door that his other belongings were in a cupboard just around the corner. Once Timo was ready, he was led along the passage and down the well-worn stone steps.

"So, are you a monk or a friar?" Timo asked, hoping he didn't sound too much like an ignoramus.

"Neither," Edwig said over his shoulder, "I am a candidate novice, hoping to become a Lay Brother soon."

"So, you are fairly new around here, right?"

Brother Edwig paused on a landing to chase away a tiny rat that quickly scurried past them. It darted down another passageway lined with doors.

"I chose to become a monk two summers ago after working as an accountant. I became quite ill for a while and during that time, I began to question my life. After recovering, I made a decision to give up all of my belongings and lead a life of meditation and prayer."

"What's down there?" asked Timo, looking into the passage.

"This section of the building includes domestic quarters, kitchens and workshops. Our Abbot has rooms on the top floor. The area that used to be the Great Hall before the monastery was established in the fifteenth century now serves as our refectory."

They proceeded to the next landing, where Brother Edwig directed Timo to a window. He pulled open some wooden shutters, allowing the cool mountain air to enter. In the distance, a steep hillside covered in dense forest led up to a snow-capped peak. He then pointed to the courtyard below.

"We have a brewery, a forge, and the red-tiled roof over there is the cloisters that contain a small infirmary, and across the field is our oratory, where my fellow brothers spend their mornings in quiet contemplation. Beyond the walls, we own a fertile grange for growing food, a herb garden, and pastureland for our animals. They provide us with all of our needs."

"How many monks live here?"

"There are twelve, plus Prior Cecil and Abbot Benlow, who used to be the dean at Cambridge University."

They carried on down to the bottom and turned into a wide hallway. Walking through an archway, they passed around the cloisters, which contained a pristine lawn and a savin juniper bush in the centre.

Back under cover, they had to stop as another rat scurried over the stone floor.

"It looks like you have a problem," Timo remarked, watching the rodent disappear into the shadows.

"They are a constant irritant."

The aroma of freshly cooked food reached them.

"Something smells nice," Timo commented, his tummy rumbling at the prospect of a meal.

"The Rule of St. Benedict allows for two meals," explained Brother Edwig. "There is dinner all year round and supper from spring until late summer except on Wednesdays and Fridays. The meals consist of simple fare. There are a few rules: no talking during dinner, communication is by hand signals, and nobody can leave the table before Abbot Benlow. After the meal, you are not permitted to associate with the other brothers, only with me and the Abbot. Do you understand?"

"Yes, but I don't plan to stay for long."

"Of course not. Once you feel stronger, you will want to be on your way."

Brother Edwig gave Timo a beatific smile, revealing several gaps where some of his teeth had fallen out.

"Here we are."

They entered a large hall with a high vaulted ceiling. Two rows of brown-robed monks sat at a long bench, hungrily shovelling food into their mouths. Positioned at the head of the dining table was an imposing and corpulent man with thin, wispy hair and bushy eyebrows. He was dressed the same as the monks, except his robes were white. At the opposite end of the dining table, an elderly monk with arthritic hands read aloud from the Scriptures. Nobody looked up or acknowledged the newcomer in their midst.

After washing their hands in a lavabo basin, Timo and Brother Edwig took their seats. A bowl of custard pudding sprinkled with rose petals appeared before Timo. Sitting beside him, Brother Edwig made a peculiar gesture with his hand, and one of the monks passed a jug across to him. Timo was expecting it to contain mulled wine or mead and was disappointed to discover it held water. Nonetheless, he took a long sip because his throat was parched.

Timo was just about to dig into the delicious-looking custard pudding when he noticed his puppy was nowhere to be seen. He turned to ask Brother Edwig about it, but the monk gestured for him to be quiet by placing a finger over his lips. Instead, Timo raised his hands to mimic animal claws and panted, eliciting a bemused look from Brother Edwig. The young monk then directed Timo's attention towards the sunlight streaming through an open doorway, to which Timo nodded in understanding.

At the head of the table, the white-robed chap – he must be Abbot Benlow, Timo decided - coughed quietly and scowled but didn't look up. Giving Brother Edwig a wink, Timo picked up his spoon and tucked in.

• • •

After they had finished eating, Abbot Benlow came to his feet and left the refectory with little fanfare. Timo noticed the tension among the other brothers ease, and the diners dispersed.

Brother Edwig took him outside to where Genny was waiting. As soon as she saw her master, she started jumping up and down.

"There, there, girl. I'm feeling much better now."

They were in a small yard just a few steps from the entrance gates. Timo's eyes landed on a beaten-up moped propped against one of the gateposts. Brother Edwig saw him looking and remarked, "We keep it for emergencies and quick trips to the village. We strive for self-sufficiency, which is difficult in the twenty-first century." He added, "It was fortunate for you that one of our brothers happened to be on an urgent errand when he stumbled upon you and brought you back to safety."

Another monk appeared and went to a shed in the corner. He unlocked the door, releasing a pungent smell of yeast. Inside were sackfuls of hops.

"I'm sorry, but I have to go now. I have chores to attend to," Brother Edwig said.

"Do you need a hand?" Timo offered.

"No. You are our guest. Please make yourself at home."

Edwig placed a hand on Timo's shoulder.

"And remember what I said: it's important that you get lots of rest."

Brother Edwig joined the other monk in the shed and Timo and Genny found themselves alone.

Chapter 23

RAVEN ROCK MOUNTAIN COMPLEX
PENNSYLVANIA

KENNY AND DEPUTY GEDDES RUSHED out of the subterranean command centre and were greeted by a chaotic scene. The convoy had gathered near the helipad and most of the people had come down from their vehicles. Shouting and gunfire filled the air, while a group of men were jostling and pushing each other. Kenny was worried they were under attack and paused to get his bearings.

It became apparent that hostile forces were not ambushing them. Most of the shooting was directed into the sky, and the crowd was not screaming in panic or fear but rather in joyous celebration. Kenny observed clenched fists waving and even a few high-fives. Most of the crowd had gathered around one of the pickups, but Kenny couldn't see what was happening.

Just then, Geddes tapped him on the shoulder and pointed. A horse rider was coming through the broken fence, pulling along two people with ropes. They stumbled and fell and by the time they regained their feet they were covered in dust and scratches.

"It's Young Little Wolf," said Geddes and Kenny saw the gleeful look on Two Moon's youngest son's face, riding his horse through the crowd. "It looks like he has some prisoners."

The pair of men jogged over and elbowed their way through the throng.

They reached the centre and Kenny's heart sank at the sight which greeted him. In the bed of the pickup truck was the lifeless body of a man wearing the uniform of the Lansing militia. His face was badly swollen and blood had trickled from his ears. Kenny thought it was one of the guards from outside the town hall – Cody was his name.

The noise from the crowd grew even more euphoric when Young Little Wolf reached them. The tied-up prisoners were marched forwards through a gauntlet of screaming, spitting faces. It was a second militiaman and a woman.

"Oh, shit, you're kidding me," Kenny said when he recognized the lady.

The town mayor was a shadow of her former self. She still wore the lopsided judge's wig but had lost all of her arrogance and fake regal haughtiness. Now she looked petrified and broken. She was also stone-cold sober. The second prisoner had taken a licking; his nose was broken and one of his cheekbones had swollen up. In stark contrast to the mayor, his features were contorted with defiance.

Young Little Wolf, recently recovered from his rough handling at the hands of the militia, rose in his saddle, waved his rifle over his head, and let out a triumphant shout that echoed through the mountains and hills.

Bethany and Alex appeared alongside Kenny and she tightly held his arm.

"What's happening?" she asked over the loud commotion.

Kenny looked at her and said, "Payback."

Then he pushed to the front and came up alongside Young Little Wolf.

"Where's your father?"

The young man peered down at Kenny with a contemptuous expression as if it wasn't worth the effort to respond. But then his adolescent bravado got the better of him, and he gestured down the slope with his rifle.

"In the woods, hunting for more prisoners. They," and he pointed the barrel at the man and woman, "were watching us and waiting for their chance to attack. We found them hiding near a creek. The other soldiers ran off, but we caught these three."

"And what about him?" Kenny motioned to the corpse in the truck.

"He resisted," was all Young Little Wolf said.

Kenny didn't like the way this was going. All around him the horde of people pressed in and he had to push them back with his arms.

"Kill them!" someone shouted, and the call was picked up.

"Let's end this!" demanded another

"Remember what the bitch did to you?" called a third voice.

Kenny went over to the prisoners. The man held his stare, eyes blazing with hatred, but the mayor looked down at the ground. She was barefoot, Kenny noticed, and her feet were torn and bloody. He couldn't stop himself from feeling sorry for her, despite everything she had done. He was reminded of the massacre by the river the previous day, and before that, the ransacking of the reservation and burning of the lodges and the sacred elm bark hut, and before that, the execution of the crook outside the town hall. Then he thought that what was about to happen here was no different. A serving of rough justice, however deserved.

Young Little Wolf climbed down from his saddle, walked past Kenny, grabbed the ropes, tied them to the truck's rear bumper, and leaped into the truck's bed.

Kenny swung around towards Deputy Geddes.

"Aren't you going to stop this?"

"Me?" said Geddes.

"You're the law around here."

"Yeah, but maybe I happen to agree with them."

Kenny couldn't believe what he was hearing. "The other day you said nobody can act as judge, jury, and executioner. What happened to people getting a fair trial?"

"Likely, some people don't deserve one," Geddes shrugged.

Exasperated, Kenny watched as Young Little Wolf banged his hand on the roof of the cabin, and the truck slowly set off. The crowd parted, and the two prisoners stumbled along behind the vehicle. Young Little Wolf banged again, and they picked up speed from a walking pace to a jogging pace. There were more cheers from the onlookers.

If this display was meant to humiliate the captives, Kenny could live with that. But as Kenny watched the mayor and her compadre being towed around the helipad, some people began physically attacking them, punching with their fists and catching them with painful blows. One young woman angrily snatched off the mayor's wig and threw it into the air, and others started tossing it around like a crowd at a concert or baseball game, throwing a giant beach ball. The crowd's reaction grew more and more disturbing.

Young Little Wolf hit the top of the truck's cabin for a third time, and the driver gathered speed. With each incremental increase, the captives were forced to run faster, and it was obvious what would happen. The mayor, tripping barefoot over the rough ground, was the first to fall. She hit the dirt and her arms, bound at the wrist, were wrenched forward. She called out in pain, her scream riding on the backs of screams as the crowd cheered exuberantly. Young Little Wolf roared with laughter at the spectacle. The mayor somehow regained her feet, but her face was bloody and panic-stricken as she was conveyed in circles. Next to her, the militiaman did a bit better and started yelling curses at the crowd. But Kenny thought his bravado was born out of terror.

When Kenny thought things were heading towards a critical mass, a sudden gunshot surprised everyone. The cheering evaporated instantly, and then the pickup truck slewed to a stop. Kenny stood on his tiptoes to see over the heads and shoulders of those blocking his view and saw Two Moon astride his horse, blocking the truck.

His son, standing in the back, looked as if he was about to burst a blood vessel from his father's interruption. The hush was punctuated only by the mayor's quiet weeping. Two Moon clicked his tongue and his horse walked forwards several paces until the animal was right in front of the truck.

Young Little Wolf said something through the driver's window and the driver revved his engine loudly.

The tense standoff lasted for a few more seconds and then Young Little Wolf tapped twice on the roof, and the driver switched off the engine.

"Father, get out of our way," he said petulantly.

"What are you doing, son?"

"What do you think?"

"This is not the way I raised you. This is not the way we do things."

"It's the way I do things, father. Blood for blood. We must take up arms to survive as Curly Hair did."

Two Moon sneered as he replied, "You are not Crazy Horse, and we are not Lakota. Your mother would be ashamed of her little papoose."

"Don't call me that!" his son shouted. "I am not a child anymore."

"And you are not a man. Revenge is for the Great Spirit. Who are you to think you can kill these people?"

Young Little Wolf didn't respond. Instead, he scanned the area and noticed people hesitating, no longer swept up in the previous mass hysteria. A murmur of unease spread through the crowd.

"If you kill the lady mayor, what then?" Two Moon asked. "Will you hunt down the others and slaughter them, too?"

"Yes!"

"Use your head, son. She is more useful to us alive than dead. With the mayor, we will have safe passage to the border. You are a hot-blooded young man like I was once, but this calls for cool heads, Young Little Wolf."

His son's expression shifted from rage to humiliation and back to rage as Kenny questioned the wisdom of making Young Little Wolf eat humble pie in front of the crowd. To restore some of his lost honour, the young Indian looked to the crowd for support. But by now, some were already drifting away, either embarrassed by their actions or chagrined by Two Moon's more perceptive point of view.

"Why do you always undermine me?" Young Little Wolf snapped, his words filled with years of frustrated anger. "If I was my brother—"

"You're more like your brother than you think, my second born," Two Moon cut in. "When you were captured, I had to stop him from getting himself killed while trying to free you. But there are two ways to skin a cat."

"And look where that got us? You gave away our land and this bitch stabbed you in the back anyway!" spat Young Little Wolf.

Kenny, watching from the sidelines, had to admit the kid had a point. But an endless cycle of revenge killings would achieve nothing. Did the kid think the rest of the militia would drift away after they lost their leader? More likely, her execution would unleash another round of bloodletting.

Father and son engaged in a lengthy argument. The crowd thinned further until Kenny and his friends were the only onlookers.

"Grandfather should decide their fate," Young Little Wolf finally declared. "Not you."

The words seemed like a deliberate attempt to undermine his father's authority, momentarily leaving Two Moon speechless.

Young Little Wolf smirked as he jumped from the truck and stalked off. Bethany stepped forward and unfastened the ropes from the truck's rear bumper. With Alex's assistance, she tied the prisoners' hands behind their backs and led them away.

That evening, they found a good camping spot just north of Gettysburg. They cooked steak, ham, and grits on an outdoor griddle and drank bottles of beer. Later on, Two Moon slipped away to discuss matters with his grandfather.

"What do you think they will decide?" Alex asked.

"I don't know," Kenny said. "There's a lot of anger and resentment, especially among the young people. Young Little Wolf still has a lot of supporters. But what his dad said made sense: taking the mayor with us might make it easier to reach Canada without any more trouble."

"Kinda like a human shield? I'm not comfortable with that, Kenny."

Kenny thought that none of this felt right, but it is what it is.

For the time being, the prisoners were being closely watched while awaiting a decision about their future. Whatever the outcome, it seemed like a division had fractured the unity of the group, and their main goal – to find safety across the border and seek help for the sick girl – was at risk of being neglected.

Bethany was playing with the boy who had the kittens, and Kenny and Alex watched, grateful for the distraction. After a bit, they went inside the school bus to show the kittens to the girl. Deputy Geddes was by himself somewhere. Since their disagreement, he and Kenny hadn't spoken. Kenny hoped things didn't fester between them; he planned to find Deputy Geddes in the morning to clear the air.

An hour later, Two Moon appeared with his frail grandfather by his side, and they walked across to where the prisoners were being held. A few curious onlookers began to wander over, but they were quickly shooed away, as whatever was being said was a private matter.

Young Little Wolf waited with the others to hear about their fate. When he learned the news, his face gave everything away. He stormed off. The news spread quickly around the camp:

The mayor and her fellow captive would be spared for now.

• • •

Young Little Wolf gathered about twenty of his most loyal supporters during the cover of night. Quietly, they packed up their gear and departed, some riding on horseback while others drove away in vehicles. A rumour quickly spread among the remaining members of the group that they were planning to retrace their steps and head back the way they had come.

Two Moon, feeling conflicted, chose not to pursue his son.

World Quake 3

"If you want to shine like a sun, first burn like a sun," he said, looking south, his voice cracking with emotion.

Chapter 24

THE NORTH ATLANTIC
SOMEWHERE OFF THE US EASTERN SEABOARD

AROUND NOON ON THE THIRD or fourth day, a light, misty rain started to fall, and the wind shifted to the east.

The morning had seen the best weather since Madison returned to Earth, with clear blue skies, pleasant sunshine, and gentle swells. That changed with the arrival of freshening winds and overcast skies. She cast nervous glances at the clouds.

By dusk, the wind started to blow in strong gusts, soon rising to gale force, and rain pelted the PVC roof. By nighttime, the frenzied antics of the ocean became more extreme, making the choppy waters on the first day trivial in comparison. It was clear that a big storm was on the way. Madison observed roller after roller coming in, some reaching heights of over fifty feet. The raft was in continuous motion, pitching and heaving in the endless acres of green and fretful ocean. She gave up on keeping track of the raft's speed and direction, the weather forcing her to haul in the mooring line and then zip up the PVC entrance.

From the raft, she watched the waves through the transparent plastic window. Seafarers called them 'greybeards', and she could see why. They were more than a mile long from crest to crest, and they reared up silently, their cliff faces torn with foam. When it seemed they couldn't get any higher, their brows curled over and crashed down with a noise like gravel in a cement mixer, threatening to swamp the life raft under a million leagues of water.

Once every minute, one of these gigantic waves loomed astern, their awesomeness instilling a paralysing fear in Madison. But by some phenomenon of buoyancy, the life raft was lifted higher and higher as it climbed dizzily up the face of a wall of rampant, rearing water before teetering on the foamy crest and hurtling headlong down into the deep trough in what surely must be a death slide to the bottom of the sea, only for the whole drama to be re-enacted over again.

Throughout the night, these rogue waves left her battered and bruised. The raft was propelled through the violent seas, running before the storm at incredible speeds. It seemed to last an eternity, a long night measured in seconds, minutes, and hours until Madison became so inured to the dangers of death that her mind grew numb to the peril.

The raft started taking on water rapidly and it struggled to stay afloat under the extra weight. Madison had to frantically bail it out to keep the raft from sinking. This required her to quickly unzip the flap and work strenuously to throw the water over the side before the next wave arrived. After just a handful of minutes, her sore shoulder throbbed with a fiery pain, and her face was soaked, the briny water nearly blinding her.

As she battled against the relentless waves, Madison became increasingly disorientated and lost all sense of time. Her movements grew more laboured, not helped by the constant soaking she endured. Her fingers were numb and stiff from the cold, and the salt water made her skin turn all puffy and dead white.

Madison thought she saw a break in the clouds where moonlight shone through, which gave her hope that the storm was ending. Her relief was short-lived. What she saw wasn't the clouds parting but the foaming crest of a monster wave advancing rapidly towards her. With no time to close the flap, all she could do was thread her arms through the raft's guy lines and pray.

The wave struck the raft on the starboard beam. For an instant, nothing existed but water as the raft was caught in the seething mass. It seemed inconceivable that it would stay afloat, and Madison didn't even know which way was up as the raft was tossed and viciously flung about. Her lips were drawn back from her teeth in a silent snarl, only for seawater to flood her throat. Madison gagged, her last meal clawing its way up from her belly to the back of his throat. The contents of her stomach poured out from her mouth and nostrils, only to be thrown back in her face along with venomous barbs of spume driven by the murderous gale. They stung her skin like sharp micro-darts, and Madison vented her spleen and screamed into the teeth of the wind.

"God damn you, you bitch!"

The words were lost to her own ears, whipped away even as she shouted them.

The storm snarled back spitefully, trying to punish her for foolishly trespassing in such hallowed territory.

The vessel lurched harrowingly as it ploughed obliquely skyward up the face of the next rogue wave, still afloat but awash with seawater. Madison had secured everything, but most of her gear still ended up going overboard. At the last moment, she freed her arms and grabbed the locker holding its valuable items and one of the paddles, but everything else was lost. The raft surged over the top of the wave, slicing through an almost sheer face of green water as it plummeted into the next cavernous trough.

Madison yelled defiantly as the howling tumult went on, her mind experiencing a heady exhilaration bordering on madness. She laughed and cried herself hoarse, possessed by an angry determination to see the journey through. After absorbing everything Mother Nature and humankind had thrown at her, Madison felt she had earned it. By God, she deserved to make it.

Madison lifted her head and blinked, her eyes mere slits, the lashes sticky with salty residue. It took a few moments for her vision to clear and even longer for her memory to catch up. Then it all came back to her: the sharks, the storm, the giant waves.

Madison looked around. She was still inside the life raft. The flap was closed, although she couldn't remember zipping it shut. Grey daylight filtered through a tear in the PVC roof. She was sitting in water up to her waist, which sloshed back and forth with the gentle movement of the vessel. Outside, everything was quiet.

She felt something brush against her leg, and she saw a small fish swimming in circles inside the half-flooded life raft. The comical sight made her laugh. She picked it up, unzipped the entrance, and dropped the fish over the side. Then, Madison scanned her surroundings.

The storm had passed and was replaced by calm and quiet conditions. The vessel was surrounded by a thick sea mist, reducing visibility to fifty yards and blotting out the sun. She should have been relieved to still be alive, that her prayers had been answered, but she was too exhausted to feel excited. She still had no idea how far from shore she was. The storm could have carried her way off course, and without the compass, she didn't know which direction was which.

After getting back under cover, she spent a few minutes checking the damage. Besides the tear in the PVC roof, she found a few small rips in the floor that let in water and at least one slow puncture in the buoyancy tube. Fixing the roof by tying it together with bits of guy lines seemed doable, but the leaks were her main concern. She thought she could probably plug them somehow, but if water continued to soak through and air leaked out of the tube, it was only a matter of time before the life raft would flounder.

As well as the damage to the raft, she had lost almost everything. All of her emergency rations and drinking water were gone, along with the flares, the transmitter beacon, the first aid kit, and of course the compass. All she had was the small locker and a single paddle.

For a few minutes, Madison sat in the water with her head in her hands. It would be so easy just to give up, she thought. Just to lean back against the side of the raft and see where she ended up. To wait for the inevitable moment the water sloshed higher and higher, slowly pulling her and the raft beneath the surface. They said that death by drowning was a pleasant way to go, although she didn't see how. Or maybe she would grow weak from hunger and thirst and fall asleep, never to wake up again.

Yes, it would be so easy.

And so wrong.

Last night had been the deciding factor, Madison decided. She had survived the storm, and now she would endure. She would fight until her dying breath and her last ounce of strength gave out. Sufficiently provoked, hardly any creature on God's earth wouldn't turn to fight, no matter the odds.

Dragging her weary body around the raft, she set about repairing what she could. It might only keep her afloat for another day or two but with a bit of luck...

The thought had barely left her mind when she heard a far-off screeching sound. She stopped to listen, wondering if she was just imagining things. Then the sound came again. Madison shimmied over to the entrance and peered outside.

A cormorant was circling above. It floated through the sky, its long neck appearing almost reptilian. Madison watched it for several moments. She knew cormorants usually stayed close to land. She lowered her gaze. The foggy mists had started to break up, forming into ragged clouds. Sunlight pierced down onto the sea, and the glittering water extended into the distance. Three or four miles away, a thin grey line marked the coastline.

The hours that followed were curiously devoid of wild rejoicing. Madison was indescribably weak, and all she could manage was a muted acknowledgment that she had achieved the impossible. The shore was within reach, wind and tide permitting. It didn't matter where she washed up or even in which country — although she was quietly confident the strip of land was America. Home. It was a small moment of victory, but she still had a job to do.

First, she needed to fix the raft and hope that it held together long enough to reach land. The shoreline might have only been a scant few miles away across the water, but getting there could be a problem. The surf might be heavy, and the raft could be pounded against rocks, not to mention the floating debris and sunken vessels.

By the time she was ready to commence the final part of her journey, the remnants of fog had burned away, the sun was high overhead, the sea contained a modest swell, and the tide had turned. Everything was in her favour, so it was now or never. Madison picked up the single paddle and started to oar.

During the first hour, she struggled to make progress. Leaning over the buoyancy tube and paddling required her to stretch and contort her bruised body in an awkward posture. With her head low over the water and her long hair dangling in her eyes, it was difficult for her to keep track of her position. The gentle chop also made it hard for her to see the shoreline, and whenever she caught a glimpse of it, it never seemed any closer.

Seaweed became another problem. It increased in volume and density and would tangle up her paddle every few strokes. After a while, the amount of flotsam became yet another concern. On top of all these problems, Madison also had to keep one eye on the damaged life raft.

It became backbreaking work—paddling, shoving aside bits of debris, wiping sweat from her eyes, and ignoring her painful shoulder. Once, she paused and called out at the top of her voice, hoping for but not really expecting a reply. Other than the slap of water and her ragged breathing there was just quiet.

She worked hard for another hour, trying to establish a rhythm. When she took a break and looked towards the shore, she was pleasantly surprised to see that it was suddenly much nearer. She was near enough to see a rocky point and the spray splashing up as waves crashed on the shore. Madison searched for any recognizable landmarks.

Something tall and slender caught her eye – a structure built of red and white bricks that dominated the rocky point. Madison realized it was a lighthouse. She experienced a moment of déjà vu as something about the lighthouse triggered a hazy memory from her childhood of a school field trip. Their teacher had arranged a guided tour of one of America's oldest lighthouses, a national monument. Madison only had a faint recollection of the tour as in the afternoon they had enjoyed the rides at Coney Island, forgetting all about the lighthouse. However, floating in the life raft just offshore, it all came back to Madison.

"No way," Madison said out loud, shaking her head. "Get out of here."

She paddled furiously for another five minutes, her eyes pinned on the lighthouse. Now she could see the wooden walkways, the sand dunes, and the steps leading down to a fishing point. She remembered it all like it was only yesterday.

"I'll be blown. I'm not dreaming."

She was looking at Montauk Lighthouse, which meant the stretch of land was the eastern tip of Long Island. She had splashed down bang on target, give or take a hundred miles. NASA might scoff about the outdated Soyuz craft, but boy, did it deliver when needed. The storm had also carried her westward, from the deeper waters of the Atlantic to the shallower Continental Shelf near the US coast.

Madison gazed at the rocky point. As she had feared, the surf was heavy, with the sound of waves crashing onto the shore reaching her ears. A bit further to the west, there was a small beach, but it would be risky to run the flimsy vessel onto the sand. Additionally, there was a big increase in floating wreckage hugging the coastline. Forcing her way through the debris field might have potentially deadly consequences.

It seemed as if nature agreed with her as the currents started to carry the life raft westward, parallel to the shore. Madison decided to literally go with the flow for now, and hope for a better spot to come ashore. It was frustrating being so tantalizingly close. But to drop the ball so near to deliverance was unthinkable.

After a while, the wind shifted and blew offshore, forcing Madison to start paddling again. Progress was painfully slow. Several times she had to oar around small reefs over which the surge of the swell was breaking. By the middle of the afternoon the raft was almost abeam of the Hamptons and she watched the ruined millionaire pads go slowly by, smoke rising from the hamlets of Hampton Bays and East Quogue. The old timber pavilion at Ponquogue Beach now resembled a pile of matchwood.

Dead ahead was Rockaway Beach, once a vibrant playground for New Yorkers. Now its rows of condos, rebuilt after Hurricane Sandy, leaned at haphazard angles. The entire seafront including the iconic boardwalk was now submerged in a putrid, stagnant swamp. The place appeared to have been hit by a big tsunami.

The smell blowing off the beach made Madison retch. It was a combination of raw sewage, spilled chemicals, and the musky, cloying miasma of thousands of dead people. It infiltrated her nose and mouth, and frightful images took root in her mind. Madison paddled past as quickly as she could and, shortly after, rounded Breezy Point.

The tip of the Rockaway peninsula always gets strong winds and today was no exception. As soon as the life raft rounded the rocky spit, a gusty breeze came from the east. Zephys of air whipped the sea into thousands of little wavelets, reflecting the orange sunset. The raft was safely carried past by the current and tide. Shortly after, Madison spotted the mangled ruins of the funfairs on Coney Island and, further away, the deconstructed neighbourhoods of Brooklyn.

Ten minutes later, Madison was floating under the suspension bridge that connected Brooklyn and Staten Island, and New York Harbour lay open before her.

And there, caught in the glow of the setting sun, was Manhattan.

The greatest city on Earth was no more. An orange nimbus crowned the eviscerated carcass of toppled skyscrapers, crumbled piles of masonry, and twisted steel girders. The bridges over the East River and the Hudson had all been wiped from existence and everything was ripped asunder. To Madison, it appeared the city was still burning all these weeks later, consumed by infernos that illuminated the evening sky. Then she heard banging and crashing like a million hammers were striking metal. Madison thought it was the sounds of the largest reconstruction project the planet had ever known and it briefly filled her with hope.

But as she approached, the sound of a million cries from a million wretched souls reached her - it was the sound of hell.

Chapter 25

**NEWBIGGEN VILLAGE
GREAT SHUNNER FELL MOOR
NORTHERN ENGLAND**

EVERYONE IN THE HAYLOFT WAS fast asleep. The only sounds were gentle snoring and early morning birdsong from outside.

Scott had been awake for a while, watching the sky outside slowly light up. His insomnia was unpredictable. Some nights, he'd fall asleep as soon as his head hit the pillow, only waking up when Sara shook him. On other nights, like now, he'd be wide awake in the early hours, listening to the dawn chorus, just like back in Windermere.

Looking through the skylight, he had a good view across the village. The crooked rooflines and crumbling chimney stacks were silhouetted against the sunrise. It seemed like it would be a nice day. Later this morning, Scott would go and check the animal snares he had set the night before. He would probably take the boy with him, since most days he usually stuck with Scott. It was as if Scott was a father figure to the boy, and honestly, Scott didn't mind. The boy was good company and was slowly coming out of his shell. They also made good hunting partners. In the past few days, they had caught more and more game up on the moor, and just two days ago they had trapped a small hairy pig near the viaduct. The animal must have escaped from a pig sty and been living in the wild until the unfortunate beast crossed paths with two human predators. Scott had let the boy carry the carcass back to their temporary billet, holding the pig over his head like a prize-fighter. Everyone cheered and in good Boy Scout tradition some started to sing. It was a surreal moment, with everyone dancing around the campfire like a tribe of Neanderthals celebrating a successful hunt. They had enjoyed a feast that evening.

Scott glanced at the sleeping forms scattered around the hayloft. For the first time in a while, everyone was content. Their little campsite was secure, well-protected, and well-guarded. The hayloft over the animal pens, typically used to store fodder and grain for the animals, served as a good sleeping area. They had a designated cooking area outside next to the potato field. Initially they built their campfires close to the entrance to provide warmth and light at night but soon discovered this filled the loft with smoke, so they moved the fires further away. After some trial and error, they learned that roasting meat over naked flames tended to leave it charred, so now they built a roaring fire over flat rocks, and once the rocks had heated up, they pushed the burning wood to one side and placed chunks of meat on the hot stones to cook.

To create some privacy for changing and washing, half of the hayloft was partitioned off with tarps. Additionally,

Fabian had dug a privy at the base of a slope, positioned away from the sheds, and set up a canvas screen with torches for nighttime use.

The little band of survivors had been resting for five nights. They had decided to spend two or three more here before resuming their travels. Being well-rested and well-fed, Scott hoped to reach their destination forty-eight hours later.

Scott climbed through the skylight and crossed the drawbridge. Fabian and Saskia were keeping watch on the pub roof next door. As he approached, Scott coughed lightly to let them know he was coming. (He had caught them canoodling once or twice before). They greeted him with tired smiles.

"Hey, go grab something to eat," he said. "The others will be up soon."

"Much appreciated, boss," Fabian replied, and he led Saskia to the shed.

Scott still didn't like being the unofficial leader, but he had long ago come to terms with everyone following his direction. When his friend and fellow teacher, Alan Pritchard, had been alive, they had shared the burden of leadership. But with Alan no longer around, a responsibility he had not sought was now his alone, whether he liked it or not.

Scott took his place on the roof. He'd stick around until he caught a whiff of breakfast cooking.

Someone was banging a piece of metal with a rock, their usual call to announce that breakfast was ready. Scott's stomach grumbled at the prospect of food, and he eagerly climbed to his feet. He had barely taken four or five steps towards the drawbridge when an odd sound reached him. They had learned to identify most noises and could separate the normal ones from those that didn't belong, as a way to identify possible threats in advance. This sound was definitely unusual. Not man-made, but certainly weird. It was kind of a high-pitched tone, almost beyond the range of the human ear. Scott did a three-sixty to try and pinpoint where it was coming from.

Everything was in order, with nothing appearing out of place. He climbed one of the chimneys. By the time that he took a second look around, the noise had increased in volume. Another noise joined it, this one more of a chittering warble coming from the trees close to the crossroads. Suddenly, hundreds of birds took flight, chirping wildly as they fluttered through the branches and high into the sky, leaving behind a storm of falling leaves.

When Scott saw the birds, he also noticed what looked like a river of black mud flooding through the village. For a heartbeat, he thought it might be another reservoir on the moors bursting its dam, but then it clicked: thousands of rats were streaming between the cottages and through overgrown gardens. He remembered the rats eating the dead lady at the post office and how they had been unbothered by his presence. Something had frightened both the rats and the birds, causing them to panic.

"Oh shit," Scott muttered to himself – only one thing could scare off the animals like that.

He hadn't even finished the thought when the roof started quivering beneath him. He made a grab for the chimney pot, but it tilted and fell away. Scott nearly followed it over the side of the building. It slammed into the ground with a crash, and Scott sprawled across the roof's apex, his cry drowned out by the loud tumult of shaking buildings and the rustle of agitated trees. One of the cottages, already weakened by earlier liquefaction, collapsed like a house of cards, with the concussion ringing through the ground.

Scott dragged himself along the ridgeline of the pub's roof and then slithered down the roof slates to the drawbridge. The metal ladder was bouncing around, and he lay on it, using his weight to stabilize it to some extent. He then cautiously began to pull himself across the gap.

Below him, he saw the others fleeing from the shed, grabbing whatever they could on the way. In their haste, someone accidentally kicked the campfire, sending burning logs rolling through the shed entrance. Almost immediately, wisps of smoke curled into the morning air as the straw bales caught fire.

If the ladder didn't tumble and send him falling to his death, or the buildings collapse and crush him, then the fire would trap and burn him alive. Pulling himself along by the final few rungs, Scott came to his knees and squeezed through the skylight.

The loft space was quickly filling with hazy smoke from below, seeping through floor planks. Scott tried not to breathe in too deeply, screwing up his eyes as he looked around. Everyone had got out. He snatched up two of the left-behind bags and went across to the trapdoor. Looking down, he could see orange flames licking at the timber posts, but so far, the fire hadn't spread to the ladder. Dropping the bags through the square hole, Scott quickly followed, foregoing the ladder and instead dropping down and using the bags to soften his impact with the ground.

A loud crash from above alerted him that the shed was caving in under the powerful tremor. Scott jumped up, scooped up the bags, and rushed outside just seconds before the loft, followed by the animal pens, were flattened like pancakes.

He stumbled away, feeling a twinge where he had sprained an ankle. The rest of the band was watching from the middle of the potato field.

"Keep moving!" he yelled, waving them away. "The whole village is about to come down."

As if to confirm his prediction, a row of cottages started to sink into the ground. It looked as if the earth had turned to mud and was swallowing them whole. The strange sight was enough to make them flee. Scott caught up with them just as they pushed through a hedgerow and tumbled onto the country lane.

The children and some of the adults screamed hysterically when they saw a tide of black vermin rolling towards them like a mini-tsunami. More of the creatures were fountaining up out of the drains and manholes, their clawed feet climbing over each other's backs in their terror to escape. They closed the distance to the group of humans in no time at all and the rats streamed around their feet and legs. Scott and his friends watched them pass by. More rats were coming through the hedgerow behind, and another set was jumping through the post office window even as the building was coming apart.

When there was a break in the flow of rats, Scott pointed dead ahead.

"Over the field! Go!"

They reached the overgrown plot and ran as fast as they could from the sinking village. Scott, who was bringing up the rear, noticed at some point that the tremor had come to an end. When they were all a safe distance away they halted. Scott, clutching a painful stitch in his side, joined them.

Together, they watched the final demise of Newbiggen village.

• • •

Two days after their unscheduled departure from Newbiggen, they reached the coast. Scott looked out to sea with his binoculars and then passed them to Tammy.

"Lindisfarne, or Holy Island as it's sometimes called," he told her as he pointed. "It's a small island built on sedimentary rock hundreds of millions of years old. It's withstood everything nature can throw at it. Only the Vikings managed to conquer it over a thousand years ago. It is a perfect stronghold with good anchorage and a limestone jetty. Most importantly, you can only get there on foot when it's low tide. You have to cross a narrow causeway, which also makes it easy to defend."

"What about folks in boats? Can they come ashore?"

Scott shook his head.

"There are cliffs surrounding most of the island, with jagged rocks at their base. Any attackers in boats would have to use the jetty, and again..."

"...that's easy to defend against," Tammy finished for him.

"There is a small village with houses or guesthouses for lodging, fields for grazing animals, some old lime kilns that we could convert into ovens, and a small but well-fortified castle that dominates everything. There is another island, St. Cuthbert's Island, just offshore that would act as a final bastion if the worst came to pass. And it's all within easy reach of the mainland for when we need to scavenge for supplies. The coast around here is dotted with small communities, so finding supplies won't be a problem, and there's enough fish to last forever."

Tammy continued studying the island through the binoculars.

"I like it. I like it a lot," she finally said. "I'm just annoyed that I didn't think of it first."

Scott laughed lightly and playfully cuffed her on the shoulder.

"What if there are already people living there?" Tammy asked as he put the binoculars away.

"There's only one way to find out."

As they followed the coastal path to where the others waited, Scott found himself hoping that this time, things would work out. So far, they hadn't had much luck, finding themselves driven out of each safe haven. They couldn't keep wandering the countryside forever. Eventually, they would need to put down some roots and start over.

They gathered at the lifeboat station in Seahouses, a small village by the sea. In another time, the area became well-known due to the story of Grace Darling, the lighthouse keeper's daughter. In 1838, she bravely rowed out in a small boat during a severe storm to rescue people from a shipwrecked paddle steamer.

Scott went over the plan, and after five minutes, they set off along the road that led to Lindisfarne, several miles away. Scott's ankle sprain wasn't as bad as he had initially feared, and he had strapped it up well. But he was grateful the coastal road was easier to traverse compared to the moors, and he would be relieved when their journey finally came to an end.

Over the next few hours, they passed a few isolated communities and fishing villages. They also came across a wild, overgrown golf course where tall grass was growing through golf buggies. Further along, they saw a caravan park that had been partially damaged by fire, as well as the occasional abandoned car or bus. But they did not encounter any people, whether dead or alive.

Finally, the road curved to the east towards the shore. They stopped to read a signpost:

DANGER
HOLY ISLAND CAUSEWAY
LOOK AT TIDE TABLES FOR SAFE CROSSING TIMES

Next to it was a red notice bearing a faded photo of a car up to its roof in water and a warning:
THIS COULD BE YOU

PLEASE CONSULT TIDE TABLES.

There was a list of tide times. Red stood for high tide when it was dangerous to cross, and green stood for low tide when it was safe to cross. Because the moon had changed its orbit, affecting the world's tides, the information was outdated. They all turned to study the road ahead, which meandered over the sandflats. The sea was way off in the distance. About three miles away, the island beckoned at the other end of the causeway. A ten-minute drive – or about a two-hour walk.

It looked safe at the moment, but dusk was approaching, and Scott didn't want to be caught in the middle of the causeway at night. If they left right away, they might just make it over before the light faded. The other option was to wait another twelve hours for the next low tide.

He turned to the others, thinking of taking a vote, only to find that everyone was looking at him and waiting.

"Follow me," he said, taking Phoebe from Sara and strapping the baby to his back. "Fabian, you bring up the rear. Kids, keep in the middle."

As they started walking, the road dipped down between some sand dunes and then levelled out. The causeway was narrow and covered in sand and small seashells. Groups of seaweed-covered rocks packed tightly into both shoulders.

They travelled in single file. Scott set a fast pace, his concentration switching from the island to the distant sea as well as the children behind him, and of course his wife and child. Two hours was all they needed. As long as the high tide stayed away for another two hours, they should be okay.

As they walked, Scott felt akin to Moses leading the Exodus and parting the Red Sea. He could only hope he wasn't like King Cnut, who failed to hold back the tide.

During the first half hour, the children chatted animatedly, clearly finding the experience strange and exciting. However, as time passed, their chatter subsided and the little party continued on in silence. The sky turned purple and the setting sun cast its shadows. On the eastern horizon, clouds gathered like a group of muggers.

The light was fading faster than Scott had expected, turning the island into a dark silhouette.

They had gone about a mile when they came across an emergency refuge hut atop some wooden steps. Scott glanced at it as they passed, contemplating whether to continue or to take shelter until the next low tide. He looked to both sides, but the twilight made it difficult to gauge the distance to the sea. After a moment's thought, he chose to keep going.

It was a mistake. Ten minutes later, he felt the first splash of water under his shoes. He looked down and saw the seawater lapping over the edge of the road on both sides. In front of them, more water covered their path, making it seem like the causeway was disappearing into the sea. He suddenly stopped, causing the people behind him to bump into him. When he looked back, he saw more seawater flowing over the stretch of causeway they had just come along. It had crept up on them stealthily.

"Right," he said, trying to keep the tremor out of his voice. "Let's retrace our steps to the hut. We'll try again in the morning, folks."

He caught Fabian's eye and gave the tiniest nod of his head, hoping Fabian got the message. Calmly and with little fuss, Fabian turned about and started back, guiding the children and adults back over the quickly submerging causeway. Scott, now finding himself at the rear of the little column, ushered them along with as much composure as he could muster.

But by now, they were wading through ankle-deep, cold water. He listened to some of the children whisper with unease. Somewhere, someone started to sniffle and cry.

Scott could kick himself. The children had narrowly escaped drowning at the summer camp by seeking shelter at the top of a birdwatching tower as flood waters rose higher and higher all around them. Some of their friends had been swept away before their very eyes. Now Scott was putting them through the exact same situation. What had he been thinking? Alan would not have made that mistake.

There would be time for self-recrimination later. First he had to get them all to safety. It was too far to go back to the mainland or reach the island so the emergency hut was their only option.

The water kept rising; now it was up to his calves and the children's knees. Blackness inked across the sky as nighttime descended, making it difficult to see where they were going. Scott worried about them straying off the causeway into deeper water. He could feel the tide surging past his lower limbs, like when surf washes back out and threatens to unbalance people paddling on a beach.

Fabian must have been thinking the same thing because he switched on his LED head torch. Scott did so too, and Louise in the middle did the same. The children were growing panicky and she tried to settle them.

"Hey everyone!" Scott shouted from the back. "Let's link arms with the person in front and behind you. We're almost there - I can see the hut up ahead. We'll be there in five minutes."

But after five more minutes of trudging through the water, the chilling coldness was up to Scott's waist and the children's chests, and there was still no sign of the hut. Surely they'd know if they had strayed off course. Then where was the blasted hut?

Suddenly the young boy said loudly, "It's there, sir. I can see it."

Scott squinted into the gathering darkness. He struggled to make out anything, even with the head torch. The kid must have better eyesight than he did.

"Just keep going, Fabian!" he instructed.

They waded through the water, their arms linked together as they strained against the rising tide. Scott wondered how high it would go. He remembered the car caught in deep water, but again, it didn't mean anything. The world was different now, its geology and climate thrown upside down. The old rules had been thrown out of the window. Even the emergency hut might be inundated.

The children in the middle were struggling to stay on their feet. It was the weakest point in the human chain, even with the adults trying their best to help. If one of the children lost their footing and fell they would all probably be carried away.

Please, kids, Scott pleaded silently. Help each other stay steady.

He looked over his shoulder at Phoebe in his backpack; she was sleeping through the drama.

"I see the tower!" Fabian called. "I see the fucking tower!"

Then Scott saw it too, caught in the LED lights. It was only yards away, looming up at the side of the causeway. He watched as Fabian grabbed one of the wooden posts and hauled himself up the first few steps before helping the children one by one. Tammy went to the top and flung open the door. Scott used his upper body strength to press from the back.

Then he was at the tower himself, and he climbed clear of the water and stumbled through the door, shutting it behind him. The interior was cramped, with a few fold-up chairs, an emergency telephone and some warm blankets. The children were crying with relief and everybody was shivering from cold.

Fabian set up a light and Scott took a headcount.

"No, no, no," he exclaimed, ice-cold anxiety crushing his heart.

Sara broke off from fussing over Phoebe, who was now bawling her head off but was otherwise fine.

"What is it, Scott?"

"The young boy – where's the young boy?"

Chapter 26

MONASTERY OF THE HOLY TRINITY
BERNESE ALPS
SWITZERLAND

OVER THE FOLLOWING DAYS, TIMO spent his time exploring the monastery and its surroundings with Genny. Despite his initial impression, he soon realized that the monastery's elevated location high in the mountains wasn't as isolated or cut off as he had first thought. In fact, he discovered that the holy sanctuary was connected to neighbouring towns and villages by two well-travelled roads. In addition to these roads, there were several narrow bridleways and unmarked goat tracks leading through the mountain fastness. However, according to Brother Edwig, all communications with the outside world had been severed since the earthquakes.

Since nobody had said anywhere was off-limits, Timo investigated all of the domestic range of buildings and courtyards, as well as the fields. He rarely encountered anybody. Edwig told him the community comprised only twelve monks, a prior and Abbot Benlow, so it wasn't too surprising considering how sprawling the place was. Sometimes, monks could be observed in the cloisters, but they would hurriedly brush past with lowered heads. In the fields, a handful of figures worked hard in all weather conditions, using sickles to cut stalks of tall grass and then threshing the wheat or barley to separate out the grain. The grain was then taken to the kitchens below the refectory to be ground down to make flour. Meanwhile, others used small ploughs to turn over a furrow in the earth ready for planting or used axes to fell small trees. The monastery kept livestock such as goats and Longhorn cattle to produce milk. These animals grazed outdoors during the daytime but were brought into a penned courtyard at night. Semi-wild pigs foraged in the forests, feeding on acorns and beechmast through a practice known as pannage, and providing pork for the monks. The monastery also had beehives for honey and kept ferrets for catching rabbits.

The monks spent their mornings inside the oratory observing their religious customs and teachings. One day after they left, Timo went for a look. The chapel sat on a small rise accessible by steps cut into the earth. The oratory's shape reminded Timo of an upturned boat, and was constructed in the manner of dry-stone walling. There was just a single narrow window in the east wall opposite the entrance.

The doorway was decorated with carved stonework. On either side, there were sculptures of bishops and carvings of mythical beasts, while above the lintel, there was a scene of the adoration of the Magi as they were awakened by an angel. In front of the door was a stone holy water stoup.

Timo tied Genny to a sapling, then pushed open the door and went inside.

The inside was small and quite bare. In the dim light, he could barely see a few wooden pews and a small altar containing a crucifix and a chalice. The only attempt at decoration was an alabaster frieze over the altar depicting a Bible story. Timo spent a minute looking around, but as he was preparing to leave, he heard the sound of a second door opening, hidden away in the shadows of the darkest corner. A robed figure emerged. For some reason that he couldn't explain, Timo stepped back against the wall. From this position, he was partially hidden by a pew.

The monk, his face concealed in the shadows of his hood, made the sign of the cross and whispered the Trinitarian formula, "In the name of the Father, and of the Son, and of the Holy Spirit. Amen." Then he went down on his knees on the stone floor and shrugged off the robe to reveal his bare flesh.

The monk's back was scored with multiple lacerations, and it became clear why. The monk's hand deftly reached inside his robes and retrieved a leather whip, its thongs tipped with iron spikes. He commenced to scourge himself, each flick of the whip cracking the air and opening new deep cuts over his flesh. Timo flinched with each lash. The monk endured his self-chastisement with incredible stoicism, but after seven or eight lashes, Timo saw the monk's shoulders start to quiver. In a minute, his back was a bloody morass.

Right then, Genny started barking excitedly, and the monk froze. A shadow appeared on the stone floor and Timo turned to see a figure standing in the doorway. It was Brother Edwig.

He was scowling, and he coughed lightly to catch the first monk's attention. The figure before the altar looked back, allowing Timo to see his face. It was the old monk who read aloud from the Scriptures during meal times. Seeing Timo, the old man's face crumpled with embarrassment and he hurriedly got to his feet, pulled up his robes, and slipped back behind the far door.

Brother Edwig stepped into the shadowy chapel and approached Timo, his eyes remaining on the far door until it snicked shut. Then his features softened and he gave a little bow.

"Apologies, my friend," the novice monk said quietly. "Abbot Benlow has asked me to fetch you. He would like to meet with you."

They went outside. Timo blinked in the bright light and started to untie Genny.

"I will take your dog back to your room. Abbott Benlow insists that you come at once."

"Why the hurry?"

"All will be explained. Now please, if you don't mind? The Abbott is waiting in his private lodgings in the west range."

Timo handed over his dog's lead and then looked pointedly back at the chapel, asking, "What was that all about?"

"The Abbott will explain," Brother Edwig repeated.

A few minutes later, Timo climbed the stairs to the top floor where the Abbott kept his chambers. He entered a hall adorned with tapestries, passed a spacious bedchamber and a small lavatorium, and then knocked on the parlour door. A gruff voice responded, "Come in." The parlour was elegantly appointed with fine furniture and furnishings, a comfortable room used to entertain important visitors.

When Timo entered, he found the Abbott seated in front of the fireplace, his eyes closed and his chin resting on his chest, apparently deep in thought. Hearing the door close, the Abbott's eyes snapped open, and he took a moment to focus on Timo. His jowls trembled when he spoke.

"I've been waiting," he said in a plummy English accent. His tone made it clear that waiting wasn't something he enjoyed doing.

Timo said nothing in response. He stepped forward and made a show of looking at the room's décor rather than the man who had summoned him. This was another thing Benlow wasn't accustomed to: being ignored.

This short but interesting powerplay continued for a few seconds before Benlow asked if Timo would like refreshments.

"There is wine or ale," he said, indicating a small table containing two jugs. Next to them was a pewter plate with pieces of bread. "Perhaps you are hungry?"

Timo was, but he shook his head and forced a smile.

"You wanted to see me?"

"Indeed. Please take a seat."

Benlow waited until Timo was seated before proceeding.

"How are you? Have you settled in?"

"It's only been a few days," Timo answered, annoyed at what was obviously small talk. He wanted to know why he had really been sent for. "I was thinking of moving on. Perhaps the day after tomorrow."

"So soon?"

"Yes. I'm grateful for the hospitality that you and your brother monks have shown, but it was never my intention –"

"How is your wound healing?" Abbott Benlow cut in, his beady eyes flicking downwards.

Timo reflexively rubbed his surgical incision, saying, "It seems to be healing well. Your physician–"

"Infirmarer is the correct term."

"He did a good job," Timo said, biting his tongue.

"Good. Your welfare is our priority. Physical as well as spiritual."

Abbott Benlow reached behind him and tossed another log onto the fire. Sparks spiralled up the chimney breast.

"So, you wish to leave, do you?"

He made it sound as if permission was required, and once more, Timo bit his tongue.

"Do you have a destination in mind?"

"I do."

"It strikes me as odd that you would prefer to leave our comfortable life here for an uncertain future out there."

"As I was saying, it was never my intention to stay here permanently," Timo said. "After all, I wouldn't want to outstay my welcome."

Abbott Benlow laughed lightly.

"That would never be the case. Have you considered that it may have been your fate to wind up here? That it wasn't just luck that we found you when we did? Maybe our destinies crossed for a reason."

"Well, I don't believe in preordained destiny, kismet, or whatever you wish to call it. Happenchance or good fortune perhaps, but not divine intervention."

"Or divine prophecy?"

"It's the same thing, isn't it?" Timo asked, already growing tired of the direction the dialogue was taking. He looked around at the room's furnishings again.

"As a man of God, I would say there are distinct differences between the Lord intervening to preserve the sanctity of life and God's will to condemn a world of sinners to its sentence. Alas, you are a man of science, Mr. Lehmann, so your lack of faith is understandable."

Timo again said nothing. The room's warmth started to lull him into a soporific mood.

"Perhaps your spiritual apathy stems from a degree of..." Benlow paused like he was searching for the right term. "Guilt is too strong a word, I daresay. Remorse is more correct."

Timo turned back and looked directly at the Abbott.

"I beg your pardon?" he asked.

"Self-reproach and contrition cannot be easy for a man bearing such a heavy burden. The closest I can compare it to would be the thirteenth labour of Hercules when he—"

This time, it was Timo who cut the other off mid-sentence.

"Wait a minute. Let's rewind. You're saying I should feel remorseful? For what?"

Benlow vouchsafed Timo a friendly smile and spread his arms wide, saying, "For all of this. The end of the world."

Timo was temporarily struck dumb. He wasn't sure whether he was hearing right or if Benlow was being serious. Each long second dragged itself through an awful stasis until the penny finally dropped.

"You're blaming me for everything that has happened?" he asked Benlow. Just saying it out loud made the idea sound even more absurd.

"Not just you, Mr. Lehmann. Your fellow scientists, too."

Timo shook his head. "You couldn't be further from the truth."

"I know all about you and the experiments you have been in charge of in your deep underground laboratory, trying to find answers to the biggest question of all.

"I said that you couldn't be further from the truth—"

"Playing at being God," Benlow continued undeterred. "All you need to do is look at the Good Book to find what you are looking for."

Benlow's face adopted a sorrowful expression, and he took a deep breath and sighed.

Timo came to his feet.

"We weren't responsible. Nobody was. The moon's orbit changed, affecting Earth's core and triggering the seismic activity. It really is that simple. Even someone of an unscientific bent should be able to grasp that."

"Ah, you still have so much to learn. Well, I hope you are happy, Mr. Lehmann. Your recklessness has brought suffering and lamentation to a beleaguered people."

"Damn you!" Timo said, raising his voice. "We tried to bring the world back from the brink."

"And instead, here we are staring into the abyss."

"A lot of my colleagues died trying to manage the situation," Timo shot back.

"And there lies the problem: your vanity, your vainglorious hubris in thinking that you have the power of a deity. God can be a great leveller, and now we are all being punished for our sins. The monk that you saw in the oratory – yes, Brother Edwig told me that you witnessed him mutilating his earthly vessel – has taken it upon himself to lay bare his soul for 33½ days, one for each of Christ's years on earth, in the forlorn hope that by offering himself up he will appease the Lord."

"And what do you think, Benlow? Do you think lying prostrate before your God will make everything right again?"

"No. I'm afraid the End Times have already begun, seven years of worldwide hardship, persecution, disasters, famine, and pain, all leading to the Rapture and The Second Coming of Jesus Christ. The seven trumpets will summon every true Christian and take them bodily up to Heaven. Are you a righteous Christian, Mr. Lehmann?

Benlow came to his feet and stepped towards Timo, his tread surprisingly soft for such a corpulent man. He reached out with one hand.

"It is never too late to seek forgiveness."

Timo brushed the hand away.

Benlow reached for a small handbell and rang it.

Two monks materialized from somewhere and grasped Timo by the arms, their sudden appearance surprising him. Their grip was firm as they manoeuvered him back towards the door. Timo struggled to break free from their hold.

"Let go of me!" he shouted at them.

"Please remain calm, Mr. Lehmann," Benlow suggested.

"Where are they taking me?"

"All of these histrionics are not good for your health. Be stout of heart."

"Tell your men to let me go! You can't do this."

"This is all for your own benefit. A period of reflection to clear your conscience before you pass through a final fire to restore your faith."

The monks on either side dragged Timo backwards out into the hall and then down the stone steps. He fought them all the way, his shoes scuffing the walls or ruffling up the landing rugs as he tried to slow their passage. He shouted, but to no avail. From the west range, they took him to the domestic quarters and dumped him unceremoniously into his room. Timo landed painfully on the floor. The door banged shut and a key was turned in the lock.

Genny was cowering under the bed, and she came out and licked his fingers. She whimpered.

"You said it, girl," Timo said, scratching behind her ear.

He came to his feet and tried the door. He kicked it in annoyance and stepped away.

"We need to find a way out of here."

Genny whimpered again.

"I don't know how."

A banging sound from outside drew Timo to the window. He peered through the iron grilles. In the courtyard below, a monk was hammering a stake into the ground while two more were piling kindling around its base.

Timo looked around his room for inspiration, searching for anything he could use to jimmy the door or pry loose the window grilles. He couldn't find anything suitable, so he sat on the edge of his bed. A guard would probably be in the passage even if he could escape the room, and the window was too high to jump from. The other day, Brother Edwig had described the small room as a cell, and at that moment, the word was suddenly very apt.

• • •

Timo didn't know how long he rested on the bed. The shadows outside grew longer as the work to build the bonfire continued.

He attempted to devise an escape plan but his options were limited. He would have to try to flee when they came for him. His surgical incision was painful, and when he lifted his clothes, he noticed blood seeping through the dressing. The wound must have opened during the struggle.

Genny lay on the bed next to him, her ears twitching with every loud bang that echoed through the window. Timo spoke to her softly, trying to remain composed on the outside despite feeling a growing sense of panic building up inside of him.

The sounds outside subsided. Timo untangled himself from his dog and stepped across the small room to the window and looked down. A solitary lantern lit the courtyard, revealing the complete bonfire and stake. He couldn't see the monks. Just then, he heard footsteps approaching along the passage. Genny dropped to the floor, and together they waited for the door to fly open and some of Benlow's men to drag him out. The key was turned. But instead of the door opening, the footsteps receded.

Timo remained rooted to the spot, feeling like he was being tested or was walking into a trap. After a few minutes of silence, he cautiously approached the door and pressed his ear against it. The passageway beyond was quiet. Silently, he turned the latch, opened the door slightly, and looked out. He could see the passageway and the steps leading down, but not the other way. Worried that someone might be in the blind spot, Timo knelt down, put his face close to the floor, and then extended his head through the opening, turning his eyes upward. No one was in sight and the passageway was empty. Timo stood up, called for Genny to follow, and stepped out.

He looked in both directions, still convinced that this was some sort of silly test or a ruse. If it wasn't, it meant that someone had quietly made their way up here, unlocked his door, and then left again, suggesting that a member of the monastery didn't want him to burn at the stake in a baptism of fire. One of the monks wanted to help him.

It was an unexpected turn of events. Just minutes ago, Timo was convinced that he was about to meet a spectacular end. Suddenly, he was presented with a chance to escape. How far he would get before being discovered breaking out didn't really matter at the moment: Timo had been offered a slim chance.

First he needed to get his gear. Brother Edwig told him it was stowed nearby, so Timo went looking for it. After a few minutes he found their belongings in a storage cupboard around the corner. As he reached for his bag, he noticed something on the shelf above. There were neatly folded sets of white cotton clothes. When he picked up the top set, he saw a small logo stamped on the front of a sweatshirt – **EDELWEISS CHATEAU CLINIC**. Curious, he examined another set and found the same logo. Alongside the clothes there were several pairs of slip-on pumps neatly arranged on the shelf.

Timo returned the clothes, removed his bag, and closed the cupboard door.

Going by their room, they slipped down the well-worn stone steps to the first landing. From the cover of the wall, Timo peered around the corner and looked down the door-lined passageway. There were no signs of anyone. Timo led Genny past the end of the passageway and down the next flight, a timpani of dog claws on the stone steps the only noise. At the next landing, Timo quietly eased open the window shutters and peeked outside.

The window looked down onto the ancient cloisters, and he was just in time to observe a group of monks emerge from the refectory. Timo ducked back into the shadows. He watched them walk around the precinct, some carrying burning torches that flickered in the night. No doubt these would also be used to light the bonfire. Timo knew he couldn't delay any longer because when they discovered their prisoner missing from his room, there would be chaos as they searched for him. But before he had time to turn away and hurry down the steps, he noticed Brother Edwig. The other monks were manhandling the reluctant novice monk along, shoving and pulling him. Edwig's desperate pleas echoed through the still night.

A chill passed through Timo. It appeared Edwig was the one who had unlocked his door and now he was about to face grave consequences for being labelled a heretic. Timo felt terrible for the novice monk but could do little to help him. Besides, Timo couldn't shake the feeling that the situation at the monastery was far from what it appeared to be. A growing suspicion began to take root in his mind. If his instincts were correct, there was something deeply amiss in this place.

Timo kept an eye on the group of people until they disappeared. Then he quickly descended the steps to avoid being cut off. At the bottom of the staircase, Timo lightly padded along the hallway. Genny was panting loudly, so Timo had to place a hand around her muzzle. The cloisters were empty as the monks were probably busy with Brother Edwig in the courtyard. Timo jogged around the quadrangle and through the doorway to the refectory.

He pulled up short in fright when he saw that the dining hall was infested with rats. A line of them was running across the floor towards a small doorway in a dark corner, and more rats were on the dining table, eating the leftovers of a meal. Genny growled and tried to attack the rats, and Timo had to hold her back. They walked around the table. As they passed the dark corner, a foul smell filled Timo's senses, and he saw a pile of bodies on the floor just inside the doorway; some were wearing cassocks, but most were naked. He nearly gagged at the sight.

Timo tried not to speculate about what had led to this point, but his imagination ran wild. Most of the monks were dead, including the real Abbott Benlow. It was possible that Edwig was the last one alive, or perhaps he was an imposter as well. When Timo saw the patients wandering aimlessly outside the clinic he knew something was wrong. Initially he thought the staff had abandoned their posts after the disasters, leaving the patients to fend for themselves. Now, he wondered if the patients had killed the staff, escaped from the clinic, and then arrived at the mountain monastery to murder all the monks and take their place.

But if that was the case, why did they rescue Timo and Genny when they found them at the roadside? Why not leave them behind, or kill them? Why bring them to the monastery, operate on Timo, and let him recuperate? Who had carried out the operation, and what exactly did they do to him? What did they remove from his body?

Timo felt a shiver of fear at the thought. There were too many unknowns to consider. Right now, he needed to focus on escaping. He carefully made his way around the rats and headed outside to the yard. The beaten-up moped was still leaning against one of the gateposts with the keys in the ignition, and the entrance gates were open. Pushing the stand away, Timo moved the motorbike onto the road. Then he placed Genny on the handlebars and positioned himself behind her. Turning the key, he pulled out the choke and pressed the starter button. The engine whined loudly before finally starting with a splutter. Releasing the brake with one hand, he twisted the throttle and sped away.

When Timo reached a bend in the road, he took a quick look back. The monastery appeared dark and looked like a haunted castle from a horror movie. Suddenly, a burst of orange light illuminated the night sky and a heart-wrenching scream of agony filled the air, even over the noise of the engine. Timo quickly turned his head away and switched on the bike's headlight. In seconds, they were swallowed up by the mountain forests.

PART 3
A STIRRING OF THE HUMAN SPIRIT

Mark Hobson

Chapter 27

US/CANADIAN BORDER

ACCORDING TO THE INFORMATION KENNY Leland's party received, the large community with doctors and surgeons was situated somewhere on the northern shore of Lake Erie, on the Canadian side of the border. Its exact location was kept a closely guarded secret. They were only told to head north and then await further instructions.

The city of Buffalo in New York State, like most urban areas, lay in ruins. This required a two-day detour, circling the downtown area and passing through the suburbs of East and West Amherst towards the Niagara River. If they were fortunate, one of the bridges connecting the United States and Canada would still span the rapids. The convoy would then travel upriver to the famous waterfalls before passing through Drummond Heights to reach the lakeshore.

Their plan to avoid the highways and freeways was harder as the geography became more metropolitan. They could no longer rely solely on dirt roads. As they encountered more quake-damaged buildings and mountains of debris blocking their path, making headway slowed to a crawl. It was frustrating for everyone, especially the little girl's mother as she watched her child grow desperately ill.

The only people happy with their slow advance were the two prisoners: the mayor of Lansing and her sidekick. No decision on their ultimate fate had been made, and it was postponed until they reached their destination. From their perspective, the longer the journey took, the better.

As they travelled along York Road, they encountered the only building that was still standing - The Homestead Lodge Motel, a budget trucker's stopover. A pancake house further down the street had been demolished, and past a set of railway lines was a large breaker's yard. The convoy came to a stop and after setting up sentries, the rest of the group picked their rooms for the night. Kenny and Bethany planned to spend some quality time together in a double room. However, as soon as they kicked off their shoes and lay on the bed, they both fell sound asleep within seconds.

Too soon, a delicate rap on the door woke them up. Kenny checked his watch and saw they had only been asleep for a couple of hours. As he sat up his tired body urged him to stay in bed, but instead he crossed the carpet and looked through the peephole. A slender version of Alex with an elongated nose waited outside the door.

Kenny opened the door.

"What's up?" he asked, his mouth all sticky.

"We have company," Alex said without any preamble, jerking his thumb over his shoulder.

A small crowd had gathered, including Two Moon. They stood in silence like they were waiting for something to happen. Kenny, in just his jeans and socks, joined them. That's when he noticed the bright headlamps shining from the trees across the motel parking lot. He squinted against the dazzling light but couldn't make out anything at night.

"They appeared a while back," Alex told him. "I was on watch at the time, and they suddenly came on and lit the place up. Whoever it is seems content just to watch us for now."

"Is this our contact?" Bethany asked as she approached.

"I suppose so," was the response.

•   •   •

Chloè Bouchard watched the people at the motel. It was the third party of refugees this week and the largest one yet. Previous groups had been small, sometimes consisting of only a single family, but this particular bunch included several dozen people. It also differed in the sense that the refugees heading north had been 99% Native Americans or blacks, but in this group, Chloè saw at least four or five white people. Regardless of their ethnicity or their stories, they all had one thing in common: they sought shelter at the lake camp.

She had been tracking them for two days. Thanks to her extensive knowledge of the urban area, she was able to remain unnoticed as the convoy advanced into the suburbs of the commuter belt of the leveled city. Chloè had practiced this for weeks. She was intimately familiar with the ruined streets and sewer network, knowing exactly where to hide as the refugees passed through and when to reveal herself to them. Stealth was her watchword, and the need for secrecy was her guiding principle. It was how it had to be if the camp was to survive.

Sometimes, Chloè thought back to her old life. Had it really only been four months? It felt like a lifetime ago.

Before the Big Quake, twenty-four-year-old Chloè Bouchard, originally from Quebec, was a ticket seller for one of the tour companies operating Niagara Falls sightseeing boats. One spring morning, she set out for work like millions of other people in North America. Upon arriving at the ferry landing where the fleet of boats was moored, she was informed that due to staff shortages, she would be needed aboard one of the boats that day. Chloè was excited as she always loved being on the sightseeing boats, especially the newer electric-powered ones with their silent propulsion drives.

Her main responsibility was to scan tickets as passengers boarded the boat and then keep an eye on them during the twenty-minute round trip. With six hundred people packed onto the boat across two observation decks, this was no easy task. So far, the company had a perfect safety record. In fact, since tour boats began taking tourists to the falls, only one boat had sunk, way back in 1861.

The boat set out, its twin VL-200 hydroelectric engines harnessing the power of Niagara Falls to glide through the turbulent waters. Packed on its decks, its throngs of poncho-clad passengers eagerly snapped photos with their mobile phones and selfie sticks. As they passed by the American Falls and approached the majestic Horseshoe Falls, everyone was soon drenched with water. Kids and grown-ups alike laughed as they enjoyed a once-in-a-lifetime experience.

The boat moved closer and closer to the curtain of water, using its bow thrusters to move sideways and provide everyone on board with a good view. The noise of the waterfalls was tremendous, a deafening roar that drowned out the excited shrieks. The boat spun gracefully on its axis, like a ballerina performing a pirouette, and prepared for the return journey.

The first hint that something was amiss came when a little girl began tugging her mum's arm and pointing at something above. Her mum broke off from taking a pouting selfie and turned her head to look, and when her inflated lips formed a circular shape, Chloè found herself looking in the same direction.

Through the swirling mist, Chloè could just make out the viewpoint where visitors gathered to gaze at the spot where the Niagara River swirled past Goat Island before plunging over the crest of the falls, tumbling 188 feet to the turbulent basin. The viewing platform was breaking up. Chloè watched dumbfounded as over a hundred people suddenly fell through the sky, their fragile bodies tumbling end over end and being swallowed by Horseshoe Falls.

Chloè wasn't sure if she screamed. The noise and shock combined to leave her brain temporarily stupefied. Her fingers tightened around the boat's handrail as the sky seemed to convulse more violently than usual. The vessel strained against the raging rapids, quivering and emitting ominous groans. Even during the highest river spate following heavy rainfall, the waters had never been this turbulent.

Then, the structures lining the river gorge, including the hotels and casinos, began to sway and disintegrate in a slow-motion frenzy. She watched in disbelief as shopping plazas collapsed, burying retail outlets and food courts. The Skylon Tower, essentially a slender stone structure with a revolving restaurant at the top, started oscillating so much that it became a blur. At the same time, the Rainbow International Bridge, connecting America and Canada a half mile downstream, fell apart like a time-lapse video, its crossbeams, cement stanchions and reinforced concrete slabs cascading into the river below, dragging cars, buses and people with it.

The six hundred other people on the boat witnessed the same harrowing sight. Their expressions of joy from moments ago contorted into frozen masks of terror. For several stretched-out seconds, they stood transfixed and speechless. Then the boat lurched and started to corkscrew to starboard. The sudden tilt and turn jolted them out of their paralysis. Looking back, they saw the curtain of water from the falls appear to double in volume, sending over 6000 tons of water *per second* crashing down and swirling towards the boat. Screams erupted from everyone onboard, but the sound was swallowed by the deafening roar of the water. The boat lifted on the sudden swell and heeled over so much that water poured over the gunwale, triggering further pandemonium. Then the vessel found itself riding fifty feet up on the crest of the oncoming wave.

Closer to Horseshoe Falls, two more sightseeing tour boats floundered and capsized, taking twelve hundred passengers and crew beneath the surface. Nobody survived, and weeks later, their crushed and bloated corpses continued to fetch up miles downriver. So many people drowned that day from countless disasters that the Niagara River was choked with the dead all the way to Lake Ontario and Toronto.

In the boat's cockpit, the captain was rendered unconscious. He slumped over the console and accidentally bumped the engine controls. With what little power they had now gone, the boat slalomed through the rapids and its keel was ripped open on rocks. The vessel's bow was submerged as water rushed in, dragging it under in seconds. The stern rose clear of the river. Fifty or so people at the bow, including the girl and her mum, vanished in an instant, their ponchos weighing them down. The rest of the passengers rushed to the back of the boat, shoving and hitting their fellow tourists as they scrambled up the almost-vertical deck.

Chloè held on with all her strength as people scrambled past, crushing her against the rails and making it hard for her to breathe. Then she felt a hand under her armpit, and a kindly middle-aged man pulled her up the incline. Hundreds of people were crammed together at the stern, fighting for the limited space. The boat continued to be carried downriver at a frightening speed. Every few seconds some passengers lost their grip, were washed off their perch by waves, or were pushed overboard by frightened and selfish people. The passenger who helped her was an exception to the trend of everyone for themselves.

On the shore, the destruction continued. On the American side of the border, the ugly monstrosity that was the Niagara Falls Observation Tower, a concrete lookout deck jutting out from the clifftop, snapped clean away and toppled outwards.

Instead of offering unrivalled views of the waterfalls, it now offered an aquatic perspective of an underwater graveyard. The Amtrak trains travelling over the Whirlpool Bridge had left the rail tracks and now looked like immense centipedes, with the bogies and passenger compartments lying in zigzag patterns in the shallows.

The submerged bow grazed the riverbed, causing the craft to gracefully pivot in lazy circles. They drifted past the American Falls, and the current pushed the boat closer to the opposite riverbank. Here, the current was more placid. As the sound of the main falls faded, Chloè listened to the pitiful cries of the survivors clinging to the boat's hull, weeping and praying.

Like all the other passengers she couldn't help but wonder what had happened. Was it a nuclear attack? A comet strike? An earthquake? Whatever had happened, the violent trembling on the shoreline appeared to have subsided. In its aftermath, thick clouds of dust and smoke billowed into the air from collapsed buildings and fires that raged out of control.

A minute later, the boat snagged on the riverbank and passengers jumped clear of the craft. Some of them immediately began to climb the steep wooded slopes. Chloè didn't want to think about what was waiting up there. First she had to focus on helping her passengers. She hopped over the side and landed in knee-deep water, then turned to assist a family behind her.

"Get your hands off my kids, lady," snarled a man with a moustache, and he shoved her in the chest. Chloè fell back onto the sandy beach. The man then rushed past with his partner and their children and joined the exodus away from the river.

Chloè sat there, shocked by the man's reaction.

"I'm only trying to help, dammit!" she shouted at the man's back, her voice cracking, but he either didn't hear or didn't care. Tears welled up in her eyes and she angrily shook them away. In the meantime, the last stragglers evacuated from the boat, which was already breaking into pieces.

"He's a jerk," a voice said nearby.

Chloè turned to see someone sitting on a boulder and pouring water from their sneakers. It was the middle-aged man who had helped her on the boat.

"He's just frightened," she answered.

"Maybe, but he's still a jerk. That family won't last long with an asshole like him in charge."

Chloè looked up at the hundreds of distant figures ascending the riverbank. She asked herself how long any of them would last.

"Just a heads up, the first rule of survival is not to be a clown. Either he'll put his family in danger or someone will be pissed at his attitude and shoot him dead. The second rule is to stay on top of things and think rationally. If you can manage that, then you might just make it out okay."

"Wouldn't it be better to just wait for help?"

"Who do you think is coming? International Rescue?"

"I was thinking of either FEMA or the Red Cross."

"Well, that brings me to the third rule of how to survive the shit hitting the fan: don't just wait around hoping to be saved."

He put on his sneakers, tied them, and stood up. Then he began walking along the riverbank, pausing to glance back.

"Are you coming?"

"Where to?" she asked but found herself scrambling to her feet and hobbling after him over the rocks.

"I know a few folks who have a spot."

"What, like preppers, that kind of thing?"

"Something along those lines," replied the middle-aged man.

Chloè Bouchard watched the people at the motel. She thought back to her old life and how it came to an end that spring morning. She also thought about the middle-aged man who helped her. He was dead now. It was ironic that of all the ways to go, he had passed away from tetanus after cutting his hand on a rusty nail, his body wracked with agony and lockjaw.

That chance encounter on the stricken vessel led to Chloè joining a fledgling group of survivors camped on the shore of Lake Erie. They survived by staying below the radar. When they went scavenging, they did so in small groups of three to six to avoid attracting unwanted attention. They were very selective over who could join them: surgeons, pediatricians, tradesmen, engineers, agricultural experts and others with the right survival skills. Even pizza delivery boys who knew all the shortcuts and dead ends were needed more than company CEOs. Chloè often asked herself why she was allowed to stay and what essential skills she had to offer.

Perhaps the middle-aged man saw something in her that suggested she had what it took to survive.

As the weeks progressed, the group heard stories of atrocities and ethnic cleansing, a settling of centuries-old scores. Finding refugees was normal, but it was the ones fleeing persecution and discrimination that struck a chord with the camp leaders.

So, without any fuss or fanfare, they began to help those in the greatest need.

Chloè waited a few more minutes, peering through the tree branches at the people illuminated by her headlights. Then she opened her door and stepped forwards.

• • •

Kenny watched as the figure approached. It was a young black woman, he saw, heavily armed, wearing cargo pants. She had a languid demeanor with a laid-back presence, but as she got closer, Kenny noticed her hand sliding down the stock of the weapon hanging over her shoulder.

Two Moon went to talk quietly with the woman out of earshot. She looked over his shoulder as they conversed, scanning the motley collection of refugees. Then Two Moon signalled for Kenny to join them.

He introduced Kenny to the young woman, Chloè. She acknowledged him with a terse smile and a nod. "Let me see the sick girl," she said.

They crossed over to the motel and gathered around the girl's bed. She was hooked up to IV drips and sleeping. Her mother looked up at Chloè with big eyes.

"There are others in the camp who have cancer," she said to the mother. "Our doctors are the best available. They'll do all they can for her, ma'am."

Back outside, Chloè gave them brief instructions:

"Get ready to leave in ten minutes. Then turn off your headlamps and follow me. If anyone gets lost or has car trouble, I'm sorry, but we can't wait. And let your horses free. You have ten minutes."

Everyone was itching to get going. The camp, if it met expectations, offered an end to their long journey. Kenny followed Chloè's taillights along local roads, winding their way out of the suburbs. The route had been cleared of abandoned vehicles and other obstructions. After two hours of uneventful driving, the road surface changed from blacktop to hard dirt.

Chloè led them off the road at a small whistle-stop outpost and over bumpy fields. By now, it was daybreak, and in the early morning light, Kenny saw a sign that read **CEDAR CREEK**. A few miles further, they entered a wooded defile that descended sharply. The convoy then passed by a second sign that read **CAMP ERIE**.

Immediately, Kenny was struck by the scale of the campground. It resembled a well-organized military field camp more than a typical refugee hub. The area was vast, enclosed by tall fences lined with razor wire and watched over by watchtowers. Within the sprawling perimeter, tidy rows of green barracks tents were arranged alongside Quonset huts serving as the camp's Headquarters. There was a sizeable vehicle garage and two large, lightweight aluminium structures housing what appeared to be food warehouses, with several fork-lift trucks lined up outside. Tucked behind a set of roller doors, Kenny caught a glimpse of crates stacked to the ceiling, likely holding essential supplies. He also noticed a canteen and kitchen buzzing with early risers forming a queue outside. Across from these facilities, a cluster of pristine white huts adorned with red crosses caught his eye – marking the location of the field hospital. One hut, in particular, stood out with a sign over the entrance reading **INTENSIVE CARE**.

The camp sloped down to the lakeshore and a small bay. At least a dozen boats were anchored in the shelter of two breakwaters. Among them were some fishing trawlers, a catamaran for shallower waters, and a motor launch. There were also some jetskis tied to a floating deck. A part of the beach had been covered with a concrete square where a two-man WASP helicopter was parked next to some fuel blisters. From the bay, a short access road led to a field covered with solar panels.

Chloè must have radioed ahead as a group of people in white smocks came out of the intensive care hut pushing a gurney. They went straight to the school bus, where they quickly moved the girl onto the gurney and took her and her mother into the hut. A second group of men and women, all well-armed, appeared from somewhere and escorted the two prisoners away.

"Wait here while I get you all registered and some digs arranged," Chloè said.

He watched the young woman walk over to the camp headquarters.

Deputy Geddes came up alongside him.

"Looks like they have things under control up here compared to back home. Say what you like about the Canucks, but they don't panic in a crisis."

"We'll see," Kenny answered. Time would tell if Geddes was right.

Chloè returned with paperwork and ID wristbands. The papers included a list of rules, which seemed fair. They included handing in their weapons. Every adult had to sign the forms.

"If anyone breaks the rules, they will be asked to leave," she explained. "We've already had to evict several people. This isn't a prison camp, but we do have to keep some discipline. Camp security is our prime concern."

She explained that the wristbands, some blue and some purple, indicated your work shift – everyone over thirteen had to contribute in exchange for food and a place to stay. There was a kindergarten and classroom for the younger kids.

She then collected their weapons and placed them in her vehicle; they would be locked away until they decided to leave, she explained.

That last comment came as a surprise to Kenny. Maybe he was being naïve, but he thought this was to be their permanent home. Again, time would tell what Chloè meant.

She led them over to the rows of tents and held open a canvas flap, motioning for Kenny, Bethany, Alex, and Deputy Geddes to go in. She joined them. The tent's interior was quite bare, containing several camp beds, each with a rolled-up blanket, a towel, a toothbrush, a bar of soap, and a roll of toilet paper laid out on top. Metal lockers served as wardrobes for their belongings.

"For the first few days, we keep families and groups together to allow them time to adjust. But as new arrivals come in, you'll be asked to bed down in one of the larger tents."

"How often do people show up?" Bethany asked.

"We have a steady influx of refugees," Chloè answered, somewhat guarded.

"What's the maximum capacity of this place?"

"We can accommodate up to five thousand guests and a thousand camp staff. We have a steady turnover but are consistently full."

Chloè finished answering Bethany's questions and then directed her next comments to everyone.

"Now, do any of you have special skills? Such as a medical background or engineering know-how?"

"I was in the Air Force," Alex said.

"Can you fly choppers?"

"A little."

Kenny thought his friend was exaggerating but he didn't say anything.

"We could really use some pilots. That would be great."

Chloè wrote something on her forms.

" Anyone else?"

"I used to be a cop," offered Geddes.

"Noted," Chloè said and made more notes.

Kenny considered mentioning his background as an IAC Researcher based at Jodrell Bank but decided that his particular skills wouldn't be needed, so he stayed quiet. Bethany also chose not to disclose her previous role in the UK Government.

"Okay, then, I'll find you two priority postings," Chloè said to Alex and Geddes as she lowered her clipboard and smiled at them.

"In the meantime, please make yourself at home and don't forget to grab a bite to eat! Welcome to Camp Erie," she concluded.

She left them.

"Well, she seems very friendly," Alex said, watching through the flap as Chloè moved to the tent next door.

"She seems very efficient," said Bethany and moved to close the flap.

"Hey!"

"Let's unpack, have some breakfast, and then take a look around."

Chapter 28

NEW YORK CITY

MADISON PADDLED TOWARDS BATTERY PARK at the tip of Manhattan.

A warm breeze blew against her face, carrying small flecks of ash on the air currents. There were fires burning within the city, probably entire boroughs alight. She had seen the flames and the smoke from New York Harbour, and she had toyed with the idea of turning back and searching for a place further down the coast, but she knew she was just dancing around the issue. The mysterious noises emanating from the ruins were too intriguing. The medley of clanging sounds and tormented wailing beckoned her like a siren's song.

She guided the life raft between a set of wooden piles coated in tar and tied it to the underside of a fishing pier. She stashed the locker onboard. Then, ignoring the seagull droppings, she climbed up through the crisscross timber beams. Emerging at the top, she stood for a moment and soaked in the feeling of standing on solid ground – on American soil.

After spending so long in space and at sea, it took her a few moments to regain her balance. Everything swayed gently from side to side. Madison took in her surroundings and noticed little evidence of the earthquakes in the park. Everything appeared unchanged. The doughnut and pretzel stands were still waiting for customers, and squirrels were still scampering along the pathways. The only unusual thing was the abandoned hoverboards and fishing rods, as well as the overgrown lawns.

The noises came from somewhere up ahead, reverberating around the empty streets and through the man-made canyons. From where she stood the ruined city looked like a formidable obstacle of twisted steel girders and haphazard, lopsided city blocks. But looking closer she saw that, although many skyscrapers had toppled over, some had maintained their structural integrity. They leaned at impossible angles, supported by their neighbours. Their lopsided posture created new tunnels and concrete and glass chasms. Ribbons of smoke billowed out of thousands of shattered windows, forming a hazy cloud over the skyline, its belly glowing a fiery orange.

Madison headed through the park and crossed the first street, weaving around stationary traffic. She then spent time deciding on a safe passage through Lower Manhattan's financial district. Broadway appeared to be her best choice; it didn't look as choked with rubble as the other streets, and it ran the length of Manhattan, or at least it used to. Whatever was causing the noise, Broadway should lead her to its source.

Squeezing past a FedEx truck, she set off on foot. The towering office blocks flanking the road were oddly bent out of shape as if the recent earthquakes had pivoted them around. Some structures looked like they had squatted down, their lower floors crumpled. Madison passed through their shadows. It didn't take much to imagine them crushing her beneath their colossal weight. Each step she took was accompanied by the crunch of glass shards and the fine powdery residue of cement dust that covered the roadway.

It struck her what an incongruous sight she must make - a woman in an astronaut jumpsuit walking through the empty streets of NYC. She thought about the Apollo 11 astronauts welcomed as heroes by New Yorkers with a ticker-tape parade along these same streets, and she felt the cruel irony. No one on Earth knew what she had gone through to reach this point.

The New York Stock Exchange came into view. Designed by the man who introduced skyscrapers to the world, its Classical Revival facade of marble colonnades had caved inwards, flattening the famous trading floors and everyone inside. The only recognizable thing was the boardroom table, which now lay in the street.

Wall Street, the heart of the global financial sector, had quite literally crashed. Originally a component of New Amsterdam's defensive walls and known as de Waal Straat, or Wharf Street, by the Dutch, it was then a slave market before becoming a focal point of capitalism starting in the 1880s. Now, devastating destruction had befallen all eight city blocks from Broadway to the East River, leaving behind a landscape of ruins.

Madison's mind had been honed to shield itself from the constant onslaught of devastation, and she guessed there would be worse sights as she advanced deeper into Manhattan. But seeing Wall Street like this was representative of a nation's collapse - in an instant, the wealthiest country on the planet had descended into a third-world state.

As Madison made her way through Lower Manhattan and Midtown over the next hour, she encountered a plethora of tourist attractions. The Woolworth Building, once a majestic gothic tower, now stood gutted and charred by intense fires. The Flatiron Building, nestled between the once bustling streets of Broadway and Fifth Avenue, leaned over so much that it cast deep, almost pitch-dark shadows as Madison passed under the structure. The once towering Empire State Building was no more, reduced to rubble and dust. Its dramatic collapse left behind a deep crater that glowed like a volcanic caldera, radiating intense heat that forced Madison to keep her distance.

Picking her way around stationary vehicles, climbing over heaps of twisted steel, or moving in a crouching jog past flaming storefronts, Madison asked herself where all the people were. So far, she had seen not a single person, dead or alive. There must be gazillions of corpses trapped under the rubble and lost forever, but what about those caught in the open when the earthquakes hit? The people pinned under pieces of masonry, sliced open by falling glass, or crushed in stampedes? There should be countless bodies lying all around. Had efforts been made to dispose of the dead? And what about the living? Even if millions had been evacuated, there would always be some holdouts who stayed behind to eke out some existence in the pulverized city.

Then, amidst the increasing cacophony of banging, Madison once again heard the mournful sobbing, rising and falling in a rhythmic, swelling sound, leading her closer to the answers she sought.

She stopped at the corner of 34th Street. A large fissure in the road had split Macy's flagship store in half. The corner of the building, which used to resemble the prow of an ocean liner, now featured a huge hole, revealing eleven floors of expensive merchandise. Rows of clothes hung limply in the breeze, their once-vibrant colours now faded. Overturned glass perfume counters lay shattered, while cast-aside fashion accessories, designer handbags and fine jewellery hinted at the store's former elegance, the famous brands now worthless. Madison could even see one of the original wooden escalators exposed to the elements.

She walked across Herald Square and reached Times Square a few minutes later.

The once vibrant neon oasis had turned into a deserted and empty junkyard of abandoned vehicles. Pieces of litter blew around in the wind. With evening approaching quickly, it was a dark and dangerous place to be, so Madison hurriedly moved through it and turned onto Broadway again. Suddenly, she stopped in her tracks.

The wide avenue was illuminated, but not with the bright lights and flashy signs of Manhattan's theater district. Instead, it was lit with burning braziers and flaming firebrands attached to lamp posts. The sight was both chilling and beautiful. The avenue of light stretched into the distance, clearly marked as a passage through the dark city. The melodious human wailing harmonized with the rhythmic clanging, drawing her forwards.

As she passed the famous theatres with faded billboards advertising musicals starring big-name performers, the sorrowful, plaintive cries seemed to change. Now it was more like a mass chanting. Madison arrived at Columbus Circus and swiftly crossed over. The parade of burning firebrands continued through the park entrance. The clanging and chanting reached a crescendo, the sounds so deafening that she had to cover her ears.

The chanting and banging abruptly stopped. At a stroke, there was complete silence, so profound that Madison felt her heart skip a beat. Madison followed the pathway into Central Park and stared wide-eyed at the scene before her. There were more braziers placed at strategic points, lighting the place. A million people had gathered in the park. They were down on their knees, arms raised to the night, their rapt faces flickering in the orange firelight.

After several seconds, a high-pitched chittering trill reached her ears, making the air quiver. It was unlike any sound she had ever heard before, and it came from the mass of human throats. The piping sound seemed to coalesce before spontaneously soaring upwards like a flock of starlings taking flight. Staring in astonishment, Madison focused on the centre of the park, where she was greeted by a sight so surreal that she had to blink repeatedly to confirm that it was real.

A magnificent statue was being erected. People stood in lines, heaving on ropes and singing, experiencing a spiritual bonding in their shared endeavour. The deep timbre of their voices carried over the other sounds. More people hammered metal pegs into the ground and secured the ropes to them. Gradually, the statue began to rise, revealing its form as it emerged into the firelight. Madison saw a crown of spikes representing the sun's rays, a stone tablet inscribed with Roman numerals, and an upraised arm holding a torch of gilded copper.

The Mother of Exiles, The Lady of the Harbor, The New Colossus, Lady Liberty: transported by boat, dragged through the streets, and erected in Central Park.

With one final heave on the ropes, the statue stood erect and gazed over the multitudes. Her oxidized face seemed to shimmer, switching between shadow and light as the flames danced in the breeze. Twin, rusty tear tracks ran over her cheeks, caused by years of traffic pollution. They gave the impression that The Statue of Liberty was crying over the destroyed city. Indeed, she may have been because beyond the statue, Madison could see rows of freshly dug graves stretching away over the parkland. Central Park was not only transformed into a place to pay homage, but it was also the biggest cemetery in North America.

Madison walked along the pathway and stopped near some people who were kneeling on the grass. She looked at them closely. The crowd was made up of a mix of adults and children. She saw people using crutches, people in tattered clothing, and people wearing fur coats and pearl necklaces - the rich and poor mixed together. A man wearing an **I LOVE NYC** t-shirt looked up as she walked past, and his eyes flicked to the NASA badge on her jumpsuit. He smiled, but whether it was out of recognition or spiritual delirium, Madison couldn't tell.

Presently, she came across a large, solitary obelisk encased in scaffolding. The air was filled with the sound of chisels tapping against stone as numerous individuals carefully carved the names of their loved ones onto the memorial. The sheer number of names etched onto the stone was overwhelming, and Madison couldn't help but wonder how many more tombstones would be needed before they were finished.

Madison found a lone rock, sat back and watched.

Chapter 29

**LINDISFARNE/HOLY ISLAND
NORTHERN ENGLAND**

SCOTT FLUNG OPEN THE DOOR and hurried out onto the deck of the emergency hut. The other adults soon followed. All they could see was the darkness of night. A strong breeze brushed against their faces and from beneath the hut they could hear the sound of water gently lapping against the timber base.

Scott's heart pounded like a triphammer in his chest as he flicked on his flashlight and shone it around. The white beam reflected off the obsidian waves. Fabian did the same, and the two men circled around the deck, desperately searching and calling out the boy's name. They met up on the other side.

"Did you spot anything?"

"No."

"Where is he?" Scott asked, sounding more desperate with each passing second. "I don't see the boy."

"Everyone, make sure your head torches are on," instructed Fabian. "If he's out there, the boy might use them as a guide."

If the boy was out there, thought Scott as the others checked their LED lights, he was in trouble. How had they missed him? They had all linked arms, so someone had to notice one of their group suddenly missing. His mind raced with worry.

"I'll have to go out there and look for him?"

"Are you mad?/It's too dangerous!" Fabian and Sara blurted out at the same time.

"I don't have a choice, do I?"

Scott looked around and spotted a red lifebelt fastened to the rail.

"Pass me that. Hold the rope, Fabian."

"No way," said Sara as she grabbed Scott's arm with one hand and held onto Phoebe with the other. "I'm not letting you do it, Scott."

"She's right," Tammy said. "It's too risky."

"Listen, I won't just stand here and do nothing if the boy is lost out there. He can swim, and he might have reached a sandbar. Now, pass me the bloody lifebelt. We don't have time to stand around debating the issue."

Shaking his head, Fabian unclipped the round lifebelt and placed it over Scott's head.

"I'll give you three minutes, and then I'm pulling you back in. No arguing, okay?"

"Five minutes," Scott insisted, threading his arms through the lifebelt. "And feed out as much rope as you can."

Her face pale with worry, Sara kissed him on the cheek. "Please don't take any risks. Promise me."

Scott kissed her back and planted a kiss on Phoebe's head. "I have to do this. We lost Fawad and the boy on the land bridge, so I'll be damned if we lose another kid."

Then he moved down the steps as Fabian played out the nylon safety line, and just before he reached the water, he said, "Everybody, keep your lights on me and the water. If any of you spot him, holler like mad."

He stepped into the icy water and descended the final few steps. The water level rose past his stomach and chest and he still hadn't touched the ground, so he kicked away from the hut and paddled with his feet, while the lifebelt kept his head above the surface.

Scott tried keeping the flashlight from getting too wet as he played the beam all around. By using his other arm and flexing his legs in a loose, circular motion, he was able to glide through the waves and move back and forth in an ever-expanding circle around the emergency hut. The others helped by lighting up the sea's surface. Bit by bit, he moved further out, his eyes scanning the water. Every few seconds, he called the boy's name. He could see Sara's milky face, as translucent as clouded glass, as she watched him.

He couldn't believe how cold the sea was. In no time at all, Scott was shivering. It felt like a tight band was squeezing his chest, making his breathing speed up, and sharp pains stabbed his legs. When he called the boy's name again, his voice sounded trembly. Scott started doing the front crawl to keep warm, but the lifebelt made it difficult to extend his arms very well. Instead, he did the doggy paddle and turned 360 degrees.

The boy wouldn't last long out here; it was just a question of which killed him first - drowning or hypothermia. Swearing and fighting back tears, Scott did another circuit around the hut. His flashlight was growing dimmer by the second. Scott halted and strained his ears, praying that he'd hear the boy calling for help. But there was nothing: just his own harsh breathing and the lapping of the sea.

Then he felt a tug on the nylon rope and the next thing he knew he was being pulled back in. In a fit of temper, Scott strained against it. But even as he did so, he knew the whole endeavour was futile. Unless some miracle turned up, the boy was gone.

A few minutes later, Fabian and Tammy had towed him in. Scott sat on the top step with his head in his hands.

"You did your best," Sara said quietly as she sat alongside him.

"It's my fault."

"No, it's not. No matter how much we try, sometimes bad things just happen."

"We're so lucky we made it this far," Louise chimed in as the gang gathered around. "Back in Windermere, when all of this began, you just wanted to get your family back safe, and you did. Everything else that happened, good and bad, wasn't part of the plan. But you've rescued so many people along the way without even thinking about your own safety. What you've achieved is just incredible."

If the young teacher's assistant was hoping to boost his morale, it wasn't working. Scott felt dejected. Again, he wondered how things might have played out had Alan still been around. The geography teacher's knowledge might have prevented this latest tragedy. Then again, it had been his friend's idea to use the land bridge to get back to England, and that cost him his life. Maybe, Scott thought, all of this was meant to be.

"You're cold," Sara said, interrupting his thoughts. "Come inside and warm up."

"We'll try again at first light, chief," Fabian promised. "It will be low tide by then."

Scott shook his head and peered into the night, saying, "I'm staying here."

He knew what the others were thinking; he didn't need to see the looks passing between them. His mind was made up, and that was that.

"Do you want me to stay with you?"

"It's best that you go inside with Phoebe and rest."

"I could help you keep watch," Tammy offered. "Fabian as well."

"I'd rather be alone if you don't mind."

Someone draped a warm blanket around his shoulders, and one by one, they drifted back inside.

They found the missing boy the next morning. His body lay facedown in the sand not ten feet from the causeway. He must have got out of his depth and drowned, or become entangled in seaweed, or the boy's feet became stuck in the sludgy muck and he had suffocated. They stood in a circle around his inert form, each lost in thought. Some of the boy's friends found the episode too much, and Louise ushered them away. Somewhere, someone was throwing up.

Scott went down on his haunches and ran his fingers through the boy's hair. He thought back to that day they had gone hunting together and how the boy opened up to Scott, pledging that one day he would find his parents. Well, he was reunited with them now, Scott thought, struggling to contain his emotions. Nearby, a gull watched them from the hut roof.

"We'll use the canvas sheet to carry him to the island," he mumbled. "The least we can do is give him a decent burial."

The wet sand was reluctant to give up its prize, and they had to tug the boy free. The task was made more unpleasant because of the sucking and squelching noises. When they finally had him wrapped in the canvas, they started across the uncovered causeway towards the island. The sea had fully withdrawn and they could see it scintillating far away in the morning light.

They walked for about one hour, their progress slowed down by the heavy burden they were carrying. Nobody spoke much. It felt like a funeral procession. In due course they reached the island, and the causeway turned into a road that led to a sandy beach. On a short headland there were some old overturned fishing boats that had been cut in half years earlier, had doors added to their flattened ends, and repurposed as sheds. Someone proposed temporarily leaving the body until they found a suitable burial place. All the boat sheds were unlocked so they randomly chose one, left the boy inside, and continued.

They hadn't discussed what they would do if the island had occupants. Would Scott's gang leave and find somewhere else, or would they try to join forces? What kind of welcome would they receive? It turned out to be a moot point.

Holy Island was a small place, just a few miles long from end to end, and it didn't take long to explore. Its terrain was predominantly rocky fields fringed with rocky coves and cliffs, but its northern edge was marked with dunes as it met the causeway, while a narrow isthmus led to a long peninsula pointing over a wide bay to the mainland. Dangerous reefs acted as a natural defence against anyone approaching from that direction. There was also ample water from natural springs.

At the island's heart was an old medieval priory around which a charming village had developed over the centuries. The village comprised a few dozen cottages and tourist guesthouses. The village centre – basically, a pub and a corner shop – overlooked the tiny fishing cove and jetty.

The only place they couldn't investigate was the motte and bailey castle. Originally constructed with timber and later stone, it was perched atop a stubby little hill that offered unobstructed views all around and was within a short stroll from any part of the island. Despite numerous restoration projects funded by charity organizations, it remained in a state of disrepair. It was covered in vines, and its tiny rooms were so choked with weeds that they proved inaccessible. The stairs leading to the battlements were crumbling apart, making them unsafe to climb. They would have to postpone their exploration of the castle for later. But there were no signs of life anywhere, and by lunchtime, Scott was satisfied the island was empty.

The priory grounds were chosen as a suitable resting place for the deceased boy. Tammy arranged for a grave to be dug while Scott and Fabian went back to retrieve the body. Upon their return, a hole several feet deep had been prepared. They lowered the canvas-wrapped body down, said a few words, and then filled the grave.

By now, the afternoon was coming to a close. They decided to spend their first night in a large manor house, which before the earthquakes, was a four-star hotel. Inside was cool and smelled musty but it was clean and had plenty of rooms. For tonight, they opted to bed down together in the dining room. In the morning, they would make better sleeping arrangements and also devise defence protocols to safeguard against raiders. Until then, they would cover the windows with black drapes to keep out the torchlight.

Supper consisted of tinned sardines grilled over a primus stove, soup bouillon, honey-flavored water, and a cup of instant coffee with powdered milk for those on watch.

The room gradually fell silent as everyone else drifted off to sleep, leaving Scott and Sara as the only ones awake. Scott kept thinking about the boy, replaying events in his mind and wondering what he could have done differently. If they didn't learn from their mistakes, they would keep repeating them and more people would die. It weighed heavily on him. Sara, keenly aware of her husband's emotions, did her best to reassure him. She reminded him of how, in his former life as a primary school teacher, his biggest problem was teaching young kids the basics of reading and writing. Now he was the leader of a band of people who had completed an epic exodus to try and survive a global apocalypse. Nobody could prepare for what they had been through.

Instead of dwelling on the "what ifs," Sara asked about their future plans. Scott began to relax as the tension left his shoulders. He shared his desire to set up a small school at the manor house where the kids could learn academic subjects as well as essential survival skills such as self-defence, treating wounds and poisonings, herbal medicine, map reading and finding their way around devastated areas, semaphore and morse code, camp security, emergency contingency plans, and childbirth from pregnancy to delivery. Teaching these skills to young children was daunting but necessary for the long-term survival and growth of their community.

For a certain grace period, they'd be able to "dine out" on the leftovers of the fallen society by gathering stockpiles of canned food from supermarkets and other abandoned places. But there would come a time when this came to an end. Then they would need to be completely self-sufficient - killing the odd hare wouldn't be enough. Unlike previous generations who made things they used every day and grew their own food, Scott's generation relied on modern conveniences, a society of consumers. They had become disconnected from the basic skills their lives would now depend on. Starting tomorrow, they had to relearn how the new world worked. They would have to experiment with novel technology.

Scott believed that they couldn't do this alone. He foresaw a time when they would have to establish contact with other remote groups of survivors. That would bring risks, including violent confrontations and the spread of disease between groups. This would be a problem for the future.

Lastly, they would have to reset the calendar, thinking in terms of Before the Cataclysm, and After the Cataclysm. The past was gone. Now, the world was starting again from the year dot.

• • •

The following morning, Fabian left early with Saskia. He wrote a note for his friends, stating that he intended to set up concealed positions to cover the causeway and fishing harbour. Tammy and Scott, after having breakfast, decided to thoroughly scout the cliffs and coves beyond the castle.

The tide was out, so the island was currently surrounded by sandflats. As they walked through the deserted village to the dock, Scott thought about how they would have to adjust to the changing tides. To prevent more tragic accidents, they'd have to figure out the tide schedule and plan their trips to the mainland carefully. It took two hours to walk across the causeway, so four hours in total to go there and come back. That left them with six or seven hours to scavenge, just to be on the safe side. They had seen many small boats with outboard engines that they could use, but Scott knew the fuel wouldn't last forever. Maybe they should have a rowing boat ready at the emergency hut at all times, along with some food, water, and signal flares. It might also be a good idea to set up an alternative refuge on the mainland for when they were delayed and couldn't return to the causeway in time.

There were so many things to think about. When they had been on the road, Scott's main objectives were to find shelter each night, some food to eat, and to always have a destination in mind. Now that they had found a place to settle, their priorities had changed. Building a community would take years of hard work.

With these thoughts running through his head, Scott followed Tammy as she led the way. They soon got to the dock, where boats were sitting lopsided on the exposed seabed. At the end of the dock there was a stack of lobster pots and some stone steps leading down to a pebble beach. They crunched their way over the pebbles, following the coastline around the circular cove. From there, they approached the castle. Following a pathway overgrown with brambles, they passed through the castle's shadow. Beyond the castle, they came across an old brick structure with several arched entrances barred with wooden gates. The two of them scrambled over and went inside. Above their heads, they could hear roosting pigeons. Lined up against the rear wall were some fire pits covered with grills: the old lime kilns that Scott had told Tammy about. They could smoke out the pigeons, clean the place up, and use the kilns to bake bread.

Emerging back into the light, they kept walking. The pathway started to get bumpier, twisting and turning until it led up a steep hill and then sharply descended to the foot of a line of cliffs fringed with a small beach. The cliffs were dotted with a bunch of caves.

"Let's check them out," Tammy said. "We have time before the tide turns."

They approached the caves positioned at the base of the cliffs. The first one was shallow and not much more than a scooped-out hole. The ground inside was a jumble of smooth boulders and rock pools. The next cave was bigger, with the sea carving out a large space in the limestone cliffs. The cave ceiling was covered in mussels and limpets, and the floor was littered with thousands of cockleshells. There was a strong smell of rotting fish.

A third cave was several metres above the beach and higher than the tide line. A set of evenly spaced rocks provided a convenient passage to the entrance, but Scott still found the climb difficult. Tammy, being younger and fitter, got there first. She slipped into the cave mouth.

"Scott, come and look at this."

He found her on her knees, examining something on the cave floor. Intrigued, Scott approached to get a closer look at what she had discovered.

"Seems like we've got company," she said, looking back.

Inside the cave, there were the remains of a campfire with a tripod and a frying pan. Arrayed around the campfire lay an assortment of cooking and eating utensils bearing scraps from a meal. In one corner of the cave was a sleeping mat, blankets, and a wooden clothes chest. Slender tendrils of sea kelp had been hung from the ceiling to dry, and Scott also noticed a fishing rod and tackle box.

Tammy held her hands over the fire's grey ashes.

"It's still warm," she said, "which means somebody has been here very recently."

It also means they weren't alone on the island after all, Scott thought. Whoever was living in the cave might still be around unless they were on a foraging trip or Scott's party had frightened them off. He went over to the cave mouth. Most of the island wasn't visible from here; all he could see was the distant white-capped waves and the peninsula.

"What should we do?" Tammy asked.

"Nothing, for now."

"What about their things? That fishing rod could be handy."

"Let's just leave everything as it is. Whoever they are, they'll show their face soon enough, and we don't want to upset them too much. In the meantime, we carry on with our plans."

They left the cave and resumed their exploration.

Chapter 30

BERN
SWITZERLAND

THE BEATEN-UP MOPED BROKE down on the outskirts of Bern. Earlier, Timo had to stop in the lakeside town of Interlaken to find a pharmacy. His wound was bleeding again, and he needed to change the dressing. It was just coming light, and there was a mist rolling in off the water, lending the wrecked town an otherworldly feel. The moped's headlight struggled to pierce through the dense fog as it crept along the empty streets, its engine murmuring softly.

He located a pharmacy just across from the shattered remains of the Metropole Hotel, wedged between a chocolatier and a shop selling designer Swiss watches. Leaving the moped in the street, Timo went inside with Genny and searched through the overturned shelves until he found what he was looking for.

Back outside, his wound freshly patched up, they hit the road again.

The countryside opened up, and Timo was relieved to leave the mountains behind. The sun came out and a freshening breeze blew into their faces as they sped along, blowing away the tension of the last few days. Genny enjoyed the ride, her curious gaze drinking in their surroundings and her damp nose sniffing the air. It brought a smile to Timo's lips. He felt a sense of renewal surge through him.

By midday, Timo's keen eyes caught sight of Bern in the distance. The capital of Switzerland, Bern was built around a crook in the Aare River. Its Old Town boasted origins from the 12th Century. Although it had been many years since Timo last visited, he remembered the pretty church steeples and the wooded riverbanks. Now, as he approached from the south, he noticed a sombre haze of dust enveloping the city.

They passed the small airport with its single runway and damaged hangars and followed the river as it wound through the commuter belt. Riding past the camping sites over the river from the city zoo, the engine suddenly started making grating sounds and black smoke began to belch from the exhaust. They began to lose speed and then the engine quit altogether, causing the moped to coast to a stop. Timo cursed lightly under his breath.

He turned the key and pressed the starter button. The engine emitted a feeble whine. Timo climbed off.

"That was adventurous while it lasted," he said to Genny, who was busy relieving herself at the side of the road. Timo collected their belongings, wheeled the moped onto the grass verge, and let it rest on the ground. He noticed a troop of monkeys chasing each other up and down the far riverbank, and a short distance away, two elephants having a drink. Timo tried to recall the way to the big house where his parents lived with their hippie friends, assuming they were still alive. The residence was nestled in one of the parks in the Old Town, in central Bern. Compared to places like Zürich and Basel, Bern was relatively small with a pre-disaster population of a hundred thousand people. By car or motorcycle, in normal times, they could do it in thirty minutes. But the odds of making the whole journey by moped were always doubtful because of the quake damage. On foot, it would take considerably longer. Still, with luck, they should make it before dusk.

Timo decided that the best plan would be to follow the river north until he reached the bridge near the Einstein Museum. Then, he would take a wide thoroughfare through Casino Square and pass by the astronomical clock to reach the Old Town.

For weeks, all they seemed to do was walk through dense forests, towering mountains and streets littered with debris. Every time they tried to settle in one place, circumstances transpired to drive them onwards. Hopefully, the end of their trek was drawing closer. Returning to his birthplace carried a sense of poetic irony for Timo, even though he had been distant from his parents. Timo wasn't sure how he would feel reuniting with them after years apart. He wasn't expecting a dramatic, misty-eyed reunion; too much water had passed under the bridge for that. Yet the pull of home was undeniable. What was the old adage? "Home is a shelter from storms." Well, Timo's instincts were telling him to go home.

They strolled along the grassy riverbank, avoiding the worst of the damage. The city of Bern, much like all other places, was transformed forever. Centuries of cultural heritage and architectural marvels were nothing but a memory; now, it looked like something from old wartime newsreels. A thick shroud of dust hung over the city, blotting out the sun.

He let Genny run ahead. He trusted her not to wander or to become lost and her acute hearing and vision served as an early warning system scanning for danger. They passed by some sports fields and outdoor lidos, and soon after, the river started curving to the right. Up ahead were the mangled remains of the bridge, but fortunately the set of pedestrian steps were intact, and they found themselves on the wide thoroughfare leading to Casino Square.

The streets were marked by the aftermath of multiple earthquakes. Nature had not only shaken the city once, but had repeatedly pummeled Bern, causing it to shift up, down, and sideways. Some buildings had ended ten feet higher than their neighbours, while others had fallen into deep sinkholes or fissures. Timo saw entire tenement buildings that had been pulled off their foundations and slid horizontally, finishing up several meters down the street. Around Casino Square, every building taller than one story was in ruins. Pavements had burst open and tramlines lay twisted in huge zigzags, with trolleys filled with passengers overturned and crushed by falling debris. The sheer physical magnitude of the earthquakes was beyond comprehension, and Timo passed through the ruins like a ghost. Everywhere was eerily quiet.

They turned onto Town Hall Alley, known for its pavement cafes and beer cellars, a popular meeting place during normal times. Genny stopped and stared into one of the cellars. Timo saw her hackles rise and heard a low growl in the back of her throat. Timo held onto her collar to stop her from bounding down the stairs.

"What is it, girl?"

Timo peered into the dark opening but couldn't see anything. Maybe she had spotted a stray cat. So long as it wasn't more rats.

He was about to resume their journey when the most dreadful growl coiled its way out of the beer cellar, making the fine hairs on the back of Timo's neck stand up. A horrible stench of bad breath accompanied the sound. Suddenly, a huge fur-covered head with a jaw filled with the largest, most menacing teeth Timo had ever seen emerged from the darkness. Timo, so petrified that he felt his mouth drop open, released his hold on the dog collar. Genny was off, fleeing for her life down the street. Timo stared slack-jawed as the monstrous creature squeezed its bulk through the opening into the daylight.

He barely had time to recognize it as a brown bear before a massive paw swiped at his face. He ducked, but not fast enough to avoid the claws altogether. He felt one of them painfully cut his scalp. He leaped back from the threshold of the beer cellar. Timo fell on his back and when the bear made a grab for him he kicked and thrashed at it with his legs. One blow caught the bear on the snout, and while it was busy shaking its huge head, Timo turned over and started to scuttle away on all fours. Another roar made him look over his shoulder. The animal was coming for him, and he could see its muscles rippling beneath the fur coat - 400kg of raw power.

As the bear struck again, this time hitting his foot with a gentle swipe, it tore his boot away and rolled Timo onto his back. Then the bear rose onto its hind legs, towering at nine feet tall, its massive body casting a shadow over Timo. The bear roared at the sky, its jaws twisting in fury and sending specks of saliva flying. The animal tilted its head and looked down at Timo, who felt insignificant and vulnerable.

In the next moment, Genny reappeared. She ran around the bear, barking like crazy. Timo thought the bear looked bemused as it watched the pesky dog, but soon its intrigue turned to anger. The bear dropped onto its front paws and began chasing Genny, growing increasingly angry as the puppy dodged its swipes.

With the bear distracted, Timo came to his feet and hobbled away as quickly as possible. He spotted an abandoned car and hurried over to it. He pulled open the rusted door, fell onto the seat, and banged the door shut. He looked through the windscreen, terrified his brave puppy was seconds from being torn to pieces, but to his relief, he saw Genny racing to safety again. For a few seconds, the bear considered running after it. Instead, it turned its attention back to Timo.

The bear approached, swaying its head to and fro, trying to spot its prey inside the car. When it saw Timo, it started making a huffing sound, then emitted a low moan, gradually escalating into a deafening growl that reverberated through the desolate streets. He'd never been so scared in his life. Being crushed by falling debris or blown to smithereens by the malfunctioning Hadron Collider was bad enough. But to be eaten alive by a rampaging bear filled him with ultimate horror.

It must have escaped from the zoo or wandered out of the forest. Then Timo remembered the city's bear pit from which Bern derived its coat of arms. For centuries, tourists had flocked to Bern to catch a glimpse of its renowned brown bears. Now, those very same creatures were roaming the city streets and hunting for their next meal.

Wherever the creature came from didn't matter to Timo as it launched itself at the car. Rising on its back legs again, it slammed its front paws onto the bonnet, denting the bodywork and making the vehicle jolt. Timo yelled involuntarily as he watched the bear tear away the wipers, the grill and the engine cowling. It dropped back onto the road and lurched around the side, peering at Timo through the front passenger window, pressing its face against the glass for a better look. Then it licked the glass, smearing it with thick saliva. Suddenly, the bear slammed a paw against the window, shattering it and thrusting a front leg inside. Timo cringed away, desperately trying to dodge the deadly claws. The bear growled in fury. Then it withdrew its paw and stomped to the back of the car.

Timo cleared the blood from his eyes so that he could keep track of the bear. The animal rested its front paws on the tailgate, causing the front of the car to rise off the ground. It hit the rear window, making the glass frost over like a cobweb. A second blow shattered it completely, showering glass fragments over the rear shelf. Timo stayed in the front seat as the bear pushed its head into the car, tearing and scratching the upholstery with both paws. It was so close that

Timo could smell its sweaty, musky odour and feel its hot breath as he cowered in the footwell.

Still unable to reach its quarry, the bear retreated and in a frenzy of rage grabbed the car and shook it violently as if it were a mere toy. Timo was flung around inside, his body striking the sides and roof. The bear clutched the tailgate and hoisted the rear of the car. Then it tore off the bumper with its powerful jaws and started to chew on the boot for a moment before slamming the car down. Quickly, it turned its attention to the roof, pounding the metal. Timo watched the roof crumple in a series of dents, each one coming closer and closer to his head. He hunkered down as the car was systematically flattened like he was trapped inside a junkyard crusher. The noise was terrific; Timo couldn't even hear his own screams.

The bear, not satisfied with just crushing the car, proceeded to turn the vehicle over and roll it across the roadway. Timo's world became a kaleidoscope of light and dark, of up and down as he found himself spun around and around.

With a screech of rending metal, the bear yanked off the doors and side panels, exposing Timo to the massive animal. In the brief lull before the coup de grace, he imagined he could hear Genny whimpering.

Run, girl. Run far away, Timo thought. *There's no point in both of us dying.*

Timo had barely finished thinking this when he was startled by the loud crack of a gunshot. The bear, in mid-lunge, seemed to falter. As two more gunshots rang out, the bear abruptly lurched and staggered. Timo saw several gushers of bright blood erupt from the animal's body, immediately turning its fur coat slick. It roared and half turned just as another gunshot sounded, and this one hit it square on the forehead. The animal made a desperate effort to stay upright, reaching out to clutch the trashed car, but then it lost its grip and collapsed to the ground with a resounding thud and was still.

Timo gasped for breath, trying not to panic. He had no idea who had shot the bear or if he was in the sniper's crosshairs. He struggled to free himself but was hemmed in the car and couldn't move. He heard footsteps crunching on the road, and then a pair of brown rigger boots appeared close to his head.

In the next instant, a face appeared. A man with messy hair, greying at the temples and held back with a camouflage sweatband, peered in at him. The face seemed familiar. Older than he remembered, but familiar.

"Hey, son," the man said as he took a drag from his spliff. "Good to have you back."

Chapter 31

CAMP ERIE
CANADA

KENNY AND ALEX WALKED DOWN to the beach together. It was their second day at Camp Erie, and a sense of urgency gripped the camp as reports surfaced of a new group of exiles migrating north from across the border in America. The camp leaders urgently needed some intel on the group – their identities, current location, and intended destination. Alex, eager to contribute, had volunteered to take the chopper up and take a look. Kenny decided to go along for the ride.

Earlier that morning, Bethany brought them some good news from the intensive care hut. The girl was doing well after her surgery to remove the brain tumour and was due to begin her follow-up treatment. It seemed she was in good hands and the doctors appeared optimistic. The positive developments spread around the camp, giving everyone a much-needed boost to their morale.

Kenny and Alex arrived at the sandy cove and made their way to the helipad. A crew was unloading supplies from the catamaran onto the floating deck out on the water. The weather was sunny with a pleasant breeze rippling the lake's surface, making it ideal for flying.

"So, how are things progressing with Chloè?" Kenny asked. It was no secret that his friend was attracted to the young Canadian woman.

"Good, really good," Alex said with a quick smile as he played around with his walkie-talkie.

"Have you asked her out?"

"Haven't had the chance to do it yet. There aren't many places I can take her, in case you haven't noticed. I was thinking maybe a stroll along the lakeshore under the stars one evening."

"Very romantic."

"Yes."

"Does she even fancy you?"

"Of course she does, buddy. Have you noticed the way she always looks at me? Chloè is just playing it cool, but I will ask her out. Soon."

Alex pointed at the chopper.

"She's all fuelled up and ready to go," he added, hurrying forward.

Kenny shook his head and caught up with his friend.

"You should do, Alex. There's no time to waste and if you don't ask her out then someone else will. What's the worst that can happen?"

Alex pretended that he hadn't heard as he did his pre-flight checks.

The WASP HX-2 was small compared to other helicopters. With its vibrant red fuselage, yellow tail boom and bug-eyed canopy, it certainly resembled the insect it was named after. Alex had given him detailed specs earlier: the two-seater chopper had a cruising speed of 90mph, although its one hundred horsepower engine could go faster if required. With a maximum range of about 120 miles and a hover ceiling of one thousand metres, the helicopter was well-suited for scouting missions.

"Are you sure you know how to fly this thing?" Kenny asked as they climbed aboard, put on ear mufflers, and strapped themselves in. "I thought you were just a driver?"

"Please," came the Royal Navy man's voice through the headphones as the rotor blades whirred around above their heads. "I used to land Merlin helicopters on the back of moving ships in stormy seas. This is child's play."

He slowly pulled up the collective with his left hand, and Kenny felt the chopper lift. It immediately settled back onto its skids with a small jolt. Alex smiled sheepishly, saying, "I'm just a little rusty."

He twisted the throttle to give the rotor blades more lift, and they rose again, gaining more height this time.

"It's like riding a bike, see?"

Alex used the pedals to turn the tail boom until they were pointing over the lake. Then he tilted the blades, and they started flying over the floating dock. Kenny spotted Chloè Bouchard with the people working down there. Alex also noticed her, gave her a thumbs up, and saluted. She waved back. Maybe she had fallen for his friend's charms, after all, Kenny thought.

"So where is this place we're headed?"

Kenny studied the map they had been given.

"It's called New Bethlehem. It's about fifty miles south of here."

"That's great. We'll have plenty of fuel to get there, look around for those folks, and come back. Easy peasy."

It felt strange to be flying again. Kenny was okay with planes, but helicopters were a different story. The constant vibration and the smell of aviation fuel often made him feel nauseous, and he hoped they had some sick bags onboard. It didn't help that their last experience of flying had ended in disaster when the President's 'Doomsday Plane' crashed into the Gateway Arch.

Alex appeared unfazed by their near-death experience. He was in his element, humming The Ride of the Valkyries as they skimmed over Lake Erie. The blue water sparkled in the sunlight, a seemingly endless expanse of water stretching to the left and right as they flew south towards the far shore.

In a very short amount of time, they had crossed the invisible border once again. Kenny felt a bit anxious about returning to America so soon after their difficult journey. However, their instructions were straightforward: locate the group of refugees, report their whereabouts, and then head back to Camp Erie. They were not supposed to land under any circumstances; it was strictly a scouting mission. Nonetheless, Kenny shared his friend's desire to assist in any way possible, and helping more people to safety seemed like the right thing to do.

The lake gave way to land and Alex increased their height as they passed over Sheridan and turned east. The countryside was mostly covered in forests with the occasional small township. As they flew over, Kenny focused a pair of binoculars on them. The houses were built from brick and timber, and many had burned down, leaving charcoaled carcasses and broken chimney breasts. He saw a few with children's swimming pools and swings, as well as a few RTs parked in driveways, but no people were in sight.

They soon reached Interstate 86 and followed it for several miles. The highway was crowded with stalled traffic. The earthquakes must have struck during the early morning hours, throwing cities into chaos as people tried to flee. Some desperate drivers had attempted to veer off the congested highway, ploughing through fields and woods, but they hadn't gone far before having to abandon their cars. A mile or two further, they encountered the source of the traffic jam. The Memorial Bridge at Bemus Point had split in multiple places, with the bridge spans collapsing and leaving massive gaps. Alex piloted the chopper over the logjam, revealing traffic backed up all the way to New Bethlehem on the other side of the bridge. Just outside of town was a big multi-vehicle wreck.

"Where were those people we're after last seen?" Alex inquired.

"At a truck stop near Wegmans."

"On the south side of town, then," he said. He changed direction and flew over the small community until he reached the rail tracks. Flying barely fifty feet above the land, the sensation of speed as the ground went by in a blur made Kenny feel queasy. Alex must have noticed his pale complexion because an amused expression appeared on his face, which Kenny found annoying.

"Can't you just... you know?" Kenny said, gesturing at the land whizzing by.

"What?"

"I don't know. Fly more sensibly."

"No one made you come along. And if we fly too high, we won't be able to spot them, right?"

Alex pointed out of the cockpit window.

"Wegmans is coming up. Keep a close lookout."

They flew over the looted supermarket and soon spotted the truck stop. There were a few rigs and a destroyed diner, but they couldn't see any sign of the refugees. They circled back for another pass and hovered in the air, the downdraft kicking up dust devils.

"How long ago was the last reported sighting?" asked Alex.

"At daybreak."

"If they've left the area, they could be anywhere."

Alex was correct. If the refugees were here, they couldn't miss a chopper flying right above their heads, and they'd come into the open unless they were too frightened. Kenny started to look around for anywhere they could take cover. He saw a few half-destroyed buildings, but nothing practical stood out. He studied his map.

"There's a camping spot a couple of miles to the east. Let's try there.

"Okay," Alex replied. He tapped the fuel gauge and added, "We need to watch the time. I don't want to run out of gas on the way back."

They swung low around the southern approaches and thirty seconds later found themselves above the RV campground. It was deserted.

"Where the fuck are they?" Alex asked through gritted teeth.

"Maybe they ran into trouble. We had a tough time getting here, remember? If I was them, I'd be nervous about showing my face. Or they could have turned back."

"Why would they do that, pal, if they are so close to safety?"

"I can think of a dozen reasons, all of them bad."

Alex looked pointedly at their remaining fuel and then shrugged. "We'll go a few miles south to see if we can find them. But only for a short time, then we head home. Understood?"

Kenny nodded. "You're in charge."

They raced through the air for several minutes, leaving New Bethlehem behind. Piloting the WASP, Alex darted from point to point while Kenny searched with his binoculars. Below them, a glistening silver ribbon led them over the once-picturesque town of Lewis Run, marking the path of the east branch of the Tunungwant Creek.

"We can't go any further," Alex said. "If we do, we'll be flying on fumes."

He started to turn the cyclic control to change course, but Kenny grabbed his arm.

"Take us down," he said into his mic.

"No way. Our orders are to try and locate them — not to land."

"I don't mean put us down. Just take us lower; I think I've seen something by the creek."

Reluctantly, Alex dove the chopper down. They passed over some low hills covered in scrub and then over the creek itself. Then they spotted them: a long line of vehicles winding along a dirt road running parallel to the watercourse. They counted over thirty cars, pickups and small trucks.

"They're going the wrong way," Kenny commented. "They need to turn around."

"I can see that, pal."

"Do something. Give them a sign, or whatever."

"I ain't going any lower. D'you see that big flatbed there? They have a huge fucking gun strapped on the back. If we fly too close and some nervous, trigger-happy kid opens up on us, then we'll be toast. I don't like the thought of being burned alive in a fireball, pal."

He pulled back on the controls and took the chopper up, bringing loud objections from Kenny.

"Hold on to your horses, will you," Alex said to ward off his friend's protests. "Do you see what I see?"

Alex pointed out of the chopper's canopy at something beyond the creek. Kenny followed the line of his finger. There was another road containing another line of vehicles likewise heading south. Further away, several more roads and dirt tracks were choked with cars and trucks - hundreds of them, all going roughly in the same direction.

"There's got to be thousands of people down there, Alex," Kenny said, out of breath. "It doesn't make sense. Where are they all going?"

"Shit," his friend exclaimed. "Okay, that's it. I've made a decision. Screw the orders. We need to put down somewhere, refuel, and follow them to wherever the hell they are going."

Kenny looked around. They had left the town of Lewis Run behind; all he could see for miles was open countryside.

"How do we do that?"

"Look on your map for the nearest filling station."

"Will that work? Can we use regular petrol on a chopper?"

"I'm pretty sure the valves will get messed up and the seals will get clogged with contaminants. I'll need to strip down the engine and clean it up later. But it should work in theory."

"In theory?"

"Do you want to help these people or not? Just find me a filling station and I'll worry about the rest."

They located a filling station just outside of Custer City, landed next to the forecourt, refueled the helicopter with leaded fuel, and were back in the air within five minutes. Then they quickly flew over the barren countryside to catch up with the exodus of refugees.

When they found the group, their numbers had increased even more. In addition to vehicles, there was also a large group of horse riders trotting alongside. One rider at the front caught Kenny's attention, so he focused his binoculars on the figure.

He quietly swore to himself, then burst into laughter, causing Alex to look at him with concern.

"What the hell is wrong with you? Don't you go full Tonto on me, pal."

Kenny couldn't stop laughing. He lowered the binoculars, glanced at his friend, and then looked through them again to make sure that he wasn't imagining things. He wasn't.

"Are you going to tell me what's so funny, or do I have to guess?"

"It's Young Little Wolf. Two Moon's youngest son."

"What about him?" Alex glanced away from the helicopter's controls and looked through the canopy at the horse riders below. "What are you talking about?"

"He's down there. Dammit, he's leading them!" Kenny was rocking with uncontrolled mirth.

"He can't be. We left him behind days ago."

"Well, he must have changed his mind and come north after all. Not to escape but to gather support. They're heading back home."

"Piss off, pal, and stop pulling my leg." Alex's voice trailed away and a startled expression appeared on his face, his eyes widening. "I don't fucking believe it," he added in hushed tones.

It was an incredible sight that brought a lump to Kenny's throat. There was little doubt in his mind what they were witnessing here. What had been a mass exodus of displaced people fleeing from vengeful militia groups had been transformed into one huge armed force with one ambition in mind: to reclaim their homes. They were led by a fiery and passionate young man who had decided to make a stand.

"This isn't happening," Kenny heard his friend saying repeatedly, but they were seeing it unfold right before them.

They followed the multitude of people for several miles. Then Alex gained altitude, increased their speed and banked east.

"What are you doing? We need to keep tracking them."

"I think I see where they are heading," Alex replied.

In a matter of seconds, they soared high above a shallow valley. Nestled by a streambed, Kenny spotted a large tented camp with about two dozen parked vehicles. A distinctive flag bearing a shovel and a musket marked the camp as belonging to the New Virginian Civil Defence Force – the Lansing Town Militia. They must have been tracking refugees north for hundreds of miles, driving them onwards and committing atrocities. This was their main campsite, hidden away in the valley – or so they thought. Now, unbeknownst to the militia, an attack was imminent.

Kenny gazed down and could see tiny figures below, going about their normal duties, unaware of the impending danger. There was no sense of panic, no indication that they knew what was about to happen. Alex hovered some distance away, the chopper's presence unnoticed by the unsuspecting people in the camp.

They watched the large force slow down as it neared the valley. They gathered together into a unified mass, and Young Little Wolf rode among the refugees, issuing orders. Then his armed force split up. One detachment of horseriders approached the entrance to the valley, getting ready to launch a direct attack against their opponents. Young Little Wolf was in the vanguard of this group. They made maximum use of the terrain and cover, being careful not to reveal themselves until the last moment. Two additional detachments manoeuvered around the flanks to reach positions on the high ground at the edge of the valley. From there, they could shoot down into the camp, pinning their opponents into position. While all of this was happening, individuals driving vehicles equipped with guns headed to the far end of the valley and began setting up an *ad hoc* ambush to intercept any enemy combatants who might flee in their direction after the fighting.

From Kenny and Alex's birds-eye view, the battle plan was decidedly simple and decidedly deadly. With Young Little Wolf leading the frontal assault, they intended to trap the militia in a classic pincer movement, driving their opponents before them into the path of the ambushers. Meanwhile, marksmen manning the valley sides would cause chaos and pick off any stragglers. The valley would play a pivotal role, corralling the militia into an ever-narrowing space where they'd be too constricted to mount a defence.

Young Little Wolf's band collected together in some bushes, and then they burst out of hiding and charged headlong into the camp, firing from the saddle. Alex flew nearer and Kenny raised his binoculars to watch the drama unfold. Taken unawares, the militia barely had time to react as the horseriders closed with them. In seconds, Young Little Wolf and his warriors rode into the midst of the enemy.

With the element of surprise on their side, the attackers immediately had the upper hand. Their opponents could barely muster a defence. Here and there, Kenny saw a few bands of militiamen coalesce into small knots and fight back to back, but they were cut down by heavy fire, and as each of them fell dead they were scalped and left bleeding over the ground. Whooping, Young Little Wolf was in the thick of it, claiming a handful of kills.

Driven back through the tents, the surviving militiamen tried to make a break for it. Some attempted to leap onboard their vehicles and escape, but more of Young Little Wolf's people waited in reserve and their retreat lasted only moments. Others tried hiding in a stand of timber on the opposite side of the streambed. But they were spotted by the marksmen up above and picked off one by one.

The remaining survivors fled in a confused rout along a fugitives' trail towards the end of the valley, thinking salvation lay in that direction. Under heavy fire, they scrambled panic-stricken up the pass, jumping from boulder to boulder and seeking an escape route. A handful reached the top, threw away their weapons and ammo belts to lighten their load, and broke into a run. This turned out to be a horrible mistake because to their front a set of vehicles waited, manned by men and women armed to the teeth. The vehicle's engines roared as they accelerated forwards to meet the fleeing militia, herding them back where they came from. Watching on from their chopper, Kenny and Alex couldn't take their eyes off the gruesome scene. It was a classic example of the Plains Indians' deadliest tactic, and compared to a buffalo hunt. Swarming close to the fleeing enemy, they corralled them to the cliff edge and drove them over the side, where they fell to their deaths.

In the valley and camp, a few derisory shots rang out, marking the end of the battle.

It was all over in less than ten minutes.

•   •   •

Kenny and Alex were silent on the way back to Camp Erie, reflecting on the unexpected turn of events. It was clear that Young Little Wolf's anger was justified. He wasn't going to stand to one side and passively witness the persecution of his people all over again. In contrast, his father was older, wiser and with a calmer head. One couldn't help but wonder if, thirty years prior, he might have harboured the same determination as his son.

As they came in to land, Kenny wondered if the attack against the militia camp was a one-off. Somehow, he doubted it. All across the nation American Indians would be on the warpath, seeking to reset centuries of injustice and recover their sovereign land. The country may have stabilized after the earthquakes, but war and strife would tear it apart all over again.

"You know what? I think you were right," Alex said as they got off the helicopter.

"About what?"

"About what you said earlier. That I should ask Chloè out on a date. Before someone beats me to it."

They both glanced over at the floating dock. Chloè Bouchard was still there, lending a hand.

Kenny said, "There's no time like the present," as he patted his friend on the shoulder.

Alex nodded, squared his shoulders, and strode purposefully down to the beach.

World Quake 3

Kenny wandered off and found a tree trunk to sit on. He took out his last two Marlboros, lit one, and took a deep drag. He thought back to where it all began for him, at the Tiede Observatory on Tenerife, smoking a cigarette and gazing up at the moon and stars. So much had happened since then, so many events and experiences. He pondered what the future held for him and for all of them. Only time would tell.

Chapter 32

BERN
SWITZERLAND

TIMO'S RECOVERY WAS GOING WELL. The head and foot injuries he sustained during the bear attack were healing nicely, and the incision in his stomach was being cleaned and dressed regularly. The bruises he received from the car being crushed were fading a little bit more each day.

His father had taken him to their old home in the oldest part of the city. Timo was glad to find the place still standing. The hippie commune had barely changed at all. There were even one or two familiar faces that he recognized from his youth, albeit older now. The extensive gardens were still being used to grow produce, goats and free-range chickens roamed where they liked, and they still burned biogas to produce electricity. The strict religious teachings that Timo hated so much when he was a teenager were gone, replaced with a more libertine, carefree lifestyle. As a boy, Timo had found the place claustrophobic and overbearing, but now it was comforting and familiar.

The only major change was his mother. In the past, she had been the vibrant and lively heart of the commune, always the first to start a dance, sing a song or entertain with her wonderful stories.

But during the earthquake she was badly hurt and was now confined to a wheelchair. She spent her days on the terrace, enveloped in a haze of hemp smoke, lost in bitter thoughts, and constantly reminiscing about her lost youth. Had Timo not walked away years ago and refused her pleas to return, he would have found it heartbreaking. But considering that the world was broken, like his mother, helped frame her situation in a better context.

Genny was growing fast. She was still a boisterous puppy brimming with energy and curiosity, and she enjoyed playing with the children in the commune. However, every night she slept at her master's feet, and during the day they went for walks through the safe parts of Bern. After their traumatic experience with the bear, she had become even more protective than ever, scouting ahead through the damaged streets to ensure the way was clear. Timo was continuously amazed by her bravery. When he reflected on the bear attack and how she had fought to protect him, even risking her life, Timo couldn't imagine a stronger bond or loyalty. He owed her his life. The day he found her under the rubble was the luckiest day for both of them.

As Timo regained his health he assisted with various tasks around the commune. He lent a hand in the greenhouses, where the smell of marijuana was nearly overwhelming. He also helped insulate the heating pipes in the cellar using recycled materials to ensure that everyone stayed warm during the cold Bern winters.

He spoke with his father, but the passage of time had not fully healed past disagreements with his parents, so they stuck to general chit-chat. He purposefully refrained from asking about Timo's work or the reasons for his journey home.

During the evenings, Timo dedicated time to transcribing his notes. He would type them up on a manual typewriter, expanding upon the scientific observations and hypotheses he had gathered over the preceding months. Much of it was conjecture and too abstract to make any sense. He also chronicled his travels and experiences, the spectacles he had witnessed, and the few people he had met along the way. As he typed, Timo regarded himself more of a historian than a scientist, preserving a detailed account for posterity. The process proved therapeutic, serving as an antidote to everything he had undergone.

Timo also pondered what the future held. Personally, he felt like staying put for a while. He was weary of travelling and didn't have a home to return to anyway, unless he considered this place to be his home. Maybe he would move on eventually, but for now, he was happy where he was.

Regarding the human race and planet Earth?

Timo had spent a lot of time thinking about and exploring the future. He imagined a scenario of ceaseless strife for the human race lasting at least a generation. Since leaving the subterranean complex at CERN, Timo had hardly laid eyes on anyone. The cities, towns and mountaintop villages he passed through were largely deserted. If this was the case throughout Western Europe, then he estimated the population levels to be similar to those during the Dark Ages, around 30 million. If he applied that rule of thumb to the rest of the world, presuming every nation had suffered equal levels of devastation, Timo approximated that the planet's human population had shrunk to around 150 million, a mere one-fiftieth of pre-disaster levels. It wouldn't take much to reduce that further, be it through famine, pestilence or warfare.

Then there was the question: could the global catastrophe happen again? Timo was no astronomer. His field was quantum mechanics. But history had shown that Extinction-Level Events were not unprecedented. Earth's core and mantle were considerably damaged. Again, it wouldn't take much to finish the job of wiping out mankind.

Timo calculated that humanity faced an undeniably precarious future.

Mark Hobson

World Quake 3

EMERGENCE

Mark Hobson

Chapter 33

**LINDISFARNE/HOLY ISLAND
NORTHERN ENGLAND**

THEY NEVER DISCOVER THE IDENTITY of the person living in the cave. In the five months since reaching their island refuge, nobody from their party has seen them clearly. Sometimes, they come across signs of their presence on the island, like animal snares left in the dunes, footprints on the beach, or some of the houses broken into at night. On one occasion, two children swear they see a weathered face peering into the classroom window, but when their heavily pregnant teacher goes outside, whoever it was has vanished – if they were even there in the first place. They don't know for sure that it is a man, although what they learn seems to suggest that. Whoever they are, they are harmless and seem determined to avoid all attempts at contact. Nobody minds. They aren't a threat, and the idea of an old hermit living in the cave appeals to everyone. It makes for a nice bedtime story.

• • •

Time moves forward, and the seasons change. The birch and alder trees drop their autumn foliage, and the carpet of golden leaves are soon buried under the first snows. Days grow shorter and the wind colder, setting bare branches chattering and whirlpools of ice crystals spinning through the air. January arrives. Now the sky is a deep blue. The world seems bereft of activity.

But the stillness and silence are deceptive. White hares flit over the snowfields, foxes creep through the undergrowth, constantly on alert because death is never far away.

At cockcrow, people emerge into the new day, bundled up in furs against the morning chill.

They are led by their leader, Scott Cook. Four adults: two men and two women. All of them are lean and strong, probably the healthiest they have been in their lives. The men have beards and one of the women has braided her red hair. They walk silently past the crumbling castle on its hill and then turn north towards the peninsular. Their boots crunch the thin layer of ice underfoot as they cross small streams and brooks.

They pass over the narrow stretch of land linking the island with the peninsular and then split into pairs. No one goes hunting alone; it's better to work in pairs so they can get help if one of them gets hurt.

Scott comes to a stop, and his partner joins him as he kneels in the snow. He points at a set of hoof prints. Despite the steady snowfall since they set out, the prints are uncovered, indicating that they are fresh. Both of them recognize the animal tracks as those of a roe deer.

Scott directs his wife Sara to his left as they move forwards, maintaining a distance but staying within earshot. In his pocket, Scott carries a slingshot, a weapon he has come to rely on for hunting. Having spent countless hours scouting for game, his aim has become incredibly accurate, rarely letting him down. His strategy is to stun the animal with the slingshot before moving in for the kill, a method that he perfected during a previous encounter. But hunting small game like hares or pheasants has become routine while taking down a large animal like a deer fills Scott with apprehension. Scott feels his mouth go dry, worrying about making a mistake. It had been a harsh winter, their first big test since arriving on the island. They need nourishment, particularly Louise Swan who is only days away from giving birth.

Without warning, a clicking sound cuts through the silence. It is Sara, hitting two stones together to let him know that she has spotted their prey. Another click tells Scott to move towards the spot where the signal was given. He finds her lying on the crest of a hill. Below them, the roe deer is eating berries by a stone wall. They watch as it stops to sniff the air and paw at the snow, worried that the animal might have caught their scent. It shakes its white rump patch and then goes back to feeding.

Scott nods at his wife. As she removes a heavy cudgel, he readies the slingshot with a round stone the size of a marble. Before he has a chance to lose his nerve, in one fluid motion he rises into a crouch, spins the sling around several times, and releases the projectile. Almost immediately, the roe deer barks in alarm and staggers sideways. The two hunters rush down the slope to find the animal on its knees, its head waving to and fro. Sara, in the lead, rushes up to the stricken creature, lifts the cudgel above her head and brings it down with such crushing force that the deer is dead in an instant.

A few minutes later, Tammy and Fabian, the second pair of hunters, join them. They take out their butchering tools and, working quickly to keep their cold hands busy, dress the animal in the snow. Steam rises from the carcass as they remove anything edible, which includes the fat, the kidneys, the liver, the heart, and the lungs.

Shortly after, the triumphant band of hunters returns to the village carrying armfuls of meat. The others are waiting for them in the old lime kilns. Stacks of wood are placed over the stone hearth. Once the stone is hot enough, the fire is moved aside using a long stick. Chunks of meat are then placed onto the hot stones to cook.

The aroma of roasting meat, sizzling with juices and fat, fills the air.

• • •

Lacking access to modern natal facilities means that Scott's band of survivors must relearn how to deliver babies under all conditions. Childbirth is a natural process that usually doesn't need artificial aids. But it can be risky. Some babies will be stillborn and others will die in infancy. Infant mortality rates will inevitably rise in the aftermath of the disaster.

The ethical questions around introducing a new generation into a ruined world are irrelevant. Children might be the only long-term point of survival.

To give Louise and her child the best chances, she is given the lion's share of nutritional foods, including vegetables, iron-rich foods and plenty of protein. A room is prepared and everything is sterilized as best as possible. Her labour lasts for most of a night and the following morning, but she is never left alone, with Sara, Tammy and Saskia staying with her throughout. The father would typically attend, but in this instance the father is Scott, which complicates matters. His wife has long since forgiven him for his transgression, but she insists that he wait outside.

Early in the afternoon, Louise gives birth to a baby boy, who they name Lucas.

Mother and child are well.

• • •

Spring's arrival is a gradual process as winter clings stubbornly to its frigid grip on the world. They wonder if the pollutants released by the disaster, which are a mixture of manmade and natural ones, have affected the planet's weather cycles. They are all aware of the concept of Nuclear Winters. Could this be something similar? A harbinger of things to come in the years ahead?

It is not until April that the snows melt away and the sun begins to warm the land. An orgy of growth is soon in full swing, and the island transforms into a lush idyll. It is a good time for hunting as large flocks of geese and seabirds migrate from the south. Kittiwakes, Razorbills and Herring Gulls can be found feeding in the dunes and sandflats, and many of them fall victim to well-aimed stones. Every day, the women head out to look for downy baby birds in nests on the ground.

Spry youngsters, their faces lit up with pure joy, chase one another, glad to be free after the long winter. The grownups do their best to give them a normal childhood, but there is no doubt that the period of infancy is much shorter in this new world. Scott watches them run and leap through the village green, a smile appearing on his kind face. Let them be children for just a little while longer, he thinks.

Sara steps outside with Phoebe, who is now a year old and has grown strong enough to sit upright and even totter about by holding onto furniture. Shortly after, Louise joins them with their son, Lucas. They make a unique and loving family - three parents, each treating the children as their own regardless of the circumstances of their conception. The bond between them is strong.

Family,

Love,

Strength,

Somehow, they will triumph.

Story notes

World Quake 3 brings the Extinction-Level Event in our scenario to a finish. Like all such occasions, I find it difficult to say goodbye to the characters we have shared this journey with, particularly those who have survived all three books. I hope that you, the reader, found the conclusion satisfying.

As with Books 1 and 2, the final entry in the trilogy required a lot of research. So much so that I had to trim the story to more reasonable – and believable – levels. Still, I have sometimes allowed my imagination to have free rein. Real Extinction-Level Events from prehistory often occurred over many centuries and sometimes millennia. Even the age of the dinosaurs didn't come to an end overnight. To make the time frame of the plot more reader-friendly, events have again been condensed.

In these notes, I would like to closely examine various aspects of the plot.

Let's begin with the Russian **Rods From God** superweapon. Some might think this is just science fiction, but it's not.

During the Cold War, both the United States and the Soviet Union developed detailed plans to build these weapons and deploy them in Earth's orbit. The Americans even gave their plan a name: **Project Thor**.

A kinetic bombardment, also known as a kinetic orbital strike, is the theoretical concept of striking a target on Earth using a non-explosive projectile dropped from a satellite in Low Earth Orbit. Instead of a traditional bomb, this method involves using a solid tungsten steel rod. There would be no need for a warhead; the destructive force comes from the kinetic energy generated upon impact. These tungsten projectiles would travel at speeds of Mach 24, slowing down to Mach 10 upon entering Earth's atmosphere. Despite the decrease in speed, they would still be fast enough to reach their target in approximately 12 minutes, which is less than half the time needed for an intercontinental ballistic missile. There would be no detectable launch warning, and having a small radar cross-section, there would be no defense against it. It also has the advantage of being able to launch projectiles at a very high angle, which when combined with its streamlined shape, minimizes air resistance and increases impact. They were designed as Bunker Buster weapons to be used against hardened bunkers, secret underground sites and military headquarters. Also, there would be no nuclear fallout.

Despite international treaties prohibiting the deployment of weapons in space, both the United States and the Soviet Union continued with their plans. The U.S. had Project Thor in development for many years, while the Soviets took it a step further by creating the 'Almaz' space station. This station was equipped with spy gear, radar, and the R-23M, a heavy space cannon capable of firing 5,000 projectiles per minute.

Almaz was launched aboard a Soyuz space capsule in 1971, and the cannon was test-fired on January 24th, 1975. The Soviets never revealed the results of the test, but sources from NASA claim that the space station was accidentally destroyed. Following these events, both the Soviets and the Americans temporarily shelved their space weapon plans, reportedly due to funding constraints.

The Russians and the Americans were not the first countries to consider deploying weapons in space. During World War II, Nazi Germany developed plans for an orbital weapon called the Sun Gun. It was an orbital mirror that would have been used to focus and weaponize beams of sunlight. They also experimented with designs for a sub-orbital crewed bomber jet plane that could potentially reach a speed of over 13,000 mph and fly up to one hundred miles high. This was part of Nazi Germany's Amerikabomber Project which aimed to bomb New York. However, the prototype never became operational.

From the 1980s onwards, the U.S. and the Soviet Union again looked at sending weapons into space. America started with President Reagan's Strategic Defence Initiative program, which included Brilliant Pebbles. This concept involved launching thousands of small satellites into space, each armed with heat-seeking missiles that would take down enemy ICBMs in mid-flight. Meanwhile the Kremlin developed the Polyrus unmanned spacecraft, a prototype orbital weapons platform intended to disable American spy satellites using lasers. All of these projects were either scrapped or failed, but that doesn't mean that others have not been developed and deployed since. After all, none of us really know what is up there orbiting the Earth. So the scenario Flight Engineer Madison Leitner finds herself in when boarded by Russian cosmonauts may not be far-fetched.

The Trail of Tears is a significant historical event commonly taught to children in America. However, its recognition outside the United States is limited., so I'll provide a very short history lesson for you.

The Trail of Tears refers to the coerced westward relocation of American Indian tribes. This was a result of the U.S. government's attempt to seize their land. The population in America was growing fast and slavery was spreading across the south. Many white settlers wanted to grow cotton. More importantly, in 1829, gold was discovered on land belonging to the indigenous people, sparking a gold rush and promising vast wealth to land prospectors. There was a clamour to grab the land, and when the American Indian Tribes refused to sell up their territory, a new solution was sought. To solve what was referred to as the "Indian Problem", President Andrew Jackson signed the Indian Removal Act of 1830, which led to the forced eviction of members of the "Five Civilized Tribes" from their ancestral homelands. They were made to settle in reservations west of the Mississippi. The arduous journey took place in winter, and temperatures rarely rose above freezing. Rivers were so clogged with ice that travel was impossible for weeks. Food rationing, provided by the U.S. Army, consisted of a handful of boiled corn, one turnip, and two cups of water per day. As well as hunger, the migrants also faced disease and exhaustion. Up to fifteen thousand of them died.

More Indian removals followed throughout the 1830s. The Cherokee tribe suffered especially badly. They were forced to march one thousand miles barefoot and in scant clothing, had to pay a fee to cross rivers, and many froze to death or were murdered by locals.

Some tribes resisted, notably the Seminole peoples from Florida. In December of 1835, they ambushed a U.S. Army convoy, killing all but three of the 110 army troops, a battle that sparked the Second Seminole War. But for the most part, the tribes moved west simply to be free from white rule.

Some scholars have described this as genocide or ethnic cleansing. As a soldier, President Jackson had earned a reputation as a man who believed in creating fear in the native population, to "bleed" his enemies to serve the goal of U.S. expansion. Others argue that President Jackson had benevolent intentions and simply wanted to protect the American Indians from white inhabitants. If he had not acted, they would have been wiped out, President Jackson feared.

This is a brief overview of events. Going into detail and conducting an in-depth examination of the subject would take too long, and this isn't the place anyway. Including a comparable theme in World Quake 3 was intended to establish historical parallels. I also drew ideas from natural disasters worldwide to illustrate how people may try to gain an advantage from a global crisis. It wouldn't take much for history to repeat itself.

An Extinction-Level Event, or Mass Extinction Event, is the widespread and sharp fall in 70% or more of life on our planet, when species vanish much faster than they are replaced.

Extreme temperature changes, variations in sea levels, plate tectonic movement, supernova events or gamma-ray bursts may serve as triggers, or devastating one-off events such as huge volcanic eruptions or an asteroid hitting Earth.

During our planet's long history there may have been up to 20 mass extinctions that almost wiped out all life on Earth. There are disagreements as to what constitutes a "major" extinction event, but the "Big Five" are listed below:

- **Faint Young Sun Paradox – 4 + billion years ago. During Earth's early history, the sun's intensity was only 70% of its current level. Even so, our planet contained liquid water and early life forms, representing a precarious balance.**
- **The Oxygen Catastrophe – 2.4 billion years ago. Killed off 57% of all genera and 85% of all species.**
- **Late Devonian Extinction Event – 360 million years ago. Killed off 50% of genera and 70% of all species.**
- **The Great Dying – 250 million years ago. Killed off 70% of life on land and 90% of life in the ocean.**
- **The Medea Hypothesis – current threat. A concept suggesting that all cellular life may be self-destructive or suicidal. In Greek mythology, Medea kills her own children.**

It takes, on average, about ten million years for the planet to recover from a mass extinction. Species that perish never return and new ones take their place. The question most of you are asking is: are we headed for another Mass Extinction Event?

If we disregard the constant threat of nuclear warfare, the most probable scenario involves a naturally-occurring event.

Mass extinctions occur approximately every sixty million years, suggesting that we are overdue for one. Recent studies indicate that unprecedented heat may precipitate the next mass extinction. Supercomputer models project that as the sun intensifies, emitting more energy, our planet will experience continued warming. While mammals, including humans, have adapted to colder conditions through hibernation, they are less equipped to endure prolonged exposure to extreme heat. Scientists posit that widespread temperatures ranging from 40 to 50 degrees Celsius could have catastrophic consequences. If extreme temperatures do not finish us off, future geological shifts and plate tectonic movement will. Ultimately, the world's continents will merge into a single arid landmass, releasing significant amounts of toxic fumes through volcanic eruptions. The entire biosphere of the world may become inhospitable to all life forms, similar to what happened on Mars billions of years ago.

Thankfully, this won't happen overnight. But most scientists agree that a sixth Mass Extinction Event is already underway. They've even given it a name: the Holocene Epoch. It covers all of humanity's recorded history, the rise and fall of civilizations, and our predicted demise. It also has another name: The Rise of Man.

Mark Hobson
January 2024 – November 2024

Mark Hobson

ABOUT THE AUTHOR

British writer Mark Hobson is an emerging horror author, rapidly gaining a large following with novels such as Dweller Under The Roots, Wolf Angel, and his hugely popular post-apocalyptic World Quake series. His novels combine spine-chilling horror with captivating settings and historical elements.
He lives at home in Yorkshire with his 3 cats

If you enjoyed reading this book, please consider leaving a review on Amazon.

You can also follow the author's official Facebook page at:
facebook.com/yorkshirescribbler

WORLD QUAKE

It was a day like any other. People setting out on the commute to work or taking the kids to school or chatting to their friends in the park.

Normal. Routine. Nothing to mark it apart.

By lunchtime, everything they had ever known, every aspect of their lives, would be changed forever – marked by the most catastrophic series of global disasters to strike the planet in over 6000 years.

MANKIND STANDS AT THE GATES OF EXTINCTION

The world is being ripped apart by a great geological cataclysm. Cities crumble and entire continents disappear beneath the sea as earthquakes and mega-tsunamis lay waste to the land. For the human race there is no escape and nowhere to flee. Millions perish.

From the rubble, a disparate group of survivors emerge.

A school teacher hell-bent on finding his pregnant wife.

A scientist with the fate of the world in his hands.

The workforce of a power plant who fight to prevent a nuclear meltdown that would poison a nation for millennia.

While the politicians hide in their bunkers beneath London and Washington, these ordinary people will have to fight to stay alive in this new world, an existence blighted with violence, cruelty and death as they journey across a devastated landscape.

They must ask themselves profound questions about their own morality while humanity descends into chaos.

A new epoch in Earth's history is underway.

THIS IS THE AGE OF DEATH

ABSOLUTE PAGE TURNER, BRILLIANT, BRILLIANT STORY.
A FRIGHTENING VIEW OF WHAT MAY AWAIT THE WORLD.
WOULD MAKE A BLOCKBUSTER FILM.
AVAILABLE FROM AMAZON ISBN: 9798795916309

WORLD QUAKE 2
The old world is gone forever.
The Great Cataclysm has left the planet on its knees, and over 2 billion people are dead. Now the dust has settled, and all of mankind's greatest achievements lay in ruins, from the modern metropolis of New York to the grand old cities of London and Paris and the ancient pyramids of Egypt – everything is destroyed.

EARTH IS UNDERGOING A GRAND RESET

With nature holding sway over the fate of the world, the survivors strive to overcome the catastrophe that has broken their lives and threatens the very existence of the human race.

Scott Cook and his companions have somehow endured, but at a cost. Seemingly stranded, they unexpectedly find themselves presented with a choice: remain where they are and risk dying from hunger and disease, or join a group of young people on a dangerous odyssey across a mysterious land.

In America, Kenny Leland is saved from certain death, only to find himself accompanying a mad president hell-bent on a perilous mission.

And beneath the mountains and glaciers of Switzerland, scientists in a top-secret subterranean laboratory take desperate measures to prevent the world from falling into the abyss as a new threat emerges.

THE GREAT TRIBULATION IS AT HAND

OUTSTANDING.
I BECAME CAUGHT UP IN THE CHARACTERS AND SCENARIOS FROM PAGE ONE.
A TERRIFYING BUT ADDICTIVE STORY.
THE DEVELOPMENT OF THE CHARACTERS IS MASSIVE.
BREATHTAKING... I CAN'T WAIT FOR THE NEXT BOOK.
AVAILABLE FROM AMAZON ISBN: 9798387952166

Mark Hobson

WOLF ANGEL
AMSTERDAM OCCULT SERIES
BOOK ONE

The City of Amsterdam is gripped with fear.
A series of brutal murders have left homicide detectives baffled.
With no motive or clues to work with, they find themselves probing blindly through the city's dark and violent underworld.
But Inspector Pieter Van Dijk is not convinced this is the work of one lone psychopath.
Drawn deeper and deeper into the shadowy heart of the case, he unearths a terrifying history of family madness and occult conspiracy echoing across the decades.

BRILLIANT… GRIPPING… A WELL THOUGHT OUT AND WELL-WRITTEN BOOK.
A DARK STORY WITH LOTS OF ACTION.
THIS ISN'T JACKANORY.
THIS IS SIMPLY A GREAT READ WITH ALL THE ELEMENTS TO KEEP YOU TURNING THE PAGE.
GRITTY DRAMA… WITH THE SUPERNATURAL ELEMENTS CLEVERLY WOVEN IN.
INTRIGUE SOAKS OUT OF THE BRICKWORK OF AMSTERDAM'S ALLEYWAYS.

AVAILABLE FROM AMAZON ISBN: 9798696036946

For more info and news on upcoming releases, please visit
www.occultseries.co.uk

World Quake 3

A STATE OF SIN
AMSTERDAM OCCULT SERIES
BOOK TWO
THREE PSYCHOPATHS ARE HAUNTING THE STREETS OF AMSTERDAM THIS WINTER.

A doctor, who leaves his patients horribly disfigured.
A hunter from South Africa, determined to add to his collection of human trophies.
A kidnapper, who keeps his victim locked away in a small metal cage.
When Dutch cop Pieter Van Dijk answers what he thinks will be a routine call to investigate a case of arson, little does he realize the chain of terrifying events that are about to grip the city with icy fear.
Fresh back from a break of rest and recuperation, and trying hard to deal with the aftermath of a brutal case, he soon finds himself plunged deep into a new nightmare. What links the three crimes? Just who is behind them? And why does he feel that this time the answers hinge on his own past?
From the snowy alleyways of Amsterdam to the frigid shores of the North Sea, the hunt to put a stop to the rampage of murder and bloodshed soon becomes a race against time. Because one thing he has learned over the years is that Amsterdam is a city of shadows, hiding the worst in human nature.

A GRIPPING CRIME DRAMA.
THERE ARE SEVERAL HIGHLY DISTURBING SCENES THAT GAVE ME CHILLS.
VERY HIGHLY RESEARCHED AND WOVEN TOGETHER WITH LAYERS OF HISTORY... VERY WELL WRITTEN.

AVAILABLE FROM AMAZON ISBN: 9798724812566

For more info and news on upcoming releases, please visit
www.occultseries.co.uk

DWELLER UNDER THE ROOTS

For Lee Harris and his cohorts, it was meant to be a simple holdup; the kind of robbery they'd done many times before. Go in, scare a few people, and get away with the money. A piece of cake, with nobody being harmed. But when the job goes bad and a man winds up dead, they soon find themselves on the run with the Rozzers hot on their tail.

With little choice but to lie low for a while, Lee soon fetches up at a safe house far from prying eyes. But the small cottage tucked away in the back of beyond soon proves anything but a sanctuary. For Lee, it is the beginning of five days and five nights of dreadful terror that will test his sanity and drag him to the heart of the cottage's dark and violent past.

Who are the people in the woods watching him? Why is the cottage the foci of a malignant, unearthly force? And what lurks in the cellar, beneath the earth, and under the roots?

Lee will discover a record of secret sin stretching back to a point in history when childish rumours or vengeful allegations could mean a painful death and eternal purgatory.

The desire for revenge will span centuries.

GRIPPING FROM START TO FINISH. I LOVE OLD BUILDINGS, AND THERE IS A VERY INTRIGUING ONE IN THIS BOOK.
COMPLETELY IMMERSED IN THE STORY...STRONG CHARACTER DEVELOPMENT... A BUILD-UP OF TENSION AND FEAR.

AVAILABLE FROM AMAZON ISBN: 9798872152453

World Quake 3

GREY STONES

Carter Middleton returns to his childhood home in Yorkshire to bury his father and to reconnect with his estranged family. Yet, after fifteen years away, he quickly learns that the old bitterness and feuding that first drove him to leave is still as deeply rooted as ever.

Others in Stansfield Bridge make it clear they want him gone too. His arrival stirs memories from the past, of events best forgotten, of secrets they would prefer kept hidden.

Jessica Bates has also come home. Years earlier, her mother left their caravan one evening and never returned. Her whereabouts remain a mystery to this day. Now Jessica is determined to get to the truth, whatever the consequences.

An act of brutal violence brings Carter and Jessica together. With steely resolve, they set out to investigate, soon unearthing terrible decades-old sins and revealing a darkness at the very heart of the community.

They soon discover that everything comes at a cost. Life is cheap in the countryside.

Set against the hard and unforgiving landscape of northern England, **GREY STONES** is a shocking tale of betrayal, revenge, loyalty and grief.

A SMOULDERING BUILD-UP TO A DRAMATIC AND TERRIFYING ENDING.
NOT A RUN-OF-THE-MILL MURDER MYSTERY... I FOUND IT A GREAT READ.
WOW! WHAT AN AMAZING STORY.
AVAILABLE FROM AMAZON ISBN: 9798548418586

Mark Hobson

A MURMURATION OF STARLINGS
TWO STRANGERS. ONE SEEKING REVENGE. THE OTHER REDEMPTION

Twelve years ago, Francis Bailey was locked away and left to rot in Britain's most notorious prison: found guilty of the worst kind of crime – the murder of a young child. A crime that he did not commit.

Finally released on appeal, he returns to his home town in the Yorkshire Pennines to rebuild his life. Unable to land a job, stigmatized by society and branded a dangerous lunatic by a corrupt police force, he soon realizes that his only course of action is to prove his innocence to the world by solving the case that still haunts the small community.

But the truth lies hidden behind a wall of silence, where the bent copper who sent him down is shielded by people at the very top. When it comes to justice, truth is irrelevant.

Liam Brennan is a man haunted by his past. Living on the streets, he is a drunkard and a deadbeat.

Dangerous people are searching for him. Former colleagues who want him dead. Because Liam knows too much about their dark and violent history. There is nothing they won't do to ensure their secrets stay hidden.

Forever in fear that his whereabouts may one day be discovered, his life is one long mess of drunken brawls and petty crime.

When Francis and Liam's paths cross, they form an unlikely bond and together set out on a tortured quest seeking truth and absolution. Either they must conquer their demons and prevail, or be crushed by the horrors they carry with them.

BUT NOW ANOTHER CHILD IS MISSING, SNATCHED OFF THE STREETS. TIME IS RUNNING OUT.

A JAW-DROPPING CRIME NOVEL
AVAILABLE FROM AMAZON ISBN: 9798840016992

NOW MAY MEN WEEP
ISANDLWANA
A STORY FROM THE ZULU WAR
JANUARY 1879 – ZULULAND

Lord Chelmsford, commander of British forces in South Africa, leads an invasion into Zululand. At the head of his main spearhead column, he expects a quick and decisive campaign against a poorly armed, ill-disciplined force of tribesmen. To achieve this aim he has with him the veteran soldiers from the 24th Regiment, 'Old Sweats' as they are referred to, men with years of campaigning behind them.

Just days into the invasion Chelmsford's force sets up camp beside a strangely-shaped crag, barely a few miles from the safety of the British Colony of Natal.

The battle that develops in the shadow of that mountain, with British redcoats fighting hand-to-hand with their Zulu foe, will become the stuff of legend.

It is a story punctuated with acts of incredible courage and heroism and moving sacrifice, a human drama that will shock the world.

ISANDLWANA!

I FEEL LIKE I'M PRESENT AT THE BATTLE OF ISANDLWANA.
PAGE-TURNING EXCITEMENT... RIPPING YARNS 21ST CENTURY STYLE!
CAPTURES THE TERROR... GRIPPING MOMENTS OF ACTION.
A CRACKING READ.

AVAILABLE FROM AMAZON ISBN: 9798666828472

WHAT READERS ARE SAYING ABOUT MARK HOBSON'S BOOKS

A RARE BOOK – A THRILLER THAT IS ACTUALLY THRILLING
GREY STONES

I COULDN'T PUT GREY STONES DOWN... A GREAT READ
GREY STONES

THIS IS A GREAT STORY AND SERVES AS A GREAT SETUP FOR THE SERIES
WOLF ANGEL (AMSTERDAM OCCULT SERIES BOOK 1)

MARK HOBSON BUILDS UP THE TENSION NICELY WITH RARELY A DULL MOMENT
WOLF ANGEL (AMSTERDAM OCCULT SERIES BOOK 1)

YOU HAVE THE INGREDIENTS FOR AN EXCITING THRILLER... GREAT READING
A STATE OF SIN (AMSTERDAM OCCULT SERIES BOOK 2)

HAD ME GRIPPED FROM THE START, I HIGHLY RECOMMEND THIS BOOK
A STATE OF SIN (AMSTERDAM OCCULT SERIES BOOK 2)

I STARTED THIS BOOK AND LITERALLY COULD NOT PUT IT DOWN
DWELLER UNDER THE ROOTS

I HAVE FOUND MY NEW AUTHOR
DWELLER UNDER THE ROOTS

World Quake 3

WELL WRITTEN AND VERY FRIGHTENING... WELL-DEVELOPED CHARACTERS AND A GREAT STORYLINE
WORLD QUAKE

THE AUTHOR PAINTS A DEEPLY-RESEARCHED AND GRAPHIC PICTURE OF A POSSIBLE SCENARIO OF AN EXTINCTION-LEVEL EVENT
WORLD QUAKE

A REAL PAGE-TURNER OR FINGER-SWIPER
WORLD QUAKE

LOVED THIS DISASTER NOVEL, WELL RESEARCHED WITH LOTS OF ACTION
WORLD QUAKE

A LITERARY GEM
WORLD QUAKE

THE STORYLINE IS WELL-CRAFTED
WORLD QUAKE 2

THE CHARACTERS ARE DETERMINED TO SURVIVE AND KEEP A VENEER OF CIVILIZATION IN PLACE.
WORLD QUAKE 2

BREATHTAKING
WORLD QUAKE 2

A ROLLERCOASTER RIDE OF OUTRAGE, HORROR AND SYMPATHY... AN ENGAGING NOVEL
A MURMURATION OF STARLINGS

Mark Hobson

YOU FEEL YOU ARE THERE WITH THE SOLDIERS, FEELING THEIR
FEAR AND PAIN... ABSOLUTELY BRILLIANT
NOW MAY MEN WEEP

THIS IS A MASTERFUL RETELLING OF THIS STORY... ONE IS DRAWN
TO THE INEVITABLE CONCLUSION
NOW MAY MEN WEEP

World Quake 3

Printed in Great Britain
by Amazon